I0666131

WHEN THE WASP STINGS

A COOPER NORTH MYSTERY

by

Richard Wolkomir

ALSO BY RICHARD WOLKOMIR

SINNABAR—three foster-care youths abducted to a dying world fight to get home, but they have no homes, only each other.

FRANKIE & JOHNNY, & NELLIE BLY— Fifteen stories about what never was and never will be.

RIDERS OF THE DUST-GRAY STEPPE— dispatches from distant times and strange places—fifteen stories.

DOG DANCE OF SNIKIA—if your dog's a genius, shouldn't you do what he says? A comic e-book novella.

JUNKYARD BANDICOOTS AND OTHER TALES OF THE WORLD'S ENDANGERED SPECIES—by Joyce Rogers Wolkomir & Richard Wolkomir

Richard Wolkomir has worked as a roofer, laundry sheet folder, grounds keeper, zoo bear keeper, newspaper reporter, and award-winning magazine writer. Now he writes fiction—fantasy, science fiction, thrillers, and mysteries. He lives with his wife and partner, Joyce, in the New England hills.

Visit him at: www.richardjoycewolkomir.net

Library of Congress Control Number: 2023919976

Cover art by JD&J Design

Published by Worcester Range Books

Hardback ISBN—979-8-9892818-0-0
Paperback ISBN—979-8-9892818-1-7
E-Book ISBN—979-8-9892818-2-4

FOR JOYCE

1

"Chief LaPerle sent me over here," the man said.

He stood in Cooper North's open office doorway, staring down at his shoes.

Three minutes ago, Tip LaPerle had called from the Dill PD, next door.

"Handle this guy for me, okay Coop?" Tip said. "For Pete's sake, I've got an alligator on Main Street! And somebody stole maple logs. Can you believe that? Now here's this nutball, babbling at me, about killer bumblebees, or something."

Cooper thought: cranks push Tip's anger button.

Her visitor looked uncomfortable in his summer-weight tan suit. It looked tight. He'd put it on, anyway, she supposed, just for this visit to the police, and now to the Allen County State's Attorney's office.

A smallish man, in his late thirties, slightly plump, round head. Brown hair thinning on top. Watery blue eyes....

Man or woodchuck?

Cooper immediately felt ashamed of that snippy judgement, based just on his appearance. Fatigue, she guessed. It made her irritable.

"What can I do for you?" she asked.

He looked determined, yet diffident, as if he knew she'd give no weight to what he said. She had a sense that no one had ever given much weight to what this man said.

"I'm reporting a murder," he said.

A hesitant voice, almost a whisper.

Cooper suddenly felt sorry for him, although she wasn't sure why.

She took out a form from her desk drawer.

"Name?" she asked.

"Flute," he said. "Flute Wagner."

"That's an unusual name, Flute," Cooper said.

He looked at Cooper, stricken.

"It's not my real name," he almost whispered. "Grady, that's my real name, Grady John Wagner."

He sighed.

"Grady's my mom's maiden name," he said. "My father's John."

Cooper waited, but he stood looking at her, like an antelope staring at a lioness that suddenly sprang in front of him. Finally, still in that near whisper, he spoke again.

"Flute's because in fourth grade we got a chance to try out instruments, the high school's orchestra director wanting to get us started, I guess, to develop talent, and he gave me a flute and I liked it, playing it, learning to make nice sounds."

Another silence, then he resumed.

2

"My folks couldn't afford to buy a flute, though, so the orchestra director gave me...."

He looked at Cooper, then away. "Other kids, they were...."

He looked down.

"They teased?" Cooper said.

"Yes," he said. "They...teased."

He sighed again.

"What they called me, Flute, it stuck."

Cooper motioned to the visitor's chair, just in front of her desk, and he sat. Henry, her housemate, a Pembroke Welsh corgi, sleeping under her desk, roused himself, glanced around the desk at the visitor, judged him uninteresting, then withdrew under the desk and resumed sleeping.

"You live here in Dill?" Cooper asked the man, thinking she'd never seen him before.

Of course, he had the kind of face you might see and then, a minute later, forget.

"Just over the line, south of here, in Snowville," he said. "I moved up here four months ago, to start work at Snowville Maple."

"What do you do there?" Cooper asked.

"I'm marketing director," he said.

A surprise. Cooper would have guessed maintenance staff.

She filled in some of the blanks on her form, then pushed it away. She looked at him, waiting. He sat looking down at his knees.

"All right," Cooper said, finally. "What's this about a murder?"

Wagner drew in a deep breath. He exhaled. Then he stared fixedly at Cooper and spoke.

"It's the yellow jackets."

She thought: some political extremist gang?

Then it came to her.

"You mean wasps?" she said. "Yellow-jacket wasps?"

He nodded, a single abrupt downward jerk of his chin.

"They were in his suit's sleeves," he said. "Poor old Proctor Gibbs."

Cooper had known Proctor Gibbs, slantingly, all her life. She'd been the daughter of a banker, and Proctor the son of a hill farmer, but both families went back to Dill's colonial times. She and Proctor went through the Allen County Central Schools together, although he was three grades ahead of her, and she'd once overheard him telling his classmates, "No way I'll always be milking Jerseys."

They'd tapped sugar maples on his farm, as most farmers did, and he'd focused on that. Step by step, building up, and the result was the Snowville Maple company, which had grown bigger than Cooper realized—now, she'd just learned, it even had a marketing director. Also, recently Proctor had incorporated the company, holding most of the stock himself, with a physician and dentist and attorney and a housewife, from Dill or Snowville, on the board of directors. So still a local business.

"I read Proctor's obituary, in the *Dill Chronicle*," she told her visitor.

4

She remembered him in his older years—shock of white hair, huge white mustache, blue eyes merry and sharp, thick Yankee accent....

His wife died young, giving birth to their first child, both mother and child lost, and he'd never remarried.

He'd died a bachelor, the *Chronicle's* obituary said, of a severe allergic reaction to wasp stings. Anaphylaxis. A lifelong problem. He had an EpiPen, but workers at Snowville Maple nagged him about it, because he mostly left it home, in a drawer.

"He got stung," Cooper said. "How's that murder?"

"Because the yellow jackets got into his sleeves," Wagner said.

Now he looked stubborn, determined.

"He'd hung his suit's jacket across his office chair's backrest—he just kept it there, didn't bother taking it home, like that chair was his closet, and he'd only put on the jacket for meetings or something," Flute said. "He wasn't a suit-and-tie kind of man, you know?"

He stared at Cooper, half expecting to be dismissed, told to go away.

"Okay," she said. "And?"

He forged on, heartened.

"Wasps don't crawl into sleeves," he said. "Not one wasp in one sleeve, and for sure not another wasp in the other sleeve."

Cooper sat back in her chair, suddenly so tired she had to shut her eyes.

It's because I took on this second job, she thought.

She'd retired months ago, after decades as Allen County state's attorney, followed by a stint as the state's attorney general, finishing up as a justice on the state's supreme court. Then Mt. Augustus College persuaded her to start a criminal justice program, while also overseeing campus security.

Now this.

A week ago, the sitting Allen County state's attorney suddenly resigned, to take a job with the U.S. Justice Department, in Washington. Police virtually applauded. He'd left all investigating to the cops. No guidance on what evidence to gather. Let the police do it all. Then he'd decide: easy to prosecute? Okay. Difficult, case needs digging, extra effort? Why bother? Let the buggers walk.

Everyone in Allen County law enforcement, including the troopers, even the city council, pleaded with Cooper to step back in, serve out the man's term. Because when it came to felony investigations, as state's attorney, she'd always been totally hands on.

Three days ago she'd agreed to do it. Now she felt exhausted.

I'm sixty-nine-years old, she thought. Maybe fatigue's just normal at this age. She'd check with her doctor.

When she got a free hour.

She opened her eyes.

Flute Wagner still sat in front of her desk, waiting.

She'd almost forgotten him.

"This looks iffy, Mr. Wagner," she said.

He looked stricken.

"I'll check into it, though," she said.

She pushed a pad and a pen across the desk to him.

"Write down your address and telephone numbers, home, work, cell phone...."

She felt too tired to jot the notes herself.

He frowned in concentration, writing on the pad.

After watching a moment, Cooper shut her eyes again.

She heard him get up, walk toward the door, then stop.

"Thank you, Miss North," she heard him say.

A pause, then almost a whisper.

"When will I hear from you?"

"Soon," Cooper said, eyes still closed. "Soon."

She heard him go out the door.

For a moment she thought nothing, just resting. Then she did have a thought.

What did Tip say on the phone, about an alligator?

On Main Street?

A thousand miles from the subtropics?

She'd   need   to   find   out   about   that.

2

Three minutes after Flute Wagner left, Cooper roused herself from a near-doze, forcing herself up from her chair. Then she met with her office's two assistant attorneys, to work out the day's schedule. For her, it started with the regular Monday briefing at the Dill PD. She glanced at her wristwatch. Already a minute late.

Leaving the office, she leaned on her cane—forty-five years ago, in her second year at Harvard Law, polio lamed her left leg. Today that leg felt particularly leaden, maybe because of fatigue. Odd, she thought, to feel so tired. Flu coming on?

She pushed open the office's armored steel door, then walked by the metal detector, with Henry strutting ahead, doing his cocky corgi walk. He glanced back, out the corners of his sharp eyes, making sure Cooper appreciated how cool he looked.

No need for steel doors, he seemed to say. This woman's protected by corgi!

When she'd originally presided here, there'd been no armored door, no metal detector. No need to worry about crazies armed with Kalashnikovs barging in. Not in this old granite-quarrying town, tucked into the mountains. Since then, though, Dill had become a cyber-tech town. Dill Industries' new steel-and-glass headquarters now dwarfed its two-centuries old Gothic neighbor, the Augustus Dill Museum of Natural Science.

Times changed.

Cooper didn't always like it.

Leaning on her cane, she followed Henry across narrow Courthouse Lane, listening to orioles and warblers singing in the sugar maples. A warm June morning. She had to gird herself to plod into the fluorescent-lit Dill PD building, through another set of metal detectors and bullet-proof steel doors. She blamed Interstate highways—they'd put Boston, New York, and Montreal within just a few hours' drive. Now Dill was evolving into a town of strangers. Tech researchers and corporate managers and tourists, but also derelicts and psychopaths and pushers.

When Cooper walked into Tip's office, he was on the telephone, talking to one of his officers. He waved at Cooper.

"Okay, bring them up here," he said into the phone. "Yeah, both of them."

He listened, then shook his head.

"Well, just keep your hand away from its teeth," he said.

He put the phone down, looking at the ceiling, exasperated.

"Officer Daisy Garrett just arrested an alligator," he told the ceiling. "She believes it wants to eat her." Cooper thought: this should be interesting.

Mike Bolknor, the office's other visitor, seemed squeezed into his chair, a big man, taller even than

Cooper, looking like the heavyweight boxer he'd been in the Army MPs. He seemed faintly off-tune in his suit and tie, routine in Manhattan, where he'd been an NYPD detective. Here, however, he headed campus security at Mt. Augustus College. And this was L. L. Bean country.

Dill PD had no detective, because the city council insisted state troopers, or the state's attorney, should handle investigations, and fund the investigator. Troopers, however, had nobody to spare. And the policy of the Allen County state's attorney, until Cooper stepped back in, a few days ago, had been, don't bother me with that stuff.

Months ago, though, Cooper had engineered a workaround.

At Mt. Augustus College, she chaired the Campus Security Committee, ostensibly Mike Bolknor's boss. She made a deal with Tip—when he needed a detective, the college would loan him Mike, no charge. In exchange, when Mike needed back-up—say because some campus threat required beefed-up patrols—the Dill PD would step in.

A knock on the door.

"Bring them in," Tip called, giving Cooper and Bolknor a sardonic look.

Officer Daisy Garrett opened the door, her round face and button nose and large blue eyes making her look like a Kewpie doll. Right now, glancing behind her, she looked like a nervous Kewpie doll.

A rangy man followed her into the office, smiling broadly, tanned deep mahogany. Definitely not from here, Cooper thought. Curly black hair spilled over his forehead. He wore cargo shorts and a Hawaiian shirt, green with pink flamingos. On his sockless feet, beach sandals. Completing the ensemble, wrap-around sunglasses, with pink lenses.

For a man hauled into police headquarters, Cooper thought, he looked remarkably ebullient.

In his arms he cradled a four-foot alligator.

He held it with one hand under its butt, the other gripping a fabric dog-harness around its upper body, designed for walking the family pet.

"Hey man," he said to Tip LaPerle. "Am I, like, arrested?"

He seemed unworried about it.

Tip shrugged.

"We don't get a lot of alligators up here," he said. "Strolling down Main Street, scaring shoppers…"

Despite being held by a human, three feet off the floor, the alligator looked relaxed. It seemed to smile, showing a mouthful of teeth. Vaguely, it resembled the man holding it.

"We invited you up here to figure all this out," Tip said, eyeing the reptile.

"Hey," the man said. "Chillin!"

He waited peacefully, for the figuring to begin.

"Take that empty chair over there," Tip said, still eyeing the alligator. "Okay, you can go, Officer Garrett."

He thought a minute, watching Daisy start out the door.

"Good work," he said.

They heard a growl, and all looked at the alligator. Then they realized the growl came from under Cooper's chair, and they looked down to see Henry lying there, glaring at the alligator and growling at it. Not one of his

11

fierce, I'm about to shred you growls, however. Cooper knew all his growls, and all his barks, too. This growl just meant: I'm right here, fully on guard, so don't mess, whatever you are.

Tip pulled a report form, from a basket on his desk. He picked up a ball-point pen and held it over the paper, but didn't immediately write.

"You got a good grip on that thing?" he asked.

The detainee laughed.

"Durango here, he's just like a puppy dog," he said. "I feed him supermarket chickens—I found him in my yard, back of my RV, no bigger than my hand back then, and that's all he's ever eaten, dead chickens from the Scallop Beach supermarket."

Tip eyed the alligator for a silent moment. Mike Bolknor looked on, as usual with no expression, but Cooper sensed he might be faintly amused. Also ready to rush the reptile, if it seemed suddenly threatening.

"What's your name?" Tip asked the man.

"I'm Joey DeMercato," the man said, with a big grin. "My buddies, back in Afghanistan, they called me the Dman, or sometimes just Demon—so, hey, call me whatever, it's cool."

"Where's this Scallop Beach?" Tip asked.

"On the Gulf," D-man said. "Florida, okay? Fun in the sun, right?"

"Where are you—and this alligator—staying here in town?" Tip asked.

"My rolling home," D-man said. "Down at the RV park, in Scallop Beach—that's where I live—I just unhooked it and drove on up here, to see the sights, you know?"

12

He thought about the sights.

"Like red barns, okay? Stone walls, whatever—my great-grandfather, he came over from Sicily, you know? To work in the granite quarries here, so I wanted to see that, hey, old-time's sake, I guess."

Tip leaned back in his chair and thought.

Cooper consulted her mental files of state statutes. "Nothing in state law addresses alligators," she said.

"Well, we got about five-thousand calls from shoppers along Main Street here, and shop owners," Tip said. "A huge reptile on the loose."

"Nah, not so big yet," D-man pointed out. "Leashed, too, around civilians, you know? Durango's got no problem with his leash."

Cooper guessed some local ordinance might cover dangerous animals in public places, but city ordinances weren't her bailiwick. For that matter, neither were yellow jackets—she'd promised Flute Wagner she'd look into it, murder by sting, but she didn't know where to start.

"All right," Tip said, picking up his desk phone. "Let's get some expertise in on this."

He leafed through his desktop Rolodex, then punched in a number. A woman's voice came over the speakerphone: "Augustus Dill Museum of Natural History, office of Dr. Steven Van Tassel, director—how may we help you?"

"This is Tip LaPerle, at the Dill PD," Tip said. "I've got to talk with Steve…thanks."

While he waited, eyes on the alligator, he said: "Let's see what Van Tassel can tell us—he's some kind of animal expert."

After a moment, Steve Van Tassel picked up, and Tip quickly explained the issue.

"Actually, I'm a fish guy," Van Tassel said. "Hang with me while I look things up...Hmmm....okay, how big's this alligator?"

D-man spoke up, from across the room.

"He's three-feet, eleven-and-a-half inches, nose to tail tip," he said. "Name's Durango. Never hurt anyone."

"Hmmm," Van Tassel said over the speakerphone. "So he isn't full grown...he on some kind of restraint?"

"Back home, I just let him roam—follows me around like a beagle pup," D-man said. "Goes in the supermarket, helps pick out chickens—he's kind of a star attraction, down there in Scallop Beach."

They heard Van Tassel faintly laugh.

"I don't know local laws on this," he said. "But if you've got him in a pet harness, with a leash...."

Tip sighed.

"Thanks, Steve," he said.

"Glad to be of not much help," Van Tassel said. "Next time we've got a catfish or a smallmouth bass terrifying shoppers on Main Street, though, give me a call!"

"Yeah," Tip said glumly.

He switched off the telephone, then sat slouched in his chair. He stared across his desk at D-man and the alligator, drumming his fingers.

"Hey, man, would it make stuff cool if I mentioned that Durango here's a certified comfort animal?" D-man said.

He put the alligator on the floor, and everyone eyed it, leery. However, the alligator merely lay down, resting

14

its snout on D-man's sandal. D-man fished a wallet out of a cargo pocket, extracted a slip of folded paper, and leaned over to lay it on Tip's desk. Then he patted the alligator's head and leaned back in his chair, watching Tip read the document.

"Well, this looks official, all right," Tip said, still staring at the paper.

"Hey, that's total legit," D-man said. "That Jerome Engel, MD, on there, he's my shrink, at the VA hospital, you know?"

Everybody looked at him.

"Yeah, I came back from Stan with PTSD," he said. "Every damned night I'd wake up yelling, from explosion dreams, like really big bad ones—red, like blood exploding, spattering all over me—blood bombs!—and
I'd wake up drenched in sweat."

He reached down and lifted the alligator back up, holding it in his arms.

"My buddies in that truck, every single one, blown to bits," he said, looking down. "Me? Not a damned scratch—makes me feel…."

He sat silently looking down. Finally he sighed and looked up.

"Since I got Durango here, it's getting better," he said. "I still dream about explosions, just about every night, but now they're mostly blue, or green, you know? With just red streaks in them, or splotches"

He looked down again, thinking.

"I guess sometimes I still wake up yelling, but Durango's lying right there on the bed, beside me, and it never bothers him…doesn't even open his eyes."

Tip told him to keep the alligator on a tight leash, walking along Main Street, out of biting range of other people. Same thing at the RV park, evenings.

"I'm down with that," D-man said, getting up to leave. "Anyone want to give Durango a goodbye pet?"

Nobody did.

They watched him amble out the door, in his sandals and Hawaiian shirt, with Durango waddling at his heels.

Cooper thought: "Dreams of blood."

After D-man and Durango left, they got to the rest of the morning's briefing.

"It's all Mickey Mouse stuff, like that alligator on Main Street," Tip said.

A logger out on the Hart's Corners road reported somebody wheeled a truck into his site at night and made off with a load of sugar-maple logs. Also, a traffic stop out on the Interstate access…locked boxes in the trunk, no drugs in them, but full-up with weird bugs— more details to come….

Later, as she started back to her office, Cooper stopped at the door and turned to look back at Tip.

"I'm going to call Steve Van Tassel myself," she said.

Then she opened the door and started out, but Henry scrambled past her, to be first.

Henry considered himself as a leader.

3

Numero Uno said: "Look!"

From under the pickup's seat he pulled a narrow foot-long package.

"Watch," he said.

He unwound the package's fabric binding, slowly, as if unwrapping a mummy.

Numero Dos said: "Oh my God!"

Numero Uno presented it laid across his two palms. They both stared at it, in silence. Numero Dos finally spoke.

"That's so...."

Numero Uno allowed one side of his mouth to curl up.

"It's a Fairbairn-Sykes commando knife," he said, voice flat.

He gazed at Numero Dos, in the bucket seat to his right, as if evaluating Numero Dos's capacity for handling the technical details he was about to impart.

"Its blade is seven inches," he said.

He continued eyeing Numero Dos.

"Its total length is eleven point five inches," he said.

Numero Dos stared at the knife as if it were holy.

"It's sheath is metal," Numero Uno said, in a tone suggesting that fact was important.

Numero Dos said: "Wow—metal—so it won't get stuck in a bush or something?"

Numero Uno regarded Numero Dos, without

expression, as if considering whether the stupidity just said invalidated Numero Dos as a partner. Finally, he shook his head.

"No, it's a really hard sheath, right?" he said. "So, you bump the knife, in its sheath, and its edge stays sharp—or maybe you drop the knife, or it's grabbed away, okay, then you can stab with the sheath." "Oh," Numero Dos said.

They sat looking out the parked pickup's windshield in silence.

"So we're set?" Numero Dos finally asked. "Ready to go?"

Numero Uno sighed, as if he'd heard one stupid question too many this afternoon.

"We don't have a target yet," he said, voice taut with suppressed annoyance. "Also—as I already told you—we start with lesser targets, practice, practice, practice-mistakes will teach us, make us perfect."

"Oh,"   said   Numero   Dos.

4

Cooper's black Volvo sedan jounced over the driveway's stones and exposed roots, threatening the car's shock absorbers. So she slowed to a crawl.

Henry rode shotgun, standing upright, forepaws braced against the dashboard. He stared out the windshield, taking in everything, sunbeams shafting through the forest's leaves and needles, red squirrel on a mossy stump, munching a beechnut, staring back at Henry, saucy-eyed....

No house in sight yet.

When she'd called to arrange this visit, Cooper received a terse response.

"I'll be in a tree."

To get here, just north of town, she'd driven into forested hills, and this unpaved driveway tunneled through white pines, yellow birches, balsam firs. It bemused Cooper, so many trees. In which one should she look?

She'd called Steve Van Tassel, at the Augustus Dill Museum of Natural History, to ask who to see, and he'd answered immediately.

"If it's got six legs, Olga Fisker's your woman."

After thinking a moment, he added an afterthought.

"Olga's a little odd."

So it would seem, Cooper thought, as her Volvo finally broke through the trees and stopped in front of the house.

Actually, a log cabin. Parked on the grass, a mud-spattered Dodge Ram. On one side, a ramshackle three-story tower rose into the treetops, with a plank platform on top, half buried in branches, accessed via a jerry-built ladder up the tower's side.

Not a prepossessing home for a world-famous entomologist.

Cooper had checked on *Wikipedia*—Olga Fisker earned her PhD at the University of California-Davis, taught there for three years, racking up research awards, but then migrated from university to university, on six continents, counting Australia, places with insects she wanted to study. Two years ago, she'd settled here, maintaining a loose affiliation with Mt. Augustus College. Her zoological eminence enhanced the college's luster, and she got research funding, with an important proviso—no need to teach students.

As she'd once told the *New York Times:* "I prefer the buzzing of insects to the buzzing of brats."

Cooper knocked on the cabin's door. No response. Nobody in the tower, obviously put up for observing insects on high branches. So she scanned the surrounding pines and poplars, looking for an entomologist in the treetops. Henry, meanwhile, nose to the ground, zigzagged around the front yard, then into the forest, then back out again, stopping once to throw back his head and bark, jubilant—nothing more exciting than exploring a new place.

"Hello?" Cooper called, cupping her hands around her mouth to create a megaphone.

"Dr. Fisker?"

No sound except the rat-a-tat of a hairy woodpecker, tapping a beech tree's bark, and the warbles and trills of winter wrens prowling the forest floor like shrews.

Cooper abruptly sat on the cabin's porch steps. A wave of tiredness. Not good. She had too many responsibilities, at the college, and now as acting state's attorney—she had no time for a flu.

"Olga Fisker?" she called.

This time she did get a response, from high in one of the white-ash trees bordering the house.

"Come up—here's an Agrilus planipennis!"

Cooper struggled to her feet, then walked to the ash's base, haltingly, because her cane's tip sank into the lawn's soil. She looked up. High overhead, a woman straddled a branch, as if seated on a horse. She looked down at Cooper looking up.

"Climb the tree," Olga Fisker called down.

Cooper shook her head.

She held up her cane for Fisker to see.

Silence from the treetop.

After a moment, a thick rope snaked down from above, and a moment later Olga Fisker descended, hand over hand on the rope, sneakers clasping the rope between them to prevent an out-of-control drop.

She got to the ground, retrieving something from her trouser pocket, clasping it in a loose fist.

"I got an emerald ash borer," she told Cooper, holding out her clasped hand. "Brunching on that ash, of course—I squashed it, figuring I didn't need its head."

She opened her hand to show Cooper a partly smashed beetle displayed on her palm.

"These adults just nibble leaves, no harm," Fisker said. "It's the larvae that kill the trees—they eat the inner bark, blocking moisture and nutrients, so the trees starve."

Henry leaned against Fisker's leg, a ploy for getting attention, and waited for her to fuss over him. Fisker, however, only absent-mindedly patted his head, while studying the dead beetle in her other hand.

About five-feet-six, Cooper estimated, and rangy. Fisker wore a grimy t-shirt picturing a moth's head on the front, gigantically enlarged, and heavy-duty tan work trousers, smeared with pine sap, held up by suspenders. She wore her hair, once blond, now with gray strands, pulled back into an out-of-her way ponytail. She squinted at Cooper, her hazel eyes evaluating.

"Okay," she said. "I thought we'd go hunt a spotted lanternfly, but you're old and lame, and you look sick, so let's just sit on the porch."

She led the way and Cooper followed, thinking, do I really look so damned sick?

Henry gave up trying to get Fisker's attention and wandered off, disgruntled.

You're pouting, Henry, like a spoiled two-year-old, Cooper thought—you're an embarrassment.

She told Fisker about Flute Wagner's visit to the state's attorney's office, and his insistence that the president of Snowville Maple, Inc., was murdered, stung by yellowjackets, one wasp planted in each of his suit's sleeves.

"Is that actually a possibility?" Cooper asked. "Wasps in sleeves?"

Fisker, brow wrinkled in thought, sat looking at the squashed beetle on her palm. It shone in the late-spring sun, metallic green, its half-smashed head shiny brown.

"I'm looking for morphological changes," Fisker said. "Here's a species in a new ecosystem, so how does it adjust?"

And that, Cooper thought, has nothing to do with yellowjacket wasps, does it? What I asked about?

"They're from Asia, these ash borers," Fisker said. "They showed up near Detroit in 2002—stow-aways, probably, on a cargo ship or plane, and they've already spread to thirty-five states, at least."

Cooper waited for the conversation to get back to yellowjackets.

"You'd think they'd die here," Fisker said. "Like we would, plopped down on Mars, and lots of invasive species do die, but some thrive, like these emerald ash borers—how do they do it?"

Henry wandered over and lay at Cooper's feet. He sighed, a petulant sigh. He shut his eyes and went to sleep. Or pretended to, Cooper thought.

"About the yellowjackets…." Cooper started.

"Right, hymenoptera, accused of homicide," Fisker said. "So, what can I tell you?"

"First, could yellowjacket stings kill an allergic man?" Cooper asked.

"Yup," Fisker said. "What else?"

Cooper could see Fisker studying the emerald ash borer's corpse again. Better ask fast, she thought. Before I lose her.

"How likely that a yellowjacket would hide in a man's sleeve?" she asked.

Fisker shrugged.

"Yellowjackets are super aggressive," she said. "So there's that."

She raised her palm to peer at the dead beetle up close. Cooper could tell the woman made an effort to stay on the porch. She clearly wanted to run inside and get the beetle under her microscope. For now, though, she kept talking about yellowjackets.

"Other wasps, also bees, they lose their stingers when they sting, it gets pulled out, but not yellowjackets,"
Fisker said. "So they can sting you again and again."

She considered, searching her memory.

"They'll sting you unprovoked, but they mostly attack to protect their nest," she said.

Fisker suddenly laid the dead beetle on the porch and stood up. She stretched. Then she executed three cartwheels. Henry, forgetting he was supposed to be petulant, watched intently. A new game? Maybe he could get in on it.

"I like to move," Fisker told Cooper.

Cooper decided to hurry this interview along. Any second Fisker might climb back up in her tree.

"So a suit jacket's left draped over a chair, and a wasp crawls into the sleeve," Cooper said. "How likely is that?"

"It's possible," Fisker said. "Sometimes yellowjackets nest in attics, or in a building's walls, so they can show up inside."

Garbage attracts them, she said. Also, human foods, especially meat and sweets—"So did this dead guy have candy bars in his pockets?"

"What about two wasps, one in each sleeve?" Cooper asked.

"Possible," Fisker said.

Carefully, between thumb and forefinger, she picked up the beetle carcass she'd laid on the porch floor.

"Possible," she repeated. "But extremely unlikely, maybe a one-percent chance—so, yeah, this guy probably got murdered."

Cooper thought: Flute Wagner's got a case. A strong case.

"Let's say I decided to use these wasps as murder weapons," Cooper said. "How would I collect them without getting stung myself?"

Fisker abruptly turned and ran into her house, leaving the door open behind her.

Interview over? Cooper had no idea. She leaned back against the porch's railing, eyes closed, tired, unsure what to do now.

She heard Fisker rummaging in the house, then hurrying back onto the porch. Cooper opened her eyes and saw Fisker had brought out an empty soda bottle and a small implement. Fisker sat back down and started work on the bottle with the implement.

"Bottle cutter," she said, as she worked.

After a minute or so she'd cut off the top third of the bottle, with the narrow neck in one hand and the bottle's wide bottom two-thirds—now headless—resting on the porch floor. She hurried back inside and reemerged in a moment with a bottle of strawberry jam and a spoon.

She spooned out jam and dropped it into the bottom of the bottle. Then she inverted the cut-off top and inserted its narrow neck into the larger bottom.

She stared at her creation.

"See?" she said. "Now it's a funnel."

She hurried back into the house. Moments later, she rushed back out, holding a roll of duct tape, which she used to tape the bottle's two segments together. Then she held it up for Cooper to admire.

"Here comes a yellowjacket," she said, weaving her extended forefinger in the air to represent a wasp.

She hovered her finger over the top of the two-part bottle.

"She's smelling that sugary stuff in there," Fisker said. "And there she goes."

She pretended to swoop her finger down into the funnel she'd created on top of the bottle, and pretended to watch a yellowjacket crawling down, then dropping inside the bottle.

"Voila," she said. "Now she can't get back out— wasp trap."

Cooper stood, ready to leave.

"Thanks for making time for me," she said.

"Actually, I haven't thought about wasps in years, I've been so focused on invasive beetles," Fisker said.

"Homicidal wasps, interesting, yes?"

Cooper thought, yes, it is interesting. Maybe Flute Wagner was onto something. She'd certainly look into it, and now she knew what she'd be looking for.

"Hey, I liked talking with you, and I don't like small talk," Fisker said. "A few days ago I lapsed, let a high school science class visit here, field trip, end of the school year—bummer!"

She shook her head, exasperated.

"Zero interest in insects," she said. "Just out of college—stupid me—I married a rock-band guitarist, which one of these kids dug up on the Internet, so they wanted to hear about that, and only that, two of them, a boy and a girl, who didn't even pretend to be interested, just prowled around the outside of the house, looking at God knows what."

Cooper laughed.

"Casing the joint?" she said.

"That'd be an exercise in futility," Fisker said. "Unless they want a bunch of old sap-stained clothes or little boxes with dead insects inside."

Cooper said she'd had her own experiences with high-schoolers, when teachers invited her to tell students about the prosecutor's role in law enforcement.

"Clearly didn't grab them," she said. "I assume that's what it means, resting your head on the desk, while the guest's talking, or staring vacantly out the window."

She gave Fisker her thanks, said she'd call if she had further questions, and led Henry back to the car. Driving away, she glanced in the rearview mirror and saw Fisker about to climb back up into the tree, but pausing to stare down the driveway, watching Cooper's car drive away. I liked her, Cooper thought. Maybe someday….

A few minutes later, back in town, driving along Main Street, Cooper saw a small crowd gathered on the sidewalk, and slowed to see what drew it, looking out through her car's open window.

Joey DeMercato drew it, and Durango. Mainly Durango.

"He's like a puppy," D-man was telling his rapt audience.

Women carrying shopping bags imprinted with names of Main Street boutiques stared at the alligator, but from a safe distance, while a gaggle of high school students got up close to peer at the reptile. One boy pretended to reach down and lift up the alligator and thrust it at his girlfriend, who flinched away, until she realized he hadn't actually gripped the reptile and lifted it, and then she pretended to look disgusted with his behavior.

"What he really likes, Durango does, is to be hugged," D-man sad.

He bent over, got a grip on the alligator's flanks and lifted him, cradling him in his arms.

"Over at the Dill RV Park, where we're staying, folks pet him," D-man said. "He's a rock star, you know?."

Cooper speeded up, heading down the street to the State's Attorney's Office, shaking her head.

It had looked, almost, as if Durango enjoyed the crowd's attention. Seemingly, the reptile smiled.

28

Which is nuts, Cooper told herself. He's just showing teeth.

5

Cooper left Henry with Mike Bolknor.

No problem for Henry—he idolized the big man.

At first, though, Cooper had questioned hiring Bolknor. When a coronary felled the college's previous police chief, they needed a replacement, fast. Cooper—who chaired the Campus Security Committee—hired Mike Bolknor, sight unseen. Easy choice. An NYPD detective, highly rated. Why, though, exile himself to northern New England? And what made him so melancholy?

A telephone call from Bolknor's sister, in the military overseas, finally explained it—his wife, daughter, and son, all killed in a road-rage shooting. New York now unbearable. Too many memories. So he'd fled, to Dill.

For Henry, it was love at first sight.

Whenever the corgi vanished from Cooper's college office, she knew where to look. He'd be downstairs, sleeping under Mike's desk, resting his muzzle on the security chief's extra-large shoe.

It puzzled Cooper, because Henry expected to be fussed over, and Mike didn't fuss. Even so, she thought, if Henry had to choose, Mike Bolknor or me....

For this drive to Snowville, she'd left Henry happily snoozing under Mike's desk. She'd scheduled interviews at Snowville Maple, Inc, despite this oncoming flu's fatigue. It strained her. So she didn't need Henry's shenanigans.

Just south of Dill, the landscape turned tippy, overgrown meadows slanting up hillsides to forested crests. She passed white-clapboard farmhouses, shuttered in black, spiffed up by physicians and professors and attorneys, without a Holstein to be seen. Some of the old barns now housed riding horses.

A few miles farther, though, past the gentrification zone, the farmhouses showed their true age, after a century, or more, of July scorchers and January sub-zero freezes. Roof shingles curled. Paint faded, or peeling. Barns leaning toward collapse. Dead tractors abandoned in the fields. In the driveways, rusted pickups. Even the occasional singlewides looked ancient and decrepit.
And then, just five miles south of Dill, a flaking sign, "Welcome to Snowville, Est. 1763."

Tacked on underneath, another sign, hand-lettered by some bitter local wit: "Town That Lost Its Marbles."

It took Cooper a half minute to drive through the village. Buxley's General Store. Marble Street Bar and Grill. Snowville Diner, still offering meatloaf, or bologna on buttered white bread. Sidewalks paved with marble slabs. Two-story houses, out-of-plumb, their dark windows evoking elderly eyes, sadly remembering better times.

Once they'd quarried here, immigrants from Italy, Spain, Wales, and Quebec, cutting marble from beneath the hills and chiseling it into building blocks and cemetery monuments. Skimpy deposits, though, in this section of the Green Mountains, where granite ruled, and the marble ran out. Residents now drove snowplows and school buses, or worked in construction, or commuted to Dill to drive trash removal trucks, or tar roofs, or stack supermarket shelves.

At the town's south edge, Cooper abruptly braked, and pulled to the roadside, to stare at Snowville Maple, Inc.

She remembered shacks, a ramble of them, with sugaring gear stacked outside. All razed since she last drove by here, and replaced.

Now a new three-story headquarters, in the traditional white-clapboard style, but obviously recently built, featured triple-glazed picture windows all around. Mounted on its black-metal roof, solar panels.

On one side, in a brushy field, heaped here and there with quarrying slag, stretched phalanxes of giant solar panels, mounted on swivel bases with sensors, to automatically track the sun, turning like phototropic mechanical flowers. On the building's other side, a series of garages held the company's trucks for transporting syrup. A large barn housed pumps and other sugaring gear. Next to the barn stood a modern sugarhouse, for boiling sap into syrup, with smoke stacks sticking up.

So Proctor Gibbs, who began life on a marginal hill farm, ended up heading a thriving corporation.

Cooper thought: Proctor, you did well.

Then she remembered: Proctor's dead.

Somehow it seemed preposterous, so jovial a man, with merry blue eyes, and that enormous white mustache.

Dead.

Murdered?

Maybe.

She parked in a row of slots labeled "Visitors," with two long spaces beyond, labeled "Tour Buses."

No buses right now, but a dozen cars in the visitor slots, all with out-of-state plates. Cooper thought, we're becoming a rustic theme park. City people come here to experience the imaginary good old days, when every farm had a sugarhouse, and every March, after town meeting, Vermont farmers pounded iron taps into their sugar maples, the sap plinking into hundreds of tin buckets, filling the woods with pagan music.

Picturesque, certainly. But not the whole story, Cooper thought, on her way into the headquarters building.

No roadside placards, for instance, at least none Cooper ever saw, commemorated the many hundreds of Vermont youths who rushed to join the Union Army, to fight against slavery, but also—maybe mostly—to get away from milking cows on 10-below January mornings, and shoveling half-frozen manure, and to escape those lonely hill farms, and grim Dad.

Inside, polished hardwood flooring and windowsills. Wall-to-ceiling photographs lined the walls, showing maple-syrup harvesting underway, both old-time sugaring, with horse-drawn wagons and tin buckets, and the modern version, with white tubes snaking through the maple forest.

"I'm here to see Myron DeWitt—I've got an appointment," Cooper told the auburn-haired receptionist, who looked at Cooper blank faced, as if what Cooper said made no sense.

She's just a high-school kid, Cooper thought.

Summer job, probably.

"No Myron DeWitt here," the girl said, shaking her head. "Nope."

She looked pleased with herself, delivering negative news. She looked past Cooper, who glanced back over her own shoulder—a boy now leaned against the entryway doorframe, looking on, also high-school age, long legs, buzz-cut blond hair, smirk. In his left hand he dangled vehicle keys. For no apparent reason, a title came into Cooper's mind, a novel she'd once enjoyed, *The Left Hand of Darkness*.

Cooper thought: "So our receptionist is playing to the audience."

She felt too tired for stupid games.

Cooper put her hands on the girl's desk and leaned toward her, causing the receptionist to pull back her head, startled.

"Now that Proctor Gibbs has died, isn't the new president of this company Mr. DeWitt?" Cooper asked, quietly, tonelessly, the voice she used in front of juries, for questioning hostile witnesses.

"Yeah," the girl said.

A pretty girl, or would be, with her auburn hair, the rich reddish brown of horse chestnuts. Her green eyes, though, seemed vacant, a no-there-there look.

"From where I'm standing, I see his office door, behind you," Cooper said, in that same emotionless voice. "On that door is a sign, obviously new, and what do you think that sign says?"

A shrug from the receptionist, looking sullen.

"I'll read it to you," Cooper said. "It says 'Myron DeWitt, Chief Operating Officer'—doesn't it?"

She leaned a bit closer, forcing the girl to pull her head even farther back, not a comfortable position.
Green eyes now looking aside, avoiding Cooper's steady close-up gaze.

"So why did you say there's no Myron DeWitt here?" Cooper asked, no accusation in her voice, just a request for information.

Now the girl's green eyes looked down at her hands on her desk. She turned the hands palms down and stared at her emerald-green fingernails, as if they were magic talismans, giving her strength in a confusing situation.

Suddenly, she plunged her hand into her trouser pocket and pulled out a package of chewing gum. With effort, she managed to pull out one stick of gum, and then, like an addict preparing a desperately needed shot, she hurriedly pulled off the gum's paper wrapping and stuffed the stick of gum into her mouth, and chewed, releasing into the office air a scent of spearmint.

Cooper waited.

After a moment, as if the girl had thought this out, a real stumper, but now knew the answer, she jerked up her head, belligerence in her stare.

"Because he told me!" she said.

"I see," Cooper said. "What did he tell you?"

"He doesn't like being called Myron," the girl said.
"He likes Sonny."

Cooper considered asking the girl why she didn't say that in the first place, and why the office sign said Myron, if Sonny DeWitt didn't like that name, and why she was such a pill. She decided against it. No point going to war with a child, particularly a rude and offensive child.

Also, she suddenly thought, a profoundly stupid child.

Cooper leaned back and took her hands off the girl's desk and stood up straight, silently studying the girl.

"What's your name?" she asked.

"Winnie Rink," the girl said, looking back down at her emerald fingernails, furiously chewing her gum.

Cooper thought: if a stronger personality told you to leap from a cliff, Winnie Rink, you'd immediately go full lemming.

She turned to see if the boy still smirked in the doorway, but he'd disappeared.

"What's your boyfriend's name?" she asked, indicating with her chin the doorway, where the smirking boy had stood.

"Vic Ledger," the girl said, looking up, suddenly bright eyed, confident, proud, as if all the world knew being Vic Ledger's girlfriend put you tiptop on the social mountain.

Cooper sighed.

Since childhood she'd read people and situations, by their intonations and gestures and facial expressions. As a five-year-old, perhaps she couldn't articulate it, but even then she often saw clearly what hid behind people's words, and why they did what they did. As for this girl....

Looking steadily now, at Winnie Rink, she felt her interest wane, this small battle of wills hardly worth fighting.

Because she didn't care. Little girls and little boys, with their little preoccupations with each other, and their attitudes, seemed just...little.

She shook her head. She really needed to check with her doctor about this fatigue, she thought. Before she got even more irritable. Probably they had some kind of pill to fight off viruses.

Cooper left Winnie Rink staring down at her green fingernails. She walked around the reception desk, her cane loudly thumping on the hardwood floor, and rapped her knuckles on the door labeled "Myron DeWitt, Chief

Operating Officer."

Why did that name suddenly sound familiar?

From behind the polished-maple door came a booming voice: "Entrez!"

6

Cooper walked into the office and beheld Snowville Maple's chief executive officer, who lounged in a plush office chair, leaning back, his running shoes up on his desk, legs crossed at the ankles, revealing white athletic socklets. He held a thick half-eaten ham-and-cheese sandwich in his left hand and a large tumbler of what surely was beer in his right hand.

He regarded Cooper blankly, not knowing what to make of this visitor.

"I thought you'd be one of the kids," he said. "Wanting to leave work early or something."

"I'm the Allen County state's attorney—Cooper North," she said. "I have an appointment."

Myron "Sonny" DeWitt looked bewildered, then hurriedly leafed through the paperwork strewn across his desk. He finally disinterred an appointment calendar, and stared at it.

"Is this Monday?" he asked. "Or Tuesday?"

"It's Tuesday," Cooper said.

She thought: this guy's now the CEO?

Her first impression of Sonny DeWitt: "sloppy."

A large man, not Mike Bolknor's size, but large, nevertheless. High school football, Cooper guessed. Maybe even college. Now going to flab, his pale-blue dress shirt pushed out from his trousers by an expanding belly. His future clearly featured a fat man.

Sonny suddenly sat up, squinting at Cooper, looking canny.

"Okay, so why's the state's attorney come calling?" he said. "Hey, I'm CEO here, so I can do whatever—you want a complimentary bottle of syrup? Two bottles? A case?"

Cooper thought: he assumes I want to finagle free syrup. So that's how he thinks, everyone's wheeling and dealing.

"No syrup, thanks," she said. "I'm here about Proctor Gibbs."

He sank back in his chair, shaking his head.

"Poor old Proc," he muttered. "We all told him, keep an EpiPen in your desk drawer, for God's sake, I told him that every day, almost, but he'd just chuckle…."

His big hand still clutched the ham-and-Swiss sandwich, and he waved it, absent-mindedly, in the general direction of his office's extra chair, inviting Cooper to sit.

"I had some confusion with your receptionist," Cooper said. "Something about your name, Myron."

He groaned, and laid down his sandwich, and turned up his eyes.

"Those kids!" he said, keeping his eyes dramatically upturned.

Blue eyes.

Disheveled brown hair falling over his forehead. Face darkened. Suntan, Cooper thought. His skin's weathering suggested skiing in the winter. Also, though, something else made his face liverish.

She'd had her own problems with alcohol, like her father before her, and here sat Sonny DeWitt, drinking beer at brunch.

Did he come into work most mornings hung over? She knew something about that. Maybe he didn't even make it mornings, came in around lunchtime, with his head pounding.

"It's standard procedure," Cooper said. "We investigate, when a county resident unexpectedly dies."

She intentionally omitted the modifying phrase, "...dies, under suspicious circumstances." No point getting the new Snowville Maple CEO alarmed. She'd come to gather information, and she wanted him to speak freely, without lawyers dancing in his head. Sonny DeWitt produced a wry smile.

"Yeah, I told Winnie out there, Myron's a jerk name," he said. "What kind of parents embarrass their kid with a name like that—in school, they called me Sonny, and I use that, but right after Proc died the corporation's Board moved me here, into Proc's old office, and put up that "Myron" sign on the door, didn't check with me or anything...."

He sighed, hunching his shoulders.

"I was vice president for sales," he said.

He shook his head.

"What that meant was, I headed the sales force, right?" he said. "Except the sales force was just me—I'd drive around to grocery stores and tourist shops, all over New England, and sell them on stocking our syrup, which I was good at, and it was fun, out of the office, tooling around, but now...."

Cooper guessed "tooling around" included frequent stops at ski resorts, to hit the slope, and tavern stops, too.

Sonny stared down moodily at the paperwork mounded on his desk, and moved some of the documents around with a thick forefinger.

"So you were next in line, after Proctor, to be CEO," Cooper prompted.

She wanted to talk about wasps in sleeves. Sometimes, though, to get a witness talking freely it worked best to just let them ramble, because they might volunteer what you needed to know, or even what you didn't think to ask.

"Yeah, next in line," he said. "Who else was there? Just me and the new guy, the Flute Man."

He still stared at the paperwork on his desk, looking glum.

"I called my mother, downstate," he said.

He seemed to speak mostly to himself.

"I told her, hey, it was in the papers—your youngest kid just made CEO!"

His face darkened, as if a curtain of gloom descended.

He made his voice go high, and sharp, imitating Mom.

"Yeah, Myron, thanks to a guy dying—how long before you mess this one up?"

He stared darkly at the wall. Then he stood and walked to the office window and looked out at the parking lot, hands shoved into his trouser pockets, shoulders hunched. He sighed.

"DeWitt Fuel & Shop!" he suddenly said, making it sound like a curse.

"They took in my big brother, and my sister, too, but they wouldn't even let me...."

Cooper suddenly understood why the name DeWitt seemed familiar. She'd seen it on convenience stores, across the state.

Sonny made a sound like a snarl. He swiveled around and glared at Cooper, as if it were she who wouldn't take him into the family business, because of a history of messing up.

"Well, what is it you want?" he demanded.

Cooper thought: that was sudden, this upwelling of anger. Haunted eyes, though. So it seemed to her. Emotions galore slithering in his head. Looking at his now sullen face, Cooper thought, he's scared. He doesn't think he's up to running this company.

"I want to talk about yellow-jacket wasps," Cooper said. "Do many of them buzz around inside this building?"

"Who knows?" Sonny said.

He sank into his chair, leaning back, and stared at the ceiling.

She heard him mutter to himself: "Every damn thing I've ever touched...."

"Two yellow-jackets got into Proctor Gibbs' sleeves," Cooper said.

Sonny shrugged.

"Well, stuff happens," he told the ceiling.

"This office, when it was Proctor's," Cooper said. "Did he usually leave the door open?"

Sonny, still leaning back in his chair, closed his eyes.

"Yeah, " he said. "He liked shooting the breeze, you know?"

"So workers here could just walk into his office whenever they wanted," Cooper said. "To speak to him?" Sonny abruptly straightened in his chair, giving Cooper a squint-eyed look. He reached for the sandwich he'd left lying atop the desk's mounded paperwork, then changed his mind and grabbed the beer glass with his other hand. He took a swig.

"When he left the office?" Cooper asked. "Did he still always leave the door open?"

"Yeah, we'd leave him notes and stuff," he said. "So where's this going, these questions?"

"Just trying to get straight what happened that day, when Proctor died," Cooper said. "So people could just walk into this office at will, whether he was here or not?"

Sonny nodded, still squinting at Cooper, as if trying to understand what she had in mind.

"Did he usually have on his suit jacket?" she asked.

"If he could of, he'd have worn rubber Wellington boots to work, overalls, suspenders, that would be old Proc's style," Sonny said. "Running a business, though, there's standards...."

He sat back, staring at his desktop. Then he straightened up.

"No, he hardly ever wore the suit jacket, not when he didn't need to," he said. "He mostly kept it hung over the back of his chair."

Sonny looked down at the arms of his chair, as if suddenly realizing that Proctor Gibbs' chair was now his chair. Using his big forefinger, he began pushing papers on his desk, this way, that way.

43

Maybe he wants to get to work, Cooper thought. She doubted, though, that this big sloppy man did much actual work. He had energy, she could see that. Plenty enough for skiing or tennis. In bars, he probably got loud and vociferous. Not much energy for office paperwork, though.

"Were you here when Proctor Gibbs died?" Cooper asked.

"It was me who called 911," Sonny said. "Awful."

He'd walked into the office, he said, to tell Gibbs a general store near a ski resort wanted to set up a standing order, a monthly case of syrup. Sonny wanted Proctor to help figure out a delivery schedule, but Proctor lay on the floor, on his back, unresponsive. By the time the ambulance arrived, he'd stopped breathing.

"We thought, heart attack," Sonny said. "After they took him away, I pulled his jacket off the chair, and shook it, sort of to get wrinkles out, I guess, something to do— and a wasp dropped out of each sleeve."

"Have you ever seen wasps in this office?" Cooper asked, quickly looking at the walls and windows, to see if any yellow-jackets crawled there.

None did.

"Nah, outside sometimes, out by the sheds I think I've seen some," Sonny said. "Maybe they've got a nest out there or something."

He took another swig of his beer, then a bite of ham-and-Swiss sandwich, followed by another swig of beer.

Cooper felt a wave of weariness and sank back in her chair, eyes closed.

"You okay?" Sonny asked.

She opened her eyes and nodded. Just tired, she thought. Overwork, maybe, or this damned flu coming on.

"I'm fine," she said. "That day Proctor died, let's recreate it, okay?"

Sonny shrugged.

"Where was your office?" Cooper asked.

"Next door to this one," Sonny said, slanting his head to indicate where his former office stood.

"Could you see everyone who went into Proctor's office?" Cooper asked.

"Sure, if I spent the whole day in my doorway, but I didn't," Sonny said. "So, I guess I just saw some people going in and out."

He shrugged.

"Was Proctor in his office all day?" Cooper asked.

Sonny screwed up his face, to indicate he was thinking hard.

"Nah," he said finally. "One time during the morning he headed out to the maple shed, to check if the tubing got stored right—I overheard him telling that new guy, Flute Wagner, that's what he was doing—so he was gone for, like an hour, maybe, probably got into chitchatting with people out there, the man really liked to talk, you know?"

Cooper had a sudden memory from high school, Proctor Gibbs leaning against a corridor wall, no mustache then, entertaining a gaggle of classmates with a story about a recalcitrant cow that stepped on his father's foot and then mooed, as if bragging about it. He'd gotten a laugh.

"Do you know some people, at least, who went into his office while he was out at the shed?" Cooper asked.

Sonny put up his hands and shrugged, clearly tiring of the questioning.

"As I say," Cooper said. "We have to investigate when a citizen dies unexpectedly, just a standard procedure, so I'd appreciate it if you'd help me figure out the events just before he died."

Sonny sighed and made an "I'm thinking" face, which involved frowning and squinting down at his belly, where it pushed out over his belt, forcing one button out of its buttonhole, to reveal a sliver of white undershirt.

"Okay," he said. "I was in and out of his office myself, putting slips of paper with questions in his inbox, like what deal can we offer a store ordering more than one case of syrup a month, for instance, stuff like that.

He made the "I'm thinking face" again.

"I'm pretty sure Wagner went in a few times, probably suggesting a new look for the syrup cans or something," Sonny said. "He's at it all the time, Mickey Mouse crap like that."

It's called "marketing," Cooper thought. Flute Wagner's the vice president for marketing. And we can guess that Sonny DeWitt is not in love with Flute Wagner.

"So I saw that kid, Vic Ledger, go in there at least once," Sonny said. "He does the tours for tourists, so maybe he needed to know how fast sap drips into a bucket, or something like that." He thought.

"Lots of people went in there, I could hear them going in and out, but I don't know who they all were, maybe truck drivers, whoever," he said. "That's all I've got."

Cooper stood, reaching for the cane she'd left leaning against her chair's arm.

"Thank you, Mr. DeWitt," she said. "That's enough for today—but I may have to come back for more information."

"Yeah, whatever," he said.

Glumly, he watched Cooper leave his office.

7

As she exited the building, Cooper found a crowd at the entrance, waiting for a tour to begin. Just then the guide walked up, Winnie Rink's boyfriend, Vic Ledger.

Cooper usually decoded people quickly, their words, intonations, facial expressions, posture, gestures, but this tall boy, with buzz-cut blond hair, seemed alien, his face as expressionless as one she once saw in a zoo's herpetology section, when she'd peered through the glass pane into what seemed an empty cage.

On the pane's far side, just inches from her eyes, a long shape rose up.

Cobra.

Through the glass, its face—frighteningly blank—stared into hers.

Snakes gave Cooper the heebie-jeebies.

She decided to join the tour. Maybe she'd learn more about the company. Also, she wanted to get a reading on Vic Ledger—on the day of the yellow-jacket stings, according to Sonny DeWitt, this boy had gone into Proctor Gibbs' office.

Cooper disliked Ledger's eyes—pale blue, almost white, like January lake ice, opaque over frigid water.

"Let's go see how maple syrup's made," Ledger announced.

He turned and ambled toward the sugarhouse, not looking back, apparently uninterested in whether the tour's twelve people followed him, or not.

A shack made of rough boards, with a red-metal roof, a tin smokestack sticking up. Parked beside it a hefty pickup truck, olive green, mud spattered. Probably for off-road expeditions to set up the sap piping. Beside it stood a long trailer, with seats, clearly for taking visitors to Snowville Maple on tours of the maple groves.

Cooper walked at the back of the crowd, using her cane, just behind an elderly woman sagging in a wheelchair, pushed by her equally aged husband. Ahead of them walked two couples, in their late thirties, with four small children between them, two girls chattering excitedly, one boy looking sullen, and one boy walking backwards, maybe out of boredom.

Otherwise, the group consisted of a seventyish man, skinny, with a white Vandyke mustache and beard, wearing black jeans and a black t-shirt and carrying a notebook, in which he'd already started scribbling. Cooper guessed he must be working on an article, or a book.

Ledger stopped and turned to address the crowd.

"Here's the sugarhouse," he said. "This one's modern—old-time sugarhouses looked shacky."

He recited this memorized spiel, face and tone both expressionless, uninterested, as if he spoke to an audience of paper cutouts.

"Let's get to know ourselves," he said, from his script. "So everybody say where you're from—you start, lady in the wheelchair."

He glanced at Cooper, standing in back, leaning on her cane. Something in his eyes....Because I argued with his girlfriend, she thought. He looked away.

In a quavering voice, the lady in the wheelchair said she and her husband came from Akron, Ohio, her husband a tire-industry retiree, whose grandparents lived on a Vermont farm, so they came to see.

After that others spoke. From Brooklyn, one couple said. Vacationing in the Green Mountains to give their two girls a sense of the farms that produced their food. From Connecticut, the other couple said, just up for a few days' getaway, at their second home, a Stowe condo.

Ledger's gaze fixed again on Cooper.

"What about you?" he said.

"I'm from Dill," she said.

Ledger stared at her, as if her living locally mattered.

"House in town?" he asked.

For some reason, the question—or a sharpening of his gaze as he asked it—piqued Cooper. Whether she lived in town, or in the surrounding countryside, what difference did it make?

"Yes, in town," Cooper said, determined to say nothing more about herself.

Ledger shrugged.

Cooper thought: disappointed? That I don't live out in the hills?

It made no sense.

"What about you?" Ledger asked, looking at the VanDyke-bearded man, dressed in black, carrying a notebook.

"Absolutely!" the man said, in a voice loud enough to prompt everyone on the tour to turn and look back at him, even the four children.

"I am," he said, "Allister Chesterton!"

He paused to look at the tour members, apparently expecting faces to light up with recognition. None did.

"Department of History, Mt. Augustus College," he announced. "Chairman." Still no brightening of faces.

"Emeritus," he said.

People regarded him politely, but without recognition. Disgust passed over his face, as if he now felt he dealt with ignoramuses.

He sighed.

"Allister Chesterton, PhD," he said. "Author of *Green Mountain Boys versus Yorkers—How Ethan Allen forged the Independent Republic of Vermont, January 15, 1777 to March 14, 1791.*"

Cooper now vaguely recognized the name, and thought she might have seen the book displayed at the Main Street Bookstore, along with other local history books.

Ledger stared at him, face as blank as ever, but Cooper sensed something suppressed.

"So you live on campus?" he asked.

"Certainly not," Chesterton said, as if the suggestion insulted him.

"I have a home on a mountain, in a balsam and spruce forest, three miles outside of town," he said. "A site where no shrieking kindergarteners and yapping cocker spaniels will disrupt my work—I write books with intellectual heft, requiring intense concentration."

"Your wife okay with living out in the woods?" Ledger asked.

Chesterton shook his head, whether because this probing of his personal life annoyed him, or because he thought the issue too trivial to consider.

"My wife exited the marriage fourteen years ago," he said. "I live alone now, thank God, with my writing and my books, and every dawn begins a day of discovery and accomplishment!"

Ledger kept that blank gaze on him, as if processing important information. Then he turned, to resume the tour, but Allister Chesterton had more to say.

"I've been persuaded by the directors of the Snowville Maple corporation to write a history of this company," he announced. "However, that is too limited—instead, I've decided to tell the story of maple sugaring's evolution, starting when Abenakis roamed these mountains, and culminating in this company's founding, and I...."

"Let's get the tour moving," Ledger said, cutting Chesterton off.

He turned, opened the sugarhouse's door, and walked in, once again unconcerned whether the audience followed or not.

Cooper, at the back of the crowd, waited for her turn to go in, thinking of the exchange she'd just seen, the high school boy cutting short the college professor.

So, she thought, we know this boy's a controller. He feels so dominant he tells an adult to shut up. And that adult's an egotistical windbag. Possibly, though, Allister Chesterton's a useful windbag, she thought, because he's also probing Snowville Maple. He might have insights to share.

"It takes forty gallons of sap to make one gallon of maple syrup," Ledger announced.

He spoke tonelessly, as if this lecture bored him, and he wanted it known it bored him. Yet, he recited his prepared script perfectly. So, despite his sneering, he couldn't be accused of shirking his work. A manipulator, then.

Cooper thought: clearly, he can't tolerate being directed.

Would he resent a boss's orders? Enough to murder?

Farfetched, she thought.

This is just a high-school kid.

"Sap's mostly clear water, just two-percent sugar," Ledger said. "To get syrup, you have to boil off all that water."

Cooper watched Allister Chesterton furiously scribble notes, forehead knotted in concentration. She thought: Chesterton puts on a show, too. Ledger proves to himself he takes no orders, by sneering through his spiel. Meanwhile, it's kindergarten information, so Chesterton doesn't need notes on it. Yet, he's scribbling furiously. Maybe because Mt. Augustus College is no history powerhouse, no Yale or Princeton. As scholars go, he's a small fry. So he takes notes, forehead knotted, to convince himself he's a heavy-hitting researcher.

Cooper suddenly felt a need to collapse into a chair.

Her weariness, down into her bones, stunned her. She looked around the sugarhouse, but saw no chair. So she leaned hard against her cane.

"Early spring's sugaring season," Ledger said. "Because you need freezing nights and thawing days—that gets the sap running."

From a wall rack he pulled a poster-sized photograph showing a farmer hammering a metal tap into a maple's trunk, with tin buckets hanging from taps already hammered into nearby trees.

Cooper had a memory flash, a childhood visit with her parents to a sugaring operation, huge Belgians and Percherons hauling collection wagons up forested hills, where tractors couldn't go, snow drifts still on the ground. Farmers toting sap-slopping buckets to the wagon, for transport down to the sugarhouse. All through the forest, sap plinking into hundreds of tin buckets.

"No buckets now," Ledger said. "Taps drip sap into white plastic tubes, slung from tree to tree, with pumps pushing it down to that collecting tank over there."

He pointed, languidly, at a large vat in one corner of the sugarhouse.

Chesterton scribbled a note about that.

"Over there's a reverse-osmosis machine," Ledger said pointing. "You run the sap through that to get out a lot of the water, saves boiling time."

"Here's the arch, where the fire burns," he said, indicating the long steel stand dominating the room. "Used to be wood fires in there, but modern places like this mostly burn oil."

Cooper stepped backwards and leaned against a wall. Her weariness distressed her. Even so, she found herself staring across the room—crawling down the opposite wall, a yellow-jacket wasp.

"That's the evaporator pan, resting on top of the arch," Ledger said. "It's where the sap gets boiled down to syrup."

Cooper started toward the door, her cane thumping. She felt everyone turn to look at her. She felt Ledger's eyes on her back.

"Got to go," she announced over her shoulder. "Appointment."

Outside, she shuffled to her Volvo and sagged into the driver's seat.

She sat that way, summoning the energy to drive.

She thought: I've got to see a doctor.

8

Phone ringing.

It woke her, but she didn't know where she was.

Still in her car? Parked at Snowville Maple's headquarters?

More ringing.

Some of the fog cleared.

She lay on her bed, in her house on Hill Street. Her bedside clock's red digits said 8:13 p.m.

Another ring.

She reached for the phone, remembering—she'd driven home and fallen onto the bed like this and she'd lain here ever since, into the evening, deeply asleep.

Abnormally asleep.

"Hello?" she said into the receiver.

Her voice sounded groggy.

"Are you all right, Cooper?"

Mike Bolknor's voice. Deep, steady, but worried.

"Tired," she said.

And then she said: "Oh, for the....Henry?"

"He's right here," Bolknor said. "I'm calling from my office at the college—something's come up."

She sat up on the edge of the bed. She noticed she still wore what she'd worn to Snowville, black running shoes and black slacks and a white blouse and a lightweight black silk jacket.

"Tip LaPerle just called me, from his Dill PD office," Bolknor said. "It's about that alligator guy, Joey DeMercato —should I pick you up on my way down?"

She started to tell him to skip her, because she really wanted to go back to sleep, but then something rose in her, self-disgust for succumbing to this stupid flu, and determination. She'd do her job. She always did her job.

"I'll be on the front stoop," she said.

Sixteen minutes later, they sat in Tip LaPerle's office in the Dill PD building and it seemed to Cooper like déjà vu, because it was the same cast—Chief LaPerle, Mike Bolknor, Cooper, Henry under her chair, and the D-man, with his reptile friend, Durango.

Yet, it wasn't the same.

Tip LaPerle, called in from home by the dispatcher, this time had on jeans and a black t-shirt instead of his uniform. Mike Bolknor, working late, as usual, instead of his normal suit and tie, had thrown on a leather aviator jacket over his tieless shirt. Most transformed, though, was the D-man.

Cooper remembered him as hang-loose and amiable. He still wore cargo shorts and a Hawaiian shirt and beach sandals, no socks, but he didn't look relaxed. He paced the floor in front of Tip's desk, eyes darting. He held Durango in his arms.

"Look!" he shouted, turning the alligator to reveal a gash near the base of its tail.

"Ninjas," he said. "Out from the woods, at the RV park, evil eyes…."

Tip LaPerle made quelling motions with his hands.

"Just tell it from the beginning," he said. "Step by step."

D-man looked ready to detonate, but he took a deep breath and abruptly sat, still holding the alligator in his arms.

"I'm in my RV, having supper, okay? It's just turned dark," he said. "Window's open, and I hear stuff, twigs go snap, you know? Feet shuffling?"

His eyes stopped darting and looked inward.

"Like I'm back in that Hummer, outside Kandahar...."

He jumped up and paced again, back and forth in front of Tip's desk.

"Durango's out there, okay?" he said, as he paced. "He likes to get the night air—got his leash on him, tied to the RV's bumper."

He stopped pacing and put his head down. His neck tendons bulged. After a moment his head jerked back up.

"Those noises out there stopped, and I heard crickets, and that silence sounded wrong...Wrong!" Pacing again.

"I ran out and there's these two Ninjas, all in black, black socks over their heads, holes cut for their eyes and mouths, one taller, bigger, and that one's got this combat knife—I've seen plenty of those—and he's just gashed Durango—just knifed him....and now he's got that up ready to stab right down on Durango's neck!"

D-man put the alligator down on the office floor, gently, despite his agitation, and then he straightened.

"Here's what I did to that devil...."

He suddenly lashed out, punching the air.

"Caught him on the jaw, knocked him on his back, and he lost his knife, I went for it, but—still lying there— he reached out and grabbed it, so I figured he'd be coming for me with that knife, and I got ready to kick his face---I'll be honest, I meant to kill him, but he rolled away and got up and ran across the street, and into the woods over there, with his mini-me friend right on his heels."

He sat back down and bent over to grasp the alligator. He lifted Durango and cradled him in his arms again.

"I'm getting the hell out of this crazy place," he muttered. "Tonight!"

He stared into the eyes of each in turn, Tip LaPerle, Mike Bolknor, Cooper.

"You got evil in this town!" he said. "Demons!"

Nobody else spoke for a moment, until Tip LaPerle finally broke the silence.

"We'll go out in the morning, when it's light, and see what we can find."

D-man shook his head.

"Me and Durango, we're heading back to Scallop Beach tonight because…."

He shuddered, misery on his face.

"I've gotta get to Florida, to my VA hospital," he said. "Gotta see my shrink, see Doctor Engel!"

He got up, still holding Durango, and headed for the door.

"Blood-bomb dreams," he muttered, to himself, barely audible. "They'll be back now, every night, explosions, spattering red blood…."

He stopped at the door, frozen, one arm cradling the alligator, his free hand on the door handle.

He shuddered again.

Then he turned and stared at the other three people in the room, eyes wide.

"Hell's walking your streets," he said. "Demons!"

He opened the door, started out, then looked back.

"There's more coming!" he said.

9

In the morning, Cooper felt a bit more energetic. Just slightly, but she hoped her flu might be lifting.

As she walked into the Allen County State's Attorney building, her telephone rang—Tip LaPerle on the line, from the Dill PD next door, a conference call to her and to Mike Bolknor, up at the college.

Tip started with a curse, and a rant.

"That SOB fat-cat Cappy Dixon's on my back," he said. "Some lowlife swiped a few of his logs? So what? He's got logs coming out his ears! He's got like a million Caspar Dixon Lumber Company sites, logs and logs and logs—Jeezum Crow!"

He swore under his breath.

"Every officer here's out straight," he said. "Especially me."

Then he sputtered: "Cappy, you want action? Then pay more taxes, hire me more officers!"

A moment's brooding silence. Then he spoke again.

"So, in your great log heist, Cappy, who got killed?"

Cooper had heard that one before, down through the years. Tip's standard defense, when the Dill PD's slowness to jump on a petty felony "frosted some citizen's whiskers."

So who got killed?

"Coop, Mike, help me out, okay, while I'm doing logs?" he said. "Go check out Gatorgate?"

Ten minutes later Bolknor picked Cooper up in a Campus Security Prius, and they drove down to River Street and turned right, heading toward the town's western end. Henry had to ride in the back seat, which he accepted only because Mike Bolknor drove, his hero. Sometimes, amused by her own petty jealousy, Cooper admonished the corgi—"Hey, Mister, who feeds you organic dog chow? Who gets you distemper shots??"

They passed Tenement Row, after that a stretch of small, tired ranch houses, which gave way to stores selling carpets or patio furniture or plumbing fixtures or medical supplies or paint. They turned left onto a gravel drive, then bumped across railroad tracks. Ahead, through foliage, the Ira River glinted. They drove under a wooden arch, high and wide, with a sign on top: Dill RV Park.

Mike stopped the Prius at the entry booth, and asked where to find Joey DeMercato's parking site.

"Alligator Man!" the booth's grandmotherly attendant said.

She studied a record book.

"He checked out last night, around nine," she said. "Emergency trip back to Florida, that's what he told the night attendant—had that reptile riding shotgun."

She told them where to find the D-man's now-vacant parking spot.

"Perch Lane, Slot Sixteen."

They left her shaking her head and mouthing "alligator!"

They got lost, instantly, in the narrow streets, lined on both sides with parked RVs of every type and size, shaded by overhanging maples and beeches.

...Cedar Street, Muskellunge Avenue, Balsam Lane, Black Willow Drive, Sunfish Lane, Moose Alley....

Finally they found Perch Lane, and then Slot Sixteen.

Flanking it on one side, in Slot Fifteen, stood a super-huge RV, blue with white trim, the kind of land yacht rock bands use for touring. Two bicycles clung to its stern, slung from brackets, and it towed a Mini Cooper sedan, for sightseeing.

On the other side, Slot Seventeen, stood a vintage Airstream, backed into the slot, and not much bigger than the white Ram pickup that towed it, currently unhooked to free the truck. Tools and equipment filled the Ram's bed. In the morning sun, the Airstream's aluminum body shone.

Perch Lane ran along the RV park's edge, so the street's opposite side had no parked RVs, just forest. In Joey DeMercato's former space, sewage and water and electrical hookups stuck up, ready for the next customer.

Cooper guessed several hundred RVs currently filled the park. No residents out and about yet this morning, the volleyball and badminton and shuffleboard courts waiting for the fun to begin. Driving in, they'd passed a swimming pool, and every RV had a grill outside. At night, Cooper guessed, there'd be beer and cocktails and the mixed aromas of smoldering charcoal and searing steaks or burgers or hotdogs. There'd be music here and there, and there'd be a hum of voices and laughter.

Cooper thought: not where you'd expect your pet alligator to get knifed.

They'd parked across the street from Slot Sixteen, leaving Henry asleep on the back seat, and walked over to take a look, stopping at the macadam's edge, to avoid mixing their own footprints with whatever evidence might be on the ground. Silently, they both divided up the site with imaginary grid lines, then surveyed it, section by section, trying to miss nothing.

"First question, where'd these two Ninjas come from?" Cooper said.

"And where'd they go to?" Mike said.

They continued studying the ground.

They could see where D-man parked, because his RV's tires imbedded the soil slightly. They could guess where the door and step-down were, and where D-man tethered Durango to the vehicle's front bumper. What they couldn't see were footprints, because it hadn't rained in a week, and the ground had dried and hardened.

"D-man said these two Ninjas ran off into the woods," Mike said. "So probably that's how they got here, too, out of those woods, on foot."

They gave up examining the parking site and gazed across the road, into the trees.

"Why stab this animal?" Cooper said finally.

Bolknor shrugged.

"Grudge against Joey DeMercato?" he said. "People from the RV park?"

Cooper shook her head. She didn't believe this could be so easily written off. It felt—for reasons Cooper couldn't explain—ominous. She no longer doubted that somebody planted wasps in Proctor Gibbs' sleeves, to murder him. Now, this alligator knifing. No obvious connection. Still, it troubled her.

What was the last thing she'd heard the D-man say? "Hell's walking your streets—Demons!"

And he'd made a prediction.

"There's more coming!"

Cooper looked grim.

"Let's ask around," she said.

She felt her fatigue returning.

They walked to the Airstream, in Slot Seventeen, but before they could knock the door opened and a man in his early sixties stood on the step-down, squinting at them. Gray stubble on his face. Jeans, sleeveless t-shirt. He smelled of cigarette smoke.

Asked if he'd seen or heard anything last night, he shook his head.

"No interest in gators," he said. "Working in Florida, Louisiana, saw plenty of them."

Last night? Watching an old Clint Eastwood movie, on the TV, he said. Didn't hear anything except the show's background music and Clint's six-shooters banging.

"Got to get going," he said.

He reached behind him into the Airstream and pulled out a knapsack, which he held by its shoulder straps.

"What I do is maintain air-traffic beacons, for the FAA," he told them, opening the pickup's driver-side door. "Got three scheduled today, got to go climb mountains."

He slung the knapsack into the Ram's cargo bed, then got in and started the engine. He pulled out and turned right, heading back toward the park's entrance.

From inside the closed-up Airstream, they heard faint shouting. After a moment, they realized the FAA technician had left his radio turned on, with a political commentator loudly taking exception to something or other.

"Not the alligator knifer," Mike said. "Doesn't seem right for it."

They had better luck at Slot Fifteen, knocking on the door of the blue-and-white jumbo RV. A woman opened the door and stood on the steps, her blue eyes alert behind glasses. She wore her white hair parted on one side, not quite shoulder-length. She wore gray slacks and a blue silk blouse, and looked ready for a meeting of the corporate board.

"Just a moment," she said, after they displayed their badges and explained their mission.

She disappeared into the RV's vast innards. They heard her speak to someone. A moment later she reappeared, now with a tall man, slender, wearing a pale-green dress shirt, the kind that might be worn to an office, with a tie and jacket.

"Come in," the woman said. "We just finished breakfast—can I offer you coffee?"

Cooper felt she'd walked into a McMansion. Off to one side, they passed a full kitchen, featuring granite countertops. She and Bolknor followed their hosts past a dining room, with fine-China serving platters on the table, holding scrambled eggs and bacon and toast and jam, then into a living room, with obviously expensive furniture. It had picture windows, offering a view of Perch Lane, the forest beyond, and the now empty Slot Sixteen.

"Any animosity toward the alligator, here in the RV park?" Mike asked.

"No," the husband said. "Never saw any of that."

"That alligator was a hoot," the woman said. "So was

Joey, everybody enjoyed talking with him." Both husband and wife had faint southern accents. They said they'd lived in various sections of the country, wherever the corporation moved them. Retired now, they'd sold their home and lived in the RV, traveling from state to state, migrating north in summer, south in winter.

"We're professional sightseers now," the man said.

"We like it here in the mountains," the woman said. "We'll probably stay until October, to take in the fall foliage."

They said they heard nothing last night, until Joey DeMercato shouted, out in the dark, and when they'd looked out their window it was over. They just saw Joey crouched over the alligator, looking at the wound. They'd rushed out and he'd told them what happened.

"Damned shame," the husband said. "Sneaking in here, doing something like that."

"Maybe some teenagers, from here in the park…." Cooper said.

"No kids in here we ever saw," the woman said. "Heck, nobody under sixty—just us codgers."

"That's all we know," the man said, with an apologetic shrug. "I doubt there's anything on our surveillance camera, because it was just about dark...." Cooper and Mike exchanged a look.

"May we see?" Mike said.

A few minutes later, on a screen in the RV's cab, they saw the night view outside the picture window. It looked too murky to make out the tethered alligator, but then, out of the woods, two shadows hurried across the road, hunched over. A tall shadow and a shorter shadow. Suddenly the tall shadow reached up—light spilling from the D-man's window glinted on a long knife—and then the knife struck downwards, disappearing into the gloom.

Suddenly, the RV's door burst open, spilling out lamplight, and the D-man exploded out, already running, instantly becoming a shadow himself. In the murk, they couldn't see his fist strike, but abruptly the tall attacker fell backwards onto the ground. They saw Joey go for him, but the downed shadow rolled away, apparently grabbed the knife, and then the two Ninja shadows raced across Perch Lane, vanishing into the forest's even deeper darkness.

They saw Joey attending to his alligator. And that was all.

"Thank you," Cooper said to the RV couple. "You've helped."

"We'll go take a look in the woods over there," Mike said.

"We hope you get these creeps," the husband said.

"It's scary," the woman said. "It's like fiends came out of those woods."

"That's what we need," the man said. "An exorcism."

WHEN THE WASP STINGS

10

After they'd walked several minutes into the forest, looking for markers of the Ninjas' passage—footprints, broken twigs, bent-back branches—and found nothing, Cooper suddenly sank onto a fallen log and sat there, too fatigued to go on.

She didn't want Mike Bolknor to know she felt so weakened. She didn't know why she didn't want him to know, she just didn't.

"Sit a minute, Mike," she said. "Let's talk about these Ninjas."

He looked at her, a man hard to read, used to keeping his emotions inside. She thought, though, looking at her, he had worry in his astute eyes, and she didn't like that.

She thought: next week I'll see a doctor. Maybe. If there's time.

Mike sat beside her on the log, and continued looking at her, waiting to hear what she had to say.

Henry had gone snuffling off into the woods, amusing himself, and they heard him moving among the nearby trees.

"So far, we haven't picked up their trail, here in the woods," she said.

"No, it's a big swath of forest," Mike said. "They could have come in ten feet to our left, or ten feet to our right, and we wouldn't know."

"We'd have to get a battalion in here," Cooper said. "We'd need to do a sweep."

Mike said nothing.

"So, given what we know so far, what can we figure out?" Cooper said.

Mike regarded her, waiting.

"One thing is, there was a fight, right?" Cooper said. "D-man punched this taller Ninja, knocked him down...."

Mike nodded. Cooper had no doubt he'd already thought about these things.

"In the Army, you were a heavyweight boxer," Cooper said. "So, as a trained fighter, what do you read from that fracas?"

Mike looked down, forehead wrinkled, considering.

It occurred to Cooper, in a sudden rush of unexpected emotion, watching him think, how much she'd come to depend on this man, how much she respected him, how much he now meant to her, this former NYPD detective, forty-two years old. Her son's age, if she'd ever had one.

"All right, we know some things," Mike said. "From the surveillance video, we know both these Ninjas were slender, and they moved smoothly, light on their feet— so let's guess they're young, in their thirties, or younger, maybe even a lot younger."

He sat looking at his big hands, continuing to think.

"We know the taller Ninja took a punch to the head from D-man," Mike said. "D-man's sturdily built,

70

he's had military self-defense training, and he was infuriated, so that punch undoubtedly hit hard." He thought a moment more.

"This Ninja's had no fight training—never been in the military, police, whatever—because if he did have fight experience, he'd see that punch coming, or sense it, and block it, or dodge it, or he'd rock his head back to lessen the blow."

Again he thought silently.

"You take a hard punch to the head like that, knocked onto your back, you lose your oomph," he said. "But this guy immediately rolls over and grabs that knife, before D-man can get to it—then he's up and running away."

"So he's athletic," Cooper said. "He's fit."

Mike nodded.

"Okay," Cooper said. "What about the shorter one?" They both thought silently.

"All we know is the taller Ninja's the alpha," Mike said. "He's handling the knife, and on that surveillance video you see him taking the lead."

Cooper nodded.

"So the smaller Ninja takes orders," she said. "Probably looks up to the bigger Ninja, maybe it's hero worship, or intimidation, maybe both."

Mike spread his hands, indicating that's what they knew, and no more. Nothing about where the Ninjas came from, how they knew about the alligator, how they knew D-man's parking slot, or why they wanted to harm the reptile. Nothing to show where they entered the woods in the first place, or how they got to the RV park.

71

"We're out at the town's edge here, a long hike," Cooper said. "So probably they had wheels to get out here, or they live nearby."

Mike nodded.

Off in the woods, Henry barked, then barked again, and then kept on barking.

Cooper thought: okay Mister, you're excited, because that always turns you into an annoying bark machine.

Henry barged out from the trees, something dangling from his mouth. Cooper thought: you little thug, you've killed a squirrel. Corgis, though, were bred to herd cattle, so they like bossing other animals, not killing them.

Eyes bright, pleased with himself, Henry ran up to show off his prize.

It was a rag. A black rag.

Cooper reached out and grabbed its dangling end. Henry backed away, shaking his head, playing tug-of-war. Cooper raised her index finger and shook it, glaring at him, and Henry knew what that meant. He dropped the rag and Cooper picked it up.

"Well, well," she said, dangling it for Mike to see.

A black face mask, to be pulled over the head, with openings for the eyes and mouth.

Ninja mask.

"And look here," Cooper said, pointing with her free hand at the dangling mask's insides.

Caked blood.

Mike pulled a plastic evidence bag from a pocket and held it open for Cooper to drop in the mask.

"It looks like D-man bloodied this guy's nose," Mike said. "It bled inside the mask, not pleasant, so in the woods here he pulled the mask off."

"Then he didn't know what to do with it," Cooper said. "So he just threw it onto the ground."

Mike examined the mask through the evidence bag's clear plastic.

"No label," he said. "We've got the blood, so we can get his DNA...."

"Right, if we catch him, we can compare," Cooper said. "If he's got an arrest record, his DNA might be on file, but that's a long shot." Mike nodded.

"I doubt we could trace the mask back to where he bought it, because I'm not seeing anything like special fibers—it looks like ordinary cotton cloth."

Henry sat listening, head cocked. He yawned, bored. Then he stood, stretched, and trotted into the woods, back to where he'd found the mask. Cooper and Bolknor exchanged a look. Both got to their feet and followed the dog, into the trees.

They didn't go far.

A short walk to the left of where they'd been searching, they found Henry gleefully snuffling around the forest floor, as if he detected buried truffles. Mike suddenly knelt to look closely at a spot on the brown pine needles covering the ground.

"Blood spot," he said. "So here's where the taller Ninja threw down his mask...."

"And here's where they went," Cooper said, pointing to more blood spots, a trail of them, leading to the east.

They followed the spots, finding other signs of the Ninjas' passing, a bent-back branch, a pebble dislodged by a shoe, more blood spatters. Before long, the trees thinned and they came to the forest's edge, at a dirt road leading to the Ira River on their right, and back up across the railroad tracks on their left, toward River Street.

"Look at this," Cooper said, pointing.

Where the forest ended, the ground dipped, a low spot, where water in the soil dampened the earth, almost to mud, and the damp soil yielded information.

Footprints.

"Looks like running shoes," Mike said. "Here's the print of a larger shoe, and over here's a smaller one, and you can see the tread patterns, and even spots where the rubber soles have worn away from use.

He pulled his smartphone from a pocket and snapped photographs of the footprints, taking them from every angle.

Cooper waited until he finished, and then she pointed.

"Tire tracks," she said. "So these Ninjas drove here." Mike knelt again, peering closely at the track.

Then, still kneeling, he snapped extensive photographs of the tire track, close up. From a pocket he pulled a tiny plastic ruler and a pad and a pen. He used the ruler to measure the tread depth in the track and wrote it down.

"I'm no tire expert," he said. "We'll bring the State Police lab in on this, but I can see a few things right now—big tires, for instance, really big, maybe an SUV, but more likely a truck."

He stuffed the pad, pen, and ruler back into his pocket.

"You carry those things around ordinarily?" Cooper asked.

"For crime scenes," he said. "For gathering evidence."

He studied the tracks.

"That's a heavy duty tread, for off-road driving," he said. "There'll be wear patterns, things like that, the lab people will spot, but look at this—"

He pointed to a spot on one of the tracks. Cooper bent down, using her cane for support, and saw a shallow groove running horizontally across the treads.

"Looks like this truck drove over a piece of glass, or really sharp stone, or a dropped metal strip, and got that groove," Mike said. "Nowhere deep enough to ruin the tire, but it's a marker, so if we find the truck, we'll know it's the one the Ninjas drove."

Cooper struggled to stand back up, determined to do it without Mike's help, leaning heavily on her cane. Finally she stood upright.

"Something else," she said. "You can see, besides these new tracks, there're older tracks underneath, same tires—let's guess they've come here several times, parked, then snuck into the RV park through the woods, hunting for the D-man's spot."

Mike looked at her, leaning on her cane, inscrutable.

"Want me to get the Prius, pick you up?" he said.

"Hell no," Cooper said, anger flaring. "I'm a grownup and I can walk back to the car."

Mike shrugged.

So they walked back through the forest to the car, parked across from Slot Sixteen, currently empty, with Henry frisking ahead of them. He figured this must be a game, lots of fun.

11

Numero Uno and Numero Dos sat in the truck's cab, eating half-foot sandwiches they'd bought at Subway, each with a can of Coke.

Ahead, through the windshield, they looked without interest at sugar maples climbing a slope, leaves vibrant green in the springtime noon sun.

"Can't we use our real names?" Numero Dos asked. "It'd be easier."

Numero Uno sighed.

"I'll explain… again," he said. "It's practice, practice, practice, remember?"

He used his tired voice.

"It's so there's no slips when we're in action," he said. "No accidentally saying our names where some civilian might hear."

He sighed again.

"Like I told you," he said.

"Yeah, okay," Dos said.

Dos pointed to the black bruise on Uno's face, encompassing his right eye and his nose. It had begun turning bluish, and red around its outer circumference.

"Does it hurt?"

No response. He glared through the windshield at the hillside sugar maples.

"I guess that didn't go so well," Dos said.

Uno continued glaring, silent. Finally, without looking to his side, where his partner sat in the shotgun seat, he spoke.

"It went perfectly," he said.

He kept his voice ominously flat, as if underneath he controlled anger.

He didn't look at Dos. He stared out the truck's windshield at the trees, as if it would be too boring to look at the source of these stupid comments, irritating. Dos shrank down a little in the seat, pulling a stick of gum from a shirt pocket and unwrapping it, then sticking it into the mouth.

"As we've said, over and over, this is the training phase, am I right? For the big event?"

"Yes," Dos said, chewing.

"And why do we train?"

"To learn mistakes that can happen," Dos said, as if reciting a catechism.

"What tactical lesson did we learn from the alligator?" Uno asked.

Silence.

After a moment, Dos spoke, in a hushed voice: "I don't know."

Silence from Uno, as if mentally counting to ten.

"We learned," he said finally, "the importance of target selection—do you understand?"

"Yes."

"What targets do we choose?"

"Sort of isolated, I guess," Dos said. "Maybe not a young, tough kind of guy?" Uno nodded.

"Correct," he said.

"When will we pick out targets?" Dos asked. "Really get into it?"

Uno shook his head, as if stunned by his partner's density.

"If you'd paid attention…."

Then, voice tired, as if he shouldn't need to explain this: "I've already picked two targets, and a third possibility."

"Wow," Dos said. "So we're finally going into action, like tomorrow night maybe, or…."

"No," Uno said. "Knife control—that's still to be perfected, and target approach."

He sat silently, as if contemplating his own words, pleased with them.

"Tell me, Dos," he said finally. "Given what we've just discussed, what will we do now?"

Dos sighed.

"More practice," Dos said. "Like the alligator, but I wish…."

"Stop wishing," Uno said. "We're doing, remember? Not dreaming. Raising ourselves, above the sheep people?"

They both stared through the windshield at the trees.

"Yeah," Dos said, finally. "I guess."

12

Tip LaPerle resented Cappy Dixon's accusing rasp, so he didn't look at him.

Instead, stone faced, he stared at Dixon's maple logs, piled a story high. Mainly, he thought about Thor Ennis, the seven-year-old orphan he and Marge now fostered.

Thor had punched another boy.

"Jeesum crow, Tip, I pay my damned taxes," Dixon was saying. "Lowlifes swipe my logs—where's the cops?" He glared at the police chief.

"Three days, getting your butt out here," Dixon rasped. "Hey, that's a crap return on my tax investment!"

Tip thought: "That cigar stuck in your face stinks like your attitude."

He still mulled over last evening's call: "That little thug of yours, he slugged my Bernie, knocked him down."

Thor had anger problems.

So did Tip LaPerle.

"We've got cases backed up right now," Tip told Dixon. "If we had more officers…."

"Sure, even more taxes!" Dixon said. "God!"

He pulled the cigar out of his mouth, turned aside, and spat.

Tip thought: "Whine away, Moneybags."

He wanted to say it. He wanted to move in close to Caspar Dixon's bristly face to say it. "No free services, boo-hoo!" He didn't say it.

Cooper North had taught him to not go volcano, over their decades working together, police chief and prosecutor.

He'd be about to erupt. Some complaining citizen. Or a mouthy prisoner. Cooper knew the signs. She'd raise her eyebrows. He'd get the message. Inside him, the rising magma would subside.

And later, after the near career-ending explosion, she'd say: "Tip, all you've earned—don't blow it away."

She'd known him since he burst into her office, still a small child—"I want to be a policeman!" It hadn't been easy—drunken, thieving parents, a father who punched until Tip got big enough to punch back, his childhood in Tenement Row, the town's lowest of the low....

Now, chief of police, he stared at Cappy Dixon's timber.

"They took logs off the top of that pile, way up there?" Tip told Dixon. "They'd need, what, some kind of forklift?"

Dixon sucked on his cigar and blew out a cloud of smelly gray smoke.

"Nah," he said. "Right here's where they stole my logs, see that grass, flattened down?"

He pointed to an empty patch adjacent to the main log pile.

"We'd just started a new pile there."

"How many logs got pinched?" Tip asked.

"Five logs, prime sugar maple," Dixon said, glaring at the spot where the logs had lain.

Tip thought: he's got these roadside landings all over Allen County, tons of logs, including this mountain of logs right here, and he's all ticked off about five?

This roadside clearing smelled of sawn hardwood, mixed with the aroma of last autumn's fallen leaves, now decaying into the earth, and the reek of Cappy's cigar.

No cars passing, Tip thought. Not since I got here. Low traffic on this back road. Good spot for a log heist.

His thoughts reverted to Thor.

Second scrape this week—as usual, a bigger, older bully shoved him. This time it was Bernie Sullivan, from down the street. Thor punched him in the face, so Bernie went home sniveling to his parents. Bigger kids like Bernie never admitted they started these fights. They picked on Thor because he was now "a cop's kid," and because he was smaller, and because his clothes used to be faded and frayed and holey, and because his druggie mother, before she got murdered, scissored off his hair, when she thought about it, which was rarely.

Tip knew how this scrape with Bernie happened. Thor told him. Thor kept a lot to himself, but he never lied.

"Tough work, muscling stolen logs onto a truck," Tip told Dixon. "What inspired them?"

Cappy took the cigar out of his mouth, turned his head, and spat, an expression of disgust.

"Damned newspaper," he said. "Article about sugar-maple prices, sky high—that's an engraved invitation, 'Hey, crooks, come get it!'"

He spat again.

Tip had never liked Cappy Dixon, starting in grade school. Now, he thought, Cappy looks like a fifty-year-old lumberjack, a minimum-wage woodchuck, which he isn't.

Dixon's height was only average, but he was broad, from his shoulders down, wearing sawdust-peppered jeans and a t-shirt grimed with chainsaw oil, scowling face bristly.

Tip thought: he's Caspar Dixon the Third—Grandpa Dixon started this business, his father built it up, and Cappy here just slid into it, instant tycoon, easy as peach pie.

"What's this site here?" Tip asked.

Dixon took an angry drag on his cigar and blew out the smoke.

"We log these mountainsides," he said, pointing up the slope rising behind them.

He sounded irritated that he needed to explain it.

"We snake down logs, stack them by the roads, landing sites like this, trucks load up, haul them to sawmills."

"How many sites like this?" Tip asked.

"Fourteen," Dixon said. "What the hell's the difference?"

"Just wondering—why'd the thieves hit this particular site," Tip said, feeling the magma rising again.

He didn't like Dixon's voice tone.

"Look, our landings, they're mostly on dirt roads, back where nobody goes," Dixon said. "So who sees them?"

Another vehement suck on his cigar.

"Right here, this one's on a county road, paved, just happens that way," he said. "Any jackass driving by can see it, get ideas."

"All right," Tip said. "Let's have a look—I see a tire track over there, one of yours?"

"No way," Dixon said. "I haven't sent a truck down here in two weeks, so that's gotta be from the crooks' truck."

Tip squatted to look at the track closely. He used a forefinger to poke the soil near the track.

"Bone dry," he said.

So the truck, weighed down with logs, pressed into the dried soil and left this track. If he touched it, the track would crumble.

Tip pulled his cell phone from one of his uniform's pockets and stooped to snap pictures of the tire track, from all angles. He repocketed the phone, and then from another pocket he pulled a small pad and pen. He opened the pad and lowered it into the tread mark, careful not to touch the dried soil. He drew a line across the pad, marking the top of the tread, to record its depth.

Cappy Dixon stood with his arms crossed, watching.

"You sending all that to the state cops' lab?" Dixon said.

Tip nodded.

"Find the truck, we'll find the crooks," he said.

"Yeah, well here's a head start for you," Dixon said. "Looking at that, I can tell you it's from a big pickup, with all-terrain tires—you got eyes, you don't need test tubes."

Tip stooped for a closer look at the tire track.

"Look," he said, pointing.

84

Dixon stooped beside him and peered at the track. A shallow groove ran across the track, horizontally.

With the man stooping beside him, Dixon's cigar came within inches of Tip's face. It reeked. It smelled like an insult. Tip wanted pull the cigar out of Cappy's mouth and grind it underfoot. So he did what he always did, when the magma started rising. He summoned a memory of Cooper North, staring at him, eyebrows up.

"This truck ran over a piece of glass or something," Tip said. "That groove's not deep enough to ruin the tire, but it's a marker for us."

Dixon straightened, but said nothing, staring pensively at the spot where his logs used to be.

"Five logs," Tip said. "Worth how much?"

He could see Dixon's mouth moving around the cigar, silently making computations.

"Okay, right now, the mills, they're paying about sixty cents a board foot for prime sugar maple," he said.

He worked on further silent computations, for the first time not looking cantankerous. Because this is what he does, Tip thought. Counting the money in wood.

"These were smaller logs, say ten-inch diameter, and say twelve-feet long," Dixon said. "We use the Doyle Method to calculate, and it comes to twenty-seven board feet in one of these logs—times sixty cents, you get sixteen bucks a log, probably a little more."

He stood silently computing, making sure of his number.

"Times five logs, we're talking, say, eighty bucks," he said. "Plus or minus, probably plus." Tip felt irritated.

All this fuss.

For the price of a dinner out.

How much did the Caspar Dixon Lumber Company turn over every year? A million? Some big number. Why all this agitation over chickenfeed?

And why's my back up because Diane Sullivan called up complaining about Thor? Chickenfeed, right?

So we've all got buttons, he thought. They all get pushed.

"Pickup bed's what, six feet long, five feet?" Tip said.

"How'd they fit five twelve-foot logs in the truck?"

Dixon chewed on the end of his cigar, which had gone out, looking at the patch of ground where his logs had lain. Abruptly, he pointed.

Tip looked, and saw sawdust on the ground, in small heaps.

"Buggers chain-sawed those logs in half," Dixon said.

He sounded pained at the thought.

"So now each log's six-feet long," Tip said.

Still, that much hardwood had to be heavy. They had just the pickup. If they'd had some kind of lifting machine, there'd be marks of it on the ground. So the crooks had to manually heft the logs into the truck.

"How many men to lift one of those logs?" Tip asked.

Dixon shrugged.

"Three, for sure, or you'd risk a hernia," he said. "Four probably."

"So this truck's a crew cab," Tip said. "Two guys sit in front, two guys sit in back." He shook his head.

"Why would four guys go through all the hassle, steal logs for a lousy eighty bucks, which is twenty bucks each."

He thought: for a lark? Or because they had only a hazy idea of the logs' worth?

"Okay, Cappy," Tip said. "What's got to be done is call all the sawmills around here, ask who brought in ten logs, cut down to six-feet long."

"Right," Dixon said, taking his extinguished cigar out of his mouth and staring at its soggy butt end.

"I've got nobody to do that, we're straight out," Tip said. "You do it—you know all the sawmills anyway."

Dixon stared at him.

"Call me if you get an answer," Tip said.

Dixon started to protest, but Tip stared at him and shrugged.

He thought: Thor, I know how it is—I came out of Tenement Row, just like you. So, you slugged a bully? Good on you! And here's what I'm going to do about Bernie Sullivan—exactly nothing.

"All right," Dixon said. "I'll get some of my people on it, make the calls."

As he got back into his patrol car, Tip thought: I've got your back, Thor. But you handle what needs handling.

I know you can do it.

Because   I   did.

13

Evening on Hill Street.

Now the sun had set, but its light remained, only softer. A warm night coming, humid. Soon, maybe tomorrow, maybe the next day, the moisture would breed a storm.

In the air a scent of blooming lilacs.

Cooper stood on her front porch, the door still open behind her, watching Henry saunter down the slate walkway, pausing every few steps to exuberantly sniff the lawn and bushes growing alongside, apparently taking in important information.

In his corgi mind, king of all he surveyed.

No leash.

He wouldn't go into the street. Cooper trusted him. He always stayed close by.

Behind her, Cooper sensed her home's mass, this large brick Federal that had housed generations of Norths, ever since Ethan Allen scouted these mountains. It gave her a sense of continuity, of belonging, of stability.

Henry barked.

She looked up, to see what caused the outburst.

He barked at a pickup truck stopped across the street. Something new in his realm. Henry liked to express himself.

Cooper hadn't looked across the street until now, so she noticed the truck for the first time. She didn't know how long it had idled there. A tough-looking truck, olive green, with big knobby tires. Everything—door hinges, grill, fenders—heavy duty. A large cab, two seats in front, two in back.

Cooper thought: that's a big Jeep. An ugly truck.

She'd seen it before, but where? Or one like it.

Four people could fit in the cab, but only two people sat in it now. She couldn't make them out, through tinted windows, only their shapes. A man driving, a woman riding shotgun.

They both stared at her. Then at Henry. Then back at her.

Cold stares. She sensed it.

She started down the walkway, meaning to cross the street and rap with her cane on the truck's door, find out what they had in mind.

However, the engine suddenly revved and the truck accelerated away, down the street, making a sound like a growl.

Cooper thought: I should have checked the license plate.

Standing on the walkway, looking at the spot where, a moment ago, the truck had stood, she shrugged.

Then she trudged back up the slate walkway, leaning on her cane.

This fatigue....

She sat heavily on the porch steps.

"Henry," she called. "You come back here."

14

That night, just after eight, Cooper's landline rang.

Caller ID said it was the Dill PD calling.

Tip LaPerle's voice sounded strained. Home for the evening, Cooper guessed, then summoned back to work.

"What is it, Tip?" she asked.

"Damn!" he said.

A silence. She could imagine him holding the telephone, glaring at the wall.

"All morning I got stuck in the woods,," he finally said. "Listening to that jackass Cappy Dixon, whining about a few stolen logs, but just now Gert Lemon called, in tears— you know her?" Cooper knew her.

Gert worked in the cafeteria at Dill Industries, although she could have retired years ago. A skinny, white-haired woman, nervous, never married, lonely except for her beagle, her roommate, her friend. Cooper thought: like me and Henry?

"I drove out to see," Tip said. "God!"

Cooper guessed, Tip didn't need to bring in a prosecutor, not right now. He just needed to talk. "Gert?" Cooper asked. "Is she…." "It's her dog," Tip said.

"Tess," Cooper said. "That's her dog's name."

"Yeah, I suppose," Tip said.

Cooper waited.

"Knifed!" Tip said. "Four times—again, and again, and again...."

Tip had no special feeling for dogs, Cooper knew. He had compassion, though, mostly kept in protective custody, hidden under layers of seen-it-all police cynicism, and anger, the residue of destructive parents. Right now, in his voice, Cooper heard no cynicism. Just anger and compassion, and something like horror.

"It was like—Christ!—they were practicing," he said. "Stick it in the neck, now the belly, try the eye...."

Cooper felt sickened.

She thought: they attacked the D-man's alligator, now they slaughter this beagle.

It had to be the same two people. Ninjas. She had no doubt.

"Clues?" she asked.

Tip sighed.

"No," he said.

A moment's silence.

"She had the dog out on a leash, on the front lawn," Tip said. "She put him out every night like that, just about at dark."

No really close neighbors. Nobody heard anything, saw anything, he said. Gert didn't either, inside watching television. Her routine ever night.

Cooper thought: so these Ninjas cruise the town, see who leaves pets out. Looking for houses set apart, vulnerable.

She flinched.

That ugly truck, a few hours ago, stopped across the street from her house. Two people inside, staring. At her? At Henry?

She frowned at the wall.

All these odd crimes. So different. Proctor Gibbs murdered by yellow jacket stings. Logs stolen. Now, pets knifed.

She suddenly remembered the D-man, leaving Tip's office, with his wounded alligator, about to flee back to Florida, shouting as he hurried out the door. "Hell's walking your streets--demons!" And he'd prophesized.

"There's more coming!"

Cooper sank into the chair beside the phone table.

A voice in her ear said: "Where do I even start with this?"

It was Tip LaPerle, still on the line.

"I don't know what to do either," Cooper told him.

She hung up, too weary to keep talking.

She imagined Gert, alone in her house tonight.

If she ever found Henry like that, out on the lawn....

She cursed, under her breath.

Then, shaking her head, she mouthed what D-man said.

"There's   more   coming."

15

Cooper awoke and lay in bed, thinking about Gert Lemon, who'd be waking this morning with her beagle dead. If she'd slept at all.

Impulsively, Cooper leaned over the bed's edge to check the floor—Henry lay on his assigned patch of rug, on his back, short legs pointing straight up, asleep.

She reached for her bedside phone, and punched in the police chief's office number.

Tip routinely started work at six-thirty, to scan the night patrol's reports, so she knew he'd be there now, at seven.

"Do we have anything yet?" she asked.

"No tire tracks," Tip told her. "No footprints."

Dry road, dry lawn. So the Ninjas parked at the curb, then ran onto the grass to knife the dog, leaving no marks. Then they ran back to their vehicle and drove off.

"Took them not even a minute," Tip said. "We've got zip on this." He cursed.

"Maybe someone's mad at Gert Lemon?" he said.

"No," Cooper said. "Who'd have a grievance against that poor woman?"

Or, for that matter, against a Florida guy's pet alligator.

"This isn't vengeance," Cooper said.

She shook her head, angrily.

"Someone just wants to kill."

She clicked off the phone and drummed her fingers on the bedside table, frowning.

Because these pet killers ran free. And because they'd surely keep on killing. And because Proctor Gibbs' murderer ran free, too—so far, nothing done about it, except deciding Flute Wagner had it right. It really was murder.

So she called Snowville Maple, Inc., and told Wagner's answering machine she'd be there right after breakfast.

An hour later, she stopped at the college to leave Henry, so he wouldn't wander into mischief while she interviewed. She eyed the dog relaxing under Mike Bolknor's desk, which Mike had spread with night-patrol reports, and security equipment catalogs.

She thought: you're jubilant, aren't you, Mister. You get to spend all morning with the big man, instead of the old lady. Right?

She gave her mouth a sardonic twist, although her petulance amused her.

Twenty-six minutes later she walked into Flute Wagner's office, but stopped, staring at a huge wall poster behind his desk—it showed what seemed a shimmering car from the future, eel green, all angles and swoops, like a comic-book superhero's wheels. Printed above the image, in lurid type, the car's name— "Lamborghini Huracan." Cooper pointed at it.

"What's that thing?" she said.

Flute, rising from behind his desk, to welcome his guest, stopped halfway to upright, looking down, abashed, as if putting up the car poster constituted a prosecutable offense. With his head momentarily bowed like that, Cooper could see his brown hair seriously thinned on top, showing white scalp.

Yet again Cooper found herself feeling sorry for this smallish man, with a round head, who reminded her of a woodchuck, although she pushed that idea away, detesting her own snark. Especially since she'd been judged herself, in school, for being taller than everyone, and gaunt, with a gyrfalcon profile, and fierce hawk eyes.

She guessed they'd called her names behind her back, but hadn't dared use them where she'd hear, because she'd once punched a girl who tried it.

And then, polio at Harvard Law. A leaden left leg. A limp. A cane.

No, comparing this slightly plump man with watery blue eyes to a rodent shamed her.

"Why the car poster?" Cooper asked. "Is that what you drive?"

Flute, still looking down, shook his head.

Then he looked up, his expression wistful.

"That town where I grew up," he said. "In Connecticut…."

He motioned for her to sit in one of the visitor's chairs, facing his desk. And after she sat, he sat, too.

"All the kids there got cars as graduation gifts," he said. "It was, like, a tradition…." He sighed.

"Every kid got a luxury car, a BMW."

He looked past Cooper, at the office's wall.

"They called their cars 'Beamers,'" he said.

"So you got one, too?" Cooper said.

Flute looked at her, as if startled, then shook his head.

"My father was the high-school janitor," he said.

95

He looked down, then mumbled.

"My Mom sewed hems in a seamstress's shop, and we lived in an apartment up over a store."

He kept looking down.

"Fancy cheese, caviar, that's the stuff they sold in that store," he said. "We never bought any of it."

Cooper thought: poor family, ultra-rich town.

"Your classmates," she said. "Mean kids?"

Flute sighed once more.

"I always thought, you know, someday I'll drive a really fancy car back there...."

He looked into space, eyes vacant.

"I'd just roll around town, you know, so they'd see...."

He shook his head, as if to shake away thoughts.

"I've been saving...."

Then he looked at Cooper, face clenched against having to say any more about it.

"Let's go over the murder again," Cooper said. "Do you remember anyone at all who had a grudge against Proctor Gibbs?"

Flute shook his head.

"Everybody liked Proctor," he said. "We all did."

Cooper herself had liked the man. She'd liked that booming voice, and his twangy Vermont accent, "ayah," for "yes," and "heah" for "here," those Yankeeisms almost extinct now, along with the hill farms from which they sprang. Still, with his white walrus mustache, and merry blue eyes, Proctor had kept the look of a dairyman, even if he no longer sported bib overalls and had a close association with Holsteins.

"He was kind to me," Flute said.

96

Starting to tear, he wiped his eyes dry with the back of his hands.

"How was he kind?" Cooper asked.

"He gave me a job, when…"

Flute turned his gaze aside, as if looking away from a painful memory.

"I'd flopped at business," he said. "And I never thought…."

He shied away from talking about himself. Cooper saw that. Even so, she wiggled out Flute's story. At least, some of it.

For his own graduation present, Cooper learned, Flute's parents gave him a crisp new ten-dollar bill.

"That's what they could afford," he said. "Probably not even that, really."

He'd had nothing ahead of him. Maybe flipping burgers in a fast-food place. So the day after graduation, he enlisted in the Army. During his four years on active duty, he took every Army training course available to him.

His Army job was in supply procurement, so he trained in financial management and logistics planning. Shopping for whatever products his unit needed, from bullets to desks to food supplies, he'd made it a point to study the businesses he visited. He listened to sales people, seeing how they positioned their products, versus the competition.

"From all that, I got an idea about marketing," he said.

After he mustered out, funded by the GI Bill, he studied Business Administration at the University of Connecticut. Afterwards, he worked for a number of companies, in low-level positions, saving his money. Finally, on a shoestring, he started a business of his own.

"I sold super-fancy smartphone cases," he said. "I marketed them to upscale people, who wanted their phones to look classy, not run-of-the-mill, like ordinary people's phones, you know?"

It was tough going, at first. But then his business took off. His former classmates noted it. And after that, because of those classmates, his business collapsed.

"Seven of them—they got high salaries, working in their fathers' companies—pooled their money and started a company of their own, to compete with me," he said. "They sold the same kinds of fancy phone cases I was selling."

Flute's former classmates had far more financial backing. They told suppliers, we'll place really large orders, but you have to make us the exclusive dealer in this state.

"Everything dried up for me," Flute said. "I had to shut my company down."

Cooper felt something like an urge to murder.

Flute stopped talking about it, but Cooper saw it clearly.

A school full of rich kids, who'd made a game of taunting the janitor's boy, who wore clothes from Walmart. Now they saw this person they considered inferior, whom they'd routinely made miserable, building a successful business. So they'd deployed their daddies' money to smash him. Point proved, right? It was all about breeding. This ragamuffin couldn't do diddly.

"I didn't know what to do," Flute said. "But then I saw this little maple-syrup company needed a marketing director...."

Just then Wagner's office door flew open and Sonny Dewitt lurched in, disheveled, red eyed, clutching a messy sheaf of papers.

Cooper thought: hung over.

She knew how that felt, from personal experience.

16

Sonny DeWitt glowered at Cooper, then sighed heavily, and looked away, as if resenting the intrusion, not liking the prosecutor nosing around the company, but too nauseated and headachy to acknowledge her presence. Instead, he sank heavily into Wagner's second visitor's chair, and slouched, legs stretched out, eyes closed.

"What's this?" he said to Wagner, not opening his eyes, but weakly holding up the sheaf of papers he'd brought, then letting his arm drop, too heavy to hold up.

Flute looked at DeWitt, his new boss, and took a deep breath, girding for effort.

"That's a marketing plan," Flute said.

Sonny opened his eyes, stared at Flute, then shut his eyes again.

"What's all this stuff in here," he said. "Flavors?"

Flute took another deep breath.

"It's about adding a new product line," he said. "To draw younger customers, because our current demographic's aging and...." Sonny groaned.

"Damn," he said. "Talk English."

"It's like with e-cigarettes," Flute said. "Younger people like different vaping flavors—so we'd give them maple syrup with a hint of strawberry, or blueberry, or mint, or...."

Sonny groaned.

"God, we'd need to hire what, thousands?" he said.

"No, not much hiring for this," Flute said. "We'd get a consultant to help us choose flavors, and sources for them, and a mixing machine, for getting the new flavors into the syrup, and..."

Sonny groaned again, eyes shut. Cooper guessed his head must be pounding.

They sat silently while Sonny DeWitt slouched in his chair, radiating misery and gloom.

Cooper thought: he doesn't know how to run this company. He knows he doesn't know. So he blusters. He has to decide on this marketing plan, but he's lost.

"All right, Flutesy," he said, eyes still closed. "It's all on you—if this flavor stuff costs us a pile, but doesn't boost profits...."

"I'll take care of it," Flute said.

Yes, you will, Cooper thought. Proctor Gibbs dies, so Sonny DeWitt gets the CEO title, and the big salary, and the profit-sharing, but it requires knowhow. Flute has that. He'll do what Sonny can't handle—he'll manage this company. Nobody'll know it's Flute running Snowville Maple, Inc., but Sonny knows. He already resents Flute for it.

"You men can work on marketing later—I'm here about Proctor Gibbs," Cooper said. "What about workers in the maple groves, in the sugar houses, anyone better off with Proctor dead, especially if they spent any time in
Proctor's office?"

Still slouched in his chair, eyes closed, Sonny banged one fist against his forehead, and exhaled, exasperated.

"You're back on that again?" he said. "We're just a happy family here, all hugs and birthday parties."

He sat up, then lurched to his feet and started out, but stopped in the doorway.

"Those wasps, crawling up Proc's sleeves?" he said. "Well, all on their own they buzzed in there, because they had free will, okay?"

He glared at Cooper, red eyed.

"God, give us some peace," he said.

Sonny lurched out the door. They listened to his footsteps plodding away up the corridor, leaving a thick silence behind. After a moment, without looking up, Flute mumbled.

"He's got so much on his shoulders now, and...." Cooper thought: and you're apologizing for him. Because he's a bully. And you grew up bullied. By those spoiled brats in your school. Deep inside, you feel it's your due, being bullied.

"None of the outdoor workers, then..." she started to say, but Flute shook his head.

"Proctor liked to get outside to talk to them," Flute said. "He wasn't an office kind of guy, and he liked joking with the workers out there, got on great guns with them all—I've never seen any of them come in here, into his office."

Cooper thought: so only four people regularly wafted into Proctor's office. One of them just lurched out of this room in a hungover huff.

"What about the tour guide here?" Cooper said. "What about the receptionist?"

Flute jerked up his head, as if alarmed.

"Vic Ledger?" he said. "Winnie Rink?"

He vigorously shook his head.

"They're just high-school kids," he said.

Cooper suddenly felt weariness welling up, like a wave. She leaned back in her chair and fought against closing her eyes.

Just then, a woman hurried through the office's open door and stopped abruptly, staring at Cooper. She looked as if she'd never eaten much, starting in childhood. Her eyes, dark brown, staring intently at Cooper, had wariness in them, and her tensed face had bitterness.

"Viola!" Flute said, and then, to Cooper, "My wife."

A fraught moment. As if, for Viola Wagner, this visitor's presence triggered a cascade of moments, receding into the murky past, upsetting moments, painful. Now the woman's gaze shifted from Cooper to Flute, inquiring, and it wasn't the glare of a woman in a toxic marriage, staring at the husband she resented, even hated.

Nothing like that.

"This is Cooper North," Flute told his wife. "She's the state's attorney, for Allen County, and she's looking into what happened to Proctor Gibbs."

Viola Wagner looked from her husband to Cooper, then back to Flute, eyebrows now slightly raised.

"Is this about the wasps?" she said.

Flute nodded.

Viola looked at Cooper.

After a moment, she shrugged.

"My uncle died of a spider bite, brown recluse," she said.

Cooper thought: that wasn't what she'd wanted to say, about the spider. She wanted to say something else, but not in front of Flute. And now she stared at Cooper, studying her, making an evaluation.

Cooper felt too fatigued to continue the interview. She didn't know where to go with it anyway, seeing no clear evidence pointing to any particular suspect, and no clear way to get at that evidence, if it existed. There'd be fingerprints, but they'd mean nothing, prints of Snowville Maple's office staff, and UPS deliverers, lots of prints, all over Proctor Gibbs' office.

Sonny DeWitt's office now.

Cooper sat back in the chair, her left hand feeling for the cane she'd left leaning against the armrest.

"That's it for this morning," she said. "We'll talk again."

She got up from her chair, using her cane, not sure she'd make it onto her feet.

"Nice meeting you," she told Viola Wagner, as she left the office.

She walked into the entry area, her cane tapping the floor, and passed Vic Ledger, leaning over the reception desk, whispering with Winnie Rink, but the two went silent, staring at Cooper as she walked past.

Cooper thought, cold eyes on that boy. On the girl, imbecile eyes. It struck her as against nature, such a pretty face, but a hamster's brain.

Ledger and Rink silently watched Cooper walk out the building's front door. She started across the parking lot, thinking about home, an armchair, when she heard footsteps hurrying after her. She turned and saw Viola Wagner, rushing to catch up.

"Ms. North, I have things to say," Viola told her.

Cooper looked at her, waiting.

"Flute said you're here about Proctor Gibbs," she said. "Those yellowjackets in his sleeves?"

Cooper nodded

"Possibly someone put them there," Cooper said.

She thought: Viola Wagner looks upset, and under that, anger, an old anger, maybe going all the way back to childhood.

"Is that what Flute thinks, a murder?" Viola asked. "He called you in on this?"

Cooper nodded again.

Viola inhaled deeply, and exhaled.

"I don't want him getting involved in this," she said. "I don't want that DeWitt guy all stirred up, that's one thing."

Viola, silent now, stared fixedly at Cooper, but didn't really see her.

"That town where we grew up...."

She drew a deep breath and exhaled.

"My mother cleaned their houses, and Flute's mother hemmed their dresses."

She looked fiercely at Cooper.

"It was sixth grade, after gym class," she said. "They liked to plague him in the locker room." Cooper guessed who "they" were.

"One of them caught a wasp," Viola said. "Probably in a handkerchief—they were all changing, back into their class clothes...."

Viola deeply inhaled again, and exhaled.

"They put that wasp—while Flute was in the shower—into his pants, and after the shower he put the pants on."

She glared now at Cooper, as if daring her to understand.

"It stung and stung and stung."

She told it as if they did it yesterday.

"They laughed and laughed and laughed."

Ugly laughter, Cooper imagined. Mean laughter.

"So if Flute thinks someone put those yellow jackets in Mr. Gibbs' sleeves, you see...."

Cooper did see. Because whatever happens, she knew, it persists. Starting in the crib. All you've ever said and done. All that's said around you, and to you. And done to you. Like a sculptor's fingers, shaping clay.

"I wanted you to see, why...."

"Yes, I see," Cooper said.

"I don't want that DeWitt man knowing Flute called you in," Viola said, glaring at Cooper.

"He won't," Cooper said.

She nodded at Viola Wagner, standing there in the parking lot, small and skinny, intense.

Cooper thought: she wants to protect Flute. Because there are always bullies.

She visualized one of them, lurching up the corridor, hungover.

"When they did that to Flute, the wasp," Viola said behind her. "I came at night, to the chief bully's driveway, and I dumped a bag of sugar into his car's gas tank."

Viola Wagner looked triumphant, remembering that moment in the night.

"It didn't work," Viola said. "I thought—hoped—it would ruin his car, but it didn't."

Cooper looked at her, listening.

"I don't care," Viola said. "At least, I did something, for...."

Viola stared intently at Cooper, a vehement stare.

"My mother and father, they were mean," Viola said. "Those rich kids in school, just as mean, always making fun of my...."

Silent now, eyes focused far away, Viola seethed.

"Then I met Flute," she said. "So kind, I'd never had anyone be kind to me before."

Again she stood looking far away, back into the past.

"He was so good, but he couldn't do anything about those bullies," Viola said. "So I did for him what I could, sugar in a gas tank."

"I understand," Cooper told her, and walked toward her car.

As she got in, she glanced back and saw Viola still standing in the parking lot, staring after her.

She drove her Volvo north, toward Dill.

WHEN THE WASP STINGS

Yes, she thought, because of what happened in school, Flute is hypersensitive about yellow jackets. Probably just seeing one triggers unhappy thoughts.

Even so, he's right.

Somebody murdered Proctor Gibbs.

17

"Watch," Numero Uno said.

He balanced the Fairbairn-Sykes commando knife upright on his left palm, hilt down. With hand motions, he kept the blade pointed at the ceiling.

His moving hand made the knife dance.

"It embodies our power," Uno said.

He sat upright on his bed, back supported by heaped pillows, outstretched legs crossed at the ankles, balancing the knife on his palm.

"Wow," said Dos.

Dos sat in the room's armchair, knees bent, chin resting on knees, mesmerized by the dancing knife.

Uno smirked.

"It's nearly time," he announced.

"Hurrah," Dos said.

"First, a few more training missions," Uno said.

"Boo!" Dos said.

Uno's mouth twisted down, lips flattening against his teeth, causing Dos to jerk back in the chair, as if struck by his glare. After a moment, his face returned to emotionless neutral. Without looking at it, he pointed over his shoulder at one of the posters lining his bedroom's walls, dense black type on white posterboard—

"BEFORE INVINCIBILITY, MASTERY;
BEFORE MASTERY, PREPARATION."

Other wall posters—all lettered in black, on white cardboard—made added proclamations:

TO RISE ABOVE SHEEP, BE WOLVES
MERCY IS WEAKNESS
IN VICIOUSNESS IS FREEDOM
WAKE, ACT—OR DIE ASLEEP
CRUELTY IS MASTERY

Dos looked down, chastened.

"I've chosen two targets," Uno said.

He stopped balancing the knife and laid it atop his bedside nightstand, alongside its metal sheath.

"First will be a trial run, to identify flaws, and eradicate them," he said. "Second will be a full-scale mission."

"Exciting!" Dos said.

"No," Uno said. "Emotion is weakness—action is all."

"You really know stuff," Dos said.

"So listen to me," Uno said. "Learn."

He sat back against the pillows looking at the room's walls. Besides the posters with lettered messages, hung photos of animals—all predators—taken from magazines.

"Choose your totem animal," he said, indicating the posters with a sweep of his hand.

Dos studied the photos, indecisive.

"I'll choose for you," Uno said. "You're the pygmy shrew."

Dos looked unhappy.

"Shrews look like mice, and they're small," Uno said. "But they're one of the fiercest North American predators."

Dos looked dubious, but no longer stricken.

Uno turned in the bed, studying the photographs.

"Do you know which one is me?" he asked.

A blank stare from the newly anointed pygmy shrew.

"That one," Uno said, pointing to a picture.

It showed a snake—hooded head upraised, fangs bared, coiled to strike.

Cobra.

18

A work-study student brought in this morning's mail, including an envelope from the Vermont Forensic Lab.

"Thanks," Mike Bolknor said, not looking up.

His voice seemed to come up from a cavern.

He glanced at the mail, mostly bills for equipment orders, and gear catalogs, offering sensors and tasers and bullet-proof vests. He picked up the lab's envelope, started to open it, but then put it aside, as if reading it right now would be too heavy a task.

After a moment, he stood, and walked to his office window to stare out at the Mt. Augustus College campus, its walkways lined with sugar maples. A million caterpillars busily chewed the foliage—by late September, each leaf would be in tatters. Now, though, the chlorophyll-rich canopies, vibrant green, radiated health.

Bolknor put his big hands on either side of the window frame, and leaned forward, as if too weary to stand upright.

Just below his window, in a maple's shade, two students on campus for summer courses, a boy and girl, lay on their backs, their dropped backpacks spilling textbooks. They stared up at the leaves, intensely green, and sky, intensely blue, holding hands.

Bolknor turned away.

Slowly, he walked back to his desk, and stood still. After a while, he picked up the envelope from the forensic lab, knowing it contained an analysis of the tire tracks he and Cooper found, at the Dill RV Park, after the attack on Joey DeMercato's alligator.

They'd sent in their notes and photographs, and this was the lab's report.

After a moment, Bolknor sank into his office chair. He laid the envelope, still unopened, on his desk and drew open a desk drawer, carefully, as if a strong pull on the drawer might break something inside.

He extracted a framed photograph.

It showed a young woman, slender, dark-haired, brown eyes lively, standing with one arm over a pretty little girl's shoulders, the child her mother in miniature, and the other arm embracing a small boy, who eyed the camera impishly.

For a full minute, Bolknor stared at the photograph. Then he carefully placed it back in the drawer, and slid the drawer shut, gently.

Today would have been Abigail's ninth birthday.

Frankie's birthday would be three months from now.

He'd have been seven.

And Rachel....

Bolknor sat looking at nothing, doing nothing. Finally, he reached again for the envelope, opened it, and this time he read the report. He read it again. Then he lifted his desk's landline telephone and punched in Tip LaPerle's office number, at the Dill PD.

"I've got the troopers' analysis, of those tire tracks we found at the RV park," he said. "I can send you a copy, or just read it to you now."

"Read it," Tip said.

"Tire diameter's thirty-two point five inches," Bolknor said.

He read off more numbers, for wheel size, tread depth....

"What else?" Tip said.

"They think it likely was a Jeep Gladiator truck," Bolknor said. "That model comes from the factory with big-lug tires like this, to run in mud or off road." Silence from Tip LaPerle.

"Okay," LaPerle said. "Tell me if I'm right on this— your tire's got a shallow cut across the tread, from running over something like, say, a piece of shale, stuck in the ground, with a razor edge sticking up." "Yes," Bolknor said.

"You've got scalloping, right?" Tip said. "Tread scooped out here and there? Where stones or something whacked it?

"That's right," Bolknor said. "How did you...."

Tip went on: "Outer edge is wearing down, because maybe the alignment's a little off, am I right?" "Yes," Bolknor said.

Over the phone, he could hear Chief LaPerle's fingers drumming on his Dill PD desk. After a moment, Tip spoke again.

"I just got in my own lab report on tires," he said. "Remember, idiots stole Cappy Dixon's maple logs? So guess what—same tires as yours, same scalloping, same outer edge wear, same shallow cut across the tread."

Silence on both ends of the line, until Mike Bolknor finally spoke.

"So our pet stabber's also a log thief," he said.

114

"Looks like it," Tip said. "Problem is, Allen County's crawling with Jeeps like that...."

"So we'd have to go all over the countryside, checking the tires of every Jeep Gladiator we find," Mike said.

"That won't get done," Tip said.

They agreed to keep their patrols alert for Gladiators, checking tires if they got the chance. Maybe they'd get lucky.

"About Cooper," Bolknor said. "I'm worried."

Silence on the line. Then Tip spoke.

"Yeah, me too." Silence again.

Tip finally said. "She looks whomped."

Both men held their phones, saying nothing now, not aloud.

Mike knew what percolated unsaid, for each of them. Probably Tip LaPerle knew, too.

For Tip, his parents drunks, and crooks, Cooper North became the parent he needed, starting as a child, when he burst into the state's attorney office like a belligerent baby goat, demanding to know how he could become a policeman.

And for Mike Bolknor, who'd lost his wife and two children in a road-rage shooting, Cooper had become—although they never discussed it, didn't need to—not a replacement for his family, their loss forever a hollowness inside his chest, but something like a new family, whom he cared about, and admired.

Cooper had saved him, at one point, maybe, from shooting himself, beset by guilt, because he'd stayed in Manhattan, working on an organized crime investigation, letting his family go alone to Tampa, to visit Rachel's mother in her retirement home, and he hadn't been there when the armed fools in cars on either side of Rachel's rented Hertz opened fire at each other.

Tip finally spoke: "So we'll keep a watch on Cooper, too, besides tires."

"Yes," Mike said, and he pushed the phone's off button.

19

In extra-large letters, his mailbox shouted his name—
"Allister Chesterton, PhD."

An odd mailbox, Cooper thought, heavy steel, welded to a solid-steel post, set in a concrete base. Designed, apparently, to thwart sledgehammer attacks.

Cooper had stopped her Volvo here, after a confusing drive, even with the GPS, three miles north from Dill, along tangled back roads, snaking up a mountainside. Ahead, the gravel driveway twisted through balsam firs and spruces.

Cooper leaned back in the leather seat and shut her eyes.

Just a short rest, she told herself.

Something wet, though, on her cheek. She opened her eyes and saw it was Henry, leaning over from his perch on the shotgun seat, giving her a lick.

"You think I'm an ice-cream cone?" she asked.

Henry barked, as if he appreciated the joke, although Cooper knew what he really appreciated was attention, being spoken to, even if he didn't understand a word of it. He understood tone, though, and inflection, and facial expressions, and he knew what Cooper meant was: I really, really like you, Henry.

Or did Henry sense something wrong with her?

For a week she'd determinedly pushed away that thought, but now she'd thought it. So she gritted herself to drive on, to leave the thought behind, to attend to the business at hand. Nothing to see here, folks.

Chesterton's house proved to be a modern assemblage of cubes, with triple-glazed picture windows and rooftop solar panels. To generate additional volts, off to the house's side, a windmill. Right now, with the afternoon sunny and calm, the windmill stayed still.

It looked like a house built a century from now, but also like a fortress, its front door massive and its windows set in thick frames, which looked vaguely mechanical.

Chesterton waited on the house's porch, pacing.

He looked just as she remembered, from the Snowville Maple, Inc., tour—skinny and seventyish, with a white Van Dyke mustache and beard. Today, as then, he wore black jeans and a black t-shirt, apparently his summer uniform. In winter, she guessed, he switched to a black turtleneck.

He pointedly looked at his watch as Cooper got out of the car.

"I expected you twelve minutes ago," he said.

He spoke in a loud voice, as if addressing a lecture hall. If you were sitting in a restaurant, it would be the voice that drowned out the voices of all the quiet speakers, at other tables, and dominated the room.

Cooper had an urge to get back in her car and turn it around and drive away without ever saying a word to him. However, she knew, even a narcissistic egomaniac can be useful.

She walked around the car and opened the passenger door. Henry immediately vaulted out and his sharp eyes swept the grounds. Where to start sniffing? Up on the porch, Chesterton regarded the dog with downturned mouth of a man seeing something distasteful.

"If you don't like dogs, Henry can stay in the car," Cooper told him.

"I don't want fecal droppings on my lawn," Chesterton said.

"It won't happen," Cooper said. "If it does, I'll clean up after him."

She pulled a crumpled plastic bag from her pocket, and dangled it, to prove she could deal with any emergency.

Chesterton said nothing, so Cooper assumed it was a deal. She climbed the steps to the porch, with Henry scrambling up after her, the risers stretching his short corgi legs, and his big paws scratching at the treads.

"Thanks for making time for me today," Cooper said.

Make nice. Oil the gears. Get the witness talking freely.

"It's a citizen's duty," Chesterton said. "Assist legal authorities in investigations." Sarcasm?

No, he doesn't do sarcasm, Cooper decided. He says what he thinks. If it irritates someone, he doesn't notice. Or care.

"I don't know what you're investigating," he said.

"Proctor Gibbs' murder," Cooper said.

He stared at her, taken aback.

"Wasp stings, wasn't it?" he said. "Yellow jackets in his sleeves, anaphylactic shock?"

"We believe someone placed those wasps in his sleeves—everyone knew he was allergic," Cooper said. "Our question is, who did it?"

Chesterton still stared at her, absorbing the idea.

"Ye gods and little fishes," he muttered.

He sat on a porch chair, motioning with his chin for her to take the chair facing his.

"I see," he said.

He spoke to himself, thinking aloud.

"Two wasps, up two sleeves, the odds...."

Cooper thought: okay, the man's not stupid.

"Here's a question," Cooper said. "Who had access to Proctor's office, especially when he wasn't there?"

Chesterton looked steadily at her.

"Me," he said.

"Why don't you elaborate on that," Cooper said.

"He kept files in his office, records back to Snowville Maple's day one," Chesterton said. "I'd be checking facts for the history I'm writing."

"Did you get along with Proctor?" Cooper asked.

Chesterton turned up his eyes, indicating he regarded the question as imbecile.

"I'd contracted to write the company's history," he said. "Proctor Gibbs created the company, and ran it, so he was my prime source, and he cooperated."

Cooper thought: yes, but what about the man? Did you like him? Dislike him? Nurse a grievance?

And then she thought: no use asking. Like? Dislike? Allister Chesterton hardly knew what that meant. It would be like asking, do you like that filing cabinet over there? Does it irritate you?

Chesterton's world must be dusty as the moon, she thought. Nothing but data, and connecting theories, to thread the facts together. Momentarily, she felt sorry for Allister Chesterton. He was about her age, but she bet he'd never tapped his foot to a rock-and-roll song.

"Let's assume you didn't murder Proctor Gibbs," she told him. "You're studying this company, though, seen it in action, and you must have insights."

Chesterton said nothing, but stared intently at her.

After a long silent moment, he said: "Ask a question."

"Besides the office staff—Flute Wagner, Sonny DeWitt, Vic Ledger and Winnie Rink—who've you seen going into Proctor's office?"

"UPS delivery woman," Chesterton said. "Post office mail carrier, also a computer technician, just once, quite a while back."

He sat upright in his chair, thinking.

"Just about a month ago, the outdoor crew's foreman came in," Chesterton said. "They stood in his office doorway talking about ordering new plastic tubing, for collecting maple sap, as I remember."

"Did they seem to be getting along?" Cooper asked.

Chesterton looked at her as if he didn't fully understand the question.

"They talked business," he said.

He shrugged.

"Then, I remember, they did kid around, about the olden days, when draft horses pulled collecting wagons through the maple groves, " Chesterton said. "Something about certain horses being pals, and certain others being jerks."

Another shrug.

He thought again.

"Sonny DeWitt's wife came in once," he said. "She talked to Sonny—child-support issue, I believe—and then she spoke with Proctor briefly, just saying hello, how are you? And she left his office smiling, but I certainly don't see Sheila DeWitt as a murderess."

So, a news flash. Sonny had a wife, and children.

"Did you hear what Sheila and Sonny said?" Cooper asked.

From Proctor Gibbs' office, where Chesterton would be looking at old files, she knew he could easily hear conversations in Sonny DeWitt's adjacent office.

"Mainly about child support payments," Chesterton said.

He sat back in his chair, looking at nothing, remembering.

"Also, she wanted to know if he was still hanging out with somebody named…Possum, was it? And Dougie, and…Beast—could that be a name?"

"Anything else?" Cooper said. "How did their mood seem?"

Chesterton spread his hands, as if such a question was unanswerable.

"Well, she sounded a bit piqued, about the child support," he said. "And maybe concerned, about that Possum business."

Cooper heard a thumping sound.

It was Henry, clomping down the porch stairs, bored with their talk, ready to go exploring. Cooper thought about calling him back, but why spoil the dog's fun? In any event, she knew Henry well, and he'd stay close by.

"What can you tell me about the two high-school summer employees, Vic Ledger and Winnie Rink?" Cooper asked.

Chesterton made a disgusted face and put out his hands, palms up.

"Typical of their generation," he said. "In a nutshell, bratty—he's got a nasty edge, but keeps it suppressed, and she'd have difficulty tying her shoelaces without his step-by-step instructions, and that's all I've got to say on that…or any of the rest of this."

Cooper thought: so you actually can read personalities, but you don't like discussing people. You don't like answering questions. You don't know who killed Proctor Gibbs, and don't care, except that you've lost your information mother lode and you'll have to dig harder now. So goodbye to you, Ms. Prosecutor.

Chesterton stood, meaning interview over.

Cooper stayed sitting, sure that Chesterton could add more. However, he said nothing, waiting for her to leave. Finally she stood, too, wondering how she could squeeze more out of him. Right now, she decided, she couldn't. So give it a rest. Change the subject

"That fortified mailbox you've got out there," Cooper said. "You've had trouble?"

"Where I used to live, I did, near campus," Chesterton said. "Halloween, idiot students…."

He hadn't been a beloved professor, Cooper guessed. Probably routinely stamped on student feet, for misdemeanors, like lazily researched term papers, or felonies, like wavering attention in class, or super-serious crimes, like responding to a question about history with a stupid answer.

"This house looks solid," Cooper said.

Chesterton shook his head, as if the question reminded him of the awfulness of the modern world.

"Out there you've got psychopaths toting submachine guns," he said. "Druggies wandering around, thieves…."

Slightly paranoid, Cooper thought. But only slightly. Northern New England started changing the day the interstate highway system fully opened, making these mountains a quick drive from New York or Boston or Montreal.

Cooper scanned the house with a professional eye.

"Your one real vulnerability might be those picture windows," Cooper said. "Somebody using a rock as a smasher...."

Chesterton looked at her with his eyebrows up, and knowing twist of his mouth.

"Let me show you something," he said.

He pulled open the heavy front door, looking back to make sure Cooper noticed its massive construction and its heavy-duty locks. Without a medieval battering ram, a potential housebreaker wouldn't get through the door.

Inside the house, Chesterton led her from the white-walled entryway into a living area, also white, walls and ceiling. No decoration, just utilitarian ultra-modern chairs and reading lamps and tables. He walked to a control panel built into one wall.

"Watch," he said.

He pressed a button.

From throughout the house, a faint whirring. In this living area, as Cooper watched, each window looked like an eye shutting. From the top, a heavy steel-mesh screen descended, until its bottom edge fitted into a steel channel built into the sill, and the screen stopped with a solid clunk. Now, with most of the daylight screened out, the house had darkened.

"Every window in the house," Chesterton said. "Evening comes, down it all goes—back door's armored, too."

He gave Cooper a satisfied look.

"Place is built on a slab," he said. "No basement windows creeps could slither through."

Cooper thought about her own home, the large brick federal on Hill Street. Easy to break into. A house built in colonial times, when nobody gave a thought to security.
She felt suddenly vulnerable.

She thought: but I don't live out in the woods. I'm in town, with neighbors.

"Impressive," she told Chesterton.

Something made a scratching sound at the front door.

Chesterton strode to it, and threw it open—Henry stood outside in mid-scratch. He'd been feeling unattended to, and decided to fix that.

He strutted in looking pleased with himself.

"Who benefitted from Proctor Gibbs' death?" Cooper asked.

Chesterton, more comfortable now, having showed off his security system, actually thought about the question. She could see him considering each office worker. While he thought, they both stood silent, until Chesterton finally spoke.
"Well, from what I could see, Flute Wagner doted on
Gibbs, almost like a beloved father, you might say." Cooper thought: also, it was Flute who blew the whistle on this. Plus, he'd been better off when Proctor ran the business—now he had to answer to Sonny DeWitt, an incompetent, who bullied him.

"Those two high-school kids, Ledger and Rink?" Chesterton said, thinking aloud now, as if this were a problem in history needing to be solved, like who stabbed the king?

"Unlikely, because Gibbs dead or alive made no difference to them." he said. "Ledger's the kind of kid who resents being told what to do, but I don't think he got ordered around much."

Chesterton thought, frowning, mouth pursed.

"All that boy does is lead the tours," he said. "Show people the sugarhouse, then load them into wagons behind the truck, to haul them through the maple orchard, and that's about it."

Cooper thought: All right, let's classify Ledger and Rink as just faint possibilities. Got to learn more about those two.

"That leaves Sonny DeWitt," Cooper said.

Chesterton put out his hands, palms up, and hunched his shoulders in a shrug.

"I never heard them exchange harsh words," he said. "Gibbs and DeWitt."

He thought, then spoke again.

"But a year ago, back when the only two front-office people were Proctor, the CEO, and DeWitt, the vice president for sales, the Board met to name a successor, if Proctor died or retired," he said. "They voted unanimously, and that man's now the CEO."

Cooper thought: yes.

Who inherits the throne?

20

Tip LaPerle glowered at last night's patrol reports, all the while drumming his ball-point pen on his desk.

It meant, Cooper knew, Dill's police chief felt up against a wall.

"Damn," he said.

Cooper and Mike Bolknor sat in silence, waiting for Tip to start their regular Monday morning briefing.

Tip seethed, drumming his pen.

Cooper knew what drove these outbursts.

Fear.

Fear he'd risen too far above his origins, down by the Ira River, in Tenement Row. Fear he'd waded in over his head. That he'd flounder. He'd be shamed.

Tip suppressed that fear, so it erupted as anger.

Cooper guessed Mike Bolknor, too, could read Tip's flareups.

Mike sat upright, as always, wearing his usual suit and tie, as if he were still at the NYPD, instead of up here in flannel-shirt country. Behind that impassive face, Cooper knew, and all that size and muscle, a sophisticated intelligence hummed.

It occurred to Cooper that, in different ways, she loved these two men.

"Jeezum crow," Tip said.

He held up the reports and waved them.

"Sick!" he said.

Cooper and Bolknor waited.

"All over town," Tip said. "Stab, slash...."

Cooper sensed what must be coming.

"Down on Foundry Street, somebody's cat got sliced up," Tip said.

He glared down at the patrol reports in his hand.

"They got a cocker spaniel, on Starke Lane, then down on Snowville Street, they stabbed Harley Baker's basset hound, for crying out loud, big ears...."

Cooper felt the morning darken.

"No rain, for weeks," Tip said. "So no tire tracks, no footprints."

He sat glowering at the reports.

"No witnesses, either," he said. "They must go scouting, see when pets get let out, see when neighbors are all inside for supper."

He swore under his breath.

"I bet they even plan for these dry spells," he said. "No tracks."

He drummed his pen a while, then spoke again.

"It's like hunting ghosts." Mike Bolknor frowned, thinking.

"Why're they doing this?" he said.

Tip shrugged.

"If we can figure a motive, it might be a lead," Bolknor said.

Tip silently cursed.

128

"Got nipped as kids, maybe," he said. "So they're death on pets—who knows?"

Silence, all thinking.

"Or maybe they're ticked at various people," Bolknor said. "So they kill their pets."

Tip looked up from the paperwork strewn on his desk, brightening.

"Hey, we could check, see if one nutball's feuding with all these people," Tip said. "Figure who that snakehead is and…."

He sat up now, hoping they'd found a trail to go sniffing down.

Bolknor considered it, then shook his head.

"Doesn't add up, though," he said. "First they attacked Joey DeMercato's alligator, and he'd been in town, what, a day? No time to make enemies."

"And who'd hate frail little Gert Lemon?" Cooper said. "Enough to kill her beagle?"

Tip stared down gloomily at his desk and resumed drumming his pen.

Cooper suddenly threw up her hands, then dropped them back into her lap.

"It's worse," she said.

She sat shaking her head.

"It's worse than we think," she said.

Both men looked at her, waiting.

"First, these are psychopaths," Cooper said. "They torture and kill for pleasure."

Tip groaned.

"God, if I don't stop this…."

He groaned again.

"This town'll come for me with pitchforks," he said.

129

"And torches."

Silence now, everyone thinking. Finally Cooper shook her head.

"Killing pets is just Act One," she said.

She stared at the wall, behind Tip's desk, hung with photographs of former police chiefs, back into the nineteenth century.

"Remember what Joey DeMercato yelled at us?" she said.

She reminded them.

"Hell's walking your streets—Demons!"

Cooper looked grim.

"They're killing dogs and cats now," she said. "Their main act's coming soon."

She sat back in her chair and shut her eyes, then spoke again.

"Killing   animals   is   just   practice."

21

Just above the doorbell button, a plastic nameplate announced: "Sheila Cassidy DeWitt."

Cooper pushed the button, hearing a "ding-dong" inside the house. She waited on the stoop, with Henry standing beside her, bright eyed, because he liked visiting new places and meeting new people, whom he assumed would love him to pieces, just because.

Nobody came to the door, but Cooper heard children shouting excitedly.

She pushed the button again.

A tidy little ranch house, Cooper thought, on a middle-class residential street, Starke Lane. Lying on the front lawn, a purple frisbee. Also, a red child's bicycle, with training wheels, toppled onto its side. Parked in the driveway, a white Nissan Versa, dinged, getting on in years.

Nobody came to the door.

Cooper thought the voices came from behind the house. So she started around the side, with Henry pushing ahead of her, barking exuberantly, to announce his imminent arrival.

In the back yard, a blond girl, about eight years old, and her younger brother, equally blond, competed on a swing set, vying to swing highest, shouting.

Sheila Cassidy DeWitt, wearing a turquoise bikini, which matched her eye color, stood on a mat, barefoot, holding a dumbbell in each hand, doing curls.

Seeing Cooper, she stopped in mid-curl, a surprised expression on her face, quickly replaced by chagrin.

"Oh my gosh, Ms. North," she said, glancing down at her bikini-clad body. "I totally, totally forgot—I'm so sorry!"

Cooper smiled, to put her at ease. Henry hurried up and stood beside the woman's knee, looking up, waiting to be appreciated.

"What a cutie!" Sheila DeWitt said, laying down her dumbbells on the mat and crouching to grasp Henry's head two handed, and give it a gentle shake. Both children had abandoned the swings and crowded around Henry, petting the corgi, who glanced back at Cooper, an arch look. It meant, Cooper assumed, "Do you see how I should be treated?"

Cooper brought Henry to this interview because of his ice-breaking powers, to keep the talking easy. She'd come to ask this woman about her husband, to probe, and she didn't want her getting upset and freezing. This visit shouldn't feel like a law-enforcement interrogation of a witness, although that's what it was.

Sheila DeWitt looked to be in her late thirties, but still fit, stomach flat, with toned thighs and biceps. All that weight lifting, Cooper thought. Running, too, probably. She noticed a jump rope lying on the mat. Still a pretty woman, of the blue-eyed and blonde pixie-cut sort.

In high school, probably a stand out.

"I appreciate your making time for me, Mrs. DeWitt," Cooper said.

It made the woman wince.

"Not Mrs. DeWitt anymore," she said. "Divorced— please, call me Sheila—I'm keeping his name because of the kids, but otherwise…."

"I'm sorry," Cooper said. "Not an amiable separation, I take it?"

Sheila sighed.

She looks you in the eye, Cooper noted, straight forward.

It felt odd, vaguely, interviewing someone wearing only a turquoise bikini.

"Sonny and I, we're still friends, sort of," Sheila said. "I just couldn't put up with…."

She stopped there. She still looked Cooper in the eye, but her attention had gone elsewhere. Abruptly she came back.

"Would you like tea, or coffee?" she said. "Or a Coke?"

Cooper shook her head.

Sheila suddenly registered that Cooper leaned on a cane. She frantically looked around the yard, finally spotting two lawn chairs lying on their sides, relics of some make-believe game the kids played. Sheila hurried to the chairs, turned them upright, and set them facing each other.

"Please," she told Cooper. "Let's sit to talk."

Henry now ran around the yard's perimeter with the kids, a chasing game, which Henry clearly enjoyed, if tongue-out grinning and incessant barking were a measure.

Cooper thought: so, kids, they're more fun than a poky old woman, right Henry?

Sheila ignored the racing kids, and their shouts, and the barking dog, running beside them on his short corgi legs. She leaned back in her chair, looking at the sky. Finally she spoke.

"Sonny and me, it just got to be...you know," she said.

Cooper thought: Sheila, you've got a story to tell, and I'm guessing no really close friends to tell it to, because you moved to Dill not long ago, and you've been occupied watching over your small kids, so here's me, a stranger willing to listen.

"About four months ago, Sonny didn't come home for supper, which happened a lot," Sheila said. "I knew where to look, so I packed the kids into the car and drove down to River Street, to the Donut Dive—you know that place? Sort of a fast-food joint and bar, where a punky crowd hangs out, and I've heard there's drug deals, too?"

Cooper nodded, letting Sheila do the talking.

"Okay, so there's Sonny, sitting on the fender of the company Jeep, holding a bottle of Bud, probably his third or fourth of the evening, and he's laughing it up with Possum, and Walrus, and Beast, just like twenty-five years hadn't gone by, even though he'd promised, no more hanging out with them, and right then it totally hit me—is this it, for the rest of my life? Hooked to a high-school kid?"

"Who are the three friends with funny names?" Cooper asked.

Sheila shut her eyes and shook her head.

"Jerks," she said. "Like we all used to be, including me, stupid jerks."

In high school, she said, they'd been football stars, Possum, Walrus, Beast, and Sonny, especially Sonny. They'd called themselves "The Four Musketeers."

"For Sonny, that was his best time, you know? High school?" she said. "Well, for all five of us, actually, but you can't stay sixteen forever, can you?"

She said she'd been a trophy-winning athlete, too, on the girls' soccer team. She and Sonny had gone steady since junior high school, and they were prom king and queen.

"It felt good to be us," Sheila said, shaking her head, rueful. "But when we graduated, Sonny sort of didn't graduate, mentally—he just stayed in high school, still hanging with his old football buddies, because after school ended, it was like everything fizzled for him…his parents…."

"What about his parents?" Cooper asked.

"They're rich, the DeWitts," Sheila said. "You've probably seen their convenience stores, DeWitt Fuel & Shop? All over the state?"

Cooper nodded.

"Sonny's older brother went into the Air Force, because he'd been in ROTC, in college, and I guess he had to," Sheila said. "Sonny inherited his brother's Corvette, so we drove around in that, like some Hollywood couple, you know? And I felt so good about us, back there in high school—Boy, was I shallow or what?"

After high school, Sonny's friends, Possum, Walrus, and Beast, kept on doing what they did in school, Sheila said. Pranks. Lazing around. Chasing girls. Heavy drinking, too. They'd take a job, like delivering pizza, or shingling roofs, whatever, but they never lasted long at anything.

"And that's them now, too, just hanging around, really," Sheila said.

Sonny's parents insisted he go to college, and a minor school finally accepted him, despite lackluster high-school grades, because they needed a football player. However, that didn't work out so well. His three pals followed him to the college town and he hung out with them, although they never even tried to enroll in the school. They finally pulled a prank—running off with a campus security patrol car—that got them all into big trouble.

"Possum and Walrus, they both went to jail for three months," Sheila said. "Beast got off because he'd been laid out in the back seat, dead drunk, the idiot, and they figured he hadn't had much to do with taking the car."

Sonny, she said, hadn't driven off with them in the car, but a surveillance video caught him handing money through the window to Possum, in the driver's seat, for gas, and watching them rocket off, grinning.

"So he didn't go to jail or anything, but they kicked him off the football team," Sheila said. "After that, he limped along in college, getting really mediocre grades."

His parents had written Sonny off since elementary school, she said. Now he'd really let them down, involved in this car theft. His older brother and sister both were class valedictorians, and his brother starred in every sport, including football.

"Sonny couldn't match him," Sheila said. "It ate at him, I guess."

Sonny's parents groomed their two oldest children, brother and sister, to take over the family business, but not Sonny.

"Loser, that's what they'd decided he was," Sheila said. "Oh boy, they made that clear!"

In the Air Force, his brother became a fighter pilot.

"It made Sonny feel like a nobody," Sheila said.

When the brother finished his Air Force hitch, he started taking over the family business, along with his sister.

"Sonny just floundered along, you know? Selling used cars, mostly," Sheila said. "Something always happened, anyway, so he didn't last long at any dealership, especially after he started drinking too much."

Sheila had gone to the University of Vermont, on a soccer scholarship—her father worked in a granite quarry and her mother was a practical nurse. Sheila got a degree in business, focusing on accounting.

"That's what I'll be doing now," she said. "I got a job in the accounting department, up at Dill Industries, which I'm starting next week."

She hadn't worked until now because of the kids, she said. She wanted to be there for them, but they were a little older now, and she'd found a good day-care service. Also, she couldn't count on Sonny coming through with child-support payments.

"He drinks too much, and he gets muddled," Sheila said. "And I think his jerk friends get him into gambling a little—when he got this job with Snowville Maple, they followed him right on up here, and they're living here in Dill, like some kind of virus you can't shake off."

She sat looking at nothing, silent now. Cooper, too, remained silent, letting Sheila do the talking, and Sheila suddenly turned her head to look at Cooper.

"You're here, because...."

She looked puzzled.

"Something about poor old Proctor Gibbs?"

Cooper nodded, then gave the explanation she'd used with Sonny.

"When somebody in Allen County dies unexpectedly, we have to get the details, just to tie up loose ends," she said.

She didn't say, as she didn't say earlier to Sonny, the qualifying phrase: "When somebody dies under suspicious circumstances."

She'd alerted Tip LaPerle to Proctor Gibbs' murder.

"By wasp sting!" Tip had said. "Jeezum Crow!"

For now, they'd agreed, keep these interviews unofficial. Witnesses would speak more freely, especially before the *Dill Chronicle* took off with the story, and everyone got lawyered up. Then they'd get warrants and the Dill PD would come in on the case, with Mike Bolknor borrowed from the college as detective.

"How well did Sonny get along with Proctor Gibbs?" Cooper asked.

"Okay, I guess," Sheila said, with a shrug.

She'd liked Proctor a lot, she said. Sonny liked him, too.

"Well, except sometimes...."

"Oh?" Cooper said.

Sometimes, out on the road, doing sales, Sonny didn't exactly tell Proctor where he went and what he did, and Proctor asked about it, which made Sonny mad, she said. Probably, she suspected, he got mad because he felt guilty, for going skiing, when he should have been making his rounds, or stopping at some bar, that kind of thing.

"Flute Wagner, too—he got hired and Proctor really liked him, thought he did a great job marketing," she said. "No kids, Proctor and his wife, and I think he got to thinking of Flute almost like a foster son, or something— that's what Sonny said."

Cooper said nothing, watching Sheila think, forehead wrinkled. Again it struck her, the vague oddity of interviewing a woman in a turquoise bikini, watching her think.

"Sonny complained about Flute," Sheila said. "You know what? I just realized, to him it was like his parents, sort of, you know, favoring his older brother and sister?"

Cooper let her think some more.

"I think Sonny got into bullying Flute a little," she said. "Like he used to do in high school, picking on the nerds—we all thought it was funny back then, and now I'm ashamed I never told him to stop it."

Cooper looked at her, thinking she liked Sheila Cassidy DeWitt, bikini and all. Just as she'd liked Olga Fisker, the entomologist who climbed trees. In fact, she liked Olga because she climbed trees, one reason. She'd be calling Fisker, she thought. Another wasp question.

She thanked Sheila for her help, and stood. Leaning on her cane, she called Henry, still racing with the children. Henry stopped, and stared across the lawn at her, clearly deciding whether to obey or keep on running.

"It's up to you, Mister," Cooper told him. "If you want supper."

Then she turned and started back around the house. She heard Henry's paws pounding the ground behind her. Abruptly, he pushed past her and ran toward the street, looking back to make sure she followed.

Opening the Volvo's door, so Henry could scramble up onto the shotgun seat, Cooper noticed her right arm. She wore a sleeveless blouse.

Just above her elbow, she had a large bruise, intensely black, covering a large section of arm. She had no idea what she'd bumped, to get the bruise.

She didn't remember bumping anything.

Leaning back against the leather seat, she shut her eyes. After a minute, she roused herself. As if with great effort, she pushed the "Start" button.

"I've got to call the doctor," she told Henry.

This time, she almost meant it.

22

"Why'd we park way out here?" Numero Dos asked.

Numero Uno turned in the driver's seat to give Dos an expressionless stare.

"Because our target might escape, drive off in his car," he said. "What's to stop him?"

Dos looked dumbfounded.

"Our truck stops him," Uno said. "Because we parked out here."

Dos looked blank.

"We're blocking his driveway," Uno said.

His partner brightened.

"Oh yeah," Dos said. "Right."

"Answer this," Uno said. "Why park out here, by his mailbox, where the driveway starts?"

Dos looked like the proverbial deer, frozen in oncoming headlights.

Uno stared at Dos, expressionless, maintaining the silence. Finally he spoke.

"A visitor drives up, while we're in action," he said. "Then what?"

Dos thought hard, then answered, but hesitantly, fearing a rebuke for being wrong.

"They can't get down the driveway? Because we're parked out here?"

Uno nodded, a single downward jerk of his chin.

"Contingencies," he said. "What we plan for."

"Boy, you think of everything," Dos said.

Uno stared at Dos.

"You missed the most obvious thing," he said. "If we park out here, he won't hear us coming in."

Dos said: "Cool."

From a pocket, Dos pulled stick of gum, peeled off the wrapper, began to chew. Tense. Nerved up. Chewing gum helped.

"Masks on," Uno said.

They pulled black balaclava masks over their heads, with openings for just the eyes and mouth. Then Uno reached into the bin between the front seats—he pulled out the Fairbairn-Sykes commando knife, in its metal sheath.

He opened the driver-side door and got out.

For a moment, though, he stood with one foot still on the running board, staring up at the gibbous moon. It dimly silvered the landscape. Ahead, though, the balsam firs on either side shaded the driveway, keeping it in late-evening darkness.

"Here we go," Uno said.

Dressed in black, the two Ninjas ran down the driveway, a dark corridor between walls of trees. They seemed shadows, running through shadows.

"Remember, we go in through a window," Uno whispered as they ran.

"If no window's open, we do Plan B," Dos whispered back, pleased to remember their catechism.

"Move like a stalking tiger," Uno said.

They stopped, still in the trees, where forest ended and lawn began. Ahead loomed an assemblage of giant cubes, a modernistic house. Hidden in the balsam's shadows, they studied it.

Here the driveway arced past the house's front steps, then terminated at a garage, attached to the house's left side by a passageway. Steel bars made windows in the garage and passageway impregnable.

Atop the house's roof, solar panels glinted silvery in the moonlight.

Large windows in the house shone yellow.

Uno and Dos stayed hidden in the trees, watching.

Something whirred.

"What's that," Dos whispered, alarmed.

Uno pointed to the house's right side, at a windmill, its blades slowly turning in a light breeze.

He'd reconnoitered here in the daytime, studying the house unseen, hidden among these trees, memorizing its details, and its surroundings.

They stood a moment, staring at the house, gathering momentum for what they'd come to do.

Off in the forest, a barred owl hooted.

"Who cooks for yooooah."

After a moment, from far away, fainter, came an answering hoot.

"Who cooks for yooooah."

Uno raised the knife, up over his head, pointing at the gibbous moon.

He took one last look, making sure nobody peered out any of the house's windows. Then he brought down the upraised knife, pointing it now at the house.

"Go," he said.

They ran across the lawn, two figures in black, shadows.

At the porch, Uno held up a hand, signaling a halt. He studied the house's front windows. Something looked wrong. Maybe, inside, gauzy curtains covered the windows. Yet, when he'd reconnoitered here in the daylight, he'd seen no curtains.

Probably no big deal.

Uno pointed an index finger, signaling they'd bypass the front porch and check out the house's right side.

They ran, in silence, two crouched shadows.

On this side of the house, windows still had the odd veiled look. Yellow lamplight shone through from inside, but it seemed to come through gauze.

"Stay here, Dos," Uno whispered.

"Okay, Uno," his partner whispered back.

Silently, on his running sneakers, he walked to the nearest window and peered closely at it.

Inside, a steel-mesh sheath had dropped from the top of the frame and braced in a slot at the bottom. Uno reached out, to see if the window might be opened, so he could push the mesh out of the way, but he pulled back his hand.

Maybe this guy had alarms.

He doubted he could push the mesh aside anyway.

He whispered to Dos: "Follow me around—we'll check the rest of the windows, see if there's a basement door, too."

Dos spit out something onto the grass.

They started their circumnavigation of the house. In the back, it was the same, steel mesh protecting the windows. A back door looked heavy and strongly locked. Uno didn't try to open it. They continued on around to the far side of the house—here, too, steel mesh protected every window, except in the garage and passageway to the house, where steel bars did the armoring.

No entry to a basement anywhere.

Uno cursed under his breath.

"Let's go around front," he said. "Plan B."

Plan B meant knocking on the front door. Probably he wouldn't automatically open the door, so they'd speak through it, loud enough to be heard. We're students, they'd say. From an environmental protection group. We've come to discuss saving a threatened bog.

Then, once the target opened his door....

They walked up the steps to the front porch. Uno held the knife in his left hand. He pulled back his right hand to knock, but....

Blinding white light.

Uno squeezed shut his eyes, to keep out the light.

It came from floodlamps, set in the house's eaves, all around the building, turning night into noon. Somewhere, an alarm pulsed out deafening wails.

"Oh my God," Dos screamed.

Uno opened his eyes, but remained frozen, momentarily blind.

Abruptly, the alarm stopped.

From hidden loudspeakers, a man's voice blared out.

"You with the knife!"

Electronic crackling from the loudspeakers, then the voice again.

"You've been watched every step on infrared sensors, and videoed."

Another moment of crackling.

"You're being videoed now—stay where you are— the police are on their way!" "Oh my God," Dos said again.

"Run, you idiot," Uno said.

He started racing down the driveway, out of the circle of light, into the shadows. After a stunned moment, Dos ran after him.

At the driveway's start, by the mailbox, gasping for breath, Uno opened the truck's door and vaulted inside, already pressing the "Start" button, while Dos scrambled into the shotgun seat. With their doors still hanging open, Uno reversed the truck out of the driveway, shooting backwards, its knobby tires spitting gravel. Back on the road, he momentarily paused.

Go left? Go right?

Abruptly, he spun the wheel and pressed the accelerator and the truck shot off to the left.

"Cops'll be coming up the other way," he said, teeth gritted. "Up from Dill."

A moment later, behind them, patrol-car sirens wailed, the sound rising and falling, high-low-high-low....

Uno drove rapidly up the side of the mountain, following the road's curves, finally slowing when they no longer heard sirens.

"Oh my God," Dos moaned. "He got us on TV!"

Uno, staring fixedly through the windshield at the twisting road ahead, said nothing. Abruptly, he reached up and pulled off his Balaclava mask. His face looked grim. Along his jawline, something twitched.

"We're dressed in black," he said, teeth clenched. "We wore masks—that's all the videos can show."

"Oh," Dos said.

They topped the slope and the truck leveled, then tipped forwards, starting the descent. Ahead, the road forked. Uno turned down the leftward branch, back toward town.

"Boy, I guess that didn't work right, at that house," Dos said. "Boy, I guess it sure didn't."

Uno's hands tightened on the steering wheel. His jawline twitch became more pronounced.

"Shut up!" he said.

23

Early the next morning.

They rode up the mountain in Tip LaPerle's patrol car, slowing for banks of fog, then accelerating, with the rising sun turning the balsam and spruce tops golden. Cooper North rode in the shotgun seat. Mike Bolknor sat folded up in back, with Henry.

Cooper thought: with Mike's long legs, he needed this front seat, to stretch out.

Too late now. No matter, really. Just a small lapse in consideration. Except it seemed she wasn't paying attention.

This troubling fatigue, she thought.

At the driveway's start, by the mailbox, Tip stopped and got out. He crisscrossed the gravel driveway, peering down for tire tracks, but finally got back into the cruiser and shook his head.

"No tracks," he said. "Wouldn't be, not on this gravel, even if it wasn't so dry."

Cooper thought: there'd be no tracks anyway, because there'd been no vehicle.

Chesterton's driveway motion sensors picked up nothing last night. That was in the report from the Dill PD officers, who answered his 911 call.

Still, it's too far up the mountain to hike it, Cooper thought now. So the Ninjas certainly drove here, but then walked down the driveway. They must have parked their vehicle out here, where the driveway begins.

Cooper thought: yes, to block it.

She imagined this driveway in the late evening. Firs and spruces on both sides would keep out moonlight. In her mind, she saw the two Ninjas, wearing black, shadows gliding up the dark corridor.

Like demons, she thought.

She guessed Chesterton's sensors were tuned for two-ton vehicles, not pedestrians. Otherwise, every grazing white-tailed deer would set them off.

Chesterton awaited them on his porch, pacing. He frowned, shaking his head, glaring at them. Clearly upset, and angry.

"It'd be nice to see the police doing their job," he snarled.

Nobody responded to that, an angry and frightened man lashing out.

"What can you tell us?" Tip asked.

Chesterton, in his agitation, rose up onto his toes, then dropped back onto his heels, then up on his toes again.

Cooper thought: Ninjas in the night, coming for you?
Who wouldn't be agitated?

"I watched them on the infra-red security cameras," Chesterton said. "Both dressed in black, with black masks over their heads, ski masks, I think"

"See any details?" Tip asked.

"Just that one was tall—that's the one with the big knife—and the other one was shorter," Chesterton said.

"That knife—which hand held it?" Cooper asked.

Chesterton shut his eyes, visualizing what he saw on the tv screen.

"Left hand," he said.

"Let's look at the security camera footage," Mike Bolknor said.

Chesterton turned to lead them into the house.

"Can my dog come in with us?" Cooper asked. "If you'd rather not, he can stay in the car."

"Right now, after all this, I don't care about that," Chesterton said, and pulled open the armored front door.

As they followed him in, both Tip LaPerle and Mike Bolknor eyed the door, with its massive construction and its heavy-duty hinges and lock. Cooper had seen it before. Overkill, she'd judged it then. Now, though, she thought, this kind of thing, it saved his life.

In what probably was meant to be a large closet, Chesterton had set up a security control room, with a phalanx of tv cameras capturing views all around the house.

"They work in infra-red at night, and regular tv in the daylight," Chesterton told them. "Movement turns them on."

He had a microphone, so he could speak over loudspeakers hidden under the house's eaves. An array of readout screens showed data from sensors, around the house and up the driveway. Switches controlled floodlights mounted under the eaves.

150

He pointed to one readout screen—"Picks up a car, stopping out by the mailbox," he said. "Flashes red and beeps."

LaPerle and Bolknor, said nothing, taking it all in.

Cooper thought: ordinarily, all this might seem nuts, but this isn't ordinary. Chesterton lives out here alone, in an expensive home, a prime target for thieves. Nothing around for miles but forest—so, was the man paranoid, or intelligently cautious?

Chesterton flipped some switches, and the security camera screens lit up, showing the view around the house. If this were night, in infrared, it would look eerie.

"Motion detectors picked up movement outside, set the alarm beeping," Chesterton said. "Usually, it's a bear, or raccoons, but I checked the security cameras anyway, and this is what I saw."

He pressed a button, and the cameras whirred, rewinding, then started forward with last night's recordings.

Two figures moved across the screen. In the infrared, they looked like ghosts.

In the tall Ninja's left hand, a large-bladed knife.

Momentarily, the Ninjas stared at the house's front porch. Then, with the bigger Ninja leading, they walked around to the house's side, where a different camera picked them up.

Now the larger Ninja moved up close, to inspect one of the windows.

"Steel-mesh screens, night comes, down they drop," Chesterton said.

As the taller Ninja studied the window, his shorter partner leaned forward, turned aside, then straightened.

Cooper thought: spitting?

"Do you have sound?" Mike Bolknor asked.

Chesterton pressed a button and last night's sounds came in, along with intermittent static, crickets chirping and the windmill whirring. At one point, Cooper heard a barred owl call. Moments later, farther off, another answered.

After a few minutes, voices—whispering—came over the speaker.

"Stay here, Dos."

"Okay, Uno."

Cooper thought: microphones distort their voices. If I heard them talking in real life, I couldn't recognize their voices, not from these recordings.

"They've got weird names," Tip LaPerle said. "Uno, Dos—couple immigrants, you think?"

Mike Bolknor shook his head.

"That's Spanish," he said. "Uno's one and Dos's two—but their pronunciation's off, so I doubt they're Hispanic, just keeping their real names secret."

A bark from the front door—Henry, bored and wanting to go out. Probably needing to pee.

Cooper thought: I don't even know why I brought you, Henry,

She opened the door for him and he scampered out, excited, clearly ready for adventures.

They grilled Chesterton, trying to extract more information, but didn't get much. Just that Uno, the taller Ninja, clearly led, which they already knew. Also, that the knife looked weird. They got the surveillance tv turned on again and looked at the knife—its blade seemed oddly thick and dull.

They studied it.

"All right, that's a commando knife," Mike Bolknor said. "We'd use them sometimes in the Army—I think this one's sheathed."

He studied the screen image closely.

"I believe that's a metal sheath, not leather," he said. "Unusual." He

thought.

"Might be able to pinpoint its brand," he said. "Must not be many commando knives that come with metal sheaths."

"Trace it, maybe," Cooper said.

"Maybe," Mike said.

They finished with a look outside, with Chesterton trailing behind. They walked along the house's side, slowly, heads down, scanning the grass. Maybe a Ninja dropped a Kleenex. Or something.

Except for slightly trampled grass, they saw nothing. Meanwhile, believing a game was underway, Henry scampered ahead of them, jubilantly checking the ground himself, although he wasn't looking for clues.

Dropped food, Cooper thought. That's what Henry wants.

Abruptly, the corgi stopped, sniffed at the ground, then threw back his head and barked. He bent forward again to pick up whatever prize he'd found.

"Stop him!" Cooper said.

Mike Bolknor strode ahead, and put his big hands around Henry and lifted him into the air. Henry turned and give Mike a big corgi grin. What a great game. Fun!

Cooper and Tip LaPerle caught up and bent over to look for what snagged Henry's attention.

Something lay buried in the grass, small, shapeless, gray.

"Who's got gloves?" Cooper asked.

Mike put Henry down and pulled a pair of evidence gloves from his suit jacket's pocket.

Of course, Cooper thought. Mike always brings latex gloves. A former NYPD detective. Tip forgets. I forget. Mike never forgets to bring gloves.

He pulled the gloves on, then reached down to pick up the small gray blob. He held it up, between thumb and forefinger, for all to see.

It looked like nothing in particular. Not quite like a raccoon dropping, say.

Cooper thought she sniffed spearmint. Faint. Faded.

"It's gum," she said.

Now she noticed tooth marks.

"Do you chew gum?" Tip asked Chesterton. "Any chance you dropped this?"

Chesterton snorted.

"Good Lord no!" he said

Mike Bolknor already had pulled a plastic evidence bag from his jacket pocket. He dropped in the gum and sealed the bag and slipped it back into his pocket.

"You think these gum-chewing jerks came here to steal something?" Chesterton said.

Cooper looked at him, momentarily silent.

"No, they didn't come to steal," she said finally.

"What then?" Chesterton asked, puzzled.

Cooper stared at him.

"They came to butcher you," she said.

24

After keying in her physician's phone number, Cooper put the receiver to her ear, then silently cursed the recorded message—

"All our receptionists are currently helping other patients. Your call is important to us. Please stay on the line, and your call will be answered in the order in which it was received."

Then, over the telephone, came Mozart's *Eine Kleine Nachtmusik*, intended to soothe the on-hold caller, but it didn't soothe Cooper North.

To free her hands, she clenched the receiver between her head and shoulder, waiting for a human voice, while she surveyed the file folders spread across her desk, considering assignments for her two assistant Allen County State's Attorneys, standing in front of her desk, notebooks poised, awaiting their day's to-do list.

Still early morning. Tip LaPerle had just dropped Cooper off at her office, after their visit with Allister Chesterton. A profoundly unsettling visit.

What if Chesterton hadn't armored his home like an M1A2 Abrams Battle Tank? He'd be dead. Now, because he escaped, the Ninjas would be frustrated. Pressure building. They must slaughter.

Uno and Dos.

Homicidal psychopaths.

Soon now, they'd attack someone else.

And what, exactly, could the Allen County State's Attorney do about it?

Eine Kleine Nacthmusik started over, from the opening notes.

Cooper fantasized strangling her telephone.

Henry, lying on the floor near the door, raised his head, took in the two young lawyers waiting for Cooper to add to their work load, and Cooper's frown, then let his head sink back down. He knew Cooper's irritation wasn't directed at him. So he resumed sleeping.

"All right, sit down you two," Cooper said, motioning her assistants to the two visitor chairs, facing her desk.

She kept the telephone clenched between her ear and shoulder. She thought about hanging up, calling again later, but didn't do it. If she did, she'd go through the annoying rigamarole all over again. "Your call is important to us...."

Looking at her two assistants, with her head tilted aside, to hold the phone, she scanned the folders, figuring priorities, and which new task to give to which assistant, in addition to all their current work.

Cooper held up a folder.

"First," she said, "here's a complaint from a married couple, and between us, complete idiots—they demand we file criminal charges against Thor Ennis—that's the kid Tip and Marge LaPerle are fostering."

She looked now at the attorneys sitting in front of her.

Who should handle this one?

Ozzie Knick's brown eyes stared unblinking at her, from behind round wire-rimmed eyeglasses.

Looking at him—short, curly dark hair, round headed—Cooper tried to remember which terrier breed he reminded her of. Or was it an owl?

Ozzie had a gripe.

He believed, vehemently, that he should be sitting in Cooper North's seat.

When the previous prosecutor resigned, to take a job in Washington, Ozzie assumed he'd step into the top position. Super smart, right? Quick, right? Totally up on the legal code, right?

However, city counselors, the Dill PD, Allen County Sheriff's Department, and the State Police, too, unanimously lobbied to reinstall Cooper in her old position, to fill out the term.

Ozzie still smoldered over it, but tamped it down.

"Thor Ennis is seven years old," Cooper said.

She gave them the boy's background. Before his mother, a down-and-out fentanyl addict, got murdered, she sent Thor to school in rags. So, a deprived kid, alone—naturally he got bullied. In particular, a group of older, larger boys constantly picked on him.

Thor's tormenters would sneak up behind and shove him. They'd slap him, too, until he struck back. Then they'd complain to the principal. Gosh, they'd say, that little Thor kid, always punching and kicking, for no reason. Comes from Tenement Row, you know. These boys were sons of prominent citizens. So the principal believed what they said, or chose to believe it. So did many teachers. They regarded Thor with cold eyes. Other students knew the truth, but stayed quiet.

Cooper guessed why Tip LaPerle decided to take in this orphan: Thor reminded him of himself. Both came out of Tenement Row, down by the Ira River. Both had awful parenting. In any event, Tip's and Marge's kids were off at college, so their house had room to spare, and—Cooper thought—so did their hearts, although Tip kept his own heart hidden, maybe even from himself.

Now, though, the gang of bullies had a new rallying cry—"Hey Ennis, you a cop kisser?"

Cooper paused, to see if either assistant had a question.

Kalisha Rains just had a comment.

"That poor kid."

Cooper knew Kalisha had endured her own experiences with bigotry and bullies, a smart black girl in a white suburban high school. She'd learned how it feels to be outcast, and beset. She had empathy. She'd earned it.

"That's absurd, criminal charges against a seven-year-old," she said. "It shouldn't be done, for God's sake, and it actually couldn't be done." Cooper nodded.

"That's exactly right," she said. "You just missed one part—these Prescotts are big deals in Dill, and if we just flat out told them they're jerks, they'd get fussed up."

"So let me guess," Ozzie Knick said. "Once again the Ennis boy defends himself, and hits back—but this time the bully's parents throw a hissy fit, the injustice! Their
little darling attacked!"

Cooper nodded.

"Tyler Prescott, that's our bully," Cooper said. "Three years older than Thor, twice his size, and his Daddy's number-one vice president up at Dill Industries—not to mention his mom's on the City Council.."

She held up the case folder.

"Who wants it?" she asked.

Ozzie leaned forward in his seat, reached out, and took the folder from Cooper's hand.

"What's your plan?" Cooper asked him.

He smirked. Of course, in the last half minute, he'd already devised a plan.

"I'll let them know we seek justice, in this brutal attack their son sustained," Ozzie said. "To do that, folks, I'll explain, we'll need your help, prepping for the jury— what I won't say is, a seven-year old? A criminal trial? Are you two nuts?"

He grinned, anticipating the encounter.

"Our thrust," he said. "Pretend to be trying to support their case, but making it really clear they don't have a case."

He thought a moment.

"Lots of ideas on that, and the killer evidence will be Exhibit A," he said. "Currently secret."

Cooper held up her hands, almost losing the telephone clenched between her head and shoulders.

"Okay, there go the Prescotts," she said. "Out the door, tails between their legs."

Ozzie grinned.

Cooper thought: if something happened to me, Ozzie Knick really could step in.

Cooper shuffled through the folders on her desk, selected one, and held it out to Kalisha Rains, who laid it in her lap while she lifted the reading glasses she slung from her neck on cords and placed them low on her nose, so she could look over the tops of them. Now, though, peering down through the lenses, she opened the folder and leafed through the papers inside.

After she finished, she looked at Cooper over the tops of the glasses.

"Stolen sugar-maple logs?" she said. "We never had any crimes like that in Philadelphia."

"Welcome to flannel-shirt country," Cooper said.

Then she gave Kalisha a run-down on the log thefts from the Caspar Dixon Lumber Company. Right now, Cappy Dixon had his workers checking area sawmills, to see who came in with a pickup truck carrying ten logs, chain-sawed in half, to six-feet long, worth eighty dollars, total.

"Tip LaPerle will investigate, finger the perps," Cooper said. "I know you've already got lots on your plate, Kalisha, but when you have time, start figuring how we should charge these jerks, four of them, Tip figures, so something like twenty dollars each, that's their wages for sin and risking arrest."

"Anything in the state law books about stealing wood?" Kalisha asked.

Cooper shrugged, eyes turned up.

Just then, *Eine Kleine Nachtmusik* stopped and a voice came into her ear—"This is Laura, how may I help you?"

160

Cooper unclenched the phone, straightening her head and dropping her shoulder, while simultaneously gripping the handset with her right hand and motioning with her left hand for her assistants to get back to work.

"This is Cooper North," she said. "I need an appointment."

Henry raised his head, looked at Cooper, then turned his head to watch Kalisha and Ozzie walking out of her office. He stood, clearly considering, then followed the two assistants out the door, betting they'd do something more entertaining than talking on the telephone.

"Date of birth, please," Laura said.

Cooper told her.

"Is your information still the same?" Laura asked. "Insurance, address, phone numbers…."

Cooper said, "Yes, I need an appointment with Dr. Goldstein."

"And what will you be seeing the doctor about?"

"Chronic fatigue, getting worse," Cooper said. "Some kind of virus, I imagine."

She heard the clack of Laura hitting computer keys.

"Also, I doubt it has anything to do with the fatigue, but I've been getting odd black bruises on my arms and legs, but I haven't bumped into anything to account for them."

More clacking keys.

"Dr. Goldstein is currently booking appointments two-and-a-half months out, so I could slot you in for…." Cooper interrupted.

"I want you to do something for me, Laura," she said. "You're new in the office, I believe, so you couldn't know, but I've been a patient of Phil Goldstein's for something like twenty years now, and we're also personal friends—so I want you to give him the message that Cooper North called and needs to be fitted in, as soon as he can."

Silence.

Then Laura spoke again.

"That's not our office protocol here, so...."

"So I'll have to call him at home, at night, then, won't I?" Cooper said. "I'll explain to him that I had to bother him at home, because office procedures prohibit you from giving him my message?"

Silence over the phone. Laura breathing. A sigh.

"All right, I'll give him the message."

"Thank you Laura," Cooper said. "Bye now."

She slid the handset back into its holder.

25

Cooper parked her Volvo next to Olga Fisker's mud-splattered Ram pickup, in front of Olga's log cabin. When she'd first visited here, this house seemed too rustic for a world-class entomologist. Not now. Not for a woman who held up her britches with suspenders. Who wore sap-stained t-shirts. Who climbed maples and oaks.

Cooper leaned against the car's leather backrest, resting with her eyes shut, while Henry, standing in the shotgun seat, front paws braced against the dashboard, stared out the windshield, bright eyed.

He barked.

It meant, let's go!

Through the car's open window came bird calls and songs. Crickets chirped. Among red clover and daisies, bumblebees buzzed.

Cooper thought: this is why I've come.

She had a question to ask, about wasps, but such a simple question could be answered over the telephone. No, she came here for a respite.

"You still breathing, Ms. North?"

Cooper opened her eyes and saw Olga Fisker beside the car, looking down at her with concern.

"My friends call me Coop," she said.

She wanted to be just Coop, for now, because that relentless prosecutor, Cooper North, felt exhausted, and stymied.

Proctor Gibbs' murder—no clues. Uno and Dos, the homicidal Ninja psychopaths, preparing to kill—Cooper felt powerless.

Tip LaPerle's foster kid, too, Thor Ennis. A different worry. After his mother's murder, Cooper sheltered him in her house, hiding him from the killers hunting him. Seven years old. So much trauma. Now bullying at school. Would these cruel older kids make him feel worthless for life?

Like Flute Wagner?

Cooper opened the door and got out and stood looking at Olga, in her suspendered work trousers, and her stained t-shirt, imprinted with a neon-green dragonfly, and her gray-streaked blond hair pulled back in a ponytail, out of the way.

A woman who climbed trees. Cooper liked that.

"Did you have a pleasant childhood?" Cooper asked.

Olga considered, as if it were a perfectly natural question. Finally she shrugged.

"Yeah, I guess," she said. "For an Army brat."

Cooper sighed.

"I came about the wasps again," she said.

Not really, she thought. I came because my friend Mona Dill Saunders is off hunting art in Europe, and I have no one to talk to. She had Tip LaPerle, of course, one of her oldest friends, and Mike Bolknor, one of her newest.

Talking with them goes only so far, though, she thought. They're men.

"Want some chamomile tea?" Olga asked.

A few minutes later, they sat on Olga's front porch, each with a mug of aromatic herbal tea. At least, Cooper sat.

Olga stood, leaning against a post supporting the porch's roof, feet crossed at the ankles.

"I envy you the peace of this house," Cooper said.

Olga fixed her hazel eyes on Cooper, then looked off across the small lawn.

"Bugs galore," she said, staring at the grass.

Abruptly, she set her mug on the porch floor and started across the lawn at a trot, staring intently at the grass ahead, and ignoring Henry, who'd darted out from the side of the house and now scampered beside her, convinced this must be a game.

Without stopping, Olga bent from the waist to scoop up something from the grass, then whirled around and trotted back, hand cupped. When she reached Cooper, she opened her hand to reveal what seemed a long brown twig, but then the "twig" spread six fragile legs and began a slow walk across Olga's palm.

"Diapheromera femorata," Olga said, staring admiringly at the thing in her palm. "People call them the 'walking stick insects.'"

Because the walking stick reached the edge of her palm, ready to topple over, Olga brought up her other hand and let the insect move onto the new palm. After a moment, it spread wings—where they came from Cooper couldn't imagine—and awkwardly flew toward the lawn's bordering trees.

"I don't know why it was in the grass," Olga said, watching it fly away. "They like to be in trees."

So do you, Cooper thought. So did I, as a child. She remembered now the exultation of climbing with no help, of perching so high you felt your head got into the sky.

"Have you always climbed trees?" Cooper asked.

"Yup," Olga said.

She thought about it.

"Lots of bugs up there," she said.

She thought again.

"They're compact bio-mechanisms, insects are," she said. "Little battle tanks and fighter planes, just about infinite morphological and behavioral variety, and there's thousands to study, just up in these trees here, so every dawn I wake up full of expectations."

As if so many words at one time required rewinding, Olga got up from the porch, walked onto the lawn, and performed three consecutive cartwheels.

Cooper thought: and every morning I wake up thinking about bad people, preying on good people, and I'm ready to go get them.

Except lately.

For many days now she'd awakened tired.

"Here's my wasp question," Cooper said. "You showed me how to make a wasp trap, using a soda bottle with its top lopped off—but if I'm a murderer, how to I get the bottled wasp into the jacket sleeves of the allergic man I want to kill?"

Olga thought a moment.

"Two ways," she said. "First, you could wear really thick gloves or mittens and shake the wasp out of the

166

bottle into that mitten, close the mitten to keep it trapped, then open the mitten so the wasp can crawl into the sleeve."

"Wouldn't that risk crushing the wasp?" Cooper asked.

"They're tough little buggers," Olga said.

"And the other way?" Cooper asked.

Olga shrugged.

"You'd take off the funnel top and push the bottle's open end into the sleeve, then let the wasp crawl out."

Cooper suddenly saw a problem.

If the murderer walked around Proctor's office in the middle of summer wearing thick mittens, somebody might see it, an oddity. It would be remembered. Maybe they'd ask you about it. Same for emptying the wasp directly from the bottle into the sleeve—it would take time, it would be obvious, carrying that doctored bottle around, and you might be seen.

Now her scenario for murder-by-wasp seemed shaky.

"That walking stick," Olga suddenly said, clearly talking mostly to herself. "Most of the variants live more to the south, feeding on trees that mostly grow down there, like certain oaks, locusts, cherries, walnuts...."

I've lost her, Cooper thought. She now has a bug on her mind.

Cooper had a sudden thought: Thor will be all right.

Flute Wagner's made of soft white pine inside. Thor's made of solid oak. He's got Tip and Marge behind him. He's got me. He'll withstand these older bullies.

Olga turned and stared at Cooper, addressing her directly.

"So, we've got this variant we just saw, with wings, which they all don't have, and it's interesting, what changes allow it to live so far north…diet? Behavior? Physical alterations…."

Or what iron you've got inside you, Cooper thought.

"One idea about those wasps of yours," Olga said. "They're inactive at night, so if a murderer wanted to…."

Cooper remembered what she'd been told about Proctor Gibbs' jacket.

He left it hanging from the back of his office chair, left it there day and night, never took it home, put it on just for a meeting, or some important visitor.

So, in the night, a bottle-bearer goes to the jacket.

"Thank you, Olga—you've just helped to solve a crime," she said, standing, and starting for her car.

She stopped to call Henry, who came racing around the house on his short legs.

"Come again," Olga said. "I enjoy talking with you."

"I will," Cooper said.

Then she drove home.

When she and Henry walked into the house, she saw her phone's message light flashing.

"Hi, this is Phil Goldstein, over at the hospital, my office—why don't you come in this Saturday, and I'll see what you've got—one-thirty, okay? If I don't hear from you, I'll assume that's good and I'll meet you there."

Cooper thought: Phil's coming in special on the weekend, to help me out.

She felt a wave of appreciation for this friend, for all her friends.

It seemed odd, though, arranging this special weekend visit.

She shrugged off that faintly unsettling thought before it took shape.

Getting this flu fixed, that's what mattered.

26

Ozzie Knick stopped at the Dill PD to pick up Exhibit A. Then on to what he called, in his own mind, the Prescott Trial.

They demanded the Allen County State's Attorney prosecute a seven-year-old, for assault and battery.

Ozzie wanted to say, "That's nuts—go away."

Apparently, though, you must be nice to local bigshots. Cooper had made that clear. For one thing, Mrs. Prescott, on the City Council, had fingers in the city budget.

All right. Ozzie had a solution.

He'd put the Prescotts' demand itself on trial, and the jury would be the Prescotts. They'd hear the evidence. Then they'd decide: forgetting it's not even possible, does trying this child as a felon make sense?

He'd already arranged the "trial" with Tip and Marge LaPerle, and with Exhibit A, too. It had taken explaining, but in the end, all agreed to the plan. Except the police chief insisted on coming, too, as backup for Exhibit A, and he stipulated they all arrive in his Dill PD cruiser.

"Visible weight of the law," he muttered.

Ozzie thought about it, for a half second, and decided, yes, it would provide a reality check, a squad car in their driveway. See what you're bringing on yourselves?

Possibly it would be faintly intimidating, even to highly placed people, used to being the intimidators.

Also, with Tip LaPerle there, the Prescotts must realize the police chief supported this orphaned boy he and his wife fostered, a solid vote of approval for Thor.

Ozzie liked jury trials. He liked figuring the moves.

As they drove over in the police SUV, with Exhibit A sitting in the back, Tip asked: "Do you think Cooper looks okay?"

Ozzie hadn't thought about it, his usual focus being what he wanted to do, and how he planned to do it, but he had a flash memory, from just now, as he left the State's Attorney's office—Cooper slumped in her desk chair, eyes closed.

"She looks tired," he said.

"Overwork," Tip said. "I guess."

Tip pulled into the driveway of the Prescotts' sprawling neo-farmhouse, white clapboards with black shutters, and four times the size of any actual farmhouse Ozzie ever saw. This house stood on ten acres, among other McMansions, in the hills across the Ira River from Dill, with a panoramic view of the town and the mountains beyond.

Tip and Exhibit A stayed in the cruiser, waiting to be called into the "courtroom."

Ozzie entered the house alone, carrying his briefcase. He noted the living room's vastness, with its luxurious furniture and drapes, but didn't care. It took him another tenth of a second to evaluate the Prescotts. Both tall, slender, silver-haired. He instantly decided his opposing attorney would be Mrs. Prescott, based on how she looked down at him, pale-blue eyes scornful, a disapproving downturn of the mouth.

Yes, he thought, with something like pleasure, I'm short. I look like I work with wrenches and power screwdrivers. So I must be dumb.

Both Prescotts seemed dressed for a White House luncheon. Carlton Dumont Prescott wore a gray suit, perfectly fitted, with an indigo tie. Pamela Hatch Prescott wore a black-silk pants suit, with pearls.

Ozzie thought: okay, I made a tactical error. Probably I should have worn a suit.

He'd worn his usual Nikes, blue jeans, and a corduroy jacket.

Well, he thought, too freaking bad.

"We expected Cooper North to come," Pamela Prescott said. "We assumed she'd handle this prosecution herself."

Just imagine, Ozzie thought. Instead of kowtowing to you VIPs, the state's attorney sent over a janitor.

"Cooper's overloaded, just now, with a murder investigation," Ozzie said. "I'm assistant state's attorney, and I'll be working to achieve justice here."

"Ms. North comes from a very old and prominent Dill family," Mrs. Prescott said.

Ah, we're going full snob, Ozzie thought. Intimidate the little prosecutor, let him know he's got no class, so he'll be humbled, and do just what we want.

He gave her his blank look.

From his briefcase, he extracted a legal pad and a ball-point pen, and carefully wrote the Prescott's names, double-checking the spelling with them.

Message: this is official, folks. You're now on the record. Everything must be done precisely right. Only the truth, folks. Otherwise....

"And the complainant's name?" he asked, pen poised.

Now the two Prescotts exchanged a glance.

"We're the complainants," Carlton Prescott said. "Pamela and I."

Ozzie   shook   his head.

"No, who claims to have been attacked, viciously, by one Thor Ennis?" he said. "That's the name we need for the court record."

"Tyler," Mrs. Prescott said. "But we don't want our boy involved in this, getting his name on court records, since he's just a child."

Ozzie looked at her.

"Actually, the accused is also a child," he said.

Mrs. Prescott looked taken aback, but just momentarily. She followed up with an angry glare.

"What prep school did you attend," she suddenly demanded.

"A public school in Queens," Ozzie said. "My dad's a firefighter, and my mom's a bank teller."

Carlton Dumont Prescott looked as if he'd swallowed something unpleasant. Revolted by Ozzie's lowly origins? Or upset by his wife's prep-school slap? Hard to tell.

Ozzie thought: okay, Carlton, you'll be the judge in these proceedings.

"In this trial, we'll be up against sharp defense attorneys," Ozzie said now, looking worried at the prospect. "They'll be calling lots of witnesses to undermine your case, to prove this attack on your son is bogus, so we'll need to refute them."

Pamela Prescott looked startled, then irritated. Open and shut, she'd assumed. Just tell a judge what a monster Thor Ennis was, and the state would put him on Death Row. She hadn't thought the Ennis boy would have defenders, even witnesses.

"So, here's the first point the defense will pick at," Ozzie said. "You claim your son suffered severe injury in this attack, so what evidence can we present?"

Carlton Prescott looked befuddled. Pamela Prescott looked outraged.

"We say it, that's our evidence," she said. "We certainly can judge if our son's been injured."

Ozzie gave her one of his blank looks.

"This is a legal trial," he said. "A jury will demand concrete evidence."

Silence from the Prescotts.

"How about an affidavit from the doctor," Ozzie said. "You know, the physician who treated Tyler's injuries?"

Pamela Prescott stared at him, aghast.

"Ridiculous," she muttered. "Our word, all that's...."

"Okay, but you'll be under oath, remember, so if you swear Thor Ennis battered your son, yet can't produce medical proof, well, that could be perjury right there."

Ozzie shook his head, as if that would be the last thing he'd ever want to see.

Pamela Prescott stared at him open-mouthed.
Carlton Prescott looked slightly ill.

Ozzie shrugged.

"Okay, moving right along," he said. "Next, the defense will demand to know exactly how Thor Ennis actually did the damage, considering he's three years younger than your son, and considerably smaller."

Neither Prescott said anything, but Pamela Prescott looked increasingly angry and upset.

"Where'd you study law," she suddenly demanded. "Some obscure state college, I suppose?"

"I graduated from New York University," Ozzie said. "Then I went to Harvard Law."

Mrs. Prescott looked at him in disbelief.

"And how did someone like you, may I ask, pay for all that?" she said. "Rob a bank?"

Ozzie gave her his blank stare.

"ROTC paid for my undergraduate studies, actually," he said. "And after the Army, at law school, I had work-study jobs, and just plain jobs, and I had loans, which I'm still paying off."

He shrugged.

Pamela Prescott sniffed, disdain on her face. Carlton Prescott eyed his wife with a hard-to-read expression. Admiration, maybe, of her clever sneak attack on this lawyer, who said things they didn't want to hear? Or embarrassment?

"Now, let's go over this," Ozzie said. "Remember those defense attorneys will be ready to pounce."

He sat a moment with furrowed forehead, eyes downcast. His worried-man look.

"Okay," he said. "In court, you'll assert that Thor Ennis savagely attacked your son, unprovoked—do I have it right?"

Carlton Prescot nodded. Pamela Prescott mouthed "yes."

"How do you know it happened that way?" Ozzie said. "That's the first thing those defense attorneys will hit you with."

Pamela Prescott turned up her eyes and looked disgusted.

"We know it," she said, "because our son Tyler told us."

"And you're sure Tyler gave it to you straight?" Ozzie asked. "All the facts?"

"He's a solid, honest kid," Carlton Prescott said, speaking up for almost the first time. "He's quarterback on the town's junior football team, you know, a star player."

Ozzie pretended to think.

Surreptitiously, he saw Pamela Prescott looked pleased. They'd asserted Tyler's honesty. No more to be said. Carlton Prescott looked concerned, just slightly. He probably recognized that athletic prowess didn't prove honesty, even if the boy's quarterbacking filled Dad with pride.

Ozzie thought: do you grasp that your boy's athleticism's juice for the defense—if Tyler's so athletic, how did this little kid beat him up?

176

Actually, there'd be no defense attorneys, no trial. There'd be no guilty verdict coming down on Thor Ennis, not for assault, attempted murder, or whatever the Prescotts dreamed of, so besotted with their son they believed whatever he said, demanded revenge for his wrongs.

Ozzie wanted the Prescotts to realize it all on their own. This was wasting the time of the State's Attorney's office. This was nuts.

"Let's have Tyler in now," Ozzie said. "Let's hear what happened in his own words."

After an exchange of glances, Carlton Prescott shrugged and left the room. A moment later, he returned, ushering in his son, a hand on the boy's shoulder.

Tyler stared at Ozzie unblinking. In that stare, Ozzie saw disrespect, and arrogance, and great confidence.

Tall for his ten years, nearly Ozzie's height. Slender, like his parents, but his athletic talents clear in the ease of his movements. Unasked, the boy took a chair, crossed his legs, and stared at Ozzie.

"Tell us what happened," Ozzie said. "Remember, in a courtroom, there will be defense lawyers listening to your every word, looking for mistakes, or even lies, so tell it to us straight."

Tyler shrugged, and looked disgusted. This bored him.

"I was just talking with my friends and that Ennis kid came up and started punching me," he said. "Just out of meanness, I guess."

"Did he knock you down?" Ozzie asked.

Tyler snorted.

"I'd like to see that," he said.

He glanced at his father, who nodded approval.

"Can you show me any bruises?" Ozzie asked.

Tyler stared at him.

"They all cleared up," he said. "Went away."

Ozzie regarded him thoughtfully.

"All right, let's reenact the assault," he said.

He fished his cellphone out of his jacket pocket and punched in a number.

"Come in now," he said.

A minute later Tip LaPerle stood in the living room, in his police chief's uniform, with Thor Ennis at his side, Exhibit A. Thor looked stoic, a boy who'd faced tense situations all his seven years.

Ozzie motioned Thor to stand beside Tyler Prescott and then said nothing, letting the Prescotts take in the comparison and draw their own conclusions.

Next to the bigger, older boy, Thor looked tiny. His head reached Tyler's chest. Thor, with his buzz-cut blond hair and robust build didn't look puny. Even so, the contrast was David and Goliath.

Ozzie surreptitiously eyed the Prescotts. Pamela Prescott looked disconcerted. She hadn't expected the monster thug of her imagination would turn out to be just a little boy. He could see her mind working, reorganizing what she saw before her eyes, making it conform to the scenario in her mind—a little thug, radiating menace and meanness, stood beside her son.

Carlton Dumont Prescott looked uncomfortable. He hadn't anticipated this. Ozzie guessed he realized how a jury would see it, the contrast between these two boys.

And the villain he and his wife imagined turned out to be just a small child.

As they'd prearranged, Tip LaPerle said nothing, just standing beside his foster child, with an encouraging hand on his shoulder. Thor maintained silence.

Ozzie let the scene sink in, then spoke.

"Tyler, you say Thor attacked you—would you demonstrate how he did that?"

For a moment, Tyler stood silent, glaring down at Thor. Abruptly, he pointed an accusing finger at the smaller boy.

"We were in the playground at the school, some friends and me, just standing there talking, and all of a sudden, this one ran up and came at me, punching, you know?"

He kept the accusing finger pointed at Thor.

"I see," Ozzie said. "Now, if we go to trial, be prepared for defense attorneys—they'll have collected testimony from witnesses to the attack, and they'll be presenting all that in court."

For a moment, Tyler looked startled. Then his expression turned mean.

"Big deal," he said.

"Yes, it is a big deal," Ozzie said. "To get ready for what we'd face in court, my office has gathered statements from other students at the school, who saw the encounter—would you like to hear them?"

Tyler shrugged.

Ozzie thought, he knows what's coming. He and his football teammates kept the younger kids intimidated,

179

too scared to speak, he figured. However, some of them really wanted to speak out, and several of them did.

Ozzie reached into his briefcase and pulled out a handful of typed pages. He made a show of riffing through the documents, brow furrowed.

"All right, here's a girl in Thor's class speaking," Ozzie says. "She testifies that you and your friends have been picking on Thor ever since he started at the school."

Ozzie looked at Tyler, concerned. Then he looked back down and resumed reading.

"Now, here's what she saw of the incident with Thor, where you claim he attacked you out of the blue, unprovoked."

Again he studied the document, then shook his head, as if he couldn't understand the conflict between what Tyler said and what the witnesses saw.

"She says you and your friends cornered Thor on the playground that day, and surrounded him," Ozzie said, studying the testimony. "She says you took turns cuffing him—he'd turn to confront a boy who cuffed him, and another of you, standing behind him, would cuff, and so on."

That went on a while, Ozzie said, studying the testimony.

"Finally, you cuffed Thor, and when he turned, you slapped his face, laughing," he said. "At that point, goaded beyond control, Thor punched the hand slapping him, tried to knock it away—at least six students witnessed this, and they all describe it exactly the same."

Ozzie put down the papers and gazed speculatively at Tyler.

Tyler stared back, belligerent, annoyed.

"They say you then went into the principal's office— they all followed you in—and they heard you telling the principal Thor had attacked you, for no reason, and something should be done about him—they say you left the principal's office smirking."

Ozzie riffled through the other witness statements and then shrugged, meaning all the same, no point repeating each of them. He slipped the interviews with the students back into his briefcase.

Then he stared at Tyler and spread his hands, palms up, meaning, what do you say about all this?

Tyler looked disgusted.

"Oh, beans, so we had some fun with this jerk kid," he said. "Big hot deal!"

"According to classmates, you'd been having that kind of fun with this boy for a long time, you and your friends," Ozzie said.

Tyler shrugged, indicating it didn't amount to anything.

"Why did you and your friends pick on this boy?" Ozzie asked.

Tyler looked irritated and then pointed at Thor, who stood silent, looking small.

"He came to school wearing all cheapo raggy clothes," Tyler said. "Miserable little brat—and it's like my Mom's always saying, those low-lifes from Tenement Row are a disgrace to the town and those tenements should be bulldozed, turned into a park for decent people, right Mom?"

He looked to his mother for backup, but for once Pamela Hatch Prescott had no words. She stared at her son at a loss.

Carlton Dumont Prescott looked sick.

Prescott stared at his son, then at Thor Ennis, then at his wife, then back at his son.

"That's it," he said, voice sharp. "There's going to be no trial, we're dropping it, so all of you, please leave right now—we've got things to discuss as a family."

Ozzie shrugged, and stood, lifting his briefcase, then motioning with his head for Tip LaPerle and Thor to leave with him.

As they went out the front door, he turned and saw both Prescotts staring down at their son, who looked confused. Pamela Hatch Prescott looked unwell. Carlton Dumont Prescott looked angry.

Back in the police SUV, driving down from the hills to the river, then across the bridge into town, Ozzie said nothing, staring at his hands in his lap.

When they parked in back of the Dill PD, he said thanks. He said it weakly, not his usual voice tone. Then he vaulted out of the vehicle.

He muttered: "I've got to talk with Cooper about this."

Then he trudged across Courthouse Lane, not hearing the orioles and warblers singing in the sugar maples, looking at his feet, frowning.

27

Cooper watched Ozzie Knick walk into her office, just back from his face-off with the Prescotts. He looked glum.

He dropped into Cooper's visitor's chair, thumped his briefcase onto the floor, and slouched.

"How'd it go?" Cooper asked.

Ozzie shook his head.

"Good and bad," he said.

"Oh?" Cooper said.

"They dropped their trial fantasy," he said. "So Thor's safe from Old Sparky."

That electric-chair euphemism might have amused Cooper, if Ozzie didn't look so gloomy.

"And the bad?" she said.

Hand's spread, palms up, Ozzie signaled resignation.

He'd planned, he said, to quickly prove they couldn't indict the child. Seeing the light, the Prescotts would thank him, and they'd say goodbye.

It hadn't worked that way.

"I got into assassin mode," he said.

Pamela and Carlton Prescott, he said, pushed his I'm-not-taking-your-crap button.

They believed their son a golden boy. Ozzie saw him as an insufferable little bully, arrogant and disrespectful.

Pamela Prescott proved a bully in her own right, trying to intimidate Ozzie to do her bidding.

Cooper suspected Ozzie Knick didn't intimidate easily.

"Their son's a mean SOB, and I made sure they knew it," Ozzie said. "I proved he'd been constantly picking on Thor, this little orphan kid."

Ozzie shook his head, disgusted.

"Then their golden boy actually blamed his mother," he said. "Apparently, she hates Tenement Row, says it makes Dill look bad, so bulldoze it, I guess, deport those sub-humans to somewhere deserving, like New Hampshire."

Ozzie didn't mention a volcanic eruption, so Cooper imagined Tip LaPerle, a Tenement Row alumnus, stayed cool. Good on you, Tip, she thought.

"So you set these people straight," Cooper said. "And the problem was?"

"I murdered their happy family," Ozzie said.

When he'd arrived, they'd been pleased with themselves, with their station in life, with Tyler's golden glow.

"I shredded all that," he said. "I just kept at them."

By the time he left, Ozzie said, the Prescotts virtually glared at each other, and Tyler no longer glowed golden, reduced to tarnished tin.

"I'm supposed to prosecute criminals," Ozzie said. "These people aren't criminals."

He slouched farther down into his chair.

Cooper sighed.

"Buck up," she said. "It's just how prosecutions go."

Ozzie squinted at her, dubious.

"Laws get broken," Cooper said. "Our job's to prove it, and get the law-breaker appropriately punished, so that's good for society—but there's inevitably going to be collateral damage, which isn't our fault."

Ozzie continued squinting at her, still dubious.

Cooper cited a serial rapist. Suddenly his wife discovers the solid citizen she married is a creep. Collateral damage. Ditto for his kids, parents, whoever. collateral damage. Maybe the rapist had a thriving tire store, and he's going to jail, his store closes, and his employees lose their jobs. More collateral damage.

"And so on," Cooper said.

"Yeah," Ozzie said. "I guess."

He picked up his briefcase and started out.

At the door, he turned.

"Here I go," he said. "Off to commit collateral damage."

And he left.

Cooper, looking at the empty doorway, wondered what would happen in her own case, Proctor Gibbs' murder.

She shrugged.

"Collateral damage."

She mouthed it, silently.

28

Next morning, Saturday, clouds began streaming in from the west, over the mountains. Light-gray clouds, at first. By the time Cooper finished breakfast, they'd darkened to the color of lead.

Good, she thought. There'd been no rain for weeks, and the soil needed it.

Cooper took Henry for his morning walk, the corgi cockily strutting ahead, down Hill Street to Abner Park, where Cooper unhitched his leash and he began serious sniffing. Cooper leaned against the trunk of a butternut tree. She'd slept long last night, yet she still felt weary.

On their way back from the park, sudden gusts swirled up curbside dust. Then fat drops began to fall, creating dark circles on the sidewalk's gray concrete. Cooper inhaled the aroma sent up by the raindrops, an earthy scent that always preceded a long-withheld rain.

She'd be enjoying this, she thought, if she didn't feel so tired.

They got home just as the heavy rain began. Within minutes water gushed along the house's gutters and gurgled down the drainpipes.

Cooper gave Henry fresh water, and his post-walk treat, a dog biscuit shaped like a bone. Then she collapsed in the living room's recliner. She noticed another black bruise had appeared on one arm.

Odd.

She had an appointment to see her doctor, Phil Goldstein, at one-thirty this afternoon, and he'd explain the bruising. He'd know.

She leaned back in the recliner and shut her eyes, thinking about the Proctor Gibbs case. On the walk, she'd come up with a hypothesis, a possible motive.

She opened her eyes.

Might as well start now, she decided, and rummaged among the notes heaped on the telephone table next to the recliner. Finally she found the list she'd made of Flute Wagner's phone numbers.

Cell phone, she decided. That's the best bet for a Saturday.

He answered after two rings.

"Do you know anything about drugs at Snowville Maple?" Cooper asked. "Anyone using, or selling, maybe transporting product in the company's trucks?"

At first, a stunned silence over the phone. Cooper waited. Flute finally spoke.

"Oh no, there's nothing like that."

"Would you know if there was?" Cooper asked.

Another silence.

"I'm sure I would," Flute said. "This company's small and…"

"Nobody in the outdoor work crew?" Cooper asked.

"What about those two summer-job kids, Ledger and Rink, or even, let's say, Sonny DeWitt?"

Sonny had been her first thought. Him and his get-in-trouble pals.

"No, nobody," Flute said. "This company...."

Cooper suddenly understood. Flute Wagner loved Snowville Maple. A home. It had Sonny in it, but Flute seemed able to bear that one hitch. He wanted no dark streaks in his company.

Except for the murder.

Cooper knew no facts backed up her hypothesis. Still, it seemed plausible—somebody at the company dealt in drugs, Proctor sniffed it out, and so Proctor got extinguished.

Sheila DeWitt didn't think her ex-husband to be truly criminal. At least, so her comments about him suggested.

Even so....

"A nice area like this," Flute said. "Are there really drugs here, like fentanyl or heroin or whatever they use, cocaine...."

"A brisk trade in illegal drugs," Cooper said. "Just go down to the Donut Dive on River Street, any night, and you can buy whatever you need to ascend into the ionosphere."

Flute said nothing. His silence somehow sounded like disappointment, as if his image of an idyllic Dill had now tarnished a little. At least, so it seemed to Cooper.

"One thing more," she asked. "Does anyone have access to the headquarters building after hours, at night?"

Olga Fisker had suggested yellowjackets go dormant at night. They'd be more easily handled then. So night would be the best time to slip them into Proctor Gibbs' jacket sleeves.

Flute thought about it. Cooper imagined him focusing on each employee in turn, seeing who might go in at night.

Actually, that would be any of us, at least the office people," he said. "We all have keys, because sometimes you need to go in, maybe to finish a report, or look up some sugaring statistic, all sorts of reasons, or you left your glasses on your desk."

He thought more.

"I'm there at night sometimes," he said. "Also, once or twice, working late at home, I needed a report or something, and my wife volunteered to go fetch it, so I could keep working, and I'm sure Sonny must go in at night sometimes, maybe sent in Sheila, when they were still married—Vic Ledger and Winnie Rink have keys…or do they?"

More silent thinking.

"No, but I know they have access to keys—there's a spare set in the receptionist's desk drawer—and they could have had them copied, I suppose, but why would they do that?"

Cooper suddenly felt too tired to continue.

"Thanks," she said. "We'll talk more about this another time."

She hung up the phone.

Then she leaned back in the recliner and shut her eyes. When she opened them again, it was five minutes after noon, and she had an appointment with her old friend Phil Goldstein, M.D., at one-thirty.

29

Henry knew this route. It led to Mike Bolknor's apartment, just north of the Mt. Augustus College campus, on Maple Street. So he stood up on the shotgun seat, forepaws braced on the dashboard, barking in excited anticipation.

Cooper, at the wheel, glanced at him and sighed.

"You get all afternoon with your hero," she said. "Right?"

Henry kept barking.

"No hanging with the boring old lady," she said. "Right?"

She gave him a sardonic look.

A few minutes later, Henry lay sleeping on Mike's couch, on his back, four short legs up in the air.

"I'm leaving," Cooper told him, while Bolknor, amused, watched the ritual unfold.

"Do you miss me yet?" Cooper asked, but the corgi just opened his eyes, gave her a glance, then shut them again, delighted to be here.

Henry regarded Mike Bolknor as his best bud.

Six minutes later, after a slow drive through heavy rain, Cooper turned into the Allen County Medical Center's parking lot. She wove through rows of locked cars until she finally found an empty spot. Even on Saturday afternoon, a nearly full lot. She decided: at the next hospital board meeting, she'd suggest enlarging the parking area.

After she turned off the engine, and the windshield wipers stopped clacking, she listened to rain drum on the Volvo's roof. Finally, she mustered the will to open the door and step out into the downpour.

Cane in one hand, furled umbrella in the other, she used her elbow to shut the car's door. She already felt drenched.

She leaned her cane against the fender, freeing her hand to struggle with the umbrella, finally getting it unfurled. Immediately a gust almost wrenched it away, while rain pounded on its fabric.

Cooper trudged, head down, toward the hospital's entrance, gusts repeatedly jerking the umbrella aside, letting rain soak her face and shoulders. Water flowed across the parking lot's macadam, pooling in spots, seeping through her sneakers. Her jeans, soaked from the knees down, stuck to her calves and shins.

Inside the building, finally, she furled the umbrella, then leaned it dripping beside the entrance door. Too sopping to bring up. If any of the patients and staff walking through the hospital's lobby stole it, she'd survive.

She rode the elevator up to the third floor, in the wing containing physicians' offices, and found Phil Goldstein waiting for her in his reception room.

They'd been friends for decades, both serving on various boards of directors, often socializing together, but when he met her in his physician capacity, their relationship always shifted slightly to formality.

"Coop, you tell me you have chronic fatigue?" he asked, closing the Richmond Lattimore translation of *The Iliad* he'd been reading. He dropped the heavy tome onto a chairside end table. It hit with a thud.

"Some kind of virus got me," Cooper said. "There must be anti-viral medicines...."

Goldstein regarded her thoughtfully.

"Come into the examining room," he said. "Let's take a look."

Today his offices were silent, closed for Saturday. No nurses bustling about, no other patients awaiting their turns.

It felt eerie.

Everything white in the exam room, walls, ceiling, cabinet doors. From the window, this rainy dark afternoon, just dim light. Ceiling fluorescents lit the room harshly.

Goldstein eyed her, up and down.

"How's the prosecutor business," he asked, applying a stethoscope to her chest. "Cough."

He moved the stethoscope to her back and instructed her to cough again. Then he started slipping a blood-pressure cuff over her right arm, but froze, staring.

"Where'd you get these?" he asked, indicating with his chin two large bruises, black.

"Who knows?" Cooper said. "I don't remember bumping anything."

Goldstein, brow wrinkled, thinking, finished pumping up the blood-pressure cuff and watched the dial, as it deflated, then beeped. He pulled off the cuff.

"Heart sounds good," he said. "Blood pressure's okay, for someone your age."

He sat back on the rolling stool he used for examinations and studied her.

"Tell you what," he said. "I'll take a blood sample, see what it has to say—we've got a machine for analyzing it right here in the office."

After he used a hypodermic needle to extract blood, he told Cooper he'd give her a call. She thanked him, they said goodbye, and she walked toward the elevator. Waiting for it to open, she looked back and saw Phil Goldstein standing in his office's doorway, watching her go, a man of average size, with thinning blond hair shot with gray, but with a far-above-average intelligence, she knew, and a caring nature.

She thought he looked worried. Something at home, she guessed. Marion ill?

A minute later, getting back into her car, she decided to leave Henry with Mike Bolknor for the afternoon.

She thought: you'll like that, you disloyal little corgi.

Go home, she decided. Get dry clothes.

Just out of the parking lot, she changed her mind. Minutes later, she parked at the state's attorney's office. Paperwork piled up. Might as well tackle it.

She walked into an empty office, this Saturday afternoon. No assistants bustling and conferring, no secretaries tapping keyboards, or answering telephones, no visiting police officers wanting to discuss a case.

This office, like Phil Goldstein's, seemed eerie.

She scooped up a handful of forms and reports and legal papers, started to look through them, but after a minute dropped them back onto her desk.

Too tired to work.

I'll drive home, she decided. Rest awhile.

Twenty minutes later, she collapsed onto her living room's recliner, and instantly slept. For how long, she had no idea, only that at some point, she awoke.

Phone ringing.

Caller ID said it was Phil Goldstein.

She listened, still groggy, not fully awake.

"Coop," he said. "I've got really bad news—you've got acute myelogenous leukemia—you need to go into the hospital right now."

Cooper tried to remember what acute myelogenous leukemia was.

It must be serious, she thought. Otherwise, why do I need to be in the hospital this second?

"Meet me up here in fifteen minutes," Phil said, and ended the call.

Cooper sat holding the handset, looking at it, with no thoughts, just listening to its dial tone.

30

She'd now been in the hospital one night and a morning.

When she arrived, Phil Goldstein met her and arranged for a private room, to isolate her from viruses and bacteria. She had virtually no immune system.

They'd ordered an emergency delivery of blood for her, and pumped it into her system as soon as the courier delivered it. Leukemia had dangerously decimated her own blood cells. She'd be needing periodic transfusions.

Later, they wheeled her into the operating room, where a surgeon inserted a Hickman catheter into her chest, its tube running through a vein directly into her heart.

"We'll be pumping in a lot of chemo," Phil told her. "Also antibiotics, and maybe intravenous feeding—with a catheter, you won't get constant needle pokes."

At first, though, the surgeon botched the catheter installation. Weary, after operating all day on other patients, he slipped, jabbed her lung. Now she had blood in the lung.

An inauspicious start, Cooper thought.

She watched a nurse tapping notes and observations into the room's computer.

"Good thing you're in the hospital," the nurse said, eyes focused on the screen, hands tap-tap-tapping the keyboard. "If you'd waited another week, you'd be dead."

Cooper's clothes lay folded in the room's closet. She wore a humiliating hospital johnnie. A computerized machine periodically pinged, white letters and numbers moving across its green screen, reporting her blood pressure and pulse rate and other data about which she didn't care. A jagged graph line ticked up and down. If that line flattened, it meant she'd died.

On her wrist, a paper ID bracelet, her new hospital identity.

Her identity had always been Prosecutor. She'd been a player, statewide, often pictured in the *Dill Chronicle*. She'd guarded the civic peace. She'd hunted down evildoers, weeded them out.

Now a sign hung on her door: "Lowered immune system—no fresh fruits or vegetables. No flowers. Surgical mask required."

Before getting into this bed, she'd trudged around the ward, with her cane, taking it in. This section of the hospital centered on a glassed-in island, the nurse's station. It served as an office and a storeroom for medicines and a computer workspace. Here doctors congregated to review reports on their patients' vitals, and to confer with nurses, and to kid each other, and to talk medicine. Patients' rooms ran along this wing's outside walls, each with windows looking out on meadows or mountains.

In each room lay a patient, like her.

She doubted many patients raised themselves in their beds to look out at the world. She didn't.

Soon her assigned oncologist would arrive.

Chemotherapy would begin.

Just before she left for the hospital, she'd telephoned Mike Bolknor. He promised to look after Henry. Tacitly, silently, never actually discussing it, they'd agreed—Mike's apartment would be Henry's new home, if Cooper died. Odds were she would.

They'd given her a brochure on acute myelogenous leukemia. It said the bone marrow generates myeloid cells, which develop into the blood cells the body needs to function: red cells, white cells, platelets. In leukemia, the myeloid cells mutate, and those mutants reproduce rapidly, crowding out the normal cells.

Survival rate: 29.5%.

"Two decades ago, it was 4%, so we've made good progress," the nurse who gave her the brochure said brightly.

With age, Cooper guessed, the survival rate dropped. She'd passed her sixty-ninth birthday.

Now she lived on another planet—the world of the sick.

Here machines attached to her body by wires and plastic tubes blinked and beeped.

Masked attendants moved through this world, dressed in white.

They brought her food on a tray, but she didn't want to eat.

She should make calls, she thought. To Mt. Augustus College and the Allen County State's Attorney's office. She should make arrangements.

She didn't feel like it.

Those responsibilities seemed light years away.

She listened to the machines hum and beep.

She slept.

Later, she opened her eyes to see a tall man, masked, staring down at her, wearing white.

"I'm Manny Lopez," he said. "Phil Goldstein asked me to be your oncologist, if you agree."

If Phil chose this man, approved of him....

Fortyish, dark haired, brown eyed. Because of his mask, though, she couldn't see his face., just eyeglasses pushed up onto his forehead.

"We'll be starting chemotherapy," he said. "Your bone marrow's producing bad cells, so we'll pump in powerful chemicals—they'll just about wipe out your bone marrow."

He looked at her. Eyes sharp, but concerned.

"After the bone marrow grows back, if all goes as it should, it won't produce any more bad cells."

Cooper thought: except the likelihood I'll die is 70.5%.

"Okay," she said.

She slept.

Later, she awoke to find a nurse working on a treelike contraption beside her bed. Cooper lay back against the pillows, fatigued, watching the woman hang plastic bags filled with liquids colored red and green and amber from the steel branches, as if decorating a Christmas balsam. Glancing back at her, the woman saw Cooper had wakened.

"Now your life will change," the nurse said, still hanging bags of chemicals.

Cooper thought: this comes out of her life, she's gone through something like this, so she knows.

This nurse had a melodious voice, soft. Her posture, her arm movements, graceful.

"Your relationships with people, and with yourself, too—they'll all change," the nurse said.

She smiled at Cooper, a smile with sadness in it, yet triumph, white teeth dazzling against her coal-black skin. She wore no mask.

"Before coming into your room, I self-tested—no viruses, no bacteria," she said. "I'll be your leukemia nurse, and I wanted you to see how I look, without a mask, because we'll be together a lot."

Cooper thought: good.

"My name's Emma Ford," the nurse said.

Cooper thought: please be my friend, Emma. I'm frightened.

Emma lifted a white-plastic tube, and attached one end to a hanging chemical bag.

"Antibiotics and other medicines in these bags," she said. "They'll pump through these tubes into your catheter."

Cooper thought: my life will end now, lying in this bed, with chemicals pumped into me, surrounded by machines beeping and blinking.

My graph line will flatten.

Then it will be night.

31

Numero Uno stepped from the truck onto soggy ground, still wet from yesterday's rain. His hiking boot left an imprint.

Numero Dos, also just out of the truck, pointed down at the footprint, then looked at Uno inquisitively.

"Yes, we had a rule, no missions after a rain," Uno said. "But this is Action Time—now we forget old rules."

Dos looked upset.

"Maybe they could trace that footprint," she said, nearly a whisper.

Uno looked at Dos without expression.

"I'll be throwing these boots out," he said, voice dry. "Afterwards."

"Okay, but no black Ninja suits?" Dos said. "They always wear them in the videos, okay? And ski masks, too."

Uno continued regarding Dos without expression.

"So, maybe there's surveillance cameras," Dos said. "And we've got no masks…."

Uno clenched his teeth. He waited a moment to speak, calming himself.

"We've already checked out this house," he said. "All sides—remember?—no surveillance cameras— remember?"

Silence.

"Oh yeah," Dos said, finally. "I remember now."

Leaning into the cab, Uno opened the between-seats storage bin, and pulled out the Fairbairn-Sykes commando knife, in its metal sheath.

He held out his two palms, side-by-side, with the knife laid across them, and they both gazed at it, silent, as if it were a saint's relic, or the Holy Grail.

Dos grinned, excited and nervous.

"We'll do it!" Dos whispered. "We'll really do it!"

Uno gave Dos a measuring stare.

"Remember," he said. "I speak, you don't."

Dos nodded.

Uno now shrugged out of his tight t-shirt, opened the rear door, and threw it onto the seat. From the same seat he pulled a folded Hawaiian shirt, just bought, ocean blue with golden shells decorating it, and put it on, a floppy shirt.

"Just like that alligator guy wore," he said. "Where I got the idea."

He slipped the knife in its sheath under his belt, on his right hip, and buttoned the shirt over it. Under the loose shirt, the knife made no bulge.

He stared at the house, silent.

Nearly noon. Lunchtime. Putting out food, probably. Uno had figured the target would be home at this hour. Likely to be. He planned everything. Considered the odds. No detail escaped him.

A cool day, for summer. Gray clouds, leftovers from yesterday's rain, scudded across the sky, sunny one moment, dark the next.

Uno nodded, as if reviewing all steps to this point.

He stopped nodding, and stared ahead, at the house. All done right. Now, the planned moment had come. Now they'd liberate themselves from the herd. Afterwards, forever, they'd roam the world free.

Uno looked at Dos. He smiled. Dos smiled back.

"Let's go," Uno said.

His voice sounded taut with suppressed excitement.

They walked away from the parked truck, across the lawn. Dos followed Uno up the single step onto the porch. Uno lifted his fist, held it—a moment, a second moment—abruptly, he knocked.

Another moment, silent, motionless.

Sounds from inside, footsteps on a wooden floor.

Suddenly the door opened.

"Hi, sorry to bother you at lunch time," Uno said. "We're from the Ecology Club, at Snowville High School, and we're doing a survey, how Allen County residents feel about turning Jasper Bog into a wildlife preserve—may we come in?"

With a nod, the homeowner invited them in and shut the door.

Silence from behind the closed door.

It lasted a moment. Then another.

Then, from inside, a yell.

A woman's voice.

Startled.

Frightened.

Enraged.

A crash.

Yelling.

Another crash, and another.

A scream.

Pain.

Another scream, trailing to a moan.

Silence.

Abruptly, the house's front door flew open--Dos and Uno ran out, grinning, exultant. Uno, elated, held up his knife as they ran, displaying it to the world.

Its blade, now reddened, dripped blood.

After a few steps, Dos stopped, leaned over, vomited.

"Oh, for God's sake," Uno snarled.

Dos straightened and ran after him, to their parked truck. They threw open the doors, driver's side, passenger's side, scrambled in, and slammed shut the doors, locking them for no clear reason. Then they sat leaning back in the seats, breathing heavily, eyes excited, faces flushed.

"Where's the knife's sheath?" Uno demanded.

Silence from Dos.

"Well?"

In a small voice, a whisper.

"I don't know."

Uno made a sound like a snarl.

"I gave it to you to hold."

Silence.

After a while, Dos, in a small voice, "Should we go back in and look for it?"

"You go," Uno said.

Silence. After a while, Dos spoke again, that same whisper.

"I can't."

Stony silence from Uno.

"All right," he said finally. "It's just a sheath—they can't trace it to us, and we wore the rubber gloves."

Uno started the truck and backed it around, so it faced back down the driveway. Then he drove ahead rapidly, leaving tracks behind in the wet gravel.

Dos looked at him, guiltily, but a little defiant, too.

"Look—she ripped a piece out of your new shirt."

"So what," Uno said. "It's just a shirt."

He turned left, out of the driveway, and then gunned it down the road, although no cars came from ahead or behind. Traffic a rarity, on this mountainside road, through a dark-green forest of balsam firs and white pines and spruce. He'd thought of that, targeting this house.

"Your ear's bleeding," Dos said.

He put up a hand and felt it, then looked at his forefinger, now with his own blood on its tip.

"She put up a lot of fight," he said.

He thought.

"That made it even better."

32

Cooper felt too weak even to lift her arm.

Powerful chemicals pumped into her.

Red chemicals. Orange chemicals. Purple chemicals.

Clear-plastic bags held the chemicals. They hung from the steel post beside her bed, like holiday ornaments on a tree.

Plastic tubes ran from the chemotherapy bags to the catheter imbedded in her chest, so the chemicals could flow into her body.

Leukemia fighters.

Poisons.

Cooper thought: my dangerous friends.

She watched a nurse adjusting the bags—to handle those chemicals, pumping into Cooper's bloodstream, the nurse wore a rubberized protective gown, and goggles.

Now the nurse left. Cooper lay alone.

Thinking.

She thought about death.

She imagined it as a roar, ever louder, from an oncoming wall of black water, a tidal wave. Or it might be like sitting by a lake, watching wavelets sparkle, growing ever sleepier in summer's sunshine, until you sleep.

Earlier today, her oncologist, sliding his stethoscope across her chest, listening to her lungs, had muttered—to himself—"I hope I can give you two good years."

Optimistic, Cooper knew.

She'd read the statistics.

Her body already felt heavy, immobile. To slip away from this hulk....

Once, in a barn south of town, a suspect aimed a hunting rifle at her forehead, about to shoot. That was different, though, because then she had no time to face dying, her only thought how to escape, how to keep living.

Now she had time to face what must be faced.

She thought about Proctor Gibbs, stung by yellowjackets in his sleeves. Death from sting allergy. She'd Googled it—Proctor would have slipped away, without pain, and was gone.

He'd striven all his life, Cooper knew. To escape his father's hill farm, to build a company. No more obstacles to surmount now. No more striving.

She'd been the same. All her life she'd striven.

Home from elementary school, she finds her father sprawled on the sofa, in his banker's pinstripes, but with his tie askew, reeking of bourbon, and she furiously shakes him awake, yells at him, "Stop doing this to us!" She crusades for his sobriety, and fails.

Decades later, she awakens to find herself sprawled, on her own sofa, clothes in disarray, reeking of scotch.... It seemed a small victory, choosing scotch, shunning her father's bourbon.

To overcome that family curse, she strove for years.

Harvard Law. A professor, snide, demeaning her for some nit in a paper, an imagined nit, because women weren't wanted here, not in those days, but a classroom full of men laughed. It fired something inside her, a fierce determination.

She'd outshine them all.

More striving.

Polio, a lamed leg, a lost fiancé—setbacks to overcome.

Striving.

Malefactors staining her town. Root them out. Hundreds, over the decades.

Investigations, convictions—always striving.

Then hundreds more malefactors would appear, replacements for those she'd had imprisoned.

So strive all over again.

Or, finally, say no to striving.

She lay in her hospital bed, too weak to move.

No.

No more.

No energy left in her. No will. No caring.

Let others strive. She would lay back on these pillows.

Waiting.

33

Tip LaPerle sat with his elbows on his Dill PD desk, his head in his hands.

He'd shut the door, so his officers wouldn't see him like this.

Weakened.

He'd sat up in bed at 3:23 a.m., in the dark, because it finally sank in—Cooper North might die.

Probably would die.

Thor Ennis, their new foster child, didn't know it yet. Tip and Marge hadn't told him. How he'd take it worried them, this seven-year-old who'd already endured loss and lethal danger, whom Cooper took in and protected when his mother's killers came hunting her son, too. Thor now, in his silent way, revered Cooper, and regarded her corgi, Henry, as his best friend.

A tough little boy. Yet, fragile, too.

As for Tip LaPerle, who'd depended upon Cooper for backup and guidance, ever since his own childhood, this woman was his Athena.

Shouting outside his closed door, in the station.

He jerked up his head, just as his door banged open, and the doorway filled with Cappy Dixon, a fat cigar sticking out the side of his mouth.

Jeans stained with chainsaw oil. Sawdust peppering his red-and-black checked flannel shirt.

Radiating red-hot belligerence.

Behind the lumber baron rushed Sergeant Jerry Doyle, who'd been manning the front desk, red-faced and already yelling to Tip—"This guy pushed right past me!" Doyle looked ready to draw his service revolver.

Tip sighed and turned up his eyes, mainly for Doyle's benefit, meaning, what we put up with in this job.

Then he motioned Cappy Dixon inside and gave Doyle a chin nod, meaning, okay, I'll handle this ignoramus, and waited for Dixon to explode, which he immediately did.

"Damn it, Tip—where've you been on this stolen log business?"

A person I love's dying, Tip thought. Your stolen logs? Who cares?

Tip said: "We left it, Cappy, you'd check all the sawmills around here, see who brought the logs in."

"Yeah, I pay taxes, but I've got to be my own cop," Dixon said.

Tip wondered: how could a man yell and snarl, at the same time, with a fat cigar stuck in his whiskery walrus face?

"So, what've you got?" Tip asked.

Dixon, in anger, bit off the tip of his cigar, which momentarily silenced him. He fished in his mouth with a thick, filthy index finger, and finally pulled out the cigar bit. He stared at it, then started to throw it onto the floor. However, seeing Tip's eyes filling with fury, he revised his plan and tossed it into Tip's deskside wastepaper basket, where it landed with a thump.

"So, what've I got?" Dixon said, sinking into Tip's visitor's chair. "Well, no damned sawmill. Because my swiped logs never got hauled to any sawmill."

Tip wrinkled his brow.

"Odd," he said.

Thor Ennis wandered into the office. He'd been carefully—as instructed—staying to the sides, out of the way, to watch the station's functioning. Thor rarely talked, even more rarely said anything about himself, but he had revealed he wanted to grow up to be a policeman.

Tip knew why, given what lawlessness the child had experienced, the same reason Tip had fixated as a child on being a cop, the opposite of his parents and brothers, down on Tenement Row.

Tip brought Thor to work with him, this summer day, thinking there'd be a right time, at some point during the day, to tell the boy about Cooper's sudden hospitalization.

Cappy Dixon saw the boy enter the office, then turned his attention back to the police chief.

He took a big drag on his unlit cigar, no smoke, but maybe some flavor. Then he leaned forward in his chair and pointed the cigar's end at LaPerle.

"A couple of my guys, driving the back roads this morning, scouting for a good stand of maple to lumber, they gave me a call," he said. "What do you think those boys found?"

Tip shrugged.

"You know those backroad palaces? Mountain getaways bigshots from Boston or wherever build for themselves?" Dixon said. "One of those places, just dumped in the driveway, my guys see a log pile—they get out, check, and it's all my stolen maple logs."

He sat back and stared balefully at Tip, meaning, so where were you cops in this? How come my guys had to do the finding?

Because, Tip thought, I don't have the manpower to patrol back roads. He guessed several-hundred miles of dirt roads meandered through the hills and mountainsides around Dill.

"What did your men do with the logs?" Tips asked.

"Nothing, yet," Dixon said. "Not until you check it out, do your cop thing."

"All right, let's go have a look," Tip said, getting up. "Thor's coming with me, in the patrol car—we'll follow you to the scene."

"What's the kid for?" Dixon asked.

Tip didn't bother answering.

He shrugged into his uniform jacket and put a hand on Thor's back, guiding him out of the office and into the back lot, where the Dill PD parked its patrol cruisers.

Fifteen minutes later they were following the mud-spattered blue Ford 450 pickup, with "Caspar Dixon Lumber Company" painted on each side, and Tip found himself estimating that the truck cost Cappy at least $57,000, and probably a lot more, depending on what extras Cappy required.

Tip thought: probably a built-in cigar humidor.

Mostly hardwood forests on either side of the dirt road, opening up here or there to a meadow, although few of the meadows had cows grazing, in this era of declining dairy farms, factory farms now taking over, where the cows stayed inside, eating and periodically being milked by machines.

"Thor, I've got some bad news," Tip suddenly said, as he drove. "Ms. North's in the hospital, and it's a serious disease."

Thor didn't react, just continued staring out the window at the maples and beeches and meadows.

"Henry's staying with Mike Bolknor," Tip said.

Thor continued his silence, staring out the window.

Up ahead, the Ford 450 pulled to the side of the road, beside a driveway entrance, and stopped. Tip parked behind the pickup, and he and Thor got out and walked to the spot where the driveway started.

A log pile blocked the driveway. Tip looked down the drive and saw the big house. It looked empty. He guessed the owners wouldn't be up until the weekend, which was good, because by then the logs would be gone.

Tip thought aloud: "Why steal logs, saw them in half, load them onto a pickup, all that heavy work, then drop them off in some rich guy's driveway and vamoose?"

Dixon, listening, shook his head, irritably.

"How the hell should I know?"

Tip circumnavigated the log pile and found an emptied can of Budweiser lying in the weeds beside the driveway. He pulled a plastic evidence bag from his pocket, nudged the can into the bag with his foot, then held it up.

"From one of your guys maybe?" he asked.

"Not if the jerk wants to keep his job," Dixon said. "Besides, my men came along here really early this morning."

Tip dropped the bagged can into the back seat of his cruiser, then came back to study the ground around the driveway, looking for tracks, which he found. Apparently the thieves backed onto the macadam driveway, dumped the logs, then took off at high speed—at the end of the driveway, they veered off the macadam, onto ground still soggy from the recent rain, then onto the dirt road and away.

Tip used his smartphone to snap photos of the track.

"I can see it's got the same cut mark in it we saw back where they heisted these logs," he said.

"Yeah, well they wouldn't be getting new tires, would they?" Dixon said. "You don't need a badge to figure out stuff like that."

Tip already didn't like Cappy Dixon, hadn't liked him since elementary school, and he didn't find the man's pointless sarcasm charming now. So he ignored the comment, tipped his head toward the parked patrol car, to signal to Thor they were leaving.

Before getting back into the cruiser, Tip shouted to Dixon: "Your guys can pick up these logs now—sooner the better, before the householder gets back and has a conniption."

He turned the SUV around in the road and started back toward town.

Thor sat silently beside him. Upset about Cooper? Tip guessed he must be.

"So, what're you thinking?" he asked the boy.

After a moment, silent, Thor surprised him by speaking, almost a whisper.

"It was like kids playing," he said.

"What was?" Tip asked.

Thor sat silently a moment, looking straight ahead through the windshield, then spoke again.

"Stealing those logs—just for fun, just for a trick," he said. "Then just throw them away, like kids would do."

Tip thought: absolutely right. It's the only good explanation—stupid kids pulling a stupid prank.

He nodded, to show Thor he agree. Silent, they drove another half mile. And then Thor suddenly spoke again.

"I want to visit Miss North," he said. "And to see Henry."

Tip nodded. He didn't know what to say, just then.

A few minutes later, with Thor beside him, he walked into the Dill PD building to find Jerry Doyle pacing, looking stressed. Doyle looked up when the police chief appeared and rushed toward him.

"Tip," he said. "There's been a murder."

He shook his head.

"Troopers just called," he said.

He shook his head again.

"It's bad."

34

Mike Bolknor left Henry in the Campus Security office, so work-study students could dote on him, as the corgi expected. Then he and Tip LaPerle left for the murder scene in a Dill PD patrol SUV.

They drove north from town, up into forested hills, checking the cruiser's GPS on these back roads. Neither man, by tacit agreement, spoke about Cooper North, lying in a hospital bed.

Acute myelogenous leukemia.

Both men had looked it up.

They found the gravel driveway, then jounced along it, through white pines and balsams and yellow birches, stopping where the driveway ended, at a log house. Rising into the trees at the house's side, a three-story tower of nailed-together lumber. Yellow police tape stretched across the front of the house, imprinted "Do Not Cross."

Parked in front of the house a Dodge Ram, mud spattered. Also parked there, at odd angles, two State Police cruisers and a van from the state's forensics lab. As LaPerle and Bolknor got out of their SUV, three troopers—khaki shirts, green trousers with a gold stripe,

Stetsons—crowded out the front door. On their sleeves, triple gold chevrons, signifying detective sergeants.

A shorter man with a bushy gray mustache followed them out. He wore a detective lieutenant's single gold bar.

He checked his watch, then looked up and saw LaPerle and Bolknor walking across the lawn toward him.

"Forensics inside, doing their thing," he said, eyeing Bolknor.

"You the NYPD guy Cooper North brought in?" Bolknor nodded.

"So, us yokels, we'll be getting big-city crime-fighter tips, right?" he said.

Bolknor didn't respond to that, so the trooper looked pointedly back at the house.

"You boys got strong stomachs?" he said.

Neither answered.

Now the trooper looked at Tip.

"Like I told your guy, on the phone, our Major Crime Unit's handing this over to the Dill PD—we're out straight, statewide, you know?"

Tip pointed two-handed at the trooper, with a flourish, for Mike Bolknor's benefit.

"Meet   Detective   Lieutenant   George Gildersleeve," Tip told him. "He's busy—not like us do-nothing Dill cops."

Gildersleeve grinned.

"Hey, Chief, don't be so thin-skinned," he said. "This here's your jurisdiction, isn't it?"

Tip nodded.

"Where's Cooper North?" Gildersleeve asked. "She let you out unsupervised?"

Tip's face tensed. He didn't want to talk about Cooper's illness. It felt disrespectful of her, and it felt too painful.

"Coop couldn't come," he finally said. "So fill us in." Gildersleeve said a FedEx driver stopped by, delivering a package, and saw the house's door wide open. She looked inside, dropped her package, and screamed.

A woman lay on the floor, stabbed scores of times, all over, even her face, her blood pooled on the floor. Chairs and lamps overturned, rug kicked aside....

"So the victim fought like hell," Gildersleeve said. "That's clear."

He pulled a computer printout from his shirt pocket, unfolded it, and studied it a moment.

"Vic's name's Olga Fisker," he said.

He glanced at Mike Bolknor.

"Associated with the college, so that's your turf," he said. "Some kind of scientist."

A man and a woman walked out onto the porch, taking a break. They wore white jumpsuits, with face masks, booties, and hairnets.

"Okay, here's forensics, just landed in their UFO," Gildersleeve said. "Talk to them, we're out of here."

He motioned his men to their cruiser with a head jerk, and started for his own. Halfway there, he turned, looking back at LaPerle and Bolknor.

"Nothing seemed stolen," he said. "So they just did this for what? Chuckles?"

Without waiting for a reply, he headed for his own cruiser, opened the door, but then turned back again.

"Tip, for God's sake, get these crazies!" he said. "It's a slaughterhouse, weasels in a henhouse—sickening!"

Then he got into the cruiser, started the engine. As if unable to resist one last gibe, he leaned out the window.

"If you boys need wisdom, give me a ring," he said. "Maybe I'll have some free seconds."

Then he sped off down the driveway, with the other cruiser following close behind.

Tip muttered: "Working with troopers—so much fun you get giddy."

They walked up to talk with the forensics team, who'd retrieved a thermos of coffee from their van, and paper cups. Tip had worked with them before, and he made the introductions. Karen Del Vecchio led the team, assisted by Ted Dawes, new to the troopers, just out of college.

"Rained the other day," Tip said. "Hope all your vehicles didn't mess up the mud, drive over the perps' tire tracks."

Karen Del Vecchio pulled off her hairnet, and gave her head a shake, to loosen her short-cut black hair. Pulling off her mask, she revealed the face of a thirty-six year old, more striking than pretty. Her eyes, dark brown, nearly black, spent an astute micro-second assessing Mike Bolknor. Then she turned to Tip LaPerle.

"No, we found tracks," she said. "We've got photos, plaster casts—some kind of pickup truck, likely."

She reached into a jumpsuit pocket and pulled out a smart phone, fiddled with it, then held it up to display a close-up of a tire track in mud. Running horizontally across the threads, a shallow groove.

"Looks like they ran over a sharp stone sometime,"

Del Vecchio said. "Or a broken bottle, maybe."

Mike Bolknor stared at the image.

"That's the same truck the Ninjas used, attacking Joey De Mercato's alligator," he said. "Same horizontal cut across the treads."

While Mike explained to the forensics team about the alligator attack, Tip peered at the image on the screen.

"Damn!" he said.

Bolknor looked at him.

"Those guys who stole Cappy Dixon's logs?" Tip said. "That's got to be the same truck."

Neither man spoke for a moment, taking it in.

"Odd, isn't it?" Tip said. "Murderers, but also log-heisting pranksters?"

Bolknor shrugged.

Del Vecchio held up a plastic evidence bag, containing a bit of fabric. They'd found it clenched in the dead woman's hand, she told them.

Just a scrap, with ragged edges, threads sticking out, clearly ripped from some larger fabric. Deep blue. Off to one side, half a decorative spot, gold. Bolknor peered at the yellow spot.

"Might be a scallop shell, half of one," he said. "Could be from a Hawaiian shirt."

He handed it to LaPerle who also examined it, then handed it back to Karen Del Vecchio.

"Think you can figure out what this got ripped from?" Tip said. "Something a perp wore, maybe, or the victim, got torn off in the fight?"

"Not from the vic," Ted Dawes said. "We checked—you'll get a report on this from the lab."

They could tell the newbie tried to sound blasé, seen in it all before, we're on top of this, folks.

"Analysis of the tire track, too," Dawes said.

"Hope the lab can ID the truck model," Tip said. "That'd be like Christmas in June."

All four looked at the house's open door. Finally Karen Del Vecchio spoke.

"Ready to check out the carnage?"

Inside, Tip stared at the dead woman's stab wounds. Unconsciously, an automatic response, he crossed himself. Mike Bolknor stood in one spot, carefully not stepping on any possible evidence, taking in the victim. Then he scanned the shambles of the room, sector by sector.

Karen Del Vecchio watched him.

"We've already done a floor sweep, preliminary," she said. "We found a hair, not the victim's, and it seems victim got a perp's skin under her fingernails, clawed off in the fight."

Bolknor continued his silent survey of the room.

Del Vecchio watched him.

"You worked Manhattan, I heard, with the NYPD," she said.

He nodded, still looking.

"Moving up here, your wife okay with that?" she asked.

Bolknor stopped looking and his face darkened. After a silent moment, he spoke.

"She died."

Del Vecchio grimaced, sorry she'd brought it up. Finally, not saying anything, she nodded.

Acknowledgement.

Bolknor abruptly turned and walked—carefully, so he wouldn't step on evidence—to an overturned couch. He reached between two cushions, where a glimpse of something gray had caught his eye.

He pulled latex gloves from a pocket and slipped them on. Then, out from between the sofa cushions, he pulled a flattened metal tube, about a foot long. Open at one end, closed at the other.

"What's that thing?" Tip La Pearle asked.

"It's odd," Karen Del Vecchio said, staring at what Bolknor held up before his eyes, to study.

"Evidence bag," he said.

Karen produced one from her pocket and held it open, so he could drop in the metal tube.

"In the MPs, I'd see Special Forces guys carrying these things," Bolknor said. "It's a metal sheath for a commando knife."

He studied the sheath, now inside a clear evidence bag.

"I'd say that's from a Fairbairn-Sykes commando knife," he said.

"Hey," Tip said. "That's finally solid evidence—they got sloppy."

Karen Del Vecchio handed the sheath, in its evidence bag, to Ted Dawes, to be added to the other evidence they'd accumulated. Then they all stood, looking at the body, thinking.

"No sign of forced entry," Tip said. "She must have let them in, maybe even knew them."

"Or they gave her a plausible story, no Ninja outfits this time," Mike said. "They were cranked to kill, and figured it wouldn't matter if the woman saw their faces."

More silent thinking.

"Interesting—they didn't worry about surveillance cameras," Mike said. "Blood lust got so overpowering they stopped thinking?"

"Yeah, or maybe they'd already scouted this place, knew there weren't any cameras," Tip said.

Mike looked at Karen Del Vecchio. "How tall are you?"

"Five-six," she said.

They looked at the victim.

"Same height," Tip said.

"Built like Karen, too," Mike said, eyeing her. "Trim, fit—no Amazon, this victim, but she put up a fierce fight, so these attackers weren't so jumbo they could just overpower her."

"Going after that alligator, people's pets, what was that about?" Tip asked.

Mike quoted Cooper North—

"Killing animals is just practice."

They all went back outside. Karen Del Vecchio, stepping out of her jumpsuit, looking much slenderer in jeans and a t-shirt, said they'd finished their preliminary inspection. They'd be back later, when the medical examiner came to remove the body to the morgue, for an autopsy. Then they'd do a more microscopic search, looking for tracked-in grit or fabric threads or whatever else they could find.

"Not a cheery scene," Karen said, indicating the house. "I'm going for a run, clear some of this from my head."

She eyed Mike Bolknor.

"You look athletic," she said. "Do you do running?"

"I should get back into it," he said.

"Try the recreation path, starts behind the high school," Karen said. "I go every night after work, start around four-thirty."

Bolknor looked at her.

She shrugged.

"Maybe I'll see you there one afternoon," she said.

Bolknor still looked at her, face inscrutable.

Finally, he spoke.

"It's a thought," he said.

35

Cooper North stared at the ceiling tiles, listening to her chemotherapy pump beeping.

Poisons flowed through her catheter into her blood stream. She couldn't feel them. They didn't burn. But they robbed her of energy, and appetite, and will.

She waited.

Her world—the college, the state's attorney's office, the Dill PD, all she'd ever done in the world, who she was—all now receding into mist. She'd jailed thieves and killers, only to have new thieves and killers appear, over and over.

She'd done enough. No more striving.

Just rest. Nothing more.

While she waited.

She thought, without emotion: I'll get weaker and weaker. Wearier and wearier. Then I'll slip away.

So it had been for Proctor Gibbs, fatally stung. So it would be for her.

Her door opened and she heard the voice of her leukemia nurse, Emma Ford.

"Good morning, my dear," Emma said. "How are you feeling?"

What could she say? I'm just waiting, Emma, that's all, to slide out of this world?

"How did you become a nurse," Cooper asked.

Emma adjusted the tubes connecting Cooper to the chemotherapy pump, and checked the pump's liquid levels. She bathed Cooper with an alcohol-soaked sponge, all the while inspecting her skin with expert eyes. As she worked, she answered Cooper's question, in her calm, quiet voice.

She spoke of a childhood in Harlem, years lived mostly in hospitals.

Sickle-cell anemia.

In the hospital, she read voraciously. She sat in her hospital bed doing her schoolwork. She helped the nurses— one favorite chore, collecting all the old ladies' false teeth and cleaning them.

Doctors warned her: no physical exertion. By now, though, she'd become a teen, with a dazzling smile, a strong will.

Emma wanted to dance.

From an eighth-grade classmate, she heard about a high school for the performing arts, which sounded to her like "The High School of the Reforming Arts."

Knowing nothing about dance, she prepared for the audition by watching dancers on television talent shows, and in commercials. She handed the judges a recording of the *Nutcracker Suite,* then threw herself around the stage, smiling radiantly. They laughed at her. Then they admitted her, because of her smile.

Forget ballet, they said. It's not for a black girl. So she studied modern dance.

WHEN THE WASP STINGS

After she graduated, she danced with troupes, like the Alvin Ailey Dance Company. She danced on Broadway in *The Wiz,* and in the movie version.

Then her husband died, leaving Emma with a small daughter and a son. She decided she wanted "to be of use." She earned a degree in psychology, and then a second Bachelor's Degree, in nursing. She came to this hospital.

She knew what pain her patients experienced, and what fear. She knew it well.

All her life she endured sickle cell's extreme pain. She became diabetic. Then she developed an autoimmune lung disease, pulmonary sarcoidosis. A day came when she collapsed with thrombic thrombocytopenia purpura—her blood's platelets cohered, causing her kidneys to fail and her breathing to stop. She spent three weeks in a coma, then six weeks recuperating in the hospital.

Cooper North listened to this unfolding story. She watched Emma typing a report into the room's computer terminal.

Cooper thought: Emma knows she will die soon.

Six months? A year? Tonight?

Cooper thought: Emma's not waiting.

She's "being of use."

Cooper drifted off to sleep.

36

Kalisha Rains, wearing a surgical mask, carrying a briefcase, almost wept.

It hurt, seeing Cooper North this way, lying in this hospital bed, so depleted—and, somehow, defeated—by this horrible illness, with these chemicals pumping into her, which had already taken away her hair, a woman with the face of a fierce hawk, looking now like a naked-headed condor.

A dying condor.

Kalisha's leader. In fact, her heroine.

"I'm here to report," Kalisha said, businesslike, her tears suppressed into her chest, heavy as an iron anvil. "New cases...."

A nurse came into the room, shorter than Kalisha, older, her skin a shade blacker. Her ID badge said "Emma Ford."

Between the two women, a nanosecond of acknowledgement.

As always, Kalisha felt confusion meeting someone who looked like her. She'd been adopted, into a white family, into an upscale Philadelphia suburb, her adoptive father a heart surgeon, her adoptive mother an attorney. Her brothers and sister white. She'd hardly noticed how much melanin she had in her skin, except at school. Overtly, and covertly, they'd reminded her.

So, she'd striven. Student Council president. Straight As. Soccer stardom. Valedictorian. She'd striven as a Princeton undergraduate and at Harvard Law. To prove she could do it, whatever "it" might be.

"I'll be just a minute, folks," Emma said, applying the stethoscope dangling from her neck to Cooper's chest, and listening, serious faced.

After a moment, she dropped the stethoscope and moved to the computer. She had a graceful way of moving.

"Dr. Lopez wants to start you on a new antibiotic," Emma told Cooper, as she fingered the keyboard. "I'll be back with that, Dear, in just a little while."

Then, with a smile for Kalisha, Emma left the room.

A radiant smile, Kalisha thought. A caring woman. Cooper's in good hands. At least that.

"Tip LaPerle's working on that log theft, which now looks like a prank, more than anything," Kalisha told Cooper.

She felt foolish, somehow, talking about such matters, when Cooper's chemotherapy pump kept pinging. They'd decided, though, she and Ozzie Knick, that they should do this. Don't let Cooper feel she no longer mattered.

Cooper looked at her as from a distance, as if she gazed at a miniaturized figure, far off.

"Also, we've had a murder," Kalisha said. "A horrible murder, a stabbing, many times, a woman."

Cooper looked at her with more attention.

Kalisha read from one of the printouts she'd brought in her briefcase.

"Victim's name is Olga Fisker," she read. "An entomologist, actually famous, they killed her in her home out in the…."

She stopped speaking because she'd glanced up and seen Cooper staring at her with an entirely different expression in her eyes, an expression that mutated, as Kalisha watched—shock, into anger, and then into something like ferocity.

A woman who climbed trees.

Suddenly, fire in her eyes.

"Mound up these pillows behind me, Kalisha," she said. "I need to sit up."

Sitting more upright now, she glowered at images in her mind.

"So the Ninjas finally did it, they hungered for it, and they did it," Cooper muttered, speaking to herself. "Olga, she was…."

Cooper fell silent, thinking, eyes fierce.

"All right," she said. "Bring me certain things."

She sounded weakened, as if she could easily drift asleep. Yet, she fought it, Kalisha thought, like a ship's captain, wounded, beset by mutineers, but holding them off, retaking the command.

When she walked into this room, Cooper lay ready to die. Kalisha saw it in Cooper's dulled eyes, and in how she lay in bed, as if already inert.

Then everything changed. Something about Olga Fisker's murder.

Kalisha thought: She's back at work.

"Bring me my laptop computer," Cooper said. "Bring me copies of all the paperwork for all the current cases—especially for Olga Fisker's murder."

Cooper thought, then spoke again.

"Bring me my cellphone—I left it on my desk, at the office—who's working the Fisker murder?"

"Mike Bolknor is," Kalisha said. "Also Chief LaPerle—they said the troopers started it, but then dropped out."

Cooper sat back, eyes closed. Then they opened.

"Alright," she said. "Mike, Tip—I want them both up here to talk about this, as soon as they've some clear time."

Kalisha nodded.

"You're going to be my liaison with the office, and the Dill PD," Cooper said. "You'll need to be up here a lot—I don't want any of this wimpy crying."

Kalisha thought: Cooper saw it, even though I kept it inside.

She gathered her briefcase and started out of the room. At the door, she turned, to say goodbye, but Cooper had now lain back, eyes closed.

She'd   fallen   asleep.

37

Flute Wagner's office phone buzzed.

"Okay," he said into the handset. "I'll be right down."

He shook his head, by way of apologizing to his two visitors, Kalisha Rains and Mike Bolknor.

"Sorry, I'll only be a minute," Wagner said. "A bottling glitch, down in the processing room."

He said it sheepishly, backing out the door.

A humble little man, Kalisha decided. He'd been bullied in school. She'd read it in Cooper North's notes. For being short, probably, and not athletic. For looking like a woodchuck, or just for being humble. More than anything, in a wealthy town, for being poor. Walmart sneakers. Tracfone flip phone. Walgreens cheap eyeglasses.

Kalisha glanced at Mike, to see what he might be thinking, but she couldn't read the big man's face. She never could. A face like a granite cliff. Impassive. Yet, she felt in him no meanness. Only, maybe, deep down, something sad, and heavy, and grim.

They'd left Cooper's hospital room twenty minutes ago. She'd looked exhausted. Case folders lay strewn across her bed's covers. Kalisha saw how it was: Cooper yearned to lie back, to sink down into sleep, but she fought it. Kalisha guessed Mike Bolknor saw it, too, that terrifying weariness, that battle. Mike's face, though, remained granite.

Alone now, in Wagner's office, the two investigators sat a moment in silence.

"Interesting," Mike said finally. "They've got a bottling problem, and they call in the marketing director, not the CEO, or the maintenance supervisor—what do you make of that?"

Kalisha had been reading Cooper's notes, from her interviews with Flute, Viola, Sonny, and Sonny's ex-wife. Now she pulled her glasses down to the end of her nose and dropped her chin, to look at Mike over the tops of the frames.

"Maybe it means people here rely on that little man," she said.

Bolknor nodded.

"Maybe the new CEO's not so popular," he said.

They both considered, trying to create mental maps of the internal dynamics at Snowville Maple.

Mike pointed to the blown-up photo on the wall behind Flute's desk, a Lamborghini sports car.

"What do you make of that?" he asked.

Kalisha shook her head.

"Spaceship?"

She knew nothing about cars.

Just then the office door opened and a wiry woman hurried in, carrying a brown-paper bag. She stopped, her intense dark eyes fixed on the visitors.

"Who're you?" she said.

They told her.

"I'm Viola Wagner," the woman said.

She wore black jeans and a black t-shirt, with her black hair pulled back and tied with a black ribbon. She sat in Flute's office chair, behind his desk.

"Flute forgot his lunch again," she said, holding up the paper bag.

She placed the bag carefully on the desk, moving it about, to find a spot handy for Flute, but also out of his way, while working.

"We're investigating Proctor Gibbs' death," Kalisha said.

Viola Wagner grimaced, shaking her head, a gesture that could mean anything.

"Yeah, murdered with yellow jackets," she said. "Flute's convinced of it."

She shrugged.

Abruptly, she threw up both arms, fingers spread, sign language for disagreeing with her husband, not believing the murder idea, but not wanting to argue about it.

Kalisha thought: Viola Wagner reminds me of some high-energy animal, quick, intense, skinny.

"Let's say someone working here did kill Gibbs," Mike Bolknor said. "Who'd have a reason, like a grudge, for instance."

Viola started to reply, but just then Flute walked back in.

"Viola!" he said.

He said it with pleasure, delighted to see her.

Kalisha thought: she's his support.

Viola held up his brown-paper lunch bag, and waved it, giving him a raised-eyebrow look, sardonic, but amused. Apparently, many mornings he forgot his lunch, left it lying on the kitchen counter, and his wife brought it in for him.

Viola got up, so Flute could sit at his desk, and moved to one of the office's visitor chairs.

"So who's the murderer?" Viola asked Flute. "They're asking."

Flute drooped his head and stared at his desktop. In that position, he shook his head.

"I told Ms. North, nobody here would do it," he said. "No reason."

Viola suddenly snorted.

"Grady John Wagner!" she said. "You know who had reason!"

She looked at him fiercely, then at the visitors.

"That's his real name," she said. "Grady John Wagner—back in Connecticut, those rotten rich kids called him Flute, in high school, making fun, but he went along with it."

"It's sort of an interesting name," he mumbled. "I think it is.'

Viola leaned forward in her seat, frowning, eyes sharp.

Kalisha suddenly knew the animal she associated with this woman.

Ferret.

Viola now stared at Flute. She'd said he knew who had a motive. Now she waited for him to say who. He wouldn't say it, though, continuing to stare down at his desktop, so she said it for him.

"Sonny DeWitt."

Flute leaned his elbows on the table and hid his face in his hands.

"We shouldn't make accusations," he muttered into his hands.

Viola ignored it, eyes boring into Kalisha and Mike.

"Okay, this is long before Flute ever came to work here—Proctor willed all his stock in this business to DeWitt, if he died," she told them. "Okay, if Proctor keels over—his wife's long dead, and he's got no kids— so now Sonny DeWitt owns the company."

Flute, his face still hidden in his hands, made a sound like a moan, and muttered.

"That doesn't mean Sonny would…."

Viola looked at Flute, then at the visitors, and shook her head.

"DeWitt's incompetent, which he damn well knows," she said. "Rich boy, nasty, just like those bastards back in Connecticut—they made Flute's school years awful, and mine, too, for that matter—and that's who Sonny DeWitt's like."

Having said that, she sank back in her chair, arms folded across her chest, and stared at Flute, as if daring him to disagree with her assessment. When her husband said nothing, and Kalisha and Mike also said nothing, processing what she'd just said, Viola leaned forward in her chair and said more.

"So right after Flute got hired here, everyone saw it— competent big time, okay? Not like Sonny the Jerk," she said. "Good chance, you'd figure, Proctor might change his will, right? Too bad for Sonny, right? Except, uh-oh, Proctor died first."

She let that sink in, glaring at everyone in turn.

Silence.

"Viola…" Flute said.

"You know it's true, Flute," she said. "This murder-by-wasp stuff's crazy—but, you want a motive, well, there you go."

She got up and started out the door, but stopped in the open doorway and turned, looking back at her husband.

"Flute, you know he'll run Snowville Maple straight into the damned cemetery," she said.

She shifted her gaze to the two visitors.

"Like last week, I came out of the supermarket, in Dill," she said. "And there's Sonny driving by—middle of the workday—with his three idiot buddies, not even using his own car, larking around in the company Jeep!"

She raised her two arms, shaking her head, and disappeared out the door and down the corridor.

Silence in Flute's office, but then a voice boomed outside.

"Hey Flutsie, I just saw your wife hurrying out, what're you doing, conjugal visits in the middle of the workday?"

Sonny DeWitt filled the doorway, still chortling. Seeing the visitors, though, he went silent, and stared.

"State's attorney's office, these folks," Flute explained. "And the Dill police department."

He took a deep breath, flabbergasted after all that had been said, and turned to the visitors.

"This is Sonny De Witt," Flute said. "He's our CEO."

DeWitt stood in the doorway, irritation battling with confusion on his oxlike face.

Kalisha saw a large man, although not as big as Mike Bolknor, and already going to flab, stomach bulging under his shirt, collar unbuttoned, tie loose, face red.

He looks drunk, Kalisha thought.

236

"We're done in this office, for now," Mike told DeWitt. "Let's go to your office, and we'll talk with you."

He stood, making it clear it wasn't a request.

38

DeWitt led them outside the building, instead of to his office.

"I've got to look inside the Jeep," he said.

They followed him along the front of the building, then around one side, and to the back, where Snowville Maple parked its tractor, and snowblowers, currently dormant, and other equipment, including its Jeep Gladiator truck.

"That Jeep pulls a wagon, with seats in it," DeWitt said. "For tourists, you know, a maple-orchard tour—boring, right? Trees?"

He opened the truck's driver-side door and peered inside. Bending in over the seat, he scanned the interior, including the floor. After a moment, he reached in under the driver's seat and pulled out a wallet, which he shoved into his back trouser pocket.

"I figured I dropped it there," he muttered. "Last night."

Now he sat on the front bumper, looking up at Kalisha Rains and Mike Bolknor.

"What can I do for you folks?" he said. "I already told Cooper North whatever I know, including that I think it's bull, good-old Proc getting murdered, and with wasps, for God's sake."

"If someone did kill Proctor Gibbs, who here had a motive?" Mike said.

DeWitt looked at him, and sighed.

"That's what Cooper North asked," he said. "It's all bunk, this murder thing."

Neither Kalisha or Mike said anything, just looking steadily at Sonny.

"That old man, nobody'd ever hurt him," Sonny said.
"He treated everyone great."

He sat brooding, looking off into the trees behind the company's building.

"Hell, just one person in this company had a motive to kill Proc," he said.

He looked at them defiantly.

"Which would be me."

He waited for questions, but they didn't come, because Kalisha and Mike already knew Sonny's possible motive. So they stared at him, until finally Mike did ask a question, but nothing Sonny expected.

"How do you like running the company?"

Sonny looked up, startled. His mouth moved, talking silently before he finally spoke aloud.

"I like the money…."

Faintly, from around the front of the building, came the muted racket of a car needing a new muffler, the noise steadily louder.

"Okay, getting this business willed to me, I felt I'd just won the Oscar, like Proc really thought I had ability," Sonny said. "It took me an hour to start feeling sick—like I'd been hoisted atop a swaying pole, you know, set up to fall off and...."

A faded-red Chevrolet convertible, eleven years old, rust patches everywhere, roared around the building and skidded to a stop.

Three men sat in the open car, thirty-somethings, wearing muscle t-shirts, with straps instead of sleeves, all grinning at Kalisha.

She thought: this looks like a circus car.

Each man looked clownish in a different way.

Driving, a man with the long face of an opossum, wearing a porkpie hat and violet-colored sunglasses.

In the front passenger seat, a fat fellow, face mostly hidden behind an enormous bushy walrus mustache, with stringy blond hair falling over his forehead.

Sitting in the back, a man whose flaming-red beard fell to his chest. Crown bald, red hair on the sides of his head long and tangled.

These three sat grinning at Kalisha.

Walrus Mustache shouted: "Hey, Sonny, you got a new girlfriend?"

He pointed at Kalisha.

"Primo!" shouted Red-Beard, in the back seat. "Ultra-primo!"

Sonny turned up his eyes.

"Hey, guys," he told the men in the car, voice loud for emphasis. "Not a good time, okay? I'm working with the police here, understand?"

He emphasized the word "police."

"Wow, the Long Arm," said the porkpie-hatted driver.

He used his fingers to mime checking the length of Mike's and Kalisha's arms, from a distance.

"Possum, please go away," Sonny said to the driver. "I'll see you guys tonight, okay?"

They ignored him, simultaneously opening the car's doors and climbing out.

"We maybe left a valuable in the truck last night," the driver said, whisking off his porkpie hat, twirling it around an upraised index finger, then slapping it back onto his head.

He walked to the back of the pickup and peered into the bed.

Joining him at the truck's tailgate, the other two men also stared into the bed.

"Hey, cool!" Walrus Mustache said, and he slapped Red Beard on the back and pointed to something in the truck.

"Climb in there and get that, will you, Beast?" he said. "I've got this artificial leg, you know?"

He wore cut-off jeans and held up his leg, obviously not artificial, covered with hair.

"I can't climb, Walrus," said Red Beard. "I've got a really hurtful hangnail."

By now, it had sunk in with the driver that law officers watched. He swung into action, clearly meaning to leave fast, and climbed into the truck bed and reached down. Triumphantly, he held up a six-pack of beer.

"Coors!" he announced. "Nectar of…what? The gods, or something?"

He opened his convertible's trunk and stowed the beer.

"Okay, crew, let's belt in for takeoff," he told his friends.

"Hey, Possum," Walrus-Mustache told him. "Let's stick around, get to know this pretty lady over here."

He executed what was supposed to be an elegant bow in Kalisha's direction.

Sonny DeWitt looked ready to implode.

Mike Bolknor now walked up to the men by the convertible, and stood looking down at the driver, with the porkpie hat.

"What's this stuff on your arm?" he asked. "It got on you when you reached into the truck."

Porkpie-Hat looked at him, confused. Then he lifted his arm and peered at it. After a moment, he pulled down his violet-colored sunglasses and looked at his arm over the top of the frame.

"Sawdust," he said. "I think...."

He brushed off the t-shirt and his arm.

Sonny broke in, speaking fast.

"Out in the maple orchards, you get limbs breaking off, okay?" he said. "So we go in with this Jeep, haul out the sawed-off pieces, that's all."

Mike nodded, then turned to the three men now sitting in the convertible.

"We'll need your full names, addresses, and telephone numbers," he said.

"I've got all that," Sonny said. "I can print it out for you—will you guys please get out of here?"

They watched the convertible with three heads showing roar out along the building and away.

"They're okay guys," Sonny said. "Just, you know…."

Mike and Kalisha exchanged a glance.

"That's a Jeep Gladiator," Mike said, staring at the truck. "We'd like to look that over and…."

Sonny's face turned even redder than it had been, and he glared at his two interrogators.

"I've got work, you know?" he said. "I've talked with Cooper North, and now I've answered the same questions from you, so goodbye!"

He walked fast, rounded the corner of the building, and was gone.

Mike looked at Kalisha, eyebrows raised.

"Search warrant?" he asked.

She nodded.

They started their walk back to the front parking lot, and the Dill PD cruiser they'd used today.

"Why the interest in the sawdust?" Kalisha asked.

"No reason," Mike said. "Just when you've got a case like this, no clues really, you start checking out every anomaly, who knows, maybe it'll lead to something."

Kalisha started to speak, but just then a young man walked around the side of the building toward them.

Seventeen or eighteen. Tall. Lanky.

He glanced at them, then away, and spoke in passing.

"No more tours today," he said, voice flat. "Come back tomorrow."

Markedly cold eyes, and a frozen face. So it seemed to Kalisha.

Mike took out his wallet, flapping it open to display his Dill PD badge, which he used whenever he functioned as the department's detective, on loan from the college.

Kalisha sensed the boy flinched, seeing the badge.

"We're looking into Proctor Gibbs' death," Mike said.

Hearing that, the boy relaxed, Kalisha thought. He shrugged.

"Beats me," he said, and kept on walking, back toward the parked Jeep.

Kalisha and Mike watched him disappear around the side of the building.

"We'll have to look into that one, I think," Kalisha said.

Mike nodded.

39

Cooper North sat up in her hospital bed, pillows piled behind her back, staring at case folders she'd spread out on her blanket.

Once more she leafed through the Olga Fisker file, the case that gnawed at her most.

A woman who climbed trees.

They'd slashed her, again, and again.

Brutal.

Not a murder to hush a witness, or to steal, or even to avenge a slight, not this frenzied slashing.

No, they did it for pleasure, for entertainment, for excitement, for a thrill.

They killed to feel like giants.

Monsters.

Cooper thought what must be done: arrests, evidence gathered, weighed, arranged for a jury to hear. Left free ranging, these Ninjas would kill again, and then again.

They'd infect the community.

Cooper needed her assistant state's attorneys, along with Mike Bolknor, and Tip LaPerle, to be out in the world, on the hunt. She could only lie in this bed. They'd bring her information to sort out, to think about. For that, she needed time.

She feared she had none.

Because of what was coming, a crucial test.

Emma Ford had just been in the room, checking the chemotherapy pump, and giving Cooper a plastic cup of water and another pill to swallow, this one blue.

"Dr. Lopez will do a bone-marrow biopsy, later this week, after you've finished this first chemotherapy round," Emma said. "Fingers crossed, Dear—I'll be here with you when he does it."

A wave of something like relief. Emma Ford would be with her.

She'd always been independent, prided herself on it.

Now, this neediness.

Cooper faintly smiled.

Leukemia showed her new facets of herself.

She fell back against her pillows. Just a moment's rest, she thought. She shut her eyes.

She slept.

Sometime later, not knowing how long she'd slept, she opened her eyes. Tip LaPerle and Ozzie Knick, both wearing surgical masks, sat in two of the room's visitors' chairs, silent, eyes on her.

How long, she wondered, had they sat there, watching her sleep?

She knew how she looked. Hair gone. Wasted. She'd lost twenty pounds already, and she'd never been fat.

They beheld a skeleton.

"Don't worry," she told them. "At this point, I only look dead."

She resisted the urge to lean back, close her eyes, to sleep again.

Tip LaPerle spoke first: "Coop, we've come to go over some cases, unless you're not up to it right now."

Cooper lifted an arm, then let it drop back down on the blanket.

"Talk away," she said. "I've been working on cases all this morning."

She waved a hand, indicating the files spread out on her blanket.

"First thing is tires," Ozzie Knick said.

It pleased Cooper that neither man blurted out sympathy or sorrow or regrets, although she could see it in their eyes. In Tip's eyes, especially.

Keep it to business, she thought. Please.

"What about tires?" she asked.

"We got reports from the trooper lab," Ozzie said. "There's a long list of things, like tread size and tread wear and tire diameter, but what it comes down to is this—the truck used in the maple-log heist, and the truck used in the attack on the alligator, definitely the same truck."

Tip leafed through his own copy of the reports.

"They're still figuring what make of truck it probably was," he said.

"What about the Olga Fisker murder," Cooper asked. "Anyone find tire tracks there?"

"That report's still to come from the forensic lab," Ozzie Knick said. "It'll go to Mike Bolknor, probably today or tomorrow."

Cooper felt certain what it would show.

"For now, let's assume the same people are stealing logs and also attacking pets with knives," she said

Silence, all three considering that. Tip spoke first.

"That log heist," he said. "Turns out, right after they sawed those logs in half, and heaved them up onto their truck, the thieves drove down the road a mile and dumped them into a summer home's driveway."

Ozzie Knick suddenly stood, walked a few steps in front of the bed, brow wrinkled in thought, then dropped back into his chair.

"Like a college-frat prank, right?" he said. "Slashing pets, that's a different thing—hard to put them together."

After a moment's silence, to consider that, they moved on to other current cases, burglaries, drug selling, embezzlement from a local church....the usual.

Cooper leaned back and closed her eyes, listening.

After a few minutes, fear of the coming bone-marrow biopsy interwove with the discussion of a robbery at a highway convenience store, and after that she no longer listened.

She   slept.

40

That afternoon, as Mike Bolknor reviewed campus patrol schedules, and thought about Cooper North, his office phone buzzed.

A woman's voice.

"Hi Mike," she said. "It's Karen Del Vecchio, at the state crime lab—remember me?"

"Yes," Mike said, and waited.

"We've got reports ready for you," she said. "I'll be going for a run at the recreation path around 4:30 today, after work—can you meet me there?"

Mike stared at the top of his desk, at nothing in particular. She could, of course, mail him the reports, or fax them, or email them, as PDF attachments.

"Would that be convenient?" she prompted.

Finally, he answered.

"Yes."

"Path starts behind the high school," Karen said. "I'll see you there."

She ended the call.

For a while, Mike sat listening to the dial tone.

Later, at 4:10 p.m., in his apartment near the campus, he stood looking down at a photograph he kept on his night table, taken one summer Sunday afternoon, not so terribly long ago, a family outing, at the Central Park zoo.

Rachel grinned at the camera, with an arm around each child, little Abigail on her left, little Frankie on her right.

Last night they'd watched an animated film about zoo animals flying off on a plane, having an adventure, and the kids wanted to see real animals, in a real zoo.

Mike stared at the photograph, stone faced, thinking of nothing.

A memory slid into his mind.

Rachel talking, over the telephone with her mother, recently widowed, now living in Florida. Mike had just come home from work, and was unstrapping his holster, with his service pistol, and then locking the firearm away, so he heard only the conversation's end.

"Yeah, well, Mom, the fact is Dad's gone—you know what he'd want," Rachel was saying. "He'd tell you, 'For Pete's sake, Gloria, if this guy's okay, and you like him, give life another try, and if you're too chicken, do it for me, yes?'"

Another minute of staring at the photograph.

Mike then walked to his dresser and slid open the bottom drawer. He pulled out a gray track suit, unworn since he left New York. He put it on. Then he pulled on his size-sixteen New Balance running shoes, also unworn since he left the city.

It took him five minutes to drive to the high school, then around to the parking area in the back, where the recreation path began. Karen Del Vecchio stood leaning against her white Ford Mustang's left front fender, reading reports. She'd brought them in a brown manila envelope, now lying on the Mustang's hood.

A fit woman, wearing bright red running shorts and a white t-shirt, her black hair short and loose, her wideset black eyes on him.

Intelligent eyes.

Not a pretty face, precisely, but a striking face.

She waved to Mike, as he parked the campus-security Prius he used, a stipulation in his contract, in exchange for being on call, if needed, all day and night, every day.

He thought there might be an awkward moment, but as soon as he walked up Karen handed him the report she'd been reading—an analysis of the tire tracks they'd found at the Olga Fisker murder site.

In the report, the lab listed the tire type, the lug size, wear on the lugs, wear on the tire's outer edge because the truck's alignment needed adjusting, plus added information. More importantly, they'd made it official— as he and Tip already figured, the same truck had been used in the log hijacking, in the attack on the alligator, and in Olga Fisker's murder.

One new bit of information: probably the truck had been a Jeep Gladiator, because this make of tires came as standard equipment on that model. It could have been a different kind of truck. Most likely, though, a Jeep Gladiator.

"I've got all this memorized," Karen said, holding up the sheaf of printouts. "How about if I tell you what's in the reports while we run?"

"Fine," Mike said. "I've been out of it a lot of months, so keep it below warp speed."

In fact, as they ran, it felt good. This recreation path ran alongside Beecham Creek, a tributary of the Ira River, fast flowing, gurgling musically over its rocky bed. Black willows and hornbeams lined the banks, with warblers and goldfinches and kinglets flashing orange and crimson and azure as they flitted in the foliage. Their sneakers striking the macadam path made a percussion backing to the birdsong.

It felt good, moving like this again. Maybe he'd join the Dill Keep-Fit Health Club, lift weights. Get back into boxing, if they offered sparring.

He wondered how many Jeep Gladiators might be in Allen County. Hundreds, he supposed, a rugged truck, good for driving off-road, and up logging trails.

"You were dead right about that knife scabbard," Karen told him. "It's the metal sheath for a Fairbanks-Sykes commando knife."

"Fingerprints?" Bolknor asked.

It pleased him, running like this, to find himself breathing so easily, after so many months, talking as he ran with no difficulty.

"Just smudges," Karen said. "Nothing clear enough to ID a perp."

Otherwise, no useful prints at the murder scene, she said. Just the victim's, and prints of the FedEx driver, on the porch.

They ran on in silence a while.

"If I ask how your wife died, will you be angry?" Karen suddenly asked.

"No," he said.

Running together like this, side by side, created an odd companionship, as if they'd known each other a long time.

"Road-rage, in Florida, two opposing drivers with handguns, Rachel and my son and my daughter caught in the crossfire, collateral damage," he said.

He said it as if he were giving a police incident report.

No emotion. He said it that way because he didn't want Karen to ask more questions about what happened, or offer condolences. She didn't.

For the next quarter mile, they ran again in silence.

"I ran track in college, married a guy on the team," Karen suddenly said. "After we graduated, we discovered it was all about the track team, not about us really, so...."

Silence again, for an eighth of a mile.

"We have a report on that scrap of fabric, which the victim clenched in her hand," Karen finally said.

Mike waited. No need to ask a question to encourage her to speak. Somehow, the running together made the usual social protocols unnecessary.

"It's from a shirt, not the victim's," Karen said. "It's new, never washed, so probably never worn before, likely a Hawaiian-style shirt, deep blue, decorated with golden scallop shells."

Mike, thinking aloud, said: "Maybe bought it to wear to the murder—got the idea, maybe, from the pet-alligator guy."

He thought a moment, then spoke again.

"We'll check local stores, maybe a clerk will remember who bought it."

At the three-mile marker, they turned around and ran back, finally stopping where the recreation path began, behind the high school. They stood a moment, leaning against their own cars.

"Hey, good run," Karen said. "Hope we can do it some more."

Mike took the sheaf of reports from her and stuffed them into the manila envelope, and dropped them onto his car's passenger seat.

He walked around to the driver's side and opened the door and started to get in. He stopped, though, and looked over the car's roof at Karen.

"Good idea," he said.

He got in behind the wheel. He sat a moment, staring through the windshield, then leaned over the passenger seat and lowered the window on that side.

"I'll give you a ring," he said.

41

Cooper North's mind sank into mist.

She fought it.

"After I'm buried," she thought. "Not yet."

She forced herself to look at the paperwork she'd spread out across her blankets. Investigative reports. Forensic lab printouts. Hand-written notes. They came in from Tip LaPerle and Mike Bolknor, and from Kalisha Rains and Ozzie Knick.

Cooper aimed to find threads connecting the pieces of evidence, to seek clues in patterns.

She tried to ignore her bedside pump—every few seconds, with a ping, it pushed cell-killing chemicals into her bloodstream. Also, antibiotics, because the chemotherapy chemicals had destroyed her immune system. Yesterday, her oncologist, Dr. Lopez, added intravenous nutrition to the mix, because her treatment made her too sick to eat.

She remembered a phrase from a long-ago war—"It became necessary to destroy this town to save it."

She thought: will destroying this body save it? Statistically, probably not.

Dr. Lopez would soon perform a bone-marrow biopsy. Then she'd know her chances.

She'd tracked down hundreds of murderers, tried them in court, jailed them. Now she faced a different kind of killer, acute myelogenous leukemia, on trial in her mind for attempted homicide—the upcoming biopsy would the judge's ruling.

For now, she focused on clue-connecting threads.

For instance, they now knew, for three separate crimes—log theft, alligator attack, Olga Fisker's murder—the perpetrators drove the same truck.

So, three crimes, one truck, equals one set of perps? Or did different sets of perps drive the same truck? If three separate sets of perps shared one truck, how so? Friends? Relatives? Something else?

Cooper needed Tip and Mike, Kalisha and Ozzie, to dig up more information.

She wondered, too, about Proctor Gibbs. No truck used for that murder-by-wasp. Yet, it nagged her. Three crimes, plus Proctor Gibbs, all in one short time period. So could the Gibbs murder be connected? In Cooper's mind, a possibility.

Could there be a central point, a hub, from which these four crimes radiated?

Find the truck, she thought. Find the truck.

Her eyes shut involuntarily and she sank back against her pillows, too fatigued for more work. So she lay there, fighting sleep. Often, when she started to slip away like this, as if life offered just weariness, she thought of Henry and apples.

Behind her house on Hill Street, in the yard, grew an apple tree. When she let Henry into the yard, he raced to the apple tree, barking. He barked at the tree, so exuberant his black eyes glinted. Then he turned and barked at Cooper, his message clear: "Throw me an apple!"

So she'd hurl an apple, far out onto the grass. Henry would run, joyfully barking, to grab it in his teeth, then execute a U-turn and race back up the lawn, on his short legs, to drop it beside Cooper's sneakers, already barking a demand for the next throw.

At first, Cooper thought Henry liked to eat apples. A few experiments, though, proved he had no interest in eating apples. He just liked to run after a thrown apple and bring it back, eyes glittering with exuberance.

Joie de vivre.

Cooper had taken to picturing tiny corgis, running through her blood stream, gleefully chasing away leukemia cells, barking.

A knock on the door, and Kalisha Rains walked into the room, followed by Mike Bolknor, both wearing surgical masks, as required, because Cooper now had no immune system, her bone marrow destroyed by chemotherapy. Kalisha looked at Cooper, lying in her bed, and Cooper detected a flicker of distress in the young woman's eyes, but Kalisha quickly hid it and assumed a businesslike expression. Mike Bolknor's face, the usual granite, showed nothing, a hard man to read.

"We've been out to Snowville Maple," Kalisha said. "We're here to share a few things we noticed."

"Good," Cooper said.

She forced herself to sit up straighter against the pillows supporting her back, to look more alert than she felt.

"They've got a Jeep Gladiator, for visitor tours," Mike said. "Also for general work in the sugar-maple groves."

Cooper now remembered seeing a Jeep parked there. Also, didn't she once see people in a Jeep seeming to surveille her house?

"We couldn't check the tires," Mike said. "Sonny DeWitt refuses any more cooperation unless we get a search warrant, because he resents being questioned, and we'd need him to roll the truck backwards and forwards, to see the tire treads all the way around."

"Resents it, does he?" Cooper said. "Then absolutely get a search warrant—let's especially poke through DeWitt's personal office, this man who resents us investigating a murder."

Kalisha jotted a note on a pad she carried.

"A question about persons of interest," Kalisha said.

Right now, she said, they focused on Sonny DeWitt—what about other workers, like the outdoor crews?

Cooper thought a moment, then spoke.

"First, let's eliminate Sonny, the man with a motive," she said. "If we looked into all possibles, we'd bog down—there'd be the company's outside workers, but also delivery drivers and salesmen, repairmen, maybe people in Proctor's personal life, if he had any at this point."

Kalisha frowned and glanced at Mike.

"We noticed a high-school kid who leads tours there," she said. "He seems a little creepy."

Cooper remembered him, Vic Ledger, and his hamster-brained girlfriend, Winnie Rink. Hard to see how they'd benefit from Proctor Gibbs' death, but still....

"Use velvet gloves checking on them," she said. "Go after school kids too hard, you're likely to stir up the town—I know how it goes around here."

Kalisha jotted another note on her pad.

"Couple more things," Mike Bolknor said. "First, the trooper lab got back to us on that piece of fabric, the one clenched in the murdered woman's hand."

He told her what the lab found: probably the victim ripped a piece off her attacker's shirt, as they fought. Probably a Hawaiian style shirt, brand new, never washed. Rayon fabric, color's royal blue, with gold scallop shells.

Mike said they'd check local stores, see if any sold a shirt like that, although it could easily be bought online, in which case they'd never trace it.

"Also, we've got the metal sheath, from the murder knife," he said.

They knew the knife's brand. Surely bought online.

Local stores didn't carry it. They'd already checked. Tracking it would require high-level digital skills.

"On that, we're in luck," Mike said. "Darlene Bobowaski's coming back."

Cooper found Darlene a bit hard to take. Mainly because, as a genius, she disregarded normal social rules. Darlene studied cyber whatever, at Mt. Augustus College, just babble to Cooper, except she knew Darlene, way back at the end of her freshman year, had already surpassed all her professors. These days she showed up at the college just to finish her degree, otherwise migrating around the world to top digital research centers, taking on temporary projects and earning her college fees many times over. She'd soon graduate, choose among scores of job offers, already received, and then go upend the world.

She'd just returned from a month in Austria. Now, until classes started again in the fall, she worked at the new Artificial Intelligence Institute located on the campus. Cooper didn't want to hear about her project there, because it would only confuse her and leave her vaguely upset, a feeling of the world rocketing ahead, while Cooper North remained becalmed in the age of wristwatches with hands.

"Darlene's agreed to help Campus Security again, in her spare time," Mike said. "She'll dive into the internet, look for who sold that knife, and who bought it."

Cooper didn't hear what he said.

She lay now in a different bed, a long ago summer evening, with a sore throat and a fever, feeling peevish because—through her open bedroom window—she heard the shouts and laughing of her brother and other kids their age, playing, and she resented her exclusion.

She did a thing she'd been admonished by her mother never to do, no matter what. She shouted a curse.

A moment later her father came into the bedroom, just home from the family bank, so still sober.

"What's all this?" he demanded.

"It's not fair, being so sick!" she yelled, and then immediately swallowed, because yelling hurt her sore throat.

Silence from her father. She could feel him staring at her, disapproving.

"We don't complain, Soldier," he said. "We take whatever comes at us, whether it's a medal or a bullet, and we keep shut up about it—that's what a marine does!"

"I'm not a soldier, I'm not a marine! Just because you were!' she shouted. "I'm just a little girl."

Silence again. More than anything, she remembered the silence.

"I don't care if you're a little girl or a little bunny rabbit," her father said. "You're still a marine, and I want you to live by the code, Soldier!"

She opened her eyes to an empty hospital room. She heard the pinging of the pump.

Kalisha Rains and Mike Bolknor had slipped away, how long ago, she didn't know, except the light coming through her window had dimmed.

Her eyes closed and she slept, this time with no memories and no dreams.

42

Tip LaPerle and Mike Bolknor walked into Snowville Maple's lobby, empty except for a teen-aged receptionist. Her auburn hair reminded Tip of childhood Octobers, when Tenement Row kids, like him, searched under the trees out front for fallen horse chestnuts, so richly reddish-brown, so shiny, they seemed gems, worth millions, although they weren't even edible, too bitter. Pretty girl.

"We're here to see Sonny DeWitt," Tip told her.

She took in Tip's uniform, and her green eyes widened. Tip thought, she looks nervous.

"Mr. DeWitt went to Dill," the girl told them. "Be gone a couple of hours, that's what he said."

Tip considered showing her the search warrant, and telling her they'd be going through Sonny DeWitt's office.

However, she now looked frightened.

Just a kid, he thought. No need to give her conniptions. He supposed Mike Bolknor's size and granite-cliff face probably unnerved the girl as much as his own unform did.

"Okay," he told her. "We'll just go look at your company's Jeep, and wait for Mr. DeWitt to get back."

As they turned, to walk out the front door, Tip glanced back and saw her sitting behind her desk staring at them, wide-eyed.

Back outside, he looked at Mike, eyebrows up, meaning what did you make of that?

"We scared her," Mike said. "I wonder why?"

Tip followed him around the building, to where Mike remembered he and Kalisha Rains saw the company's Jeep parked. No Jeep now.

Quiet back here, just birdsong and the faint rumble of an engine, up in the maple orchard behind the building, and a thudding sound. It grew loader, and then the Jeep Gladiator's squared-off snout poked out of the woods, coming down a dirt trail cut into the trees, and they heard voices, talking, laughing, and saw the Jeep towed a wagon—source of the thudding, as it dropped into ruts—with a gaggle of tourists sitting in it, just back from a maple-forest tour.

"Kid who's driving, we told you about him," Mike said. "Acts vaguely hostile, nothing overt."

They watched the Jeep tow its wagon past them, the teen-aged driver moderately tall, trimly built, with a face held blank.

As the Jeep passed, the driver looked at them, unblinking. Then the Jeep towed its wagon along the building's side, turned left around the corner, and disappeared out front, ending the tour at the visitors' parking lot, where the tourists left their cars.

"Did you get his name?" Tip asked.

"Cooper told us—it's Vic Ledger," Mike said. "That receptionist's his girlfriend, Winnie Rink, both from here in Snowville."

"Yeah, well, they're just schoolkids," Tip said. "Hard to believe they'd kill Proctor Gibbs, with wasps in his sleeves, no less."

Mike shrugged.

Policing in New York, he'd seen all kinds of unbelievable atrocities that were, nevertheless, real.

Abruptly the day dimmed, and both men looked up—a cloud bank, dark-gray, had slid in from the west, low enough to clip the western mountain range's tallest peaks, and now it blocked the sun. A schizophrenic sky, its western half iron gray, its eastern half blue and sunny, but the cloud wall—driven by winds aloft—moved rapidly eastward, soon to cover the entire sky.

A sudden gust tried to steal Tip's uniform hat, but he jerked up his hand and saved it.

"It's going to rain," he said.

They started around the side of the building, where the Jeep had driven, and reached the front parking lot just as passengers climbed out of the wagon, fanning out to their parked cars, with out-of-state plates.

Another gust, and brown dust swirled up from the Jeep's cargo bed.

"That's sawdust," Mike said. "Kalisha and I saw that, when we were here before."

Vic Ledger watched without interest as the last passengers climbed out of the wagon. He slid back into the Jeep, behind the steering wheel, just as Mike and Tip walked up. He glanced at them, then looked away and started the Jeep's engine.

"Hold it," Tip said.

Ledger swung his head around, something cold in his eyes.

"I've got work to do," he said.

"So do we," Tip said. "We're investigating a murder."

Ledger stiffened, almost invisibly, his face as emotionless as a snake's face.

"Anyone here have it in for Proctor Gibbs?" Tip asked. "Maybe had a grievance?"

Ledger's face subtly relaxed, as if he'd anticipated a different question.

Tip thought: maybe he got his girlfriend to steal front-office paperclips or printer paper for him, to do his homework, and he thought we're after him for that, but he didn't murder Proctor Gibbs. He's just a kid.

Ledger shrugged.

Somehow, the gesture seemed disrespectful, as if it meant, grievance against Proctor Gibbs? Stupid question. If you tried to pinpoint why it seemed disrespectful, though, you couldn't. Tip couldn't, anyway.

"Why kill old Gibbs?" Ledger said. "He was just a grandpa, with a big white mustache."

"We need to check this Jeep's tires," Tip said.

"I told you, I've got work to do," Ledger said.

Tip decided Vic Ledger irritated him. Nothing he could name. An underlying attitude. He glanced at Mike Bolknor, but couldn't tell if the boy irked him, too. What the big man thought, or felt, Mike kept to himself. Tip wished he had that ability. Right now, he fought an urge to get in this boy's face.

"We need to check these tires," Mike Bolknor said. "Right now."

He sounded neutral. No anger or threat in his voice. Just stating the situation. Something about the man's size, maybe, kept Ledger from protesting. He made no attempt to drive on, just sat behind the steering wheel, staring out the Jeep's windshield.

Bolknor took the front tires, Tip checked the rear tires, both men pulling out their cell phones and using the built-in flashlights to light up the tire treads.

Nothing to be seen.

"Okay, roll this Jeep ahead, just a foot or so," Mike told Ledger, eyeing the tires.

"Stop!" he said.

Now the section of the tires previously underneath, pressed against the macadam and hidden, had rolled into view. Tip and Mike resumed examining the treads, using their cell-phone flashlights.

Tip abruptly stood upright. Bolknor, crouched over the right-front tire, looked back at him, and Tip used his chin to signal, look at this. Bolknor straightened and walked back to where Tip stood, and he looked where Tip pointed.

For a half minute, both men stood looking at the tire. Then Tip used his cell phone to snap pictures of the tread, various angles.

"Well," he said, "The plot thickens."

Bolknor looked thoughtful.

"We'll need to change how we look into all these things," he said.

He walked up to the open driver-side window and silently studied Vic Ledger, who sat looking stonily ahead through the windshield.

"Who here drives this Jeep?" Bolknor asked. "Besides these tours?"

Ledger rolled up his eyes, bored with these questions.

"Everybody drives it," he said. "Like, you need to drive over to Dill, to get a bigger wrench, or something."

He lowered the driver-side visor.

"Key's kept up here," he said. "Everybody knows."

Mike nodded.

"Anyone here been using this truck to chainsaw fallen limbs, up in the woods, haul them out?" he asked.

Ledger stared ahead through the windshield, his silence suggesting the question was stupid and obvious and an annoyance.

"No," he said finally. "No work like that, chainsaws, not this summer, not since I've worked here."

Bolknor glanced at LaPerle, who nodded.

"Okay," Bolknor told the boy. "Drive away, do your work, we'll talk to you again."

He and Tip watched the Jeep drive out of the parking lot, with the wagon rumbling behind, and disappear around the side of the building.

Out on the highway, a car beeped. It beeped again, closer. And then a cherry-red Corvette sports car, top down, veered off the main road, beeping, and sped down the Snowville Maple, Inc., driveway and suddenly stopped nearly on the front-entrance's steps, with another loud blast on the horn. At the wheel sat a large man, well on the way to flab, with a drinker's reddened face, grinning at the Snowville Maple workers, gathering outside the front doors, drawn by the beeping.

"That's Sonny DeWitt," Bolknor told Tip.

43

Grinning at his assembled employees, the new CEO of Snowville Maple, Inc., lurched out of his low-slung sports car, lost his balance, and slapped a hand on the hood to steady himself and stay upright.

"He's drunk," Tip thought.

Sonny waved a hand at the car, as if introducing an important visitor to the assembled staff.

"Hey, Worklings—meet my new Corvette!" he said.

More workers began hurrying in, from the sheds out back, drawn by the horn blasts. On the building's front stoop, Flute Wagner already stood beside Viola Wagner, both staring at the car, along with Winnie Rink, quickly joined by two gray-haired men, nearly seventy, wearing brown workpants and gray work shirts, one of them holding the wrench they'd been using on some part of the building's physical plant, the man without the wrench wiping his hands on his trousers and leaving shiny grease stains.

"Hey, she's a honey, right?" Sonny said, beaming. "Super deal—she's only three years old, hardly driven, like fresh from the showroom."

He stepped back and ogled his new car, jubilantly grinning

Tip, eyeing Flute Wagner on the porch, used his chin to point out the man to Mike.

"Whistle-blower, right?" Tip said. "In the Gibbs murder?"

It seemed to Tip that Flute Wagner stared at the Corvette as if he'd just been stomach punched, face sagging. Some painful memory? Viola Wagner, meanwhile, glared at Sonny DeWitt.

Sonny now leaned his backside against the Corvette's fender, arms crossed over his chest, basking in his audience's stares at his new car.

"So, you know, I own the company now? From Proctor's stock?" he said.

He shut his eyes and shook his head, as if his good fortune astonished him.

"Okay, there's child support," he said. "And I've got to keep my ex in caviar, but I've got left-over bucks, so now I can howl."

He flourished an arm, indicating the new car.

"Man," he said, grinning. "When my folks, downstate, they see me thunder home in this baby, well, they'll finally...."

A sudden loud clap of thunder, as if a bomb hit the parking lot.

Giant raindrops spattered on the macadam and on the Corvette, with its top down and its interior exposed.

"Damn!" DeWitt shouted.

He lurched to the driver's door, leaned in, and stared at the dashboard, clearly befuddled.

Tip looked at Mike Bolknor.

"Hit him with the search warrant?" he said.

Mike shook his head.

"Finding that Jeep..." he said. "We need to rethink."

269

Abruptly, the scattered giant raindrops became a downpour. Tip and Mike hurried up onto the building's porch, under the roof. Meanwhile, still at the open-top car, staring at the dashboard, Sonny DeWitt looked ready to sob.

Flute Wagner ran down from the porch, yelling "Start the engine!"

Sonny looked at him, then got in and started the car. Flute ran up and scanned the dashboard, then reached in and fingered a control. Now the Corvette's retractable hardtop began rising from behind the seats, unfolding, and dropping into place, keeping out the rain.

"Better roll up the windows," Flute said.

Sonny clenched his teeth, irritated, but he buzzed up the windows, sealing himself into the Corvette, as the rain poured down.

Flute Wagner, soaked now, ran back up onto the porch, where his wife stood glaring at Sonny, slouching behind his car's windows. She said something Tip couldn't hear, although her mouth's twist made it look like a snarl.

Tip took it in, but his thoughts were on their investigation.

"Okay, we'll put off searching DeWitt's office," he told Mike. "Probably nothing in there anyway."

Sonny DeWitt now lurched out of the car, slammed the door shut, and ran up onto the porch with everyone else. He pushed through the small crowd of workers to confront Flute Wagner, frowning down at him.

Tip thought: Thank the man!

Sonny obviously drove off in his just-bought car without learning its controls, and Wagner saved the Corvette's interior from a drenching.

"You had a Corvette yourself?" Sonny demanded, angry.

"Oh no," Wagner said. "I could never afford...."

Sonny interrupted.

"So, you reach in, grab my car's switches, whatever, when you know zilch about Corvettes?" DeWitt shouted. "Damn, you could've broken the thing!"

Tip saw that Viola Wagner, eyes fiery, meant to shout at DeWitt, but her husband put a hand on her arm, and spoke himself.

"I go to showrooms, Sonny," he said. "I sit in cars like this, learn the controls, sort of imagining...."

"Oh, beans!" DeWitt said.

He turned and pushed through the crowd and disappeared into the building.

For a moment, both LaPerle and Bolknor stood looking at the now closed door.

Tip finally spoke.

"This tire thing," he said. "Let's get Cooper's take, how to handle it."

Mike glanced at his wristwatch.

"Tomorrow," he said. "I'm due at the recreation path in twenty minutes, meeting someone for a run."

Tip wondered: run with who? He suddenly remembered the child he and Marge fostered, Thor Ennis, because at lunch he'd watched Thor run with Cooper's corgi, Henry. Mike cared for the dog, with Cooper hospitalized, but he routinely left him with Thor for the summer day, Henry being Thor's best friend.

Tip had promised Thor a hospital visit. How much longer could he stall?

Cooper once protected this orphaned boy from terrible danger. Thor said little, but he clearly now worshipped her. Could he withstand seeing her ravaged by leukemia, and by chemotherapy?

Tip worried about this boy's emotional stability. Yet, he'd promised....

Just drizzling now. As they walked to the cruiser, Tip looked up and saw the dark cloud bank hurrying eastward, leaving blue sky behind, the sun turning the western peaks golden.

"Cooper's got me worried sick," he muttered.
"Actually, I'm scared."

44

Cooper North willed herself to sit up in bed, then swing her feet over the floor. Unsteadily, she stood. She shuffled three weak steps, pushing the Christmas tree pole, its bags of medicine swinging. Finally, she turned and dropped into a chair.

They'll see me sitting up, she thought. Not slumped against pillows.

I'm not gone yet.

She wore the required hospital johnny, apparently designed to maximize humiliation. She'd brought a thick bathrobe from home, which she wore over the johnny, so they'd see at least a semblance of her former self. Except that the chemo had taken away her hair, and she wore a purple African-style head scarf, given to her by her oncology nurse, Emma Ford, who'd tied it around her head for her, just so.

When they knocked, she tried to speak firmly.

"Come in."

It sounded to her like a sigh.

They filed in, all surgically masked, as Emma's sign taped to her door required. Tip, Mike, Kalisha, and Ozzie Knick. She'd told Emma she needed three extra seats for visiting associates, besides the two chairs that came with the room, and Emma produced them, folding card-table chairs, but good enough.

Before she left, Emma stopped at the door and looked back.

"Give 'em hell, Sweetheart!" she said.

Then she gave Cooper her dazzling smile, which lingered in Cooper's mind, as her team walked in.

Cooper checked their faces, as they took their seats, what she could see above the masks. Pitying eyes would irritate her. None of that, though. They knew how she wanted it. All business. Even Kalisha.

"We've got a complication," Tip told her.

Ozzie muttered: "Or maybe a simplification."

"So?" Cooper said.

She watched them tacitly decide who would speak. Ozzie looked ready for the job, or any job, but kept silent, still a junior member of the team. It occurred to Cooper, in a sudden upwelling of emotion, how much these people meant to her, each of them, even Ozzie, though he'd imagined himself the new state's attorney. It hadn't turned out that way, but Cooper felt he'd swallowed it and he'd come to accept her, and respect her.

Even so, she thought of Proctor Gibbs, and she hoped, wryly, that Ozzie had no pet wasps to tuck into her sleeves.

"Coop, remember those tire tracks?" Tip said. "That slash mark across the tread?"

Three cases—maple log theft, alligator attack, murder of Olga Fisker. At each crime scene, tread marks from the same truck, one tire cut by a sharp stone, leaving a shallow slash. Like a fingerprint.

"We found the truck," Tip said.

He made the thumbs-up sign.

"It's the Jeep Gladiator, at Snowville Maple, Inc."

Cooper thought: there's our hub.

All the crimes started at Snowville Maple.

Proctor Gibbs' death, too, she thought. No truck used for that, but she now felt sure, a Snowville Maple employee killed him. At least, someone connected to the company.

Possibly a business rival?

Snowville wasn't the state's only maple-syrup distributor, and when you included Quebec.... Still, if Proctor died, everyone at the company knew, one Snowville employee would win big. Now, he actually had won big. Focus on him, she thought.

Hey, Coop--what's our battle plan?" Tip said.

She'd always been the investigation strategist. This time, she needed to deploy her limited troops on four fronts.

No, she thought. Three fronts.

"Forget the alligator attack," Cooper said. "That was just practice, to knife Olga Fisker."

Olga's murder bothered her the most. Because she'd admired the brilliant scientist up in the tree, but also it wasn't a grudge killing. Cooper had the Dill PD and Mike Bolknor's campus police check out Olga's life. No spurned boyfriends. No envious rivals. Nothing. No reason to kill her.

So psychopaths did it, for the thrill. To satisfy the urge. Now they'd need to slaughter again. Because slithering cobras hissed in their heads, and mambas.

She shut her eyes, to think. After a moment, she opened her eyes again.

"First, we've got that maple-log heist," she said.

Ozzie Knick turned up his eyes. A nothing case. A frat prank. He wanted a murder to dig into.

"You're right, Ozzie, log rustling is trivial," Cooper said, startling Ozzie, as if she'd read his thoughts, which she had done, in a way.

"Every case, same truck, so it all dovetails, same cast of characters," she said. "Each case could offer clues to the others—no truck for the Gibbs murder, but that one, too."

They all looked at her, waiting. It had been like this all her career. She gave the directions.

Mike Bolknor needed no guiding hand, an experienced big-city detective, and yet he did. Because he hadn't marinated in this small town, and she had.

"So we'll start with the swiped logs," Cooper said. "Tip?"

He made a disgusted face.

"Yeah, I get my morning call, Cappy Dixon's loving voice, 'Hey, LaPerle—I pay your damned taxes!" He shook his head. .

"His cigar even stinks over the phone."

Kalisha raised both hands.

"Mike and I have a lead for you," she said.

They'd met Sonny DeWitt's friends, at Snowville Maple, she said. Three clowns. Mike mentioned the sawdust in the truck's bed.

"From what they said, DeWitt and his pals use the Jeep at night," Mike said. "Drinking while driving, and other adventures."

Cooper remembered DeWitt's ex-wife, Sheila Cassidy, telling her that Sonny still hung with his high school buddies, whom she described as jerks.

"Just a minute," Cooper said.

She rummaged in the papers spread on her bed and finally pulled out a sheet.

"Sonny listed his friends' names for me," she said. "Addresses, phone numbers."

She handed the list to Tip.

She said: "Ozzie, you help Tip on this one, let's get it done fast."

Then she shut her eyes again.

She thought, yes, you Ozzie. Because I've known Caspar Dixon all his loud-mouthed, obnoxious life, and he'd browbeat Kalisha, a woman, and black, and then Tip would explode, and it wouldn't be productive. And just being a guy, and closer in age than Tip is, you'd have better insight into DeWitt's clown friends, if you question them.

She opened her eyes.

"Olga Fisker's our main focus," she said. "Gibbs' murder was a one-off, but Olga's killers will kill again, and again—we've got to stop them."

She leaned back in her chair, again shutting her eyes.

Not thinking now. Drifting. Sinking, deeper....

A voice in her mind, her own voice, shouted, "No!" Her eyes snapped open.

She saw them looking at her, waiting, worrying, and she let them look a moment, swimming up from the fog.

Were the log thieves also Olga Fisker's murdering psychopaths? It didn't quite fit. Yet, it could be.

"Mike, you and Kalisha, focus on the Fisker murder," she said.

Mike nodded.

"Darlene Bobowaski's due in," he said. "She'll fish for us, in the computer—that fabric swatch, and the murder knife, and we got crime-scene analyses, from Karen Del Vecchio, at the State Police Lab...."

Cooper leaned back in her chair. Once again, she shut her eyes.

"Keep me posted, everything you find," she said, her voice weakening. "I'll be mulling it all."

A silent moment.

"Thank you," she said.

She didn't hear them filing out. Not really knowing she did it, she shuffled back to her bed.

Bone marrow biopsy.

An ugly sound.

Dr. Lopez would be coming any day now, to do it.

45

Ozzie Knick thought: this isn't Queens.

No traffic roar from over on Astoria Boulevard. No shop-lined streets. No jets, to and from LaGuardia and JFK.

Stillness, and a scent of sawn wood.

Up on the mountainside, a rivulet trickled. Thrushes sang, like ethereal harps.

Ozzie thought: you could go nuts out here. No action.

Tip LaPerle had stopped his SUV cruiser at the log-theft site, to check for anything he missed before. Now he crisscrossed the clearing, stooped over, staring at the ground.

Ozzie made an effort to help look, then stood aside, feeling the emptiness—forest all around, deserted back road, huge logs piled a story high. He sensed the logs' weight, and imagined the muscle and sweat it took to chainsaw these trees, trim them, then snake the logs down the mountain and heap them here for hauling to sawmills.

Since he'd come to Dill, just a few months ago, he'd spent his days in towns, or driving main highways. This was his first real foray into the mountains.

Culture shock.

Tip straightened, looking resigned.

"Let's go hear Cappy Dixon curse taxes," he said.

Ozzie climbed into the cruiser thinking how the road leading here branched off from another obscure back road, then twisted through woods. It would twist on through white pines and balsam firs and sugar maples, passing a few summer homes, connecting to a series of back roads, some paved, some dirt.

A maze.

They'd seen no other vehicles.

"You drive back here much?" Ozzie asked.

"We don't patrol this far out," Tip said. "I'm using the GPS."

"Traffic on these roads?" Ozzie said.

"Just logging crews," Tip said. "Land's mostly posted, or it's steep, up a mountainside, so even in hunting season…."

Tip turned the SUV onto a paved road, slightly broader, drove a half mile, then stopped at a tin-roofed ranch house, serving as an office building, painted blue, with pickup trucks in various colors and ages parked in front, surrounded by a cleared area, several acres, where big machines roared between log piles.

Over the building's doorway, a sign: "Caspar Dixon Lumber Company."

Ozzie thought the machines looked like dinosaurs, rushing to heaps of newly harvested logs, unloaded from trucks. Bending down their long steel necks, the machines lifted mouthfuls of logs, pivoted, then hurried to spit them out atop one of the existing storage piles.

Some of the machines crawled on tank-style tracks, others rolled on giant wheels, heavily lugged. More machines rested on flatbed trailers, ready for hauling to logging sites.

"That's a shovel logger," Tips said, pointing to a steel tyrannosaurus.

Ozzie watched it drop a mouthful of logs onto a pile.

"Over there's a knuckle-boom loader," Tip said.

This one looked like a giant steel insect, standing on four legs, lifting a mouthful of huge logs as if they were toothpicks.

Both men watched the machines, listening to the industrial din. Ozzie surprised himself—he wanted to climb into a cab, work the controls. Law, he thought, in a rare moment of self-doubt, what a dust-dry way to pay for groceries.

No, he thought. It's not so simple. It's not true.

"Fun's over," Tip said. "Let's go hear a citizen complain."

Inside, the office reeked of Cappy Dixon's cigar smoke.

Ozzie felt his throat swelling.

He thought the burly man behind the desk, with a whiskery face and a big cigar stuffed in his mouth, knew the smoke's stench offended visitors, and he liked it, because it gave him an edge.

"You finally catch those creeps?" Dixon demanded.

"We're working on it, Cappy," Tip said.

Dixon's eyes flared, ready to take the Dill PD to task, but Ozzie spoke first.

"That road past the robbery site," he said. "Hardly anybody drives by there, right?"

"So what?" Dixon said.

He eyed Ozzie as if he'd suddenly noticed an earwig crawling up his green-and-yellow plaid shirt's flannel sleeve.

"It's about the odds," Ozzie said.

Dixon sucked in smoke from his cigar and then expelled it, as if spitting the smoke out.

"Mostly, only your own crews drive past that theft site," Ozzie said. "Suddenly, though, here comes a truckful of crooks, with a fueled-up chainsaw?"

Ozzie saw Tip LaPerle staring at him, following his thought. Dixon, however, scowled.

"Go do something real!" he said.

Even inside the building they heard the roar of the log-moving machines.

Ozzie thought: he's invested millions in all that equipment, and more millions in salaries and benefits and insurance, plus hefty interest payments on loans, so he's up to his stinky cigar in worry—it makes him irritable.

Aloud, he said; "Odds are, these guys knew about that log pile, and drove straight to it—they planned this out."

Dixon stared at him, for once mute.

"They didn't do it for money," Ozzie said. "They just dumped the logs up the road, in somebody's driveway."

Dixon's eyes narrowed, thinking. He'd stopped drawing on his cigar.

Ozzie thought: something about this guy, not bothering to shave, that cigar. I bet he never married, or he's divorced.

No, he thought. He is married. He's married to the Caspar Dixon Lumber Company. And stealing his logs, that's like stealing his wife. So he's really ticked.

"What are you getting at?" Dixon demanded.

"Those logs were worth only piggybank change," Ozzie said. "Cutting them up, hoisting them onto their truck—that's heavy work for a few coins."

"So?" Cappy said.

"They stole the logs to poke you in the eye," Ozzie said. "Guys with a grudge."

Out the corner of his eye, Ozzie saw Tip LaPerle nodding.

"Competitors?" Tip said. "Hassles with any of them?"

Dixon pulled his cigar from his mouth and held it up in front of his eyes, to inspect. It had gone out. He reached into a pocket of his jeans and pulled out a wooden matchstick, which he flicked with a grimy fingernail, igniting it, and then used it to relight his cigar.

"Nah, peaceable kingdom, us loggers," he said. "Hell, we even loan each other equipment, you get a breakdown."

He inhaled, making his cigar's end flare red, then blew the smoke out.

Ozzie felt his throat swell even more.

"What about men working here?" Tip asked.

Dixon shook his head, looking like a bear shaking off honeybee stings.

"I pay top wages," he said. "Woodchucks, they stick with me, okay?"

Ozzie guessed "woodchucks" must be Yankee slang for "lumberjacks."

All three men sank back in their chairs, Dixon furiously smoking. Ozzie felt let down. He'd been sure he had the right slant. Now it seemed they'd hit a dead end. Where to go from here, he had no idea.

"All right," Tip said finally. "We'll look into it some more."

Ozzie knew they wouldn't look into it more. They had nowhere to look.

Tip and Ozzie both got up, nodded to Dixon and walked to the door. Tip opened it, and the industrial din suddenly got much louder.

"Hey, wait right there!" Dixon shouted behind them.

They waited while he pulled open a desk drawer, then leafed through hanging files. Abruptly he pulled one out, opened it, and searched through the printouts inside, until he finally pulled one out and held it up.

"Yeah, I forgot," he said, squinting at the document. "Two or three weeks ago, I fired this idiot."

He told them he'd sent a new hire out on his own, in a company pickup, to collect a chainsaw left at the site where logs would later be stolen. Iffy, this new man, a dubious hire. Apparently didn't even own a car, had to have friends drive him to work. Dixon decided to drive over himself, to check on the guy.

"Jerk!" Dixon said.

He found his new employee sitting on his pickup's front bumper, drinking beer from a can. Parked beside the pickup, a beat-up convertible. Sitting on the pickup's front bumper, beside the new employee, two pals of his, also drinking beer.

Dixon slammed on his brakes and stormed out of his truck. All three lounging on the bumper held up their beer cans, a demented greeting.

"I'm Possum," one man said brightly.

"Walrus here," the guy sitting next to him said.

"You know me," the employee said. "Beast, remember?"

"Hey, man," Possum said. "Want a cold one?"

Emptied beer cans lay scattered around their feet. All three men crocked.

Dixon fired "Beast" right then. Told him to leave the company pickup where he'd parked it, and get the hell out in his buddies' rusty convertible.

"His pals drove him to work in that car wreck," he said.

Cappy, glowering, smoked, silent, then spoke again.

"No drinking on the job, that's the rule," Dixon now told Tip and Ozzie. "Jeezum, we've got chainsaws going, machines, trees falling, and this joker's getting wobbly— in the middle of the workday—and also not working."

Tip and Ozzie exchanged a look.

"Damn," Dixon said.

He shook his head, disgusted.

"What moron calls himself Beast?"

46

Numero Uno stopped on Hill Street, in Dill, across from a large brick house, federal design, with a Palladian parlor window.

A home with two-and-a-half centuries of stories to tell, although still perfectly maintained. Uno stared at the house through the truck's side window, annoyed.

"Doing one, right here in town?" Numero Dos said.

After a moment, Dos added: "Sort of risky, I guess, people around…."

Uno clenched his teeth harder.

"Bossy, that old woman," he said. "Had an attitude."

"So, we're going to do her?" Dos said.

"We were," Uno said. "I wasted time checking this place out, learning her schedule, figuring our moves."

"We're not doing her?" Dos said.

Disappointed.

Uno said nothing, staring at the house. Dos stayed silent, too, to ward off the ice-eye stare. Uno finally spoke.

"Old bat's got herself sick, in the hospital," he said. "She'll be there a long time—I called up, to ask, said I was her grandson, worried about her, and all."

He leaned back in the seat.

"So we aren't doing another one?" Dos said, disappointed.

"Who said we aren't?" Uno demanded.

He put the truck in gear and drove ahead, through the Mt. Augustus stone arch, onto the campus, then past classroom buildings and dormitories, and out on the campus's far side, a turn to the right, Maple Street. Single homes on this street, older, but kept up, with many of them converted to apartments, for college instructors to rent.

Uno stopped across from Number 25, engine running, and they both stared at the well-kept Victorian, painted salmon, with green trim, hiding behind a front-yard spruce.

"That's where that big cop lives," Uno said. "I followed him here one night."

"Wow," Dos said. "Are we going to do him?"

Uno gave her his stone-faced look. He let the silence grow. Finally he spoke, his voice toneless.

"What did we discuss about strategy?"

Silence while Dos stared at him, wide-eyed, thinking hard.

"Mountain lion?" Dos said. "Something about...."

Uno shook his head, disgusted.

"At least you remember that much," he said. "Question—do mountain lions prey on grizzly bears?"

Dos looked down, and spoke in a small voice.

"No?"

"That's right," Uno said. "Because the grizzly is bigger, and dangerous, and what?"

"Maybe the mountain lion would get hurt?" Dos said.

"And?"

Silence. Thinking. Then Dos's face brightened.

"Energy—spend a lot of energy—so mountain lions hunt, I don't know, a rabbit, maybe, or a deer?"

"Yeah, a deer," Uno said.

He put the truck back in gear and drove on down Maple Street, slowly, stopping again, one block down. Another well-maintained Victorian, this one painted green, with yellow trim, and a forsythia bush out front, in flower.

"Woman working with that bossy old bat, she lives here," he said. "Black woman."

Dos stared at the house, squeezed between two other Victorians, one painted tan, the other blue.

"She's up on the second floor," Uno said.

Dos stared, brow furrowed.

"How do we do it?" Dos said. "Without, you know, people living there seeing us, hearing…?"

Uno gave her a cold look.

"We choose our battlefield, remember?" Uno said. "Play to our strengths?"

"Oh," Dos said.

They sat in silence, Dos unwilling to risk a question.

"Just about every evening, she goes walking on the Dill recreation path," Uno said. "Path runs between trees and bushes, thick on both sides, mostly isolated."

"Cool" Dos said.

"Ninja attack, out of the bushes," Uno said.

He sat back.

"Shock and awe," he said. "Advantage, us."

He opened the between-seats storage bin. He took out the commando knife, and looked at it, turning the blade, so it caught the sunshine through the window.

"I've ordered a new metal sheath," he said. "Our first one got lost, remember? By a dummy?"

47

Cooper North lay in her hospital bed, eyes closed, but awake, thoughts running through her mind, like Tip LaPerle's call a half hour ago, asking if he could bring his and Marge's foster child, Thor Ennis, to visit tomorrow, because he didn't want to put the boy off any longer.

Yes, she thought. Wait too long and there may be no Cooper for Thor to visit.

She felt no bitterness in that thought, no emotion at all, just a facing of reality.

Then she thought about Henry, with his bright corgi eyes and his corgi grin, and his corgi glee. Mike Bolknor said Henry spent these summer days with Thor Ennis, the two of them pals. Maybe she'd never see Henry again, and that did sadden her.

So she focused on work, the Snowville Maple, Inc., investigations.

Except for Proctor Gibbs' murder by sting, each case involved the syrup company's Jeep Gladiator truck.

Cooper abruptly sat up in bed.

That truck.

Not long ago a Jeep truck idled across from her house, on Hill Street. Was it the Snowville Maple truck? Had she been under surveillance?

Which meant what?

She'd visited Allister Chesterton. A few nights later, they tried to kill him. He escaped only because he'd set up his home as a fortress.

Olga Fisker.

She visited Dr. Fisker. A few days later, they killed her.

Cooper thought: if I visit, do you die? If I know you, are you targeted?

She reached for the bedside phone and punched in Mike Bolknor's number, first at the college, then at home. No answer in either place. Then she remembered: he now ran most evenings, at the recreation path. She called his cell, but he didn't pick up. Left it in his car, she thought.

Kalisha! Ozzie!

She dialed the State's Attorney office and got Ozzie Knick. She told him her fear. Silence a moment, while he thought about it.

"All right," he said. "Consider me on guard."

"Good, now Kalisha," she said. "I need to warn her, too."

"She's walking on the recreation path," Ozzie said. "She goes every evening, you know, to unwind."

"Cell phone?" Cooper said.

She heard rummaging sounds, Ozzie looking through the paperwork on Kalisha's desk.

"Actually, she left the phone here, on her desk," he said. "She didn't take it with her."

Cooper felt a chill.

"It's all surmise, though," Ozzie said. "She's just taking a walk."

Cooper felt dread.

292

"Ozzie," she said. "Get in your car, go fast to the recreation path, run along it, find her, tell her, be with her!"

Silence over the phone. Then Ozzie's voice again.

"Okay, Cooper, I'm on it."

A click, Ozzie hanging up. Cooper listened to the dial tone.

Who else, she wondered?

Would they dare attack Mike Bolknor?

No, maybe with a gun, but not up close, with a knife.

They'd be sorry.

Tip LaPerle? Chief of police? No, ridiculous.

Thor Ennis?

She sighed.

That seven-year-old saw his mother destroyed by drugs, and murdered. Her murderers then hunted him. How much trauma could he withstand?

She hadn't visited Thor, though. Not since these killings began. So if they actually did watch her, Thor wouldn't be on their radar screen.

Then she remembered: the *Dill Chronicle* had reported Thor's story, including Cooper protecting the orphan, and finally Tip and Marge LaPerle taking him in, as a foster child, so....

Cooper lay back against her pillows and shut her eyes.

She thought: am I an alarmist? Or a Typhoid Mary?

As a child, she'd had a dog, a border collie, Maureen. With a father, a decent man, but alcoholic, and a mother who maintained the New England keep-your-distance tradition, little Cooper basked in Maureen's openly expressed affection. Maureen, meanwhile, kept constant

watch over Cooper, convinced the girl's well-being depended on collie vigilance.

Cooper thought: am I a border collie?

That amused her.

And she thought: if Thor Ennis wants to visit me, good.

I need his grit.

Still, the Maureen in her worried.

48

Kalisha Rains walked along the Dill Recreation Path, listening to warblers and goldfinches. They sang unseen, hidden in the shrubs and trees lining the path's sides, green walls of foliage, dense as a jungle. No jaguars lurking, though, Kalisha thought. Or anacondas.

This stroll wasn't exercise—for that, she worked out at the Dill Keep-Fit Health Club. She walked this path most evenings to shed stress, from evidence chains and affidavits. Instead of writs, and combative head-to-heads with defense attorneys, she watched maple and beech leaves wave in summer breezes.

As she walked, she let her thoughts wander.

Would she, in this small northern town, find a boyfriend? Did she want to, at this point in her young life, just starting her career? Mostly, though, Cooper North filled her mind.

Leukemia.

She felt Cooper's danger as a weight in her chest, and she felt it in her vision, too, as if thick clouds darkened the day. Her last visit with Cooper shocked her. Always nearly gaunt, Cooper now looked emaciated, lying inert in that hospital bed, weakened, weary, yet those eyes seeing you, clearly, and seeing into you.

WHEN THE WASP STINGS

Kalisha came to Dill just a few months ago, after law school, mainly to work with Cooper, to learn from a woman she admired, more than anyone she'd ever known.

Cooper, gone—imagining that, she felt lonely, alone.

She walked now along the path's most isolated section, its center point. Through the bushes on her right, she saw bright glints, sunlight on Beecham Creek. To her left, a break in the thick foliage, the only break, a maintenance shed, where crews stowed tools and a small tractor, with an attached mower for summer, and a snowblower, to be hooked on in winter.

It seemed spooky, this little stone structure, backed into the trees and shrubs, moss growing in the seams of its tin roof.

Kalisha abruptly stopped, to listen. Footsteps. Far behind her, hurrying up the path. Rubber-soled sneakers slapping the path's macadam.

A runner.

Good, she thought. So I won't be alone.

She always felt faintly uneasy, in this isolated section of the path, and she felt uneasy now. Cool it kid, she told herself. This isn't Philly.

Her adoptive family lived in the suburbs, but she'd often walked along city streets at night, coming from an art show, maybe, or a concert, or from the city library. Hardly knowing she did it, she'd constantly scanned for threats, behind her, and in darkened doorways she passed, and she habitually packed protection into her pockets.

Those running footsteps behind her sounded just a bit closer.

A yell.

Startled, she looked toward the sound and saw a tiny red squirrel perched on the maintenance shed's metal

roof, berating her, its fur puffed up. It apparently amused the squirrel to hurl imprecations at a passerby. Kalisha smiled, amused herself. To be yelled at by a rodent.

Abruptly the squirrel went silent in mid scream, and twisted to look into the bushes behind the shed. It yelped, then leapt to a lower branch in an adjacent butternut tree and disappeared silently upwards, into the foliage.

"Wow, am I that scary?" Kalisha thought, but immediately saw it wasn't her who startled the squirrel, because the bushes next to the shed thrashed, and then a figure wearing black, masked in black, thrust out from the foliage, followed by a taller figure dressed the same, and gripping a large knife.

"Get her, get her!" the shorter figure screamed. "No, no, let me do it—my turn!"

For a moment, the taller Ninja stared at Kalisha. Then he handed the knife to his partner, and that shorter Ninja came at her.

Kalisha froze, for just a fraction of a second—she'd practiced for attacks like this, on Philadelphia's dark nighttime streets. She reached into her track shorts' left pocket and drew out a red whistle, which she stuck into her mouth and blew.

It screeched, piercing, high pitched.

It stopped the Ninja with the knife, eyes wide, startled. No protector came. So the Ninja resumed the attack. Kalisha reached into her shorts' right pocket, pulling out a metal tube, meanwhile producing another screeching blast on the whistle.

Out of the tube in Kalisha's hand issued a spray, which caught the attacking Ninja in the face, eyes and mouth both visible through openings in the ski mask.

Now the footsteps that had been running up the path seemed louder, almost upon her, and she heard a yell.

"Hey!"

She knew that voice.

A moan from the knife wielder, hunched over, free hand rubbing eyes, coughing. "Kalisha, I'm coming!"

Ozzie!

Kalisha saw the taller Ninja glance at his hunched partner, then at Ozzie, pelting up the trail.

A muttered curse, like a growl—he grabbed the knife from his partner's hand, started toward Kalisha, then looked again at the running Ozzie, and cursed again, as Ozzie charged him.

"No, Ozzie," Kalisha yelled. "He's got a knife."

Ozzie dove low, aiming for the knees, but the Ninja stepped aside and Ozzie sprawled on the macadam. Kalisha saw the Ninja taking in the situation—just steps to the targeted victim, her protector prone on the path. Decision made, he started toward Kalisha, knife raised to strike.

Kalisha aimed her pepper spray cannister at him and pressed the button. Nothing. Emptied. Ozzie started scrambling up, ready to attack again, but just then, coming down the path from the other side, heavy footsteps and Mike Bolknor suddenly loomed, seeming a giant, with a woman running beside him.

Bolknor didn't stop, but ran toward the Ninjas, just as the taller attacker grabbed his partner and ran crashing into the bushes, shoving his half-blinded partner ahead of him.

"Are you all right?" Bolknor asked Kalisha.

She nodded.

He looked at Ozzie, now half up, saw he was uninjured, and then ran into the bushes, after the fleeing Ninjas, but immediately slowing, forcing his way forward as branches tangled around his legs and waist. They heard him thrashing, and after a half minute the thrashing stopped.

A moment later Mike emerged from the bushes, shaking his head.

"Couldn't get through all that brush," he said. "Smaller and skinnier, apparently, gave them the edge."

From previous explorations, Kalisha knew the vegetation-covered ground slanted up, until it came to a secondary road. From up there, they heard a vehicle's engine roar, and then tires screech, as it sped away.

"You're all right?" the woman with Mike asked.

She looked fit, with black hair cut short, and alert eyes. Striking, actually.

Kalisha nodded.

"This is Karen Del Vecchio, from the state police crime lab," Mike said, looking from Kalisha to Ozzie, making sure neither had been damaged.

Ozzie shook his head, disgusted.

"I screwed that one up," he said.

Kalisha looked at him, and reached out, resting a hand on his arm.

"You were wonderful," she said.

She repeated it silently, to herself.

Wonderful.

Tears now trickled down. Because the attack's shock was over, and because of what she'd just learned.

In this town far in the north, to which she'd only recently moved, she felt warmed, surrounded by friends, protected.

She looked at Ozzie and suppressed an urge to kiss him.

"That smaller Ninja," she told everyone. "That voice."

She had no doubt.

"A woman's voice," she said.

"Maybe a girl's."

49

Cooper watched Emma Ford attach new chemotherapy bags to the bedside pole.

"Your last infusions," Emma said. "For this round, anyway."

She added: "You've got no bone marrow left, Dear."

Cooper supposed that must be good, in a way, because her bone marrow produced the mutant leukemic cells.

"More rounds ahead, but now we wait," Emma said. "Until your marrow grows back."

If it does, Cooper thought.

She believed in realism—face what you must.

"Dr. Lopez will be in next week," Emma told her, attaching the last bag. "To do your bone-marrow biopsy."

Cooper sighed.

Maybe, in whatever shreds of her marrow remained, the biopsy would show no leukemic cells. Remission. Or it could show only weird cells, the treatment failed, to be followed soon by an obituary.

"I'll be with you for the biopsy," Emma said, on her way out. "I'll be here."

Cooper sat alone, thinking about a second round of treatment, and then a third. After that, maybe a fourth, if her savaged body could withstand it.

"My dangerous chemical companions," she thought, wryly.

A knock on the door stopped her brooding.

Her colleagues filed in, to report on their investigations, and decide what to do next.

Cooper thought: an hour's escape from leukemia.

Ozzie Knick appointed himself speaker, and he got up from his chair and paced as he talked, as if addressing a jury, which amused Cooper, just a bit

Describing the Ninja attack on Kalisha, he stood behind her chair, supportively resting his hands on her shoulders, which interested Cooper. She'd always sensed some competitiveness between these two young attorneys, especially on Ozzie's part. He'd begun work here before Kalisha arrived, but she'd quickly proved herself equally bright, although—unlike Ozzie—not aiming to step into the state's attorney position, certainly not right out of law school. Ozzie, on the other hand, had a year's prosecutorial experience, in New York.

Cooper thought: you like Ozzie's hands on your shoulders, don't you, Kalisha.

"What he's not saying," Kalisha now told Cooper, "is that he *threw* himself, straight at that Ninja!"

Cooper thought: "Aha."

And she thought: You saw Kalisha attacked, Ozzie. Did you feel something you hadn't known you felt?

She thought about Kalisha, too. Raised by a white family, but not white. Yet, foreign to Black culture— when Kalisha met Emma Ford, she'd hesitated, not sure what to say or how to say it, and Cooper noticed.

302

Always apart, Cooper thought now. Subtly maybe, but separated, from everyone around you.

Cooper thought: Ozzie, you be her friend.

Then she thought about Ninjas.

"They'll need to strike again," she said. "Snakes in their brains, they'll have to."

She leaned back against her pillows and shut her eyes. That biopsy....

She opened her eyes.

"Let Proctor Gibbs' murder slide, for now," she said. "We'll focus on the Ninjas."

Tip LaPerle shook his head.

"That log theft, though," he said. "We've got the perps, just about sure."

He told her what he and Ozzie had found—Sonny DeWitt's three high-school buddies, one of them fired by an angry Cappy Dixon. Tip had no doubt they stole the logs.

Cooper said: "So where was Sonny DeWitt, while his three pals used his Jeep, for a felony?"

Tip shrugged.

"Heaving those logs onto the truck," he said. "Probably it took four men."

"Okay, go catch these idiots," Cooper said.

See if Sonny's part of it, she told them.

"It might be leverage for us, if he did kill Proctor," she said. "Keep that search warrant on ice, and when it's time, use it."

She fell back against her pillows, suddenly too fatigued to continue. She didn't want them to see her like this.

"Give me a moment to think," she said, trying to keep her voice above a croak, shutting her eyes.

She let her thoughts wander, but shooed them away from biopsy worries.

One of those Ninjas, a woman. Kalisha heard her voice. A woman, or a girl.

Abruptly, puzzle pieces reorganized in Cooper's mind, and she had a thought like a lightning flash.

I'm wrong!

It wasn't that the Ninjas watched me, targeting people I visited. No, they targeted people who visited Snowville Maple, including me. Or people they'd somehow run into.

That Jeep idling outside my house—they were checking where I lived. They planned to kill me.

But then they couldn't.

Ironic, she thought. Leukemia saved me. I got hospitalized.

Allister Chesterton visited Snowville Maple.

Olga Fisker? No, but a high-school biology class visited her, and two students wandered off. Checking out her house?

Ninjas drove Snowville Maple's Jeep.

Cooper opened her eyes.

"I think we've all suspected who the Ninjas must be," she said.

Everyone nodded.

"All right, but no arrests until we've got evidence," Cooper said. "Rock-solid."

She'd seen it before. A little town like this, down on its luck because the marble quarry closed, they'd rally around locals accused. They'd put the prosecutors and police on trial. It would be a mess.

"Evidence!" Cooper repeated. "Laser focus on that."

Mike Bolknor spoke.

"Karen Del Vecchio's keeps me updated on what the crime lab finds," he said. "Darlene Bobowaski starts tomorrow, doing deep-web digging for us."

Cooper nodded, then shut her eyes again and leaned back against the pillows.

Her last thought, before she slipped away: "Lo, a genius college girl shall lead them, unto the Land of Arraignment."

50

Tip LaPerle pounded his fist on the door.

After a while, the door opened, and a red-nosed man, gone to flab, with a blond walrus mustache, stared blearily at them, taking in Tip's blue uniform, then the digital recorder, small as a deck of cards, which Ozzie Knick carried in his left hand.

"Huh?" he said.

"Police business," Tip said. "We need to chat, you and your friends."

For a moment, Walrus Mustache stood transfixed, clearly reviewing his team's possible misdeeds, then emphatically shook his head.

"We totally don't speed, no way!" the man said. "It's like our sacred religion—exceed not thine limit! Hey, we worship at the altar of cruise control!"

Ozzie grinned.

"Traffic violations, not an issue," he said. "We're investigating a theft, need the public's help."

"Yeah?" the man said.

He swung the door open, and stood aside, to let them walk into the apartment.

"Welcome to our estate," he said. "Don't spill champaign on the Persian carpets."

Tip thought: you jerks live like this?

Emptied beer cans littered the floor, along with oily pizza boxes. A mangy t-shirt hung draped over a lamp, apparently to dry after a stab at laundering in the kitchen sink. Half-emptied bags spilled popcorn and Fritos and beef jerky onto the coffee table, where a medium-sized mixing bowl, serving as an ashtray, overflowed with butts.

A musty background stink.

Tip thought: "Pigpen."

A second man, bald, with a greasy red beard, lay on his back on the sofa, with one leg up over the sofa's backrest, tossing up popcorn kernels and trying to catch them in his mouth, but with most hitting his nose or missing his face altogether.

A third man, sprawled in a faded and frayed armchair, watched a soap opera unfolding on a small battered tv, but reduced the sound to a murmur and turned his head to take in the newcomers. He wore a porkpie hat, pulled down over his forehead, and round wire-rimmed glasses. His face, long, with a pointed chin, resembled an opossum's.

Ozzie faintly smiled, amused, but Tip saw nothing funny about three slobs in a sty. He'd started here in Tenement Row himself, but climbed far above it, with Cooper North's guidance, and the slovenliness disgusted him. Also, embarrassed him.

"I'm Walrus," the man with a walrus mustache told them.

"Good," Ozzie said, producing a notebook and pen from his summer-weight jacket's inner pocket. "What's your real name, Walrus?"

"Douglas Plokski," Walrus said, as Ozzie wrote the name in his notebook. "Dopey name, huh?"

Ozzie looked at the man in the armchair, and waited.

After a time, voice tired, the man gave his name.

"Possum."

Ozzie waited, and finally the man said his real name: "Martin Malloy."

After writing the name in his notebook, Ozzie looked enquiringly at the red-bearded member of the team, lying on the sofa.

"I'm Clifford Ticknor," the man said. "But my Secret

Service code name is 'Beast.'"

He tossed up another popcorn kernel, shifted his head, trying to catch it in his open mouth, but it hit his forehead and rolled off.

Ozzie glanced at Tip, meaning, that's the guy Caspar Dixon fired. Then he held up his recorder.

"Got tendonitis in my wrist, from note-taking," he said, thumbing the switch to "On." "Mind if I record our conversation, saves a lot of jotting, so okay?"

Beast looked at him blankly, then spoke.

"Hey, go for it."

Walrus-mustache shrugged, said "Yeah." Possum pulled his porkpie hat even further down over his eyes, and announced: "Guys, we'll be podcast celebs now— stars!"

"Great," Ozzie said, and slipped the faintly humming recorder into his jacket's outer pocket.

Out of sight, out of mind.

"By the way, good knowing you guys don't speed," Ozzie said to Walrus. "So many crazy drivers out there, right?"

"Yeah, we just crawl," Walrus said. "Because you blink, cops thumbtack a ticket to your forehead, like two-thousand bucks, every mph over the limit, Jeez!"

"Where'd you get those harsh facts?" Ozzie asked.

"Some guys we met, at the Donut Dive—that's down the street here," Beast said. "They told us, you go, like sixty in a fifty zone, that's twenty-thousand you owe, and if the cops don't get their boodle, because who can afford that, it's twenty years in the slammer, for crying out loud, no parole—that's what they said."

Ozzie said. "Wow, solid intel from the Donut Dive." Tip thought: these birds are morons.

"Speaking of driving, what're your wheels?" Ozzie said. "That old convertible parked out front?"

Beast, still lying on the sofa, snickered.

"Yeah, except at night," he said. "And weekends— our old football buddy, at the maple sugar place, we go cruising in his company Jeep, which is a primo ride."

"He trusts you with that truck?" Ozzie asked.

Beast snickered again.

"Hell no," he said. "He's got to chaperone, and he drives."

Tip gave Ozzie a look, now seeing where this line of questioning might be going. He thought: okay, Kid, you're sharp.

He tried a question of his own.

"What kind of high jinks do you boys get into," Tip asked. "Tearing around in that Jeep at night?"

"Not much," Beast said, suddenly wary. "Just fooling around."

Ozzie chuckled.

"Hear about Cappy Dixon? Got some logs heisted?" Ozzie said, shaking his head and grinning. "Mean loudmouth, finally got taken down—neat prank, so hats off to whoever pulled it off."

He chuckled again, as if it tickled him, that rich SOB lumber tycoon, getting his butt kicked, by some cool dudes.

Beast, still supine on the sofa, gave Ozzie and Tip a sly look.

He tossed up another popcorn kernel, and successfully caught this one in his mouth. Chewing, he winked.

"I could tell you who gets credit," he said.

"What," Ozzie said. "You heard gossip at the Donut Dive?"

Beast looked smug.

"Hah," Walrus said, pulling at his mustache's ends, two-handed. "Let's say we got it from eye witnesses."

Ozzie shook his head, dubious.

"Ah, tons of guys, probably, trying to get bragging rights," he said.

Tip shrugged.

"Yeah, half the town will claim credit," he said. "Kicking Dixon's butt."

Silence while Tip and Ozzie both grinned, shaking their heads, as if thinking with relish about Caspar Dixon's takedown. They let the silence grow, with Walrus and Beast looking ready to burst out with a secret.

On his tv chair, Possum got there first—he pulled his porkpie hat farther down, now entirely covering his face, then spoke up, from behind the hat.

"We did the butt kicking," he said. "Got him right in the timbers."

Tip and Ozzie exchanged a glance.

"Wait a minute," Ozzie said. "We heard there was a ton of logs hoisted onto a truck, and I don't believe just you three guys could have handled that, so…."

Beast sat up on the sofa, spilling popcorn that had collected on his shirt onto the cushions, and stared triumphantly at his guests.

"It wasn't just three of us," he said. "It was four of us, damn it, because Sonny DeWitt was right there with us—told you, he says no using the Jeep ourselves, so Sonny was in the thick of it, all right."

Ozzie looked down at his hands, to keep from laughing.

"Okay," he said. "I guess the credit's all yours, and Sonny's, too."

Everyone sat silently now, Beast, Walrus, and Possum basking in the memory of their nighttime caper, while Tip and Ozzie had different thoughts, such as whether to get out the handcuffs. Tip started to speak, but Ozzie held up a hand, signaling he had more to get out of the interview.

"You guys seem a fun-loving bunch," he said. "But there's Sonny, sweating at Snowville Maple, corporate slave labor, doesn't seem fair."

Possum pushed his hat back up and shook his head at Ozzie.

"You kidding?" he said. "He just got himself a fancy Corvette, for Pete's sake, and runs that company now, so he's sitting on top of the honey jar."

Ozzie bit his lower lip, thinking.

"Must have been something for him, working up there, knowing if old Proctor Gibbs kicked off, he'd be next in line, but Gibbs kept trucking along."

Beast lay back down on the sofa, and resumed trying to catch tossed popcorn in his mouth.

"Well, he really liked old Proc, that's what Sonny told us," Beast said. "Okay, he'd get a phone call from his folks, back home, and he'd go all sour, and he'd say, 'well, they'll see a different me, if Proctor Gibbs ever finally falls off a cliff.'"

"Hah!" Possum said, from under his porkpie hat. "He'd kid around, you know, like bring a tactical nuke to work, or stick dynamite under Proc's car seat, but that was jokes, right?"

Tip stood.

Ozzie stood, too.

"That's it for today," he said.

"What about that theft you're investigating?" Walrus said. "Needing help from the public and all?"

"Got to go right now, important law-and-order issues to see about," Ozzie said.

Tip said: "We'll be back in touch."

Tip and Ozzie said nothing more until they got out onto the sidewalk, beside the Dill PD cruiser they'd driven here.

"Let's see how Cooper wants this handled," Tip said.

"Yeah," Ozzie said, shaking his head. "These saps don't even know they committed a felony."

Tip said: "Meanwhile we've got Sonny DeWitt, driving the getaway Jeep…."

"And talking about offing his boss," Ozzie said. "Kidding around about it, I guess, but…."

"Yeah," Tip said. "But!"

51

Thor Ennis stood beside Tip LaPerle, staring at Cooper North in her hospital bed.

His face revealed nothing.

Cooper thought: he's like Mike Bolknor, locks it all inside.

Tip, not an especially tall man, towered over Thor. His blue uniform seemed to magnify him. So did his hip-holstered handgun.

He looks sinewy, and strong, Cooper thought, but there's pain in his face. And see how his mouth turns down.

She thought: he doesn't want the boy seeing me like this. Tip hates seeing me like this.

I'm skeletal now, I suppose, slumped against these pillows. And this steel post by my bed's creepy, festooned with bags of poison—every time the pump pulses, these medicines flow through plastic tubes, into the catheter imbedded in my chest.

With each pulse, the pump beeps.

I don't hear it anymore.

Beep....

I think Tip wants to cry.

Who knows, maybe Thor's tougher.

A chunky seven year old. Buzz-cut blond hair. Blue eyes haunted by wrenching sights seen. A mother lost to fentanyl. A mother horribly murdered. Every school day, battling bullies. Once, not long ago, this child shot a man, and killed him, because he had to, because Tip had needed him to.

How had that settled into Thor's soul?

Who could know?

"I hear from Tip and Marge you're doing well," Cooper said. "I like hearing that."

He stared at her, unreadable, but taking her in, the way she was now, absorbing it, this altered Cooper, somebody who mattered to him.

"Henry visits me," he said.

Tip nodded and rested a hand on Thor's shoulder.

"Yeah, in the morning, Mike Bolknor drops off the dog," he said. "That'll be until school starts."

Say it, Cooper thought.

"Maybe, in September, you'll be back home, with Henry."

Nobody said it.

Nobody believes it, Cooper thought. Except—maybe—me.

"Henry likes exploring," Cooper told Thor. "Do you and Henry go on adventures?"

He looked at her.

Those eyes.

Thor asked: "Do you miss Henry?"

"Yes," Cooper said, pleased that Thor asked a question.

Living with Tip and Marge, his foster parents now, maybe—slowly, tentatively—they were helping him emerge from himself.

It suddenly irritated her, two visitors, standing side by side, looking down at her.

She thought: "Like looking at a corpse in a coffin."

"Sit down, you two," she said.

Tip, seated now, balanced his hat on one knee.

"That log heist," he said. "We taped Sonny DeWitt's idiot friends confessing—and they blurted out some evidence about Sonny, and the Proctor Gibbs murder, too."

Tip sat looking at his hat, thinking.

"Ozzie Knick got them blabbing," he said. "Kid's sharp."

Thor turned his head, looking up at Tip.

"What does Mr. Knick do?" he asked.

"He's an assistant state's attorney, a lawyer," Tip said. "Helps Cooper."

When a prominent local family wrongfully accused Thor of assaulting their much larger son, Thor watched Ozzie Knick force them to drop the nonexistent case and recognize the true villain, their son, a bully.

Thor said: "When I'm a police officer, like Mr. LaPerle, could I be a lawyer, too, like Mr. Knick?"

"Sure," Cooper said. "FBI agents, for instance, lots of them are attorneys."

So young, she thought, to be concerned about his adult self, but—for this child—there'd been no childhood.

"We'll all meet, tomorrow, on the log case," she told Tip. "And I want an update on the Olga Fisker murder— that's number one for us."

Fatigue now coming on, eyes heavy, wanting to close, then closing. She opened her eyes, saw Thor now standing by the window, looking out.

"Can you walk this far?" he asked.

"Sometimes," Cooper said. "I like to look out the window."

Tip, seeing Cooper's tiredness, started toward the door, signaling with his hand for Thor to follow him.

Cooper opened her eyes again and saw that Tip had gone out, but Thor lingered in the doorway, looking at her, unreadable.

She'd protected him, once, from killers hunting him. She'd come to mean something to him, but she didn't know what, exactly. Thor rarely spoke.

He didn't speak now.

With a last look, he turned in the doorway and stepped   outside   and   was   gone.

52

Numero Uno balanced his knife on his palm, hilt down.

With minute hand movements, he kept the knife upright, slow dancing, until it finally toppled onto his bed.

"Wow, you kept that going the longest yet," said Numero Dos, sitting on the bed beside him.

Uno stared at the wall.

"They blindsided us," he said.

Dos's forehead wrinkled.

"Because she was Black?"

Uno shook his head.

"No, because of that Cooper North woman," he said. "She figured who we'd target."

Dos's brow furrowed again.

"But how do we know she did?"

Uno gave Dos his basilisk look.

"On the recreation path, remember?" he said. "Our target blows a whistle, remember?"

Dos nodded.

"Then what happens?"

Dos looked blank.

"Her friend comes, doesn't he? On the run?" Uno said. "Like he was waiting for the signal?"

Dos nodded.

"Then what?" Uno demanded.

Dos thought hard. Uno waited, but Dos kept thinking.

Uno said: "Remember? Then that big cop comes running, too?"

He picked up the knife, where it lay on the bedspread.

"They set that woman as bait," he said.

He held the knife up in front of his face and glowered at it.

"Okay, they're smarter than we thought," he said. "Especially that North woman."

Dos said: "So we lay low?"

Uno's face contorted. He lurched to his feet, holding the knife by its blade's tip, glaring at a bullseye target, nailed to the wall. Abruptly, he hurled the knife. It thwacked into the target, one ring off from the bullseye, and stuck there.

"No, not lay low," he said. "We smash them—in their private lives."

"Wow," Dos said. "How, though, with the North woman in the hospital, and all??"

Uno lay on his back on the bed, with his sneakers resting on the bedspread and his hands clasped behind his head, staring at the ceiling, and he spoke to the ceiling, reciting from some text he'd read, possibly in an action comic.

"If your enemy gains a combat edge, you dodge, before you're hurt, then immediately counterattack, where the enemy's weakest—in his unprotected home."

"Burn down Cooper North's house?" Dos suggested.

Uno made a spitting sound, expressing disgust.

"Weaklings toss matches and run," he said. "We—the strong—strike with knives."

Dos got up and walked to the bedroom's window and glumly looked out.

"Maybe they'll find us—it scares me," Dos said. "You said they're smarter than we thought…."

Uno rolled off the bed and walked to the target and pulled out his knife, then walked back.

"Smarter than we thought doesn't mean smart," he said. "I've told you, we've already out-thought them, left no clues for them, so they'll never find us, because they can't."

He stood a moment, glaring at the wall target, and then his mouth flattened against his teeth and he hurled the knife, which hit the target sideways and dropped to the floor, clattering on the floorboards.

Dos flinched, as if expecting a blow.

"Don't scrunch like that," Uno said. "It looks weak, and it's creepy."

Dos straightened and shrugged, then spoke.

"So how do we get these people, where it hurts?"

Uno walked to the wall target and picked up the fallen knife and walked back.

"We slaughter what means something to all of them," he said.

He waited for Dos to ask a question, but none came.

So Uno filled the silence.

"That kid!"

Uno stared at him, processing.

"I read all about it in the *Dill Chronicle*," Uno said. "He's the police chief's foster kid, okay? And the North woman helped the kid once, so he's special to her, and I've watched—that big cop stops at the chief's house

every morning and drops off a dog for the kid to play with, so he's soft on the brat, too, like they all are."

He hurled the knife and this time it thwacked into the target and stuck, two rings from the bullseye. He walked back to the target and retrieved the knife.

"Gee," Dos said. "Just a kid…."

"You eat veal, don't you?" Uno said. "Lamb chops?" Silence, until Uno spoke.

"Every day—I've watched this—that kid goes to Abner Park, to play with the dog, and that park's almost always empty."

Dos looked at him.

"So we…."

Uno, eyes narrowed, mouth pressed against his teeth, suddenly hurled the knife with full force, and it thwacked loudly into the target.

This time it stuck in the bullseye.

Uno stared at it, across the room, and spoke.

"Right!"

53

Cooper North lay in her hospital bed, thinking about the Ninjas, and what to do about them.

She ignored her bedside pump's continuous beeping.

In two days, the beeping would stop—this first round of chemotherapy would end. Dr. Lopez would come in then, with his cutting and grinding instruments, to do a bone-marrow biopsy. Maybe the biopsy would say she had a chance to live. Maybe not.

So she focused on the Ninjas.

Who they were, she knew. Yet, she couldn't order their arrests. Not yet. She needed hard evidence.

So they'd be out there, and they'd surely try to kill again.

Soon.

They must.

Pressure to kill's building inside them, Cooper thought. Especially because we checked them. They attacked Kalisha Rains, on the recreation path, but we sent them running. We nicked their pride, and their self-esteem, and—especially—their need for blood.

Cooper thought: Yes, they're vampires. Except they can strike in bright sunlight.

She leaned back against the pillows, trying to think like them.

She'd dealt before with homicidal maniacs. She knew some feel like giants among midgets, wizards among morons.

Yet, on the recreation path, we morons blocked them, which means....

Cooper suddenly sat up in bed, alarmed.

They crave revenge!

Her bedside telephone buzzed.

Marge LaPerle's voice.

"Hi Coop, do you feel up to walking to your window?"

"I can do that, Marge."

"Wonderful, because Thor has something to show you."

She eased out of bed slowly, and clung to the bedside steel pole to stand. Because its pump ran on batteries, and it rested on a wheeled base, she could move about, rolling it with her. It seemed an epic journey to the window, step by step. Her youthful bout with polio had lamed her left leg, but now both legs felt weak.

She finally reached the window.

She had no roommate, because leukemic patients' near-zero immune systems require isolation. Her room was on the hospital's quieter north side, away from the parking lot, looking out over forests and meadows, stretching to the Green Mountains. A path circled the building, and back here it passed through a small park.

WHEN THE WASP STINGS

Cooper looked down from her third-floor window, and saw Thor Ennis looking up. Sunshine made his blond buzzcut seem to glow. Beside him stood Henry, on his short corgi legs, also looking up at her.

It seemed forever since she last saw the dog, held him between her two hands, felt life pulse inside him. Thor must have understood that. So he brought Henry here for her to see, the best gift he could manage.

His face, looking up at her, showed no emotion, but Cooper knew strong emotion pulsed inside Thor. She unlatched the window and pushed it up and leaned out.

"Thor," she called down to him. "Thank you."

Henry heard her, stared up at the figure in the window, sniffed, and then—with recognition—he barked jubilantly, eyes glinting. With each bark, he jounced upwards.

Cooper thought: so, you're actually glad to see me?

She didn't cry. Even as a child she'd almost never cried. She felt something like tears inside, though, because of Henry's enthusiastic recognition, and because this silent child, who understood stress and danger, who'd seen it so much in his short life, felt something for her, and brought her dog to show he did.

Better than words.

"Thor," Cooper called down to him. "This is a wonderful gift."

Thor just looked up at her, expressionless, and Henry barked and pranced.

Marge LaPerle, who'd been keeping out of the way farther along the path, now walked up and waved to Cooper.

"Do you have pain?" she called up.

Cooper shook her head, and Marge made the thumbs-up sign.

"I'm on my way to the dentist," Marge said, glancing at her wristwatch. "I'm dropping Thor and Henry off at Abner Park, to goof around—they go there most days."

"I appreciate this," Cooper said.

"Thor wanted you to see Henry," Marge said. "He's been pushing for it a bunch of days now—well, off we go."

Cooper watched them walk together toward the parking lot. Just before they rounded the building, out of sight, Henry turned and even so far away she could see his eyes glint.

He barked to her.

Then they were gone.

Cooper pulled down the window and made the slow trek back to her bed, thinking again about Ninjas and vampirism and murder.

And revenge.

Then her telephone buzzed—Ozzie Knick's voice.

"Just wanted to tell you we're bringing in the Timber Rustlers," he said. "All four of them, including Sonny DeWitt."

"At the State's Attorney's office?" Cooper asked.

"Yeah, Chief LaPerle and I, we're going to do what you told us," he said. "We wanted to keep you in the loop."

Cooper thought: in the loop, even though I'm imprisoned in this bed. Even though there's a bone-marrow biopsy coming.

Yes, keep me in the loop, she thought. Because I appreciate it. I need it.

I'm not dead yet.

She said: "You do the talking—if they get mouthy, Tip might detonate."

"Roger that," Ozzie said.

54

Sonny DeWitt walked into the interrogation room last, six minutes after his three buddies got there, Possum, Walrus, and Beast.

He looked irritated. Red faced, cowlick curled up in back, one missing shirt button revealing his underlying t-shirt.

"I've got to run a business, you know," he said, glaring at Ozzie and Tip LaPerle. "I've got no time for this—what is this anyway?"

"It'll come clear," Ozzie said, not looking up, fingering the buttons on his digital mini-recorder.

Tip LaPerle sat to his left, uniform hat laid on the table to one side, giving the visitors his cop's scorn-and-disgust stare.

This large room, in the Allen County State's Attorney's office, doubled for staff meetings and arrestee interrogations, to fine-tune indictments. A long polished-oak table stretched along the room's center, with chairs all around, and windows on one side, looking across maple-shaded Courthouse Lane, at the Dill PD station. A heavy volume lay on the table, *Vermont Statutes, Annotated.*

Ozzie pressed a button on his tape recorder and looked at Sonny DeWitt.

"Listen up," he said. "You'll find this riveting."

Out of the tape recorder came the voices of Possum, Walrus, and Beast, cheerfully relating how they'd swiped the logs from Cappy Dixon. They said they drove around in the Snowville Maple company's Jeep most nights, but not alone, not ever, and not alone for the log heist, either.

Beast's voice: "It was the four of us, damn it, Sonny right there with us—told you, he says no using the Jeep ourselves, so Sonny was in the thick of it, all right."

"You idiots!" Sonny said.

He glared at his three chums, collectively, then at each in turn.

"Oh, come on, Sonny," Walrus told him. "You know we were just pranking Cappy Moneybags, just kidding around, holy cow."

Sonny shut his eyes and gritted his teeth and shook his head.

"Idiots," he said again.

After that he slouched in his chair and stared down gloomily at the table.

"As I think you've gathered, Mr. DeWitt, we're talking about a felony here," Ozzie said.

He made a show of moving the heavy volume of *Vermont Statutes* closer to him and pulling drugstore reading glasses from his pocket. Peering down through the glasses, perched at the end of his nose, he studied the index and then opened to a page, and stared at it, absorbing the text.

"This is under 'Title 13: Crimes and Criminal Procedure,'" he read. "'Chapter 057: Larceny and Embezzlement, Subchapter 001: Larceny.'"

He looked up, making sure his audience listened.

"'Section 2502,'" he said. "'Petit Larceny.'"

He looked up over his glasses again, making sure they all followed, then read the text.

"'For offenses mentioned in Section 2501 of this title where the money or other property stolen does not exceed $900.00 in value, the court may sentence the person convicted to imprisonment for not more than one year or to pay a fine of not more than $1000.00, or both.'"

Possum stared open-mouthed.

Beast said, "Wow, a year in the slammer."

He ran both hands through his red beard and shut his eyes.

Walrus shook his head, looking pained, and pulled his bushy blond mustache, one hand at each end.

"Hey, it was just kidding around, you know?" he said. "We didn't, like, sell those logs or anything, so you can't call it a crime."

"Yes we can," Ozzie said. "This goes to trial, by the way, it's on all your records, bad for business, right Mr. DeWitt? *Dill Chronicle* gets hold of it?"

DeWitt groaned, staring down at the table. He looked up suddenly and glared at his friends.

"What did I say that night?" he said. "Don't do this, in my Jeep, for God's sake, with me here in it, for crying out loud, just don't do it, but you bozos went ahead anyway."

Beast threw up his hands and shook his bald head.

"Yeah, that night, we all got crocked, including you, Sonny," he said. "And Dixon had just given me the boot and all...."

Possum stared beseechingly at Ozzie, and spoke in a whisper.

"A year in the freaking slammer...."

Ozzie sat back in his chair and eyed the four men speculatively.

"All right," he said. "You seem like good old boys, so...."

He sat thinking, all four sets of eyes focused on him.

"We'll make it easier on you," he said finally. "Instead of levying a thousand-dollar fine per moron, we'll make it collective, a thousand total—so that's two-hundred-fifty for each moron."

Stares and silence from each of the four men.

"That's a good deal, generous of us," Ozzie said. "Some problem with that?"

Stares and silence continuing.

"All right, you don't like the deal, so we'll withdraw it," Ozzie said, shrugging. "Back to a thousand per low-IQ head, and...."

Possum moaned.

"I don't actually have two-hundred-fifty...."

Beast and Walrus both looked chagrined.

"I don't have it either," Beast muttered.

Walrus just shook his head, looking down, despairing.

"Jobs hard to find, kind of," he said.

Ozzie produced a commiserating sigh.

"Yeah, for you fellows, jobs also are hard to hold onto, I suppose…"

Beast nodded glumly.

"Too bad," Ozzie said. "That brings us to the go-to-prison option, and…"

Sonny DeWitt jerked up his head and made a sound like a moan.

"I'll pay the damned thousand," he said. "God, I should have listened to Sheila, right after we got married, she said…."

"Great kid, that Sheila," Walrus said.

"Yeah, a super good looker, you know?" Possum said.

Beast said: "Boy, we had great times, didn't we? Back then?"

Ozzie looked at Tip, who'd been sitting silently beside him.

"Dill PD okay with this deal?" he asked.

Tip looked disgusted.

"With these loons, I'd say death penalty, to end idiot shenanigans," he said. "But you're the prosecutor, so…."

"We've already cleared this with Caspar Dixon, and he's accepted the deal," Ozzie said. "Anybody learn any lessons here, show of hands?"

Three hands shot up. Earnest faces. Mutterings.

Sonny DeWitt sat with his eyes closed, shaking his head.

"Okay, go away now and sin no more," Ozzie said. "Except Mr. DeWitt, you wait, while we work out a few things."

Hurriedly, the three buddies—Possum, Walrus, and Beast—got up, each face radiant with relief, and hurried out of the room. Sonny DeWitt remained, still sitting in his chair, gazing glumly down at the table.

Ozzie explained the steps he needed to take, to pay the fine.

Then he sat staring at DeWitt, speculatively.

DeWitt looked up, flinched, because of the stare, and waited, grimly.

"One thing more," Ozzie said. "Investigating this case of petit larceny, we uncovered evidence bearing on an altogether different case."

DeWitt looked at him, confused.

"Someone murdered Proctor Gibbs," Ozzie said. "They hid yellow-jacket wasps in his sleeves, a man known to be allergic to the venom."

Sonny, suddenly irritated, started to speak.

"Hey, wait a minute, if you...."

Ozzie raised his arm, hand bent at the wrist, index finger pointing at DeWitt, meaning shut up. Then he pushed his tape recorder's fast-forward button, let it whir, and stopped it.

"Listen," he said, pushing the play button.

Beast's voice...

"Okay, he'd get a phone call from his folks, back home, and he'd go all sour, and he'd say, 'well, they'll see a different me, if Proctor Gibbs ever finally falls off a cliff.'"

Possum's voice: "Hah! He'd kid around, you know, like bring a tactical nuke to work, or stick dynamite under

Proc's car seat, but that was jokes, right?"

Sonny's face contorted, angry, but then he looked stricken and buried his head in his hands.

"Don't worry too much," Ozzie told him. "That's not conclusive evidence, just circumstantial, and hearsay."

Sonny looked up at him, relieved.

"Still, we want you to know," he said.

He and Tip LaPerle both stared at DeWitt.

"We're investigating the murder of Proctor Gibbs," Ozzie said.

He continued to stare at DeWitt, silent, as if taking his measure.

Finally he spoke.

"You are now a person of interest."

55

Mike Bolknor's office phone buzzed.

Caller ID said: "Cooper North."

He picked up and heard her voice, familiar, but weaker.

"Two things," Cooper said, in a hoarse near-whisper. "A half-hour ago, Thor Ennis brought Henry over for me to see, out the window—it reminded me, I owe you thanks, Mike, for corgi care."

"Henry's a colleague," Mike said.

"He's not in your job description," Cooper said.

"Protect and serve, that's the job description," he said. "Includes Henry."

He thought to say, this isn't just a job. I lost my wife and kids. I lost Rachel and Abigail and Frankie. I ran away, but I got lucky, coming here. Cooper North was here.

He didn't say it. He didn't need to. Cooper just knew such things. Those penetrating eyes.

Unsettling, though—her voice sounding so depleted.

"Ozzie Knick called a minute ago," she said. "He and Tip LaPerle just browbeat Sonny DeWitt's clown gang, like we planned—and Sonny got warned, he's on the watch list, for Proctor Gibbs' murder."

"That should agitate him," Mike said. "Maybe he'll confess, blurt it out."

"Wouldn't that save time," Cooper said.

She feels short on time, Mike thought.

"I'm here with Karen Del Vecchio," he said. "We're waiting for Darlene Bobowaski—to see what her computer says, about our Fisker-murder evidence."

"Hello to Karen for me," Cooper said.

After a silent moment, she added: "That's a smart lady, and cool—a winner."

It was Cooper's blessing.

He needed Rachel's blessing, too. He imagined what she'd say: "Hey, what's complicated about 'until death do us part?'"

Well, he thought, it actually is complicated.

"Darlene just walked in," he said over the phone. "I'll keep you posted, Coop."

He watched Darlene toss her backpack onto the floor, beside the Campus Security Office's main desktop, in an alcove off to the side, out of the way of the reception desk's work-study students, the summer recess contingent, and the patrol officers coming and going, drawing coffee from the office's Keurig machine into paper cups.

Still standing, Darlene reached down to finger the keyboard, peering at the screen to monitor changes in the code stream.

She wore her usual baggy cargo pants, and Keds, and rimless glasses, today's lenses squinty oblongs, tinted red, making the skinny girl look fiery eyed, demonic, blond hair frizzing in all directions around her bony face. Her black t-shirt's message, printed in scarlet: "Super Smarty-Pants!"

Darlene plopped down in the typist's seat and hunched over the keyboard, tapping, although she hadn't yet been told what searches to do. Revving up the machine, Mike supposed, prepping it for a cyber dive.

Satisfied with what she saw on the screen, Darlene reached down into her backpack, on the floor, and pulled out earbuds, which she slung around her neck, ready to plug into her ears.

"Set to start?" Mike asked.

"Yeah, let's Dick Tracy this," Darlene said. "Who's that good-looking woman with you? Enquiring minds want to know."

"This is Karen Del Vecchio, from the state-police crime lab," he said.

Darlene looked up, at the word "lab."

"You a tech?" she asked. "Or a cop?"

"Some of each," Karen said.

"Oh," Darlene said, looking back at the numbers and symbols streaming across the computer's screen.

Mike pulled a metal sheath from his pocket, and laid it beside Darlene's keyboard.

"This got dropped during a murder, a sheath for a Fairbairn-Sykes commando knife," he said. "We need you to check recent on-line sales of these knives, buyers in this area—doable?"

Darlene grinned.

"Hey, give me something challenging to do, okay?" she said.

Mike nodded to Karen, who showed Darlene a scrap of fabric, in a clear-plastic evidence bag.

"It's from a perp's shirt, got ripped off during the murder," Karen said. "It's a Hawaiian-style shirt, deep blue, decorated with golden scallop shells."

Darlene hit some keys, and images appeared on the screen, Hawaiian shirts. She tapped more keys, and new shirts came up, fewer, but all deep blue, decorated with golden shells.

"Can you check local stores, say within thirty miles of Dill?" Mike said. "Any of these shirts sold recently? And to who?"

Darlene turned up her eyes, insulted by a kindergarten assignment.

"If there's nothing local, search for any internet-site sales of shirts like this, to someone in the Dill area," Mike said.

Instead of answering, Darlene slipped on her earbuds. After a moment, she sat bopping in her chair to music only she heard, staring at her computer screen, fingering the keyboard. Mike and Karen exchanged a wry look.

"So away we go," he said.

While Darlene bopped in her chair, piloting her computer, they sank into chairs in Mike's office, neatly kept except for his Glock 22 disassembled on his desk, where he'd been cleaning it, with a handful of .40-caliber rounds spread out, waiting to be replaced in the clip. Karen saw Mike slouched in his chair, staring at his hands in his lap, and stayed silent.

He'd always spoken sparsely. His sister once asked how he expected to maintain radio silence, and still teach kids English, his original plan, before his NYPD-officer father, on his deathbed, shamed Mike into going into the Bolknor family trade, law enforcement.

Right now, he thought, he owed it to Karen to talk about where they stood, and where they might be going, and his concern—illogical—of being unfaithful to Rachel. He never talked about such things. Rachel always handled personal matters. Without her, he felt vaguely lost, like a rowboat blown from the dock in a storm, and now drifting.

"Tell me about Rachel," Karen suddenly said. "What was she like?"

As if she'd read his mind, he thought. Just as Rachel used to read his mind.

"Rachel was perceptive," he said.

Many other traits, too. Intelligent, strong-willed, empathetic….He didn't want to talk about her.

Did those traits also describe Karen? Maybe. She had dark hair and alert dark eyes, like Rachel's.

Mike sat looking at the Glock on his desk. He thought, if Cooper North dies, will I stay here? Go back to the city? Somewhere else?

Karen watched him. Finally, she spoke.

"It'll be what it becomes," she said.

Another silence.

"There's a new restaurant downtown, Indian," she said. "Want to try it tonight?"

"Run first, on the recreation path," he said.

She nodded.

In the other room, Darlene's keyboard clacked.

56

Thor Ennis followed Henry around the Abner Park pond, hearing voices not far off, wanting them to go away.

Sometimes people you met on these park paths stopped you, wanting to talk, and he didn't like talking. Just him and Henry, that's how he liked it. He let Henry lead him along the paths and through the trees, Henry being his best friend, and because Henry found things with his corgi nose, stopping every few feet to sniff the news—squirrel shredded a balsam cone here, snowshoe hare hid under that fern. Henry thought in scents.

Thor thought in feelings, mostly, and in pictures, like right now, an image of his mother came into his mind, prone on her bed, where they used to live, in those tenements by the river. She'd taken fentanyl—her "medicine," she called it—and sometimes it made her sing. Sometimes she cried. Sometimes she cursed Thor.

"You little piece of crap, you ruined my damned life!"

Mostly it put her to sleep.

He made the memory go away.

Thoughts like that could turn into words. Words could escape from your head and go into other people's ears. Not good. You had to watch out for other people, who might be bad.

Bullies in school.

Teachers and the principal, siding with the bullies, always.

Those men who killed his mother, and hunted him.

Some people were good. He wanted Miss North to be his grandmother, although he never said so. His fierce grandmother.

It felt good, living with Chief LaPerle and Mrs. LaPerle, in their house. Every morning, before he left for work, Chief LaPerle and Mrs. LaPerle hugged. Thor liked that. He'd never been hugged before, but now Mrs. LaPerle hugged him. He liked that.

Mr. Bolknor, too, also good. Thor didn't say much, and neither did Mr. Bolknor, but saying nothing to each other they said a lot.

When he grew up, Thor would be a policeman, like Chief LaPerle. Or maybe like Mr. Bolknor, if he grew that big. Now he'd added Mr. Knick to his list of possibilities, thinking maybe he should be a prosecutor.

Policeman or prosecutor, he'd stop bad people from doing bad things. Hurting people. When those bad men who killed his mother tried to hurt him, Miss North and Chief LaPerle and Mr. Bolknor stopped them. So, when he grew up....

Those voices, closer.

They were just beyond this thick hemlock copse now, out of sight, but close, walking toward him.

Those bad men who killed his mother followed him like this.

341

It scared him, being followed.

"Henry!" he whispered.

Henry glanced back, to see what Thor wanted.

"Here," Thor said, and he slipped into the thicket, pushing through hemlock trunks and branches, as deep as he could go, with Henry following, until the hemlocks got too thick to push through any more.

He hunkered down, and waited.

Henry liked this new game, rushing into the bushes. This was fun.

Thor couldn't see who followed him. Branches and twigs, full of hemlock needles, blocked his view, but he heard their voices, a man and a woman. Chilly voices. They'd stopped on the path, just in front of where he hid.

"That brat came this way."

"I don't see him."

"He couldn't have gotten that far ahead of us...."

Thor carefully moved twigs aside, just enough so he could peek through the needles and see them out there, looking into the hemlocks, on both sides of the path.

They looked scary. Black jeans and black shirts and black masks over their heads, showing just their mouths and nostrils and eyes. Now the taller one cursed, and held up something that glinted in the summer sun, too bright to see, but then he turned his hand a bit and Thor could see it.

A long knife.

Sunshine on its blade blinded you if you stared at it.

"Hey little boy," the man yelled. "We have something nice for you—come on out."

His voice didn't sound nice. Once, as a tiny child, in the west, where they lived then, Thor came upon a rattlesnake in the lawn, and it hissed. That's how this man's voice sounded.

A hiss.

"Come out, come out, wherever you are."

That made the smaller person laugh. A girl's laugh.

Thor heard a rumble in Henry's throat, a growl starting, or a bark. He put his hand around Henry's snout and looked into the dog's eyes and shook his head, no. He let Henry's snout go and the dog licked his hand, amiably.

Thor thought he would be okay unless they decided to push in through the hemlocks, to hunt him down. If they did....

They're big, he thought, and I'm small.

Then he heard the man suddenly shout.

"Look, dog hair on this twig—they went in here, that brat and his dog."

He heard them pushing into the hemlocks, coming toward him.

They're big, Thor thought again, and I'm small, like Henry.

Henry, low to the ground, walked more easily among the hemlocks, because their branches and twigs didn't grow all the way down. Henry could hunker a bit and move along under the branches. Thor was small, too.

He dropped down, knees and elbows on the ground, and began inching away from the bad people pushing toward him.

Faster, he told himself.

He crawled faster.

If they caught him, they'd kill Henry. He knew they would. It made him sick. They'd kill him, too, Henry and him. He knew it.

Branches thrashed behind him. A thwack and the woman yelped.

"It snapped right back in my face and...."

Thor crawled now, as fast as he could, with Henry ahead of him, moving easier through the hemlock growth, getting ahead, enjoying this adventure, this new game.

"Hey, there he is!"

From behind him, a shout. It sounded like that rattlesnake's hiss.

A hand grabbed the back of his t-shirt, then jerked him up off his hands and knees. Thor twisted his head, to look back over his shoulder at the man holding him.

Icy eyes.

Thor saw the knife.

57

Cooper North suddenly opened her eyes and bolted up in her hospital bed.

She'd drifted asleep, after talking with Mike Bolknor on the telephone a few minutes ago, about Darlene Bobowaski starting the internet search, but not really asleep, troubling thoughts sliding across her mind.

Mostly, she thought about the Ninjas, and the revenge they must crave.

They'd been blocked on the recreation path, stopped from killing Kalisha. So they'd need to prove their superiority. They needed to strike back.

When? And who'd be their target this time?

Not another attack on Kalisha Rains, she thought. They'd tried that.

Her thoughts drifted away, to more soothing things. She wondered if Mike Bolknor, silently grieving still, would get together with Karen Del Vecchio. She liked Karen and she loved Mike. So she hoped.

She thought how Thor, that little boy, wanted to show her what he felt, but couldn't say, so he brought her dog for her to see, out the window, a gift, and Thor....

Cooper cursed.

Eyes narrowed, she grabbed her bedside telephone, flicked through its contacts list, then punched in one of its saved cell-phone numbers.

"Hello?"

Marge LaPerle's voice.

"This is Cooper—it's...."

"Coop, I'm actually in the dentist's chair, and he's just started to...."

"Thor, where is he?"

"I dropped him off at Abner Park, on the way here, but...."

"Marge, did you see any other people there, when you left Thor off?"

"No, there was a truck parked down toward the other end of the park, but...."

"What kind of truck?"

"Oh, one of those Jeep things, you know, squared off and blocky and...."

"Tip's at his office?"

"Yes, I think so, but...."

Cooper pushed the off button, then punched in Tip LaPerle's office number, at the Dill PD.

It buzzed.

Then buzzed again.

It started to buzz a third time, but Cooper abruptly pressed "Off," because explaining this situation to other officers would take too long, so she looked in "Contacts" for another number, Tip's cell phone.

After the second ring he answered.

"Coop?" he said. "I see on Caller ID...."

"It's Thor," Cooper said. "They're after him, in the park, the Ninjas, and...."

Tip cursed.

"Where are you?" Cooper asked.

"I'm in a cruiser, downtown—I'm turning, heading up to the park, keep talking, tell me."

Cooper told him about suddenly realizing the Ninjas would target Thor, the most vulnerable. So they'd kept watch, for sure, and knew he went to the park with Henry, every day, and what time.

"Marge dropped him off, and saw that damned Jeep parked there, so...."

"Coop, I've got it, so click off now," Tip said.

Over the telephone, she heard his cruiser's siren now wailing.

"I'm radioing in, getting every spare cop up here," Tip said. "Fingers crossed."

Sudden silence. He'd clicked off.

Call in Mike Bolknor, too? Campus cops?

Cooper started to punch in his number then decided no. Everyone converging on the park could lead to a confused melee. They'd need to search that big park, and they'd need to keep it organized.

Better let Tip run this operation himself. If he needed backup, he'd call in Mike.

Cooper hung up the phone and dropped back against the pillows staring at the ceiling.

"That child," she thought. "Just seven years in this world, and he's seen so much horror...."

If she were a woman who wept, she would, she thought, but she wasn't that sort of woman.

WHEN THE WASP STINGS

She felt sickened, lying in this hospital bed, almost too weak to stand, while out there, alone, Thor faced savagery.

She imagined that commando knife slashing.

58

Thor felt the man holding him up in the air let go, and he fell to the ground amidst the hemlocks, his hands digging into the forest soil, as if he could tunnel away, but he couldn't, and looking up he saw the man raising the knife, to stab.

Somebody screamed, and Thor knew it was Thor who screamed.

Not fear. Not terror.

Rage.

Lying on his back, looking up at that upraised knife, his insides blazed, an inferno.

Searing.

He scrambled to his feet, clenching the soil his hands had been tunneling into, and he hurled both handfuls into the masked man's face, into his eyes.

Yells from the man, curses.

Knife dropped.

Eyes rubbed.

Thor reached for the dropped knife, wanting to stab, and slash, but the woman grabbed it first. Thor whirled and pushed off through the hemlocks, toward the park's entrance, crawling under branches, hearing the woman thrashing just behind him, and then a different sound.

Sirens.

Everything stopped—Thor, the woman about to grab him, Henry up ahead, the man with dirt in his eyes, cursing.

A shout, from near the park's main entrance, beyond the pond, so far off it seemed a whisper.

Thor!

Chief LaPerle's voice.

Behind him, Thor heard the woman speak back over her shoulder.

"What do we do?"

"Circle around the park, keep to the edge, get to the truck, before they look for it."

Thor heard them starting to move away, still talking.

"How could they know about us, here today?"

"Don't be stupid—it's that damned Cooper North woman figuring things out again, so she's getting it next, even hiding out in the hospital."

"How?"

"There's always a way to...."

Too far away now, on the run, their voices faded.

Thor rolled onto his back, looking up at the needly hemlock branches, seeing bits of blue sky where the needles thinned, not sobbing exactly, but with his chest heaving.

Remnant anger.

Relief.

He lurched up, pushed through the hemlocks. Back on the path, he ran toward Henry's barking, until he saw Chief LaPerle, with other officers, fanned out, hunting for him.

He ran to Chief LaPerle, and pointed.

"They're running that way," he said. "To their truck."

Tip had been reaching out to hug Thor, but instead he ran back toward the park's frontal road, calling for the other officers to follow. When they reached Abner Park Drive, though, he saw no parked vehicles.

His voice, when he spoke, sounded angry.

"That garbage got away."

He pulled out his cell phone and punched in a memorized number—one ring and it got picked up, as if Cooper North had been sitting in bed all this time, staring at the phone, waiting for this call.

"He's all right," Tip said. "He's here with me."

Silence, as Cooper absorbed the good news, not the bad news she'd feared. Then she spoke.

"Meet in my room, Tip, right now," she said. "Mike Bolknor just called, he said Darlene Bobowaski got what we needed, searching the internet, so he's got hard evidence now...I'm calling in for search warrants."

Thor, standing beside Tip, heard all this. Understanding only that something would happen quickly, and he felt elated.

Cooper's voice again, over the phone.

"Get them!" she said. "Get them, Tip!"

Thor heard, even without a phone pressed to his ear, because Cooper said it loudly.

He thought: my grandmother.

Then he thought again.

WHEN THE WASP STINGS

My fierce grandmother.

59

Forty-three minutes later, a police SUV—siren wailing, blue lights flashing—careened into the Snowville Maple, Inc., parking lot and braked to a stop. Behind it, a Mt. Augustus College Campus Security cruiser, a Prius, sped in and parked beside it.

Tip LaPerle, in his blue uniform, vaulted out of the SUV. Mike Bolknor climbed out of the Prius, his dark suit and tie more Manhattan than summertime Vermont. Kalisha Rains got out the Prius's passenger door, looking official in gray pinstripes. Together, the three pushed through the building's glass-doored entrance and strode to the reception desk, where Winnie Rink stopped emery boarding her fingernails, painted reddish brown, to match her auburn hair, and stared at the trio, wide-eyed, as if struck by lightning.

Kalisha carried a hand-sized digital tape recorder, and she now turned it on.

"Winnie Rink, you're under arrest," Tip said. "For the murder of Olga Fisker, and other crimes, and you'll be coming with us now to the police station in Dill for questioning, prior to arraignment."

She stared at him, eyes still wide, transfixed.

"You have the right to remain silent," Tip said. "Anything you say can and will be used against you in a court of law. You have the right to an attorney. If you cannot afford an attorney, one will be provided for you."

She stared, mouth open.

"Do you understand the rights I have just cited to you?" Tip asked. "With these rights in mind, do you wish to speak to me?"

She looked dumbfounded.

"No comment from the suspect," Kalisha said into the tape recorder. "If the suspect chooses, questioning can be delayed until she has an attorney present."

"You want an attorney?" Tip asked.

Rink looked blank.

"Let the record show Winnie Rink made no response," Kalisha said into the recorder. "It will be assumed she wishes to keep silent until she has an attorney."

Just then the door to Sonny DeWitt's office banged open and the Snowville Maple CEO lurched out, holding a half-eaten fried chicken drumstick his left hand and a half-drunk bottle of Budweiser in his right. He took in the law officers, his shell-shocked receptionist, and turned red with anger.

"Just what the hell's going on here?" he demanded.

"This doesn't concern you," Kalisha told him.

"You better hope it doesn't," Tip added. "We're already eyeing you for killing Proctor Gibbs, and this is an entirely different murder—quite a homicide hotbed, this company."

"Hey," DeWitt said. "You can't...."

"Yes we can," Tip said. "You'll need to find a replacement receptionist—this one's coming to Dill with us."

DeWitt sputtered, unable to speak coherently.

"Where's this girl's boyfriend?" Tip demanded.

DeWitt shook his head, still trying to understand the situation.

"He's leading a damned tour, for crying out loud," he said. "What's this supposed to be about, some kind of government harassment, or what?"

"It's about murder," Tip said.

DeWitt glared.

"This is Snowville," he suddenly said. "What're you Dill cops doing out here anyway?"

"Allen County towns all contract with the Dill PD for law enforcement," Tip said.

DeWitt, looking angry and befuddled, scrunched up his face, trying to clear his head.

"For God's sake, this is just a high-school kid!" he said finally.

"Really?" Tip said. "Okay, as a special consideration, us being in favor of education and all, we'll dispense with handcuffs, just this once."

Tip now escorted Winnie Rink out the front door.
She walked like a zombie.

"Hey, don't worry," Sonny DeWitt shouted after her. "I'm getting the company's lawyers on the phone right now."

355

Kalisha looked at Mike.

"Girl in the cruiser," she said. "I better go with Tip, a second woman riding along."

Mike nodded and Kalisha hurried out the door after Tip LaPerle.

DeWitt watched them go out, then glared at Mike Bolknor.

"Our lawyers will eat you for brunch," he said. "Harassing kids like this."

Bolknor looked at him, impassive.

"Vic Ledger's out back?" he said. "With tourists in that sugar shack back there?"

DeWitt stared at him, too flustered to answer.

"I'll take that as a yes," Mike said, and walked to the front entrance and out into the summer afternoon.

In the sugar shack, when Bolknor opened the door and looked in, Vic Ledger stood in front of thirteen seated tourists, languidly describing the sap-boiling process, reciting a script in which he clearly had zero interest. He glanced at Bolknor, leaning against the doorframe, and for a microsecond flinched, but then disregarded the newcomer and continued with his memorized spiel, a youth, nearly six-foot tall, but slim, blond hair buzz-cut, face expressionless.

Mike remembered Cooper North telling him her impression of Ledger's oddly blank face, "like a snake's," she'd said.

Mike kept himself positioned in the doorway, a professional precaution, so Ledger couldn't bolt without running into the cop blocking the exit, a man with the height and brawn of a professional wrestler. Tourists turned in their seats to see the newcomer in a suit, perfectly fitted for him, yet somehow seeming too small, then turned their eyes back to Ledger, who droned on, about boiler pans.

"That ends our tour," Ledger finally said. "Syrup for sale in the shop just off the lobby—have a good day."

Mike stood aside, to let the tourists file out the door into the sunshine, and begin their hike around the building, to the parking lot. Then he stepped back into the doorway, staring at Ledger, who stared back, icy anger in his eyes.

"What do you want?" Ledger said.

Mike said: "Victor Ledger, I'm arresting you for the murder of Olga Fisker and other crimes."

He strode across the room to where Ledger stood, as he walked extracting handcuffs attached to his belt in back, and spun Ledger around, face to the wall.

Ledger struggled.

"Don't," Mike said. "Resisting arrest will be added to your crime list."

Ledger stopped struggling, face pale with cold rage, and Mike pulled his arms behind him and snapped on the cuffs.

"You have the right to remain silent," Mike said, and recited the rest of the Miranda warning, with Ledger maintaining silence.

After that, with a big hand on Ledger's shoulder, Mike marched him around the building into the parking lot. Sonny DeWitt had come outside and stood at the building's entrance, watching, as Mike folded Ledger into the Prius's back seat, resting a hand on the suspect's head to keep him from banging it on the doorframe, then slammed the door, no door handles back there, so prisoners couldn't open the door and escape.

"I've already called our company lawyer," DeWitt yelled, as Mike got in behind the steering wheel. "He'll eat your livers!"

60

Forty-three-minutes later….

Dill PD interrogation room.

One table. Four chairs.

Through a one-way window, Kalisha Rains and Ozzie Knick, standing outside, watched the questioning. Headsets let them speak privately with the interrogators, also wearing headsets, and Kalisha aimed a laptop through the window, starting a Zoom session—in her hospital room, on her own laptop, Cooper North followed along.

"Sit there," Tip LaPerle told Vic Ledger, pointing to one of the seats.

Tip and Mike Bolknor took seats facing Ledger. Mike laid a briefcase on the floor, beside his shoes, then reached into it, extracting a sheaf of documents, which he piled neatly on the table.

Just then the room's door burst open and a fiftyish man, corpulent, hurried in, whistling *When the Saints Come Marching In.*

"Killer tune!" he announced. "Louie Armstrong, best rendition!'

On his head, he wore a Boston Red Sox hat. One tail of his blue dress shirt, untucked, drooped out of his khaki cargo shorts.

"Just roared in on my private Boeing 747," he announced. "Supreme Court case, national security, totally hush-hush!"

Tip gave the late arrival a tired look.

"For the record," Tip intoned, "the fourth person in the room, serving as the accused's attorney, is Harley Duckle McGee."

McGee took a seat beside Vic Ledger, and gave Ledger an encouraging bump with his elbow. After a moment, Tip said, "How's it going, Ducks?"

"Splendiferous," the defense attorney said. "Hey, broiled cops for dinner—what could be better?"

He threw up a hand.

"Wait, wait, don't tell me," he said. "I know—for dessert, baked prosecutor Alaska, yum!"

"Ducks, you know this is murder, right?" Tip said. "Not a stand-up comedy contest?"

Ducks looked stricken.

"My poor client," he said, laying a consoling arm over Ledger's shoulders. "Caught up in this awfulness, and him just seventeen, a mere child."

Tip clenched his teeth, making a jaw muscle pulse.

Kalisha's voice came through his headset, and he echoed what she told him.

"In the state of Vermont, a sixteen or seventeen-year-old can be charged as an adult in District Court, as you damned well know, Ducks, so let's cut the jackass clowning."

Outside the room, Cooper watching on Zoom, said: "He's pressing Tip's temper button—switch me through."

Kalisha made an adjustment and Cooper spoke into Tip's earphones.

"Cool it," she said. "He's baiting you, Tip."

In the room Tip nodded.

"Okay," Ducks said. "You accuse this boy of murder, so what's your evidence?"

Mike Bolknor reached down into his briefcase and pulled out a metal sheath. He laid it on the table, then pushed it over to the defense attorney.

Ducks stared at it. Then he removed his baseball cap, revealing a bald head, with a side-fringe of messy brown hair, and scratched the top of his skull. He put the hat back on, pulled it low over his eyes, and peered out from under the brim, at the sheath.

"So what?" he said finally.

"It's for a Fairbairn-Sykes commando knife," Mike said. "We found it dropped at the murder scene—slash and stab wounds on the murdered woman matched the dimensions of a Fairbairn-Sykes."

He handed Ducks one of the documents he'd placed on the table in front of him.

"Forensics report from the state-police crime lab," he said.

Ducks scanned the report, then dropped it, letting it flutter to the table in front of him.

"Pig's wings," he said. "Nothing ties it to this poor kid."

He reached a hand over and gave Ledger a consoling back pat.

Ledger smirked.

"We did a deep internet search," Mike said. "Thirty-eight days ago, an online store, called Combat Gear, sold a Fairbairn-Sykes commando knife, and shipped it to Snowville, Vermont—the buyer was Vic Ledger, the address was Ledger's parents' home."

Ledger's face remained impassive.

"That's it?" Ducks said.

"More recently, the same store sold just a sheath for that knife, to Vic Ledger, shipped to his Snowville home," Mike said. "Looks like he needed a replacement for the sheath he lost during the murder."

Ducks abruptly shot up a hand, forefinger raised.

"Hold it," he said. "So my client bought a knife and appurtenances—that proves exactly nothing."

Tip started to snap a reply, but a word from Cooper in his headset silenced him.

Ducks spoke again: "This lad bought a commando knife?"

He patted Ledger on the shoulder.

"Well, so could any crazed drughead who barged in there, after loot, and went psycho—you've got fingerprints on that thing?"

Bolknor shook his head.

"Just smudges," he said. "These killers meticulously wiped everything."

"Well, there you go," Ducks said.

362

Mike Bolknor spoke to Ledger.

"Why'd you buy that commando knife?" he asked.

Ledger shrugged.

"For fishing," he said. "Cut trout's heads off, like that."

"So you're quite a fisherman?" Bolknor asked.

Ledger shrugged again.

"Just getting started," he said. "Haven't bought the rods and reels and that sort of thing yet."

He stared back at Bolknor, looking smug.

Bolknor reached into his briefcase and brought out a plastic evidence bag, containing a scrap of fabric.

"Found at the murder site," he said. "Didn't come from the victim, clearly ripped off the assailant's shirt as they fought."

Ducks produced a dismissive snort.

"Clearly?" he said. "You were there, watching the victim rip off this bit of shirt?"

"At the trooper lab, they pinpointed this bit of fabric's colors, thread type, and so on," Mike said. "Our cyber expert's search then turned up an on-line clothing store that sold a Hawaiian shirt with precisely this fabric to Vic Ledger, and mailed it to his parents' house in Snowville."

Ducks shook his head.

"Hey, we'll admit it, the boy's got lousy fashion sense," he said. "So do thousands of other people—how many others have shirts just like that?"

Ledger glanced at his attorney, then stared back at Bolknor.

Smug.

"Oh, come on, Ducks," Tip interjected. "We got tire tracks, okay? It was the Snowville Maple company Jeep used for this killing, and before this, for other attacks, on people and animals, and Ledger here had total access to that Jeep."

Ducks sat back in his chair and whistled another snatch of *When the Saints Go Marching In*. Then he leaned forward in his chair and pointed his index finger at Tip.

"What my client's totally got is access to the U.S. Constitution," Ducks said. "Your evidence wouldn't hold up in court, and it's not enough to keep the boy locked up here—so out he goes, right away."

He put his head back and again started whistling *When the Saints Come Marching In,* stopping after a few bars to pull his baseball cap farther down over his eyes, staring out from under the brim.

"By the way, don't think you're going to bully the girlfriend into tattling on him," Ducks said. "I already talked to her, told her not a peep, and she's getting out right now, too—just keeping you boys up to date on the current headlines."

An instant later, Cooper North's voice came in over all the headphones.

"You've got search warrants?" she said.

"Yeah, for both houses," Tip said. "Rink and Ledger."

"Get up there, right now," Cooper said. "Fast— before these monsters get home and start destroying evidence."

She thought a half second.

"Tip, you and Kalisha take the girl's house," she said.

"Look for what you can find, especially see if she's got a Ninja outfit tucked away…and maybe she wrote something down about the killing, notes or something like that—go."

While Tip tore off his headphones and started out, she spoke to Mike.

"You and Ozzie Knick hit the Ledger house—look for that damned knife, especially, and try hard to get Karen Del Vecchio to meet you there, for evidence expertise, okay?"

"Okay," Mike said.

"Go," Cooper said.

As he removed his headphone, Mike looked at Vic Ledger and Ducks.

"New developments just came in, emergency, so we'll terminate this interview for now," he said. "Ledger, don't even try to leave the area—this investigation's just beginning."

A moment later, Vic Ledger and Ducks McGee sat alone in the interrogation room, Ledger looking pleased and confident.

Ducks sat back in his chair, eyes shut, forehead wrinkled, thinking hard.

61

Twenty-six minutes later.

Snowville.

A campus-security Prius pulled up in front of a cape-style clapboard house, a short walk from the Snowville Maple company headquarters.

Mike Bolknor and Ozzie Knick got out of the car and leaned against it, waiting.

At almost the same moment, just beyond Snowville Maple, Inc., a Dill PD cruiser veered left down a dirt road, then stopped after a few-hundred yards, at a double-wide mobile home, sun-faded and rusting around the seams, with kids' tricycles and frisbees scattered in the overgrown yard's weeds.

Tip LaPerle got out from behind the wheel, and Kelisha Rains climbed down from the SUV's shotgun seat.

They walked to the trailer's front door, and Tip rang the bell.

Nobody answered, so Tip pushed the doorbell button again, and held it.

Still no response. Tip pointed to a dented and rusted eleven-year-old Honda Civic parked in the gravel driveway.

"Someone's home," he said.

A moment later, patience exhausted, he tried the door handle, and the door opened. He leaned his head in, and shouted: "Hey, anybody here? Police!"

After a long moment, a woman trudged to the door, blear-eyed, clearly just awakened. Her hair, dyed purple, had flattened on one side, where she'd lain on it. She wore tight jeans, with assorted rips and tears, and a t-shirt needing a wash, and no shoes.

Kalisha thought: pretty, once, but worn down, and she saw wasting from drugs, in the woman's face and her eyes. About thirty-seven, going on sixty.

Still bleary, the woman stared at Tip's uniform. Then she stared at Kalisha, a black woman, young and good looking, in an upscale business suit, then back at Tip's uniform.

"I didn't do anything," she said.

Tip sighed, exasperated.

"Mrs. Rink?" he asked. "Prudence Rink?"

"Yeah, Rink, actually that name's my ex's, one of them, anyway," she said. "Say, if this's about what happened at O'Brien's Lounge, the other night, well, I wasn't...."

"No, Mrs. Rink," Kalisha said. "We're not here about you, remember? We telephoned?"

A blank look.

"I guess I was half asleep and...."

Doped up, Kalisha thought. Fentanyl.

"It's about your daughter," Kalisha said.

Another blank look.

"She's at pre-school, you know? So's her brother, and...."

"It's about Winnie," Kalisha said. "Your oldest—Winnie Rink?"

"Oh."

Silence.

Then: "What'd she do?"

"That's what we're here to find out," Kalisha said. "Chief LaPerle has a search-warrant to show you."

Tip produced the document from an inside pocket and unfolded it and held it up for Prudence Rink to read, but she only glanced at it.

"Damn, the place's a mess," she said. "They keep me hopping, over at the Sleepy Time Motel—that's where I clean rooms, you know?—and I haven't had time to...."

"Don't worry about it," Kalisha said. "We particularly want to see Winnie's room—does she have a room?"

It turned out Winnie Rink did have a room. Unlike the rest of the trailer, she kept it neat, with posters of rock stars on the walls, and movie-fan magazines fanned out on a small table.

Kalisha and Tip both pulled on latex gloves, then began opening drawers and closet doors. After a few minutes, Kalisha reached into a drawer and pulled out a garment, which she held up for Tip to see—black pants. She reached in again and pulled out a black shirt, and a black ski mask.

"Ninja outfit," she said.

"Don't finger it more than you have to," Tip said.

"I'll get a jumbo evidence bag, out of the car."

He left, and a minute later returned, with a large plastic bag, into which they carefully dropped the Ninja clothes, and sealed the bag.

They resumed searching.

From a night table drawer, Tip pulled a book.

"Diary," he said.

He began leafing through it, then stared at a page, and read aloud….

"Boy, that Olga Fisker woman really put up a fight, and got a slash on Vic's face, before he got the knife in her and she went down—exciting!!"

Tip and Kalisha exchanged a look.

Then he pulled another evidence bag from one of his pockets and, carefully, dropped the diary into it.

"What do you think?" he said. "Enough?"

"Plenty, for now," Kalisha said. "Later on, the trooper lab people…"

"Yeah, let's get back to Cooper with this—set up an arraignment," he said.

When they left, Prudence Rink lay on a sofa, idly leafing through a magazine.

Meanwhile, not far off, on the town's Main Street, a quarter-mile before the Snowville Maple headquarters building, a State Police cruiser pulled up behind Mike Bolknor's parked Prius, and Karen Del Vecchio got out.

She waved to Bolknor and Ozzie Knick, then withdrew a satchel from the cruiser.

"Got what I need in here for any prelim," she said, holding up the satchel. "Let's go."

They stood together a moment, taking in the house, freshly repainted, a white-clapboard cape, with black shutters, dormer windows projecting from the shingled roof, for extra rooms upstairs.

Parked in the garage's macadam driveway, a new white SUV.

"Buick Envision," Ozzie said. "Not cheap."

He added, as if the knowledge required justification: "I keep up on car models—helps with investigations we might do."

Parked in a grassy swath, alongside the garage, a mud-spattered silver Dodge Ram 1500 pickup truck. Beside it, a yellow backhoe, its segmented bucket assembly evoking a scorpion's curled tail.

"Ledger's father runs an excavation business," Bolknor said. "We did a quick look-up on these folks."

"Let's go be detectives," Karen said.

They walked up the slate-paved pathway to the front door. Ozzie Knick reached for the doorbell, but before his finger pressed it, the door opened and a woman stared at them, frozen. A blond woman, fortyish, with a strained face and reddened eyes.

She'd been crying.

"Mrs. Judith Ledger?" Mike asked.

She nodded, stricken.

Mike took out his wallet and flopped it open, showing the Dill PD badge he used, when working as the department's detective.

She pressed a hand over her heart.

"My husband...."

She left it unfinished, because a tall, sinewy man rushed up behind her, glaring over the top of her head.

"This is Ozzie Knick, assistant state's attorney," Mike said, still holding up his badge. "We have Karen Del Vecchio with us, from the state police lab, to help with evidence processing, if we find any."

Judith Ledger gasped and pressed a hand against the doorframe, to keep herself upright. Her husband grabbed her shoulders and moved her aside, so he could get at the door.

"What kind of crap are you Dill jerks pulling here?" he demanded.

"It's as I told you over the phone," Ozzie said. "We're conducting an investigation, and we need to take a look at your son's room—you're Timothy Ledger, I assume?"

Mike removed a search warrant from his suit jacket's inner pocket and held it up. Ledger grabbed it and scanned it, face clenched, then—eyes narrowed—read it again, word by word.

"Bull!" he said.

Mike reached for the search warrant, but Ledger jerked it away, and looked about to rip it up.

"Don't," Mike said.

Ledger glared at him. Mike stared back, unruffled, like a granite cliff.

"If you tear that, the warrant still holds, and you'd be subject to arrest for interfering with a criminal investigation," Mike said.

Ledger abruptly thrust the warrant at him, and Mike took it, refolded it, and replaced it in his jacket pocket.

371

"Where do you get off, harassing kids like this?" Ledger demanded. "Dill big shots, coming into the little town to make trouble for us!"

Mike didn't react, still a granite cliff.

"It's like this, Mr. Ledger," he said. "There've been attempted murders, and a murder, and we have evidence your son might be involved—this is serious."

Ledger cursed.

"Obstructing a criminal investigation is a criminal act on its own," Mike said. "It'll be best for everyone, especially this family, if you simply stand aside and allow us to carry out our responsibilities."

Ledger stayed blocking the doorway, glaring at Bolknor, his jaw working. His face and neck leathery, and tanned, from outdoor work. Eyes angry. Behind that angry glare, fear.

"You'll damn-well be hearing from our lawyer," he said.

With something like a snarl, he stepped aside, allowing the three law-enforcement officers to walk into the house unimpeded. Muttering, he led them up the stairs to his son's room, which turned out to be locked.

"Unlock it please," Bolknor said.

"Hell, we don't have a key," Ledger said. "That's Vic's private place, and he's got the key, so…."

"What's in there that's so private?" Ozzie Knick suddenly asked.

Ledger looked at him, not a friendly look.

"Vic likes his privacy, okay?" he said. "He hasn't let us in there in years—probably just a bunch of kid stuff."

"If you won't open the door for us, we'll have to do it," Mike said. "Our search warrant gives us that right."

Ledger's face reddened.

"What part of 'we don't have a key' don't you understand?" he said. "Any idiot could understand that."

Mike stepped to the door and stooped, to inspect the locking mechanism. He opened his wallet and removed a credit card.

"Sometimes this works, and let's hope it does," he said. "We'd rather not break down the door."

He inserted the card into the crack between the door and frame, adjacent to the doorknob, and fiddled with it. After a moment, he twisted the handle and pushed, and the door swung open.

Bolknor, Knick, and Del Vecchio gazed at the room.

So did the two senior Ledgers, as if beholding an Egyptian crypt, opened after three-thousand years.

Posters lined a rear wall, black lettering on white cardboard:

"BEFORE INVINCIBILITY, MASTERY; BEFORE MASTERY, PREPARATION."

"TO RISE ABOVE SHEEP, BE WOLVES"

"MERCY IS WEAKNESS"

"IN VICIOUSNESS IS FREEDOM"

"WAKE, ACT—OR DIE ASLEEP"

"CRUELTY IS MASTERY"

Other posters lined an adjacent wall, showing images of creatures. A silver star marked one of them, "Pygmy Shrew." Marking another image, a cobra, raised up to strike, hood extended, a gold star. Other posters showed tigers, lions, wolves, hawks, and other beasts of prey, several in the process of killing an antelope or elk.

Tacked to the wall over the bed's backboard, two large sheets of paper with one word on each, hand lettered in green ink—

"NUMERO UNO."

"NUMERO DOS."

Standing in the doorway, the adult Ledgers both looked dumbfounded, unable to make sense of what they saw in their son's room.

Simultaneously, the three investigators pulled on latex gloves. Mike then opened a clothes closet, scanned the insides, and pulled from an overhead shelf a neat bundle of clothing, which he unfolded: black trousers, black shirt, black over-the-head ski mask. He held them up for Ozzie and Karen to see.

"Got a large-sized evidence bag?" he asked Karen.

She opened her satchel and extracted a plastic bag, unfolded it, and held it open while Mike dropped in the Ninja outfit.

"Look!" Ozzie said.

He pointed to a concentric-ring target hung on one wall—stuck into its central bull's eye, a large commando knife. Mike and Karen walked over for a closer look, and Karen pointed to the blade.

"Crusted blood?" she said. "Looks like it."

She pulled another evidence bag from her satchel and held it open. Mike carefully pulled the knife from the target and placed it in the bag, which Karen then closed and sealed.

"I'd say that's all we need," Ozzie said. "For now."

"Just one thing more," Karen said.

She pulled a small brush from her satchel, and a small evidence bag. Then she walked to the dresser and brushed something invisible off the top, into the bag, and sealed the bag.

"Dust," she said. "A new technology we're adopting—this could be interesting."

"We'll be needing to take this," Mike said, lifting a laptop computer, resting on the room's desk.

He unplugged it from the wall, and wound up the wire to make it easy to transport.

"That's it for now," he told the two adult Ledgers, still standing in the doorway.

Judith Ledger verged on tears. Timothy Ledger's clenched face looked enraged, and deeply upset. Both stepped aside, letting the three investigators leave the room, then file down the stairs to the front door, where Mike turned to look back at the Ledgers.

"Don't remove anything from that room," he told them. "Don't let your son remove anything—in case his attorney gets him out, temporarily."

At the curb, they conferred. Then Ozzie and Mike drove off in the Prius, and Karen left in the state-police cruiser.

Standing in their house's doorway, Judith and Timothy Ledger watched the investigators drive off. When the cars were gone, they still stood in the doorway, staring down the road.

62

Dr. Lopez would be here in one hour.

First, though, Emma Ford came.

"Big day today, Dear," she told Cooper.

Emma switched off the blue chemotherapy pump, and the pinging stopped.

For weeks it had pinged, days and nights, surging chemicals into her body. Violent chemicals. They'd decimated Cooper's bone marrow, and the white cells and red cells the marrow manufactured, leaving her with no immune system, and weak.

Chemotherapy took away her hair. Emma gave her a headscarf, and tied it on for her. Chemotherapy took away her appetite. Emma brought her ice creams, from the ward's freezer. Otherwise, she subsisted on intravenous feeding.

She looked skeletal.

"No more chemotherapy, for now," Emma said. "Round one's over."

She removed the emptied bags of chemicals attached to the pump, and she detached the pump's plastic tubes from the catheter in Cooper's chest.

"You're free!" Emma said.

Cooper got out of bed, walked two weak steps, and dropped into a chair. For the first time in what seemed forever, she sat untethered.

In an hour, Dr. Lopez would do a bone-marrow biopsy.

If the chemicals—her dangerous chemical companions—worked as hoped, they'd have eradicated all the leukemic cells in her blood.

Or not. Because the odds said not.

"What happens now?" Cooper asked Emma.

"We'll wait for your bone marrow to grow back," Emma told her.

She gave Cooper a wry, sad head shake.

"And then," she said, "we'll hook you up again and blast you a second time."

As it always did, Emma's calm voice soothed Cooper. Yet, Emma also faced death. She'd faced it as a stricken child, in a Harlem tenement. She faced death now, every day.

She could die any time.

Cooper suddenly asked her: "How do you stay so serene?"

Cooper saw understanding in the nurse's eyes.

Emma shrugged, and sighed.

"Every day, I try to be of use," she said. "And if I am…."

For a while, the two women said nothing, alone together in the darkened room, the still undrawn drapes keeping out the morning light. Emma then opened the drapes and started toward the door, but stopped to look back.

"Forget the survival odds," she said. "They only apply to the overall patient population, and your personal odds of survival may be different—they may be a hundred percent."

Emma looked at Cooper, with affection in her eyes.

"I'll be here," she said. "When Dr. Lopez comes, I'll be right beside you."

Emma left, and shut the door.

A minute later, the telephone rang.

Ozzie Knick calling.

"We got indictments," he said.

Cooper never doubted they'd get the indictments.

Yesterday they'd searched the subjects' homes, finding strong evidence. Ninja costumes. A diary. A commando knife. Vic Ledger's computer.

He'd saved manifestos on the laptop, extolling murder, as proof of superiority. He'd detailed his and Winnie Rink's attacks on animals, and failed attacks on people, listing the lessons learned. Then he bragged about knifing Olga Fisker, giving facts only the murderers could know.

Damning.

Ozzie now said: "Arraignments set for this afternoon, at two."

Cooper thought: Good.

Except....

"Ducks is a wily bugger," she told Ozzie over the phone. "Keep digging—if this comes to trial, let's hand Ducks a grenade."

She thought where to look.

"Lab results, maybe, Karen Del Vecchio...."

Cooper put down the phone.

Suddenly the room seemed strange, with the blue chemotherapy pump now rolled into a corner, silent. It seemed empty.

She thought: how can I "be of use?"

At the trial, Kalisha and Ozzie would handle the prosecution. Maybe, though, she could zoom in, on Kalisha's computer, to back them up. Ducks had two obviously guilty clients to defend. What would he do? Insanity defense? No, she knew Ducks. He'd go for the win. Maybe he'd attack the evidence. Or the prosecutors.

A knock on Cooper's door—she looked at the wall clock.

An hour had passed.

Manny Lopez stood in the doorway, belatedly slipping on a surgical mask. For the first time, Cooper saw her oncologist unmasked. Until now, she'd seen only his eyes, the color of dark chocolate, and—so it seemed to her—windows into a head crammed with complicated knowledge of malignancies, and the scores of chemicals to counteract them, and the antibiotics immune-compromised patients needed, a head with wisdom in it, from decades treating the terribly afflicted.

Cooper thought: he looks confident, and resolute, and kind.

He carried a small instrument bag.

"This'll be over quickly," he told Cooper. "Just lie on your stomach—you're an attorney, so think about the

Constitution."

"All right, Dr. Lopez," she said. "I'll review the Fourth Amendment."

"Call me Manny," he said, as he extracted a needle from his equipment bag. "Why the Fourth?"

"It prohibits unreasonable searches," Cooper said.

"Okay," he said. "We'll keep this search reasonable."

Just then the door opened again and Emma hurried in, to stand by the prone Cooper's bedside.

"Right now I'm spreading a numbing agent over your pelvic bone," Dr. Lopez said. "It'll help keep this search reasonable."

Emma reached down and took Cooper's hand. Not a gesture Cooper normally would accept, somebody offering support.

She's always been her own support.

She thought: not now, though.

I do need support.

Yes I do.

"Here comes the needle," Dr. Lopez said. "Starting its reasonable search."

He explained the biopsy needle had a hollow core, and a sharp cutting edge, and Cooper felt it pushing into her flesh. It didn't hurt, because of the numbing agent. Now, though, as Dr. Lopez drilled it into her bone, Cooper felt it grinding, and she gritted her teeth.

"It's going into your posterior iliac crest, the top of the pelvic bone," Dr. Lopez said as he worked. "It's a reasonable search, no Fourth Amendment infringement —we need it to help you."

Cooper felt the grinding stop, and the biopsy needle withdrawing from her flesh.

"Now the needle's got a sample of your bone marrow in it, about the diameter of a pencil lead," Dr.

Lopez said. "I'll get this down to the lab, and they'll see what's what."

He stopped, looking down at Cooper, forehead wrinkled.

"It'll take the lab at least twenty-four hours, and...."

He stood thinking.

"You know what?" he said. "That's too long to wait, so here comes an unreasonable search, and to hell with the Fourth Amendment—I'm taking a second sample, an aspirate, so I can get a quick look at this under my own microscope, a preliminary look."

Cooper felt a second needle going in. She felt the grinding again. She felt the needle withdrawn.

"I'll get back to you," Dr. Lopez said, and Cooper heard him hurrying out of the room, before she could sit up and look.

Emma smiled. Cooper saw it in her eyes, above the mask.

"He's your fan, you know," she said. "He admires you—he told me."

He couldn't wait, Cooper thought. He's hurrying off to see my fate.

She smiled at Emma.

I'm in good hands, she thought.

At   least,   I'm   in   good   hands.

63

It started with a single letter to the editor in the *Dill Chronicle.*

> *"Two kids from Snowville, stuck in a Dill jail cell, because it's easier for the big-town prosecutors to railroad small-town high schoolers than to hunt down the real killers, if there even was a killing—who knows? A hundred-thousand dollars for bail, and where's that money supposed to come from? And whose sticky fingers get into that bail money? Just asking—a concerned Snowville citizen."*

Actually, the *Chronicle* had reported in detail on the Fisker murder from the beginning. Also, the newspaper reported on the killings of Dill pets, too, and the failed attacks on Allister Chesterton, and Kalisha Rains, and Thor Ennis. It had also detailed the evidence—laid out in the arraignments—against Vic Ledger and Winnie Rink.

Damning evidence.

Yet, enraged Snowville residents ignored the Ninja costumes, the ripped-off shred of shirt fabric, the knife, the diary entry, the confession on Vic Ledger's computer, the use of Snowville Maple's truck at the crime scenes. They didn't discuss it. Instead, they hurled accusations against the police and prosecutors, claiming the arrest of these suspects constituted an attack on Snowville, and all its citizens, for nefarious reasons hinted at but never explained.

It snowballed, with enraged letters-to-the editor pouring in, angry town meetings, a rising sense of victimization.

> *"Looks like the big-shot prosecutor in Dill wants another notch in her Gucci belt, so she's going after our little town. It's an outrage! Let's pony up, Snowville, help these poor children get out on bail, at least."*

> *"Snowville Maple's lawyer has taken on the kids' case, so somebody gives a damn about us. A really good lawyer, too--Harley Duckle McGee, rated tops. So let's hope justice gets done here."*

> *"We had a meeting at our church, with the kids' attorney, and he said we may have to sue the corrupt cops and prosecutors, put them on trial, see how they like it!"*

WHEN THE WASP STINGS

At a meeting at Snowville's town hall, Tip LaPerle and Kalisha Rains tried to answer citizens' questions.

However, they were asked no questions. Instead, they received a fusillade of verbal shots, mostly accusing them of being on the take, somehow, and "out to get Snowville." Tip tried to lay out the evidence, all over again, but got hooted and shouted down, with yells of "Made-up Murder! Made-up Murder!"

Tip got exasperated.

"For God's sake," he told the crowd. "Look at the facts."

A shout from the audience: "We're way past facts now!"

Later, at the hospital, still fuming, Tip told Cooper: "Ducks sat in back, smirking."

Cooper told him Ducks had a problem.

"Given this evidence, a jury will convict in a second," she said. "Defense's best move would be to plead insanity."

She shook her head.

"He won't do it, though," she said.

She'd known Ducks since he first came to town, decades ago, from Baton Rouge. She knew why he wouldn't use the insanity defense.

"It's his psychology," she said. "Ducks needs to win—pleading insanity would acknowledge his clients did the crime, in Ducks' mind a loss, so he's going for a public-outcry defense."

Whip up outrage in the town, Cooper said. It's all he's got. Intimidate us. Intimidate the judge. Taint jurors.

Tip cursed.

"That town's full of dimwits," he said.

Cooper shook her head.

"It's not so simple," she said.

Fifty years ago, Snowville prospered, quarrying marble, she said. Good-paying union jobs, thriving shopkeepers, workers rising to management in the quarrying companies, or into sales. Then the marble vein ran out.

"Since then, Snowville's gone downhill," Cooper said.

Workers gravitated to jobs in nearby Dill, but for a fraction of their Snowville wages. Driving garbage trucks. Holding up "Stop" signs on road repaving projects. Selling cigarettes and sodas in convenience stores.

"They feel stepped-on, disrespected, like losers, failures," Cooper said.

So they're boiling over, she told Tip. Ducks whips it up, she said, insinuating conspiracies and injustice. Just then, her hospital-room telephone buzzed— Kalisha Rains calling, upset.

"They've started fund raising, for the bail, and to pay Ducks' fees," Kalisha said. "They've even set up an internet site, for people nationwide to donate."

Kalisha sounded shook. Clearly her law-school classes never covered this sort of public uprising. Cooper thought: toughen up, girl. You prosecute, half the time they try to prosecute you back.

"It says to send money, their web site does," Kalisha said, outraged. "It says send money to rescue small-town high school kids, railroaded by ruthless prosecutors and police enforcers, and it looks like the money's pouring in, too."

Kalisha then reported another outrage.

"They've even gotten a major national cable-news network to send in a reporter—apparently an old friend of Ducks'—and she'll be featuring the story every night, little people fighting injustice, defending their kids."

Silence on the telephone, while Kalisha considered it all.

"It's scary," she said, finally. "And if these two psychopaths get out on bail—it's so easy to get knives."

"We can only do our jobs," Cooper told her. "If national tv comes around, just lay out the evidence, and keep calm."

"Well there's more, and it's stomach turning," Kalisha said.

Women from across the country, responding to the images on tv, were now sending love-letters to Vic Ledger, in jail, pledging their eternal devotion and adoration. Young women, but older women, too, and it appalled Kalisha.

Dearest Vic—I can only imagine what you're going through. I bet they're torturing you, to get you to confess to what you didn't do. Even if you did it, though, for God's sake, boys will be boys. Maybe you made a little mistake, but only he who is without sin should cast that first stone. I wish I could be

*there to put my arms around you, such
a handsome young man. P.S. I wonder
if maybe that girl in jail with you led
you astray, seductive and nasty. Maybe
it was she who used the knife. But I
don't believe you ever did anything at
all. And when this is over, and you're
free again, I want to be there for you.*

After she put the phone down, and after Tip left, now alone in her room, Cooper thought: Ducks didn't cause this, but he's fueling it, behind the scenes, whispering in the town's ears.

One thing more: their fund-raising campaign's likely to bring truckloads of cash. Who's likely to get most of it?

64

Dr. Manuel Lopez finally walked back into his hospital office, after morning rounds. He'd checked on his oncology patients, in rooms all along this medical-surgical wing.

Cooper North's bone-marrow sample, still in its biopsy needle, lay on a table, beside his microscope. It drew him powerfully, but he still had one job to finish.

He'd just visited a young mother with rhabdomyosarcoma. An attractive thirty-year-old, she now lay exhausted in her bed.

She wore a colostomy bag.

He'd heard her tell her husband: "Well, if I can stand it, I guess you can."

She worried him.

One of many worries.

Often, at the dinner table, with his wife and his own two kids, he seemed, as his wife put it, "to have left this Earth," his mind preoccupied with the cancers growing in his patients, like alien invaders, and how to fight them.

He had to choose precisely from an arsenal of chemotherapy agents. Would this one help or hurt? For this case, should he use a combination of agents? Which ones? What doses? Should he set up a cooperative effort with the radiation oncologist, because radiation-plus-chemotherapy might work best for this patient? Meanwhile, infections sprang up, sometimes as dangerous as the cancers, so he needed to pick just the right antibiotics, and the right doses.

This woman with rhabdomyosarcoma particularly troubled him, because her cancer was bad, and her family depended on her.

Her husband couldn't handle raising three children, and holding a job. Dr. Lopez had seen that clearly. He seemed a decent person, but not fully mature. His wife in the hospital bed was the strong one.

But she was dying.

She'd put off coming to the hospital for too many weeks. She needed to keep her job at a restaurant, cleaning tables and floors after hours, because her husband's road-construction job paid too little to support them. Also, they'd dropped their health insurance, unable to afford it. Then, because of some processing glitch, they didn't qualify for Medicaid, at least so far.

Because she'd waited too long, the tumor had grown large, and the cancer had spread. A surgeon had removed the tumor, but he could do nothing about the multiplying cancers in her lymph nodes and organs. She'd been receiving chemotherapy combined with radiation, and it eliminated some of the metastasized cancers, and shrunk some of the others. But only some, and she'd grown steadily weaker.

Dr. Lopez saw in her face the knowledge that she would die.

He treated her at no cost to her, and the hospital, too, charged her nothing. It meant, though, the hospital's general rates would nudge up, to cover the shortfall from treatments like this, for patients who couldn't pay.

He'd examined the woman a few minutes ago. Now he studied the latest CT scans of her inner organs, to see if he could do something more. He looked grim.

I'll fight for her, he told himself.

He shook his head, and for a moment sat staring the wall.

Finally, he picked up Cooper North's biopsy needle.

All morning he'd waited to look at it, yet dreaded what he might see.

He sat a minute, thinking about Cooper North.

She had raptor eyes. He'd noticed that when he first met her. CT-scan eyes—they saw you, and saw into you.

He admired how she faced this dread disease, leukemia, without flinching. He admired her, too, for continuing to work, from a hospital bed, still leading her team. He admired her intelligence. He'd Googled her, an impressive career. Just speaking with her, though, he sensed her mind's strength and subtlety.

He liked most people. Some, though, stood out.

His father, for one. A man who worked loading heavy bags of fertilizer and pesticides onto trucks, in El Paso, cheerfully, delighting in his family, proud he could support them. Manny Lopez admired his mother, too. She waited tables, and kept them all nourished at home, and thriving and laughing, on little money, as if love were treasure.

He admired Cooper North.

With practiced fingers, he extracted her bone marrow from the biopsy needle, and spread it on a slide, which he placed under his microscope.

Just this tiny bit of her inner body.

He would examine it under high magnification.

391

He would see her fate.

For a minute, he stared through the eyepiece. Finally, he sat back, staring at the wall.

He thought: I won't tell her yet. Maybe I'm wrong. I'll wait until the full lab report comes in.

I'll   tell   her   then.

65

Outside the hospital, events accelerated.

"They've been bailed out."

Tip LaPerle, on his cell phone.

"Jeesum Crow, there's a Snowville crowd here, applauding!" he said. "What are those two? Homicidal perps? Or movie stars?"

"That's what Ducks made them into," Cooper said. "Celebrities."

Tip cursed under his breath.

"Well, the movie they're starring in, it ought to be called *Who Gets Knifed Next?*"

A moment after Tip ended his call, Cooper's telephone buzzed again.

Mike Bolknor this time.

"I'm at the state crime lab," he said. "I'm putting Karen Del Vecchio on—she's got new information."

Karen's voice next.

"Cooper, under Olga Fisker's fingernails, if you remember, we found bits of human flesh—clearly scratched off her assailant as they fought."

"I remember," Cooper said.

"DNA in that flesh matches Vic Ledger's," she said.

Cooper went silent, then finally spoke.

"Okay, that clinches it," she said.

"Yes, but there's more," Karen said. "When we searched Vic Ledger's room, at his parents' house, I took a dust sample, which had his DNA."

Cooper thought dust analysis must be a new technique. At least, new to her.

"Dust from the murder scene, at Olga Fisker's house, had the same DNA—Vic Ledger's," she said. "So that proves he was there."

Silence over the phone, while Cooper heard Karen rustling through paperwork at the other end. Karen finally spoke.

"Also, that gum found in the grass, after the attempted break-in at Chesterton's—its DNA's a match for the girl, Winnie Rink."

Karen silently scanned the lab reports.

"One last point," she said. "That commando knife we found in Ledger's room—it had dried blood on it, and that blood turns out to be Olga Fisker's."

Cooper, untethered from the chemotherapy pump, out of bed, sat back in her chair, thinking.

"We need to set up a chat with Ducks," she said. "I'll do it."

She called Ducks immediately.

"You'd better come right up here," she said.

"Hey, Coop, I'm a busy boy just now, and...."

"New evidence, Ducks—we need to share it with the defense."

Silence from Ducks' end.

"It'll affect your strategy," Cooper said. "So hustle your busy self on up here."

A half hour later, Ducks walked into her hospital room.

He had on his usual Boston Red Sox cap. Now he wore big-boy pants, instead of cargo shorts, but an untucked shirttail still hung out in back. He looked, as usual, smug.

"How's it going, Coop?" he asked.

Cooper doubted he cared, so she ignored the question. She sat in one of the room's chairs, and waved Ducks into another, facing her. For a moment, she silently eyed him, not for the first time wondering if this particular attorney had a conscience.

Finally she spoke: "Yes, you're dutybound to defend your clients, but some tactics amount to war crimes."

Ducks made a dismissive movement of his hand.

"Hey, you're not a sissy are you, Coop?" he asked. "Get all fluttery when there's adverse public opinion?"

Cooper eyed him coldly, a man in his early fifties, balding under his baseball cap, going to corpulence, with a retained trace of Louisiana in his intonations, and a face brimming with insouciance.

"Let this sink in, Ducks," she said.

She cited, in detail, the crime lab's new findings.

"You understand?" Cooper said. "It's over—this is knockout evidence, no jury will acquit those two killers."

Ducks sat back in his chair, not responding, and Cooper watched his mental wheels grinding.

"Whip up the Snowville grievance machine all you want," Cooper said. "This case will be tried in Dill, and we'll get a jury you haven't tainted."

Ducks exhaled heavily.

"I've got to defend my clients," he said.

"Right, otherwise no jumbo fees from internet fund raising," Cooper said.

"That's nasty, putting it like that," Ducks said.

"Poor dear, so sensitive," Cooper said. "Now, about defending your clients, shall we think together?"

Ducks said nothing, scowling at her.

"Public outcry won't help them," Cooper said. "With this evidence, a guilty verdict is certain, and they're lucky this state has no death penalty—so it'll be life imprisonment, no chance for parole."

Ducks shook his head.

"These poor kids," he said.

"Spare me," Cooper said. "They're homicidal psychopaths, and if they're out there free-ranging—like they are right now because you got them bailed—they'll surely kill again, and you know it."

Ducks shrugged and spread his hands.

"Nothing I can do about that," he said.

"Yes there is," Cooper said. "Your one available move is to plead insanity, and they'll live out their sorry lives safely confined in a mental institution."

"I don't like that option," Ducks said.

"They won't like it either, but it's all they've got," Cooper said. "You better see to that before they do something in the cold-blooded murder line, which will put some tarnish on your reputation, by the way."

Ducks made a sound like a snarl, and stood up.

"Blackmail," he said. "That's low."

"It's not blackmail, busy boy," she said. "It's the ice-cold truth, and you know it, and you'd better get things moving with your clients and the judge, before something bad happens."

With a silent curse, just his mouth moving, Ducks stomped out of the room, as much as a man wearing sneakers could stomp.

66

Tip LaPerle and Mike Bolknor walked into Flute Wagner's office, at Snowville Maple, Inc., right on time. They'd telephoned ahead.

Wagner sat behind his desk, and his wife, Viola, sat alongside. She'd obviously just brought him his forgotten lunch, because a brown-paper bag lay on his desk, as yet unopened. Under it lay a manila folder, thick with papers, apparently work he'd left at home, which Viola brought in for him, too.

"Just a few questions," Tip said.

Cooper had telephoned Bolknor and LaPerle an hour ago, saying Ducks decided to plead insanity for his clients—against such crushing evidence, he had no choice. Ozzie Knick and Kalisha Rains now worked on the prosecution's paperwork for the changed plea.

"We're racing with it," Cooper said over the phone. "Homicidal maniacs, still out on bail, maybe they'll find knives."

They'd finished investigating the Olga Fisker murder, though. So now they'd refocused on the Proctor Gibbs killing. LaPerle and Bolknor decided to see if Flute Wagner had anything new to tell them.

Taking seats in Wagner's office, both officers stared over his head at the giant wall poster behind him, an eel-green Lamborghini Huracan, looking almost diabolical with its swoops and curving edges.

"That's some machine," Tip said. "You have one in your garage?"

Flute looked down, embarrassed.

"Years, saving….," he mumbled. "It's hard…."

Viola cursed, angry.

"They don't pay Flute his worth here," she said. "They made Dumbo the new CEO—without Flute, he'd just sit there, with his thumb in his mouth."

Flute made a weak hand motion.

"Flute, that's exactly how it is, and you know it," Viola said. "It's just like Connecticut, when we were kids, and those rotten bullies…."

Flute put his head down.

"They'd ridiculed both of us, the schools only two poor kids," Viola snarled. "Every time they started on me, Flute tried to fend them off me, and then they'd really go after him."

Flute dropped his head even lower.

Viola sat staring at her husband, fuming.

Mike Bolknor thought: is she angry at him? Or angry for him? He sensed it was the latter.

"Mr. Wagner, we're working on the Proctor Gibbs murder," Tip said. "Do you have any further information for us? Any new thoughts?"

Flute looked up and shook his head.

"Who'd ever…" he said. "Such a kind old man, generous…."

"Generous!" Viola muttered. "He willed Snowville Maple to that useless lump, instead of who'd earned it, and that's generous?"

Flute sighed.

Bolknor thought: that sadness is decades deep.

Flute now sat in silence, staring back over his shoulder, at the wall poster of the expensive sports car.

"I'd imagine it," he whispered.

To himself, it seemed.

"I'd drive it slowly, through that fancy town's every street—they'd see Viola sitting beside me, proud, better than any of them, who got BMWs for graduation, and we'd....".

He sighed again.

Mike Bolknor thought: that's heavy to carry down the years, over a ton of sports car.

"Has anything happened around the company, making you think again about who might have killed Proctor Gibbs?" Tip asked.

Flute shook his head.

"Dumbo got himself that Corvette," Viola said. "Rides around like it's his royal carriage, so Proctor Gibbs died? Dry eyes on Dumbo."

"Viola...." Flute said, as if in pain.

"Sonny DeWitt is a person of interest in this case," Tip said.

He thought a moment.

"We're getting our search warrant updated, so we'll be here tomorrow, to have a look in the man's office," he said. "Although, it's hard to see what's to find—a signed and notarized confession would help."

A few minutes later, as they walked back out the building's front door, into the driveway, Viola Wagner hurried out the door behind them, meaning to speak, but just then Sonny DeWitt's cherry-red Corvette roared

400

down the drive and parked beside the Dill PD cruiser and DeWitt got out.

"Luncheon meeting, in Dill," he announced, as if his absence from the building needed an explanation.

Speech slightly slurred. Face reddened. Apparently he drank his lunch.

"Hey, there, Viola—here for a conjugal visit?" Sonny said.

He laughed, as if he'd just uttered a witticism.

Viola glared at him, a glare so intense he turned away and shrugged and started walking into the building. She glared at his receding back until he was gone.

"Jackass," she muttered.

She kept staring silently, at the closed front door, until she finally spoke.

"Flute's already raised this company's profits," she said. "Every night he's working, at home, eleven-thirty maybe, sends me back to the office here to fetch a file, or a thumb drive, helping him, best I can do."

She stared at the Snowville Maple headquarters building, face knotted up, intense.

"He's work, work, work," Viola said. "For peanuts!"

Silence then, neither LaPerle or Bolknor knowing what to say.

Mike finally nodded.

Tip shook his head, understanding.

They started walking toward Tip's patrol car.

Behind them, they heard Viola speak one last time.

"You want to know who killed Proctor Gibbs?" she said.   "Guess!"

67

At nine the next morning, Tip and Mike Bolknor returned to the Snowville Maple headquarters building, with their updated search warrant.

Viola Wagner sat behind the reception desk.

"New job for you?" Tip asked.

Viola shook her head.

"Filling in," she said. "Flute asked me to—until they hire someone."

"Flute arranged this?" Mike said. "Not the CEO?"

Viola's eyes flashed, angry, and she didn't answer.

Tip pulled a document from his uniform's inside pocket and held it up.

"Search warrant," he said. "Sonny DeWitt in his office?"

Viola made a show of checking her wristwatch.

"It's only nine-ten," she said. "Our Mr. DeWitt's morning starts with donuts, in the Dill coffee shops—that's his hangover therapy."

She pretended to study the appointments calendar on her desk.

"Yes, he rolls in here ten-thirty, or so, spends an hour staring out his office window, then a beer break, after which he's off in his Corvette, gets back from lunch about an hour before we close for the day, so...."

"Who runs things all day, when he's AOL?" Tip asked.

Viola stared at him.

"Who do you think?" she said.

Tip exchanged a glance with Mike.

"We don't need DeWitt to search," he said. "His office locked?"

Viola opened a desk drawer, pulled out a ring of keys, selected one, then led the way to DeWitt's office door and opened it.

She stood back and extended both arms toward the doorway, meaning, go right on in, gentlemen. She stayed outside, leaning against the doorframe, to watch them search.

They started by drawing on latex gloves, then surveying the room.

A big desk. Two metal filing cabinets. A built-in wall cabinet. Two guest chairs, plus a rolling desk chair. Hard-maple floors.

Tip took the desk.

Lying on top, he found a letter, hand-scrawled in ink, but unfinished. Sonny had obviously run into trouble composing it, given all the cross-outs. Tip read it aloud, for Mike to hear.

"Hey Sheila—that e-mail from your lawyer! Some operator!
Yeah, I own the company now, mostly. Like big fuming deal.
I'm working from dawn to after ten, most nights. And my expenses!
Stratosphere! Like dinner for customers, etc. etc. Needed a new car,
too. CEO can't look chintzy, okay?

I'm ticked, Sheila! Call off your legal wolves, okay? Every month, already, I send you a mint. Okay, sometimes I forget, which is no biggie. Child care! How much do kids' sneakers and ice-cream cones cost you? Also...."

Still leaning in the doorway, Viola muttered: "Works from dawn to ten?—Jackass!"

Tip now looked through Sonny's desk drawers, finding nothing of particular interest, mostly heaps of memos, printouts from Flute Wagner's computer. Marketing plan breakdowns, costs versus profit boosts. Also, suggestions for smoothing operations.

"Sonny—a thought. Instead of replacing the Ledger boy, how about seeing if volunteers from the Snowville Historical Society would lead tours? Maple sugaring goes way back here, after all. Somebody retired? Lots of empty time on their hands? It'd save a salary, and we'd probably get better tours, with guides actually interested. What do you think, Sonny?"

Sonny apparently didn't think much about the idea, because he'd stuffed Flute's memo in a drawer, unanswered, along with a heap of other suggestions from Flute.

Mike, meanwhile, found nothing of interest in the file cabinets, just standard business records. Mainly they showed that Snowville Maple, Inc., prospered.

"Drawing a blank here," Mike said.

"Same with the desk," Tip told him.

Unless something incriminating lay hidden under a floorboard, the built-in wall cabinet would be the last spot to search. First, though, they carefully walked the floor, looking for any telltale signs of a pried-up board, with something hidden underneath. They found none. A quick search of the walls also turned up nothing. No secret compartments.

"Hey, what the hell!"

They looked up and saw Sonny DeWitt standing in the doorway. He'd obviously just come in from the parking lot, a cardboard coffee cup in his left hand, and a bag of donuts in his right.

"They came with a search warrant," Viola told him, shaking her head in pretend consternation.

"Hey, you can't go through my private stuff!" DeWitt said, one decibel below a yell.

"Because we might find something like this?" Tip said, holding up a bottle of bourbon, which he'd found in one drawer.

"For crying out loud!" Sonny said.

"Don't worry, it's legal," Tip said. "Just pulling your chain."

By now Sonny's face had turned red, and he glared with gritted teeth.

Mike opened the built-in wall cabinet's door and looked inside.

"That's interesting," he said.

He pulled out a glass object, which he examined, then handed to Tip.

"Looks like a soda bottle, with its top cut off," Tip said, peering at it. "Something smeared at the bottom— looks like jam."

He put his nose to the bottle and sniffed.

"Raspberry," he said. "They must've used a glass cutter, cut off the bottle's skinny neck." He stared at it, thinking.

"See, they turned the neck upside down and stuck it into the bottom half," he said. "Then they duct-taped it together—so what's it supposed to be? A funnel?"

Mike pointed.

At the bottom of the contraption, stuck in the smeared jam, lay two dead yellow-jackets.

They looked at Sonny DeWitt, waiting for an explanation. None came. He just stared at the contraption, looking confused.

"Did you make this thing?" Mike Bolknor asked.

"I never saw it before," Sonny said. "I didn't put it in the cabinet, either."

"Funny, those dead wasps in there," Tip said. "We'll show this to Cooper North."

Mike pulled a large plastic bag from one of his pockets and held it open, while Tip carefully lowered in the glass contraption.

When they looked up, Flute Wagner now stood in the doorway, between Sonny De Witt and Viola. He stared at the bottle contraption, now in its clear plastic evidence bag, thunderstruck. He looked at Sonny, then at Viola, eyes wide, face stricken.

Suddenly he turned and hurried away, toward his office.

"Fascinating, those wasps in there," Tip told De Witt.

DeWitt said: "Hey, if you think…."

"We'll tell you what we think, soon enough," Tip said. "Don't leave the state."

He and Mike left the office, then the building. Flute Wagner stood on the front porch, looking as if he'd been punched.

Sonny…."

He said it in a whisper, speaking to nobody, except himself.

Tip shrugged and walked toward his parked cruiser. Before getting in the passenger side, Mike got out his cell phone and punched in a number.

After two rings, Cooper North answered.

"We're coming in right now," he told her. "We've got something odd to show you."

Silence a moment, then Cooper's voice, sounding tired.

"When you get here, I've got news for you," she said.

"It's   not   good."

68

When Tip LaPerle and Mike Bolknor walked into Cooper North's hospital room, they found her sitting in a chair, grim.

She waved them to guest chairs. Mike carried the clear-plastic evidence bag holding the bottle device they'd found in Sonny DeWitt's office cabinet. Cooper glanced at it, without really seeing it, her thoughts elsewhere, and she looked away.

"They're gone," she said. "Both of them, together."

Both men looked blank, momentarily, but then understood.

"Are you sure?" Tip said.

"Yes, I'm sure," Cooper said.

She sounded bitter.

Out on bail, they'd been placed in their parents' custody.

"Bad idea," Cooper had told Ducks, but he'd shrugged it off.

State police patrolled between the two houses, twenty-four seven, to stop any escape attempts. Apparently, though, just after dawn, with the patrol momentarily between houses, by then knowing the troopers' schedule, they'd snuck out, probably coordinating with cell-phone calls. Then they'd met up and hiked along the deserted country roads the short way to the Snowville Maple company's headquarters building.

They'd stolen the company's Jeep Gladiator truck.

"God knows where they are now," Cooper said.

"Let's guess—headed to Mexico."

Silence in the room. Nobody saying it, but all three thinking it: how did two homicidal psychopaths, with irrefutable evidence against them, a huge danger to the public, ever got out on bail?

There'd been the community, loudly accusing the prosecution of malfeasance, insisting on the duo's innocence, despite all the evidence. Maybe that had weakened the judge's resolve.

Ducks had capitalized on that, telling the judge: "They're just kids, for God's sake!"

Before taking off, the escapees raided their households' cookie jars and their mothers' pocketbooks. They didn't steal much money, it turned out, but enough to get them out on the road, buy food, gas up.

One thing more: missing from the Ledger house's kitchen drawer, a large knife, razor sharp. Vic Ledger's father used the knife at Sunday dinners, to slice roasts.

North, to Canada? South, to Mexico?

Vermont's troopers had sent out an all-state alert, warning law-enforcement agencies across the country to watch for the stolen Jeep.

"They'll know their Jeep's a target," Cooper said. "So they'll ditch it, soon as they can, and get another ride, maybe a car at a gas station, with the keys left in the ignition, while the driver went inside to buy a coffee or cigarettes."

"Or they'll do a car-jacking," Mike said.

"Damn," Tip said. "They've got that knife!"

Cooper sighed.

Silence. Their team could do nothing, a situation out of the prosecution's hands, and out of the Dill PD's purview.

"All right," Cooper said. "Up at Snowville Maple, you just executed the search warrant—so what did you find?"

Mike slipped on his latex crime-scene gloves, then pulled the bottle gadget from its plastic bag and held it out for Cooper to examine.

"It came from a cabinet in Sonny DeWitt's office," he said.

He and Tip didn't know what it was. Just that it had two dead yellow jackets, caught in the jam smeared at the bottom.

Cooper studied it, as Mike held it up for her.

"It's a wasp trap," she said. "Olga Fisker showed me—you can Google for instructions."

She studied the dead wasps in the bottom, stuck in the smeared jam.

"All you need is a soda bottle and a glass cutter," she said. "And duct tape."

She leaned back in her chair and shut her eyes. After a silent half-minute, she spoke.

"Did you dust it yet?" she said. "Any prints?"

Mike said: "It's been wiped, no prints, not even a dust speck."

Cooper looked thoughtful.

"You've just murdered a man," she said. "You've got incriminating evidence—do you just stick it in a cabinet in your office?"

Tip shook his head.

"Yeah, you'd do that if you're really stupid," he said.

Cooper said, voice now weakening: "Yet, he hid it where we'd surely look, but thought to wipe away fingerprints…."

She leaned back in her chair. Chemotherapy's first round over now, but it would take many days for her bone marrow to grow back, leaving her weak and fatigued.

And her biopsy….

Dr. Lopez would come to tell her what it showed.

Probably today.

She shut her eyes.

Without opening them, she spoke.

"Bring him in, for questioning, at the Dill PD station," she said. "Kalisha Rains and Ozzie Knick should be there, see what they think.

"All right," Tip said.

No response from Cooper, and they saw she'd fallen asleep in her chair.

As quietly as they could, they left the room.

69

A door knock half woke her.

Where did Tip LaPerle and Mike Bolknor go?

She remembered: she'd drifted into sleep, at their meeting's end, and they'd gone to bring in Sonny DeWitt for questioning.

Another knock.

"Come in," Cooper said, still groggy.

She watched the door open.

Dr. Lopez walked into the room, wearing jeans and a blue dress shirt, and a surgical mask, with his glasses pushed up on his forehead.

"May I call you Cooper?" he asked.

"Yes, of course," she said.

He pointed to himself.

"Manny," he said.

He sat on the bed, next to Cooper's chair, silent, looking at her. Then he spoke.

"I just got the lab results," he said. "Your bone-marrow biopsy."

Cooper thought, fine, a chat about some neutral subject, maybe of scientific interest.

Then she realized.

She felt wrenched.

She'd be changed.

If Manny Lopez said she'd die, that knowledge would change her. It would change how she felt about herself in the world. Time would constrict.

Maybe, though, he'd say she might live. That, too, would change her. She'd surely change.

Either way....

"So here's the news," he said.

Later, after he'd told her, and they'd talked about it, and what lay ahead, he'd left on his rounds, to visit his other patients, almost colliding with Emma Ford in the doorway, as she rushed in, saying she'd just read the lab report. She sat beside Cooper, and held Cooper's hand, and Cooper saw that Emma's eyes swam.

After her nurse, her friend, rose to go, Cooper started to absorb what she'd heard, but just as Emma walked out and shut the door behind her, Cooper's phone buzzed, a state-police lieutenant she knew.

"They got to Ohio," he said. "Just outside Toledo, at a Quick Stop, they ditched their Jeep—out of gas—and they pulled a woman out of her car, she fought back, so they stuck a knife in her throat."

He spoke in the police-officer voice tone, no emotion, just the facts, Ma'am. Underneath, he seethed. Because the state police, like the Dill PD, and the prosecutors, had predicted freeing these two killer psychopaths on bail amounted to reckless endangerment.

Ledger and Rink had slain Olga Fisker. Now they'd killed a second innocent woman.

"Ohio State Highway Patrol has their new car's make and license," the lieutenant said. "They're hunting."

413

"Thanks for letting me know," Cooper said.

She clicked off the telephone, but sat with it in her hand, staring at her room's closed door.

A half hour later, yet another knock on her door startled her.

Mike Bolknor walked in, with Karen Del Vecchio, and Cooper nodded toward two guest chairs. Mike never discussed it with her, this new relationship with Karen. He never discussed personal matters at all. Yet, he might as well have told her everything, because she saw into this man who'd become a friend. She knew it unsettled him, this closeness with Karen, feeling he betrayed his dead wife and dead children, although he knew it wasn't so. He had to keep going on in life.

Cooper liked Karen Del Vecchio. She hoped this attachment would keep working out for Mike Bolknor.

"We finished questioning Sonny De Witt," Mike said. "Thought you might like to hear."

Cooper nodded.

First, he reported an odd wrinkle, from when they first arrived at Snowville Maple, Inc.

"We told DeWitt to come with us for questioning, at the Dill PD," he said. "Flute Wagner overheard—he got upset."

Bolknor silently reviewed his memories of the event, then spoke again.

"You could see the agitation in the way he kept blinking," Mike said. "Hands clenching...."

He thought again.

"Not a big deal, but odd, considering I didn't think they were buddies," Mike said. "Still, I suppose seeing anyone arrested, and for murder, could upset someone not used to that sort of thing."

Cooper thought about it, then shrugged.

"He blew the whistle, got us onto the case," she said.

"Maybe, seeing what it led to, he felt guilty."

She shrugged again.

"What else?"

"DeWitt denies everything," Mike said. "Insists he knows nothing about the wasp trap—we had Karen take it to the lab, see if anything showed up on it."

"We checked it up and down," Karen said. "Somebody wiped it thoroughly with Clorox—then handled it wearing gloves."

She said minute traces left on the glass suggested they'd worn kitchen gloves, rubberized, designed for washing dishes.

"That's a thought," Cooper said. "Go check where DeWitt lives, look under the sink—has he got Clorox and dishwashing gloves?"

It wouldn't prove anything she knew. Virtually every householder had a jug of Clorox and dish-washing gloves under the sink.

"Kalisha and Ozzie said let him go," Mike said. "Not enough evidence to hold him—and right about then Ducks showed up, to do his defense-attorney thing, so DeWitt's out there free-ranging again."

"I doubt he endangers anyone," Cooper said. "Except himself."

"We told him not to leave the state," Mike said. "At the moment, though, we don't know where to look next."

"I'll think about it," Cooper said.

Again she sat alone in her hospital room.

It had been a fraught day, a tiring day. Talking with Manny Lopez, hearing what he had to tell her, left her exhausted.

Evening's light, coming through her hospital room's window, faded, and the window turned black. She got into bed, to think.

She thought about Dr. Lopez, and the work he did, trying to save lives. She'd asked him how he dealt with oncology's harsh truth, because so many cancers could not be stopped, so many patients died, despite everything he did.

"Some patients do survive, who might have died if I didn't intervene," he said. "That satisfies me."

Cooper thought her work wasn't so different. She couldn't stop murder and armed robbery and men who beat their wives. Not all of it. Yet, she did stop some of it, kept some dangerous and harmful souls off the streets, human pathogens.

"That satisfies me," she thought.

Another buzz from her telephone.

Her state-police-lieutenant friend again.

"I hope it's not too late for you, Coop," he said.

"It's fine," she said.

"Well, here's the latest thrill, from Indianapolis," he said. "Victor Ledger apparently had a tiff of some sort with Winnie Rink—this was in a city park"

Silence over the telephone, and then the lieutenant finished the story.

"He knifed her—somebody saw him drive off, in that car they stole," he said. "She got ambulanced to the hospital, but she just died."

Cooper's first thought surprised her.

Stupid girl!

Yes, stupid. Because she thought a dangerous boyfriend would be exciting. And because he convinced her murder would be fun.

I suppose I should feel some pity, Cooper supposed.

She felt no pity, though.

Just sadness.

As she sat thinking, in the dark room, yet another knock on the door—Emma Ford came in, changed out of her nurse's uniform now, into street clothes, her shift over, going home.

"Good news," she said. "I just talked to Dr. Lopez—tomorrow you go home, to rest, while your bone marrow grows back."

After her marrow rejuvenated, Cooper knew, she'd need to return to the hospital, for her second round of chemotherapy.

"It must feel wonderful," Emma said. "To know you're in complete remission."

Through the hospital's microscopes, her marrow showed no leukemic cells at all, just normal cells.

"Am I cured then?" she'd asked Dr. Lopez.

"Maybe," he said. "It's a good sign, such a strong remission, after the first round of chemo."

"Why do I need more chemotherapy then?" Cooper had asked.

"Because maybe we missed a bad cell here or there, and we need to be sure they're all gone, and gone for good," Dr. Lopez said.

She must have looked disappointed.

"You're doing wonderfully," he said. "Deep down, I think you're going to be all right."

Now her nurse stood beaming at her, that brilliant white smile.

"I'll miss you," Emma said. "But you're going home!"

Emma leaned down and kissed Cooper's forehead.

Cooper thought: yes, I'm going home.

I'll see Henry.

70

Henry snubbed her.

Mike Bolknor left the corgi off at Cooper's house, then turned in her driveway and drove back to his campus office. Henry strutted into the living room, refused to look at Cooper, and ambled to the room's farthest corner and lay down, pointedly looking away.

Cooper didn't know, should she feel hurt, or amused? Apparently she'd miffed Henry by going away, even though she'd left him with his idol, Mike, and even though most days he'd larked about with his pal Thor Ennis, Tip LaPerle's foster child.

"Hey," Cooper told him. "I'm sorry I got a dangerous disease, and had to get chemotherapy, but spoiled brats get treated like spoiled brats."

She stopped looking at him, or speaking to him, but worked at unpacking her suitcase, clothes into dresser drawers, or the washing machine. She was reshelving books she'd brought to the hospital when she felt warmth against her leg, and looked down to see Henry leaning against her, looking up, bright eyed.

So she sat on the carpet and hugged the dog.

Subtly, she'd changed.

Remission.

Over time—years—with luck, "remission" would evolve into "cured." Even so, now she'd always feel followed by her shadow.

Just a matter of time.

Which posed a question: what to do with that time?

Emma had given her head scarves, and taught her how to wrap them around her still-hairless head, and she'd become expert at it. An accomplishment, satisfying.

She'd focus on such accomplishments. Also, on small moments, like relaxing in her living room armchair at night, with just one chairside lamp lit, lost in a thriller novel. And, a kind of accomplishment and a pleasurable moment—for the first time in many weeks, she walked into the Allen County State's Attorney's office.

They'd lined up to welcome her back, the assistant state's attorneys, the secretaries. Tip LaPerle. Mike Bolknor. Henry pushed in among them and grinned at her, as they grinned and applauded, as if she were an astronaut, just returned from the moon.

Finally, after an energy burst, fatigue set in, and she thanked everyone, sought refuge in her own office, and sank down at her desk. No build-up of paperwork faced her. They'd handled things for her, Kalisha Rains and Ozzie Knick, but they'd left some work, too, and she started on it with pleasure.

One of those small moments, so important now. Just doing her job.

And then her telephone buzzed.

Her friend, the state-police lieutenant.

"They've caught him, in Indiana," he said. "They're going to try him there, for murder, and maybe we'll get a shot at him, too, later—Indiana has the death penalty, though."

One homicide handled.

Good.

Cooper didn't support the death penalty.

Sometimes, though, she did.

She put it out of her mind—a done deal—and thought about the Proctor Gibbs murder.

She read through a progress report, or lack of progress—their only suspect remained Sonny DeWitt, but they had feeble evidence. Wasp trap in his cabinet? Suspicious, but nothing to actually tie it to the murder. Otherwise, they had nothing, except motive—with Proctor dead, Sonny inherited the company.

Insufficient evidence for a trial.

They'd need to dig deeper, but right now Cooper had no thoughts about where to do that digging.

A secretary looked in the open doorway.

"Ms. North," she said. "You've got a visitor."

Viola Wagner walked in, looking fiercer than ever, cold fire in her eyes. She clenched a sheet of paper. Still holding it, she took a seat facing Cooper's desk and stared, silent, just staring.

"What is it?" Cooper finally asked.

Viola handed the sheet of paper across the desk to Cooper.

"Read it," she said, through clenched teeth.

It began:

"To whom it may concern.

"If you're reading this, I'm dead.

"I bought fentanyl from a dealer at the Donut Dive, in Dill, more than enough to kill a large man, and I'm not large.

"It's painless. You just drift away.

"I'm a killer.

"I hid yellow-jacket wasps in Proctor Gibbs' sleeves. I hoped his death would mean I'd be promoted, but it wasn't so. I wanted more money, because I wanted to buy a Lamborghini sports car. I wanted to drive through our old town with Viola sitting beside me, like the queen she is, so they'd have to see her as she really is, a queen, and acknowledge her.

"I made a wasp trap—learned how to do it on the internet—and I hid it in Sonny DeWitt's office, so he'd get the blame, if anyone ever discovered the murder. Everyone knew Proctor was allergic.

"I have always loved Viola more than the world. I'm ashamed I can't leave her what she deserves.

"I can no longer stand the guilt.

"Goodbye, Viola.

"Goodbye.

"Signed: Flute Wagner."

Cooper read through the document a second time.

Then she looked at Viola, silent, but inquiring.

"I found him this morning," Viola said. "He's gone, the best man in the world."

Cooper sat back in her chair.

For a long moment, the two women sat in silence. Fierce silence, for Viola. Thoughtful silence, for Cooper. Sad silence.

"I didn't see Flute committing a crime like this," Cooper finally said. "Actually, he brought us into it, to investigate, which is odd, for a man who's just murdered another man."

Viola's stare intensified.

"Don't be stupid," she said.

Cooper looked at her, eyebrows raised.

"Only a numb-head could believe Flute ever harmed a single soul!"

Cooper held up the signed confession.

Viola stared at her.

"I won't let that wonderful man die like this, saying he murdered, and saying it for me—I won't!"

Cooper said nothing.

Viola suddenly reached over and pulled the confession from Cooper's hand. Cooper feared the woman meant to shred it. She was about to call for help, but Viola spread the sheet of paper on the desk in front of her and sat staring at it.

"You thought he was a little man, meek, timid," Viola said. "You're wrong—Flute was a hero."

Another long silence, Viola staring at the paper lying in front of her, resting her two hands on it.

"All our life, he's looked out for me," she said. "Even in that nasty rich town, protecting me, no matter what they did to him."

She read once again her husband's farewell note.

"Flute didn't kill Proctor Gibbs—I killed Proctor Gibbs," she said. "I hid the wasps in his sleeves."

By now, Cooper had flicked a switch under her desk, starting a hidden digital recorder."

423

"Why did you do that?" Cooper asked.

"For Flute, of course," Viola said. "I finally saw something I could do for him, besides bringing him his lunch—I was sure by then Proctor saw the difference between DeWitt and Flute, saw who clearly would run his company best, and changed his will so Flute would inherit."

Anger flashed across her face.

"It didn't happen—he gave the company to that nitwit," she said.

Viola sat back in her chair and exhaled heavily.

"I never cared about that Lamborghini, but Flute wanted it so badly he almost wept thinking about it, and I wanted him to have it, to find some satisfaction in life."

"What about the wasp trap in Sonny's cabinet?" Cooper asked.

"I snuck it in there," Viola said. "For one thing, if that jerk went to jail, surely the company's board would turn the place over the Flute, who deserved it so much."

"You had no concerns about pinning a murder on an innocent man?" Cooper asked.

Viola pretended to spit on the floor.

"He's just another one of those rich nothings who harassed Flute all the time we were growing up," she said.
"Harassing him just like they did, all the time, belittling…."

"You understand we'll have to arrest you," Cooper said. "You'll be arraigned, face a trial."

Viola stared down at Flute's note.

"He saw that wasp trap at home, but he didn't know what it was," she said. "Then he saw your cops find it in DeWitt's office, say what it was—he realized I put it there, and what I'd done, and why I did it."

She didn't lift her eyes from Flute's note, staring at it.

"I don't give a damn about arraignments," she said. "I'm not alive anymore."

Cooper wished she could reach back in time, to that posh town in Connecticut, where everything began. If only she could prosecute there.

Viola still sat staring at her husband's note.

Cooper thought how this should go.

Insanity defense.

71

That evening, Cooper drove home, with Henry riding shotgun, front paws up on the dashboard, bright-eyed.

Cooper glanced at the dog, so alert, so fully enjoying this moment, and she thought: me, too. I'm also alive right now.

For supper, she shared an organic pizza with Henry.

This is a moment, she thought.

After supper, a call came through from Barcelona, her oldest friend, Mona Dill Saunders, in Europe finding art to buy, with her long-time love, a Spanish actress, pretending to be furious with Cooper, for not telling her she'd been hospitalized, with leukemia, of all the horrible things.

"I just got off the phone with Manny Lopez," Mona said. "He says he thinks you're going to be okay, just a couple more chemos to go, so please stop whining about all this."

They both knew she hadn't been whining.

Afterwards, Cooper thought: another moment.

That night, Cooper sat in a living room armchair, with just the chairside lamp lit, reading a thriller in that circle of yellow light, with Henry snoozing by her feet.

At some point, the book dropped into her lap.

Drifting asleep, she thought, this has been a moment.

Another moment.

THE END

If you haven't read the first mystery in the Cooper North series, Spider's Web in the Green Mountains, turn the page to see a free sample.

SPIDER'S WEB
IN THE GREEN MOUNTAINS

by

Richard Wolkomir

CHAPTER ONE

Rain.

Darkness.

A black motorcycle rumbles west on Hill Street, moving slowly because of the downpour.

And because its headlight is turned off.

Just before the stone arch, marking the entrance to Mt. Augustus College, the biker stops, stretches out a steadying leg, and twists in the saddle to stare at a house.

It is a large house, brick, built two centuries ago, Federal style.

Silhouetted in the living room's Palladian window, a woman reads a book.

Against the lamplight, she's just a tall shadow, but the biker knows her looks: gray-haired and lanky, almost gaunt. Cheekbones prominent. Penetrating gray eyes.

She looks like a gyrfalcon.

As the biker watches, she turns a page.

Gaze still fixed on the window, the biker reaches a hand into a long leather holster, affixed to the saddle, and—slowly—draws out a rifle.

Cooper North's window lit up—lightning flash—instantly followed by a thunder detonation. It sounded like a direct hit, but Cooper's reading lamp only flickered.

She remembered an old book's opening, often mocked: "It was a dark and stormy night..."

Gust-driven rain battered the window. Water gurgled in the big house's ornate gutters.

She thought, amused: nighttime storms don't foretell mayhem. Not actually. Maybe in old novels, but not in the real world. Not in Dill, Vermont.

She knew mayhem.

Thirty-six years as Allen County state's attorney— hundreds of prosecutions. Then Vermont's attorney general—hundreds   more. Reckless endangerment. Manslaughter. Murder. But never a major felony on a stormy night.

Out on the street, the motorcyclist rests the rifle stock against a shoulder and squints through the telescopic sight.

Three months ago, after a stint on the state's Supreme Court, Cooper finally retired. She'd planned to read and watch birds, but that lasted for one Swedish mystery novel and one re-reading of *The Odyssey,* and one sunrise visit to Abner Park with binoculars. Then Mt. Augustus College telephoned.

"Coop, our new criminal justice program? Get it going for us, okay?"

She'd grumped about it, but only for show. Retirement already bored her.

Lightning again. Another thunder whack.

She put her thriller novel down on the side table and reached for her cane, laying it across her lap so she wouldn't need to grope for it if the power went out, and all the while she felt watched.

Henry.

He'd been at it two days now.

Thirty pounds of butterscotch-and-white Pembroke Welsh corgi. He sat on the living room carpet, studying her.

Rain blurs the scope, so the biker lowers the rifle and wipes the eyepiece with a handkerchief, then raises the rifle and aims again.

Last week, Cooper's nephew called from Boston to report a promotion, and a move to Brussels. Only thing is, he said, we can't take Henry. Then his wife got on the phone.

"Coop, it'll be so good for you, in that huge empty house—a dog for company!"

Two days ago they'd driven up from Boston and dropped Henry off. When the corgi realized they weren't coming back, his sharp brown eyes dulled. For an hour, he moped. Then he shook himself and methodically explored the house, room by room. That settled, he began surveillance of Cooper. Last night she'd awakened in the wee hours and there was Henry, sitting beside her bed, watching her sleep.

In her mind, Cooper heard her long-gone mother pronounce, in a sniffy voice: "Too clever by half!"

Yes, the dog's clever, Cooper thought. He's been exiled from Beacon Hill, so he needs to scout this new home, gauge this new person in his life, fit himself in.

Crosshairs on the woman's head, rock steady. Now squeeze....

Another lightning-thunder combo.

This time the lights did go black—startled, Cooper knocked her cane over, bending to grab it off the floor, in the dark.

Cracking glass.

A roar.

Receding, gone.

Now she heard only rain, and something ticked.

The lights flickered back on. Window shards glittered on the carpet. In the living-room's plaster wall, a puncture.

If she hadn't just then bent to fetch her cane, she'd have been shot in the head.

She snapped off the light. No point still being a lit-up target in the window. She sat in the dark, listening.

Tick. Tick....

It was the grandfather's clock, out by the stairs. It had kept time there for generations. Only now, though, did she notice its ticking.

Henry leaned against her leg, his fur warm, but she felt chilled. She thought about a vodka martini.

Fumbling on the side table in the dark, she grabbed the phone, and stared at the illuminated keys.

4

SPIDER'S WEB IN THE GREEN MOUNTAINS

Her house abutted Mt. Augustus College, so the campus cops were closest, and she keyed in their number.

After two rings a deep voice said: "Security."

She thought: "Mike Bolknor—it would be him."

Two minutes later a car skidded to a stop out front and a door slammed and her doorbell rang.

CHAPTER TWO

"Do you have enemies?" Bolknor asked.

Cooper shook her head. Who'd want to shoot her?

And should she have hired this man unseen?

She chaired the Campus Security Committee, and on the fall semester's first day, the former security chief dropped dead, of a cerebral hemorrhage. Cooper filled in, but they'd needed a replacement fast.

She thought: why, just when I've been shot at, am I worrying about this?

"I called the Dill PD," Bolknor told her. "Jurisdiction, right?"

He looked down at her, expressionless. Few men were tall enough to look down at her.

His application had stood out—forty-two years old, Army MP, then NYPD detective, seventeen years. Awards. Citations. Excellent references.

But why shuck a New York career for an obscure Vermont college?

"Dill PD'll dig the slug out of the wall, look for tire tracks," Bolknor said. "We'll watch the house here, keep eyes on you."

"For how long?" Cooper asked.

She thought: bodyguards? In Dill? Me?

Bolknor shrugged.

"Until we figure what's up," he said.

His New York inflection—too big-city for this small college in the Green Mountains?

Maybe too big generally. Street-tough big. Eyebrows a thick black bar. A heaviness, as if his insides were basalt. His words seemed to come up from deep silence. And that, with his size, could intimidate. Would he spook kids from hyper-protective homes? And could he handle rowdy students without going Flatbush Avenue on them?

She thought: why am I obsessing about this?

Then: it's to distract myself....

Because the shooter's still out there.....

And, yes, I'm frightened.

"It was a dark and stormy night," Cooper muttered.

Bolknor looked at her.

"Bulwer-Lytton?" he asked.

She nodded, thinking, well, that's a surprise.

Something touched her leg and she looked down, to see Henry looking up, brow furrowed, as if asking, you all right, friend? She swallowed a sob.

Shock, she realized. Trauma. Which infuriated her.

"I'll hunt that bastard down," she said.

Bolknor looked at her, but she couldn't read his expression.

"Probably no tire tracks, with this rain," he said.

He studied her, and even his gaze seemed heavy.

"Slug in the wall's not likely to offer much, either," he said.

3

He looked at her silently. It occurred to Cooper that he knew her—his putative new boss—no better than she knew him.

"So it's mostly up to you," he said.

She raised her eyebrows, unsure what he meant.

"Figure why," he said. "That's the only way we'll get to who."

He looked out the broken window, and so did Cooper, sixty-nine years old, but still with penetrating gray eyes. Through the broken pane, she heard rain pounding the slate walkway, and rumbling thunder, now distant. She thought she'd need to do something about that window, and her leg hurt more than usual, so maybe a new orthopedic shoe insert would help.

And somebody wants me dead!

A dark and stormy night.

Henry, sitting on the carpet, looked from Mike Bolknor to Cooper North, as if taking a reading, gauging what it all meant for Henry. Then he yawned, sticking out a long pink tongue. He lay down on the carpet, stretched out on his side, sighed, shut his eyes.

Almost immediately, Henry slept.

CHAPTER THREE

"Jeezum Crow!"

Cooper wished Tip LaPerle wouldn't use old Yankee euphemisms like that in front of Mike Bolknor, because she didn't want the new man from New York City dismissing Dill's police chief as a rube.

It was the next morning, a meeting in Cooper's office, above the campus-security headquarters, to coordinate the investigation. She couldn't read Bolknor, except that he wore a suit and tie, vaguely inappropriate in Vermont, where the sartorial norm was whatever, but she'd known Tip LaPerle most of his life, and she saw him bristling inside. He didn't like this big-city cop on his turf.

A memory bubbled up, from thirty years back: ten-year-old Tip LaPerle, like a sinewy kid goat, ready to butt, bursts into the Allen County State's Attorney's office. Oversized ears. Thatch of straw-colored hair. Blue eyes resolute.

"How do I become a policeman?"

If you knew what his father had been, and his mother, and his brothers....

Cooper sighed.

She thought: you need to be born here, in a small town like this, to grasp it.

SPIDER'S WEB IN THE GREEN MOUNTAINS

You'd see the college, up on the hill, if you visited, and the cupolaed Victorians and brick federals, shaded by sugar maples. Downtown, you'd see Main Street's boutiques and eateries and indie-music cafes and bookstores. Farther down, where the hill bottomed out at the river, with railroad tracks alongside, you'd see Tenement Row, where Tip LaPerle grew up.

You wouldn't see the spider web.

That's how Cooper envisioned it: invisible strands crisscrossing Dill—feuds, affairs, business dealings, marriages, divorces, envies, jealousies, kindnesses....

Those strands interconnected everyone, and they stretched back through time, too, because lives here ran deep.

Cooper's own family came in colonial days, when the Dill brothers, Abner and Augustus, trekked up from Massachusetts to the Green Mountains wilderness, to start the sawmill that spawned granite quarries and other enterprises, and finally evolved into Dill Industries, the software corporation headquartered across Abner Park from Mt. Augustus College. Other families came down from Quebec, to blast granite out of the quarries. Stone carvers immigrated from Italy and Spain. And there were Sixties people, too. They'd come during Mt. Augustus College's love beads and "Hell No, We Won't Go" phase, and many stayed in Dill, opened music stores or artist supplies shops or organic food emporiums. Some, gray now, or bald, served on the city council, and took up such causes as turning empty lots into communal gardens.

Cooper looked at the two men sitting across from her desk. Mike Bolknor remained a puzzle, but she wanted him to understand that Tip LaPerle policed this town effectively, precisely because Tip understood the spider web, sensed its mutating strands. Tip knew Dill, down to its molecular level.

On the other hand, Tip might be just a tad impulsive.

Thinking about that, she pushed aside heaped paperwork to make space on her desk to rest her elbows, and suddenly—because last night's gunshot still unsettled her, since she normally wouldn't care—her office's mess shamed her.

Leaning towers of paper, books strewn on the floor, along with newspapers and magazines, and also Styrofoam coffee cups, some not-quite empty, on the desk a mulch of Newman's Own chocolate-chip cookie crumbs....

Her home was just the same.

She thought: "I'm Cooper North, and I'm a slob."

Which reminded her of the AA meetings she'd once needed to attend and she veered her thoughts away from that topic.

"I never saw the car," she said. "I only heard it— loud."

Something about that loudness nagged at her. No muffler?

"Jeezum," Tip said, shaking his head, looking at her.

She knew that meant, how could this happen, Coop? To you? And that he'd go after the shooter like a ferret.

Mike Bolknor sat mute in his chair, right ankle on left knee. She couldn't guess his thoughts. Even Henry the corgi, now sitting at Cooper's feet, after having crisscrossed the floor, snarking up crumbs, looked more involved in the meeting, bright eyes focusing on whoever spoke. She guessed Bolknor listened, professionally, but kept most of himself entombed in some deep-down internal vault.

"Coop, it's got to be somebody you put in jail," Tip said. "Got a grudge."

Cooper shrugged.

"Four decades, Tip," she said. "How many prosecutions? Two thousand?"

Mike Bolknor finally spoke: "Anything from the tech people?"

Cooper saw Tip stiffen.

"No tire tracks—rain, and it was all on pavement, anyway," Tip said. "Slug from the wall's a .30-06, hunting rifle, truckloads of them, just here in Allen County, so unless we find the weapon in somebody's gun rack, and match the slug to it...."

And now, Cooper thought, Mike Bolknor will say "told you so." Bolknor, however, didn't respond at all, not even with a facial expression.

Tip, though, suddenly glared at him.

"I suppose the NYPD's got super-techs, right?" he said. "Wizard out stuff from that slug our trooper lab in

Waterbury couldn't get?"

Bolknor looked back blandly, and shrugged.

"Doubt it," he said

Cooper thought: Tip's lashing out because he's intimidated by the New York cop. And she felt embarrassed for him.

"I'll think about old cases," Cooper said. "But…."

Abruptly the door burst open—no knock—and a young woman rushed in, already talking.

"…so I'll need the files, all those case studies? From our evidence class?" she said. "That newspaper lady's coming again and…."

"Stacey—this is a meeting," Cooper said.

Now the woman noticed the two men, and she instantly got cute. It was subtle. A cocking of the head, so the blond hair cascaded down on that side, one hip slightly outthrust under her skirt, cornflower-blue eyes gone limpidly winsome. It was, Cooper thought, wryly, one of Stacey Gillibrand's talents, along with a genius for being annoying.

"Oh! You're talking about last night!" Stacey said. "I've got some ideas and…."

"Office hours," Cooper said, putting stone in her voice. "Come back then."

Stacey looked from Bolknor to LaPerle, eyes extremely blue. Then she looked at Cooper, did an eye roll, and shrugged.

"Okay," she said, giving the men an over-the-shoulder glance as she left the room.

Bolknor and LaPerle exchanged a look, eyebrows up, and Cooper thought maybe there was hope yet, for them to work together.

She shook her head, irritated.

"She's twenty-six, calls other students 'brats,'" Cooper said. "Divorced, been a law-office receptionist, now aims to become a superstar lawyer herself—if she starts playing Nancy Drew with you two, a little discouragement, please."

Bolknor and LaPerle both looked briefly wry, then serious again.

"Well, how about students then, with a grudge, like bad grades?" Bolknor asked. "Ticked off enough to take a shot?"

Cooper imagined Stacey Gillibrand shooting her. Motive: to take over Mt. Augustus College's Criminal Justice Program. That, however, was ridiculous, because it poured rain last night, and Stacey wouldn't risk soaking her hair-do.

"You're smiling, Coop," Tip said. "You think of something?"

Cooper shook her head, still smiling.

"Private joke," she said.

"Faculty?" Bolknor said. "Administrators? Step on any toes?"

"Everybody loves me," Cooper said.

"Dumped an old flame," Bolknor suggested, and Cooper laughed.

There'd been only one flame, at Harvard Law, where everyone, including the professors, cold shouldered her, because in that era women were unwelcome there, but one fellow student had welcomed her. They'd dated. Then polio struck and she was out a year. She'd come back with a lame leg and found her boyfriend married to somebody else. And later, in Vietnam, a sniper killed him. After that, there'd been one marriage proposal, which had mainly irritated her, but no more suitors, at least, none serious. Too tall. Too lame. And with gray eyes that looked right through you.

"Tip's probably right," Cooper said. "Somebody I sent to prison...."

They left it that Cooper would mull over old prosecutions. Mike Bolknor took the elevator down to campus security, to arrange a watch on Cooper's house. Tip LaPerle said he'd canvass Cooper's neighbors, see if anyone saw something.

Alone in her office, Cooper checked the Yellow Pages, then called a glazier. Next, she called her podiatrist, because of her aching leg. Maybe she needed a new shoe insert.

She put the phone down and something seemed wrong.

No Henry.

He slipped out, she thought. With Bolknor and LaPerle. She imagined him running through Dill on those short corgi legs.

Lost! Terrified! Alone!

She limped to the elevator, cane thumping on the floor, then impatiently rode down to Campus Security's offices on the first floor. She needed help to hunt for the dog.

Her dog.

Henry.

Three days, that's all I've known him, she thought. But if he got run over....

She barged into Mike Bolknor's corner office, and he looked up from the patrol schedules he was studying.

"Henry's gone," Cooper said.

She hoped she didn't sound hysterical. She'd always been calm. In court, nothing could shake her.

Bolknor studied her, then—with his chin—indicated she should look under his desk.

Henry lay there asleep, his snout resting on Bolknor's extra-large black-leather shoe.

Cooper thought: I'm a basket case.

She rode the elevator back up to her office, with Henry riding with her. She collapsed into her chair.

Once again she imagined a vodka martini in her hand, heard ice tinkling in the glass, felt the chill through her fingers. She thought about lighting up a Camel, inhaling its smoke into her lungs, feeling the bite.

She kept an unopened bottle of vodka in her desk drawer, alongside an unopened package of unfiltered cigarettes, each with a rubber band around it. When she needed to, she opened the drawer and thwacked both rubber bands. She did that now.

She thought: I've got to go watch birds.

Instead, she drove downtown and parked in front of The Percolator, her favorite Main Street coffee shop. Time for lunch.

END OF SAMPLE

ORDER PRINT OR E-BOOK EDITIONS OF
SPIDER'S WEB IN THE GREEN MOUNTAINS AT
AMAZON.COM.

ORDER PRINT EDITIONS AT BARNES &
NOBLE.